POSSUM HOLLOW BOOK TWO

68 WHISKEY

ERIN RUSSELL

By Erin Russell

Copyright © 2024 by Erin Russell
Cover by Erin Russell

All rights reserved.

Any references to historical events, real people, or real places are used fictitiously. Names, characters, and places are products of the author's imagination.

ISBN 979-8-9899256-3-6

BY ERIN RUSSELL

CONTENTS

A Note on Content

Possum Hollow is a fictional small town in rural Missouri. All the roads and surrounding towns mentioned are also fictional, so don't look for them on a map. The world was inspired by real places where I spent some of my childhood.

X

The backdrop for the series is one of rural poverty. Across the series, you'll find common themes of drug & alcohol abuse, family violence, parental neglect, toxic masculinity & violence, cultural homophobia and untreated mental illness.

X

This book features plotlines regarding military service/PTSD, domestic violence, gang/mafia crime, death of family members, realistic medical procedures, traumatic mutism, and on-page self injury that some readers may find triggering.

For each book in the series, I list the most significant triggers at the front, but if you'd prefer to read a comprehensive list that may contain spoilers for the story, please check my website.

www.erinrussellauthor.com/content-warnings

Dedicated to all my trauma-fueled, commitment-phobic emergency med brethren.
We give the best fucking advice, but run away from our own relationships like it's
an Olympic sport.

If you identify with anything I just said, please drink some water you dehydrated
beast.
I can hear your kidneys screaming from here.

One of the MCs in 68 Whiskey is mute, and his preferred form of communication is American Sign Language.

ASL, like other sign languages, are not word-for-word signed versions of spoken language. They're independent languages that have their own grammar, sentence structure and slang, and a huge amount of meaning is conveyed through things like body position, signing space and facial expressions, as well as the signs themselves. ASL has a different word order than English, so reading a transliterated version of it can be very confusing if you're not familiar with the language.

Because of this, please consider all of ASL in this book to have been translated into English for ease of reading. In the same way that you could write *"Hello," he said to me in French*, you'll see sentences like, *"Hello," Ford signed.*

This seemed like the easiest way to not interrupt the flow of the story or require any extra knowledge on the part of the reader, but still respect the integrity of ASL as its own language with associated culture.

While Ford speaks ASL as a primary mode of communication, he is not deaf and has never been a part of Deaf culture. This is reflected in the way he thinks and communicates. I tried to take as sensitive and informed approach as possible to his medical issues, trauma and communication style, but it is not meant to reflect any kind of universal experience. Everyone's experience of these issues is different, and this is just one version.

Chapter One

TRISTAN

The Egg McMuffin I'm shoveling into my mouth is at least two hours old. It's a stone-cold mess of congealed egg and cheese, but it's still the best goddamn thing I've put in my mouth all week.

As depressing as that is.

Eight years in the military living off MREs and chow hall slop really gives you an appreciation for any food that doesn't come out of a vacuum pack. On top of that, this has been a grueling fucking shift. It's one of those sweltering summer nights, the kind where it feels like the humidity is trying to drown you, and there's no reprieve from the heat. Even at 2a.m., I was sweating out my body weight and it's only gotten warmer since then. I'm dehydrated and I'm fucking hungry.

Possum Hollow is a teeny, tiny little town in the middle of nowhere, Missouri. It's stereotypical rural poor, so working on an ambulance I see a decent amount of action with bar brawls, overdoses, and diabetes complications, but not a lot else. Most days, the shifts feel like a breath of fresh air compared to all the lives I've lived before.

Tonight was an exception. There was a multi-car pile-up, which is not something we see that often. My partner Cade—the EMT to my paramedic—had to pop his solo-CPR cherry because there were too many casualties to triage while we waited for other ambulances to be routed from nearby counties.

He handled it, though, and I'm pretty damn proud of him. Not that I'll say so. He's been on the job a little over a year, and this is when his ego needs to be kept in check before he gets over-confident and accidentally kills someone.

I'm not judging. He'll fuck up and kill someone eventually; it's a rite of passage for emergency med. But as the person who sucked him into this messy-ass job by convincing him to go to EMT school, I feel obligated to try to shield him from the worst of it as long as I can.

Right now, he's sitting still for once in his life; his head tipped back in the passenger's seat and his eyes closed. Cade normally has the energy of a golden retriever puppy trying not to trip over his own paws. Instead, with blood and vomit on his shirt and a fresh trauma running through his mind, the atmosphere in the cab feels heavy.

"Eat," I say, throwing his own gelatinous egg sandwich into his lap.

The grimace I get in response tells me he's not feeling it, but I'm not taking no for an answer.

"Trust me. You're going to feel like shit either way, and your body needs the fuel. The shift ain't over yet. The last thing you want is for us to get called to another fucking job and you start feeling faint half-way through."

Begrudgingly, Cade reaches for the sandwich and peels back the wrapper. He looks pale, and it's weird not to see the normal current of energy running through him. I fight back the paternal sense of worry that automatically builds in me.

More and more, I'm forced to remind myself that he's not my kid to take care of. I moved here to put distance between myself and the rest of the world, not adopt every waif and stray that runs across my path. Just because his own parents couldn't give two shits about him and he's the spitting image of my little brother...

I have to get a grip.

Beep beep beep.

Of course, the sound of our motherfucking tones interrupts us.

Shoving the rest of my breakfast in my mouth like a chipmunk, I confirm our response and then listen to dispatch rattle off the address as I try to chew through the wad of cold food as quickly as possible. The call is for a 22yo male who's been stabbed, which is a lot spicier than most of our calls. I have a vague idea of where the address is, but I've only lived here for a couple of years, so I don't have the same internal GPS that Cade does.

Which is why I look across the cab to see if he recognizes the location. Instead of a normal response, I find him staring at me wide-eyed, all the blood drained from his face, looking like he's about to hurl his single bite of food onto the dash.

"That's Ford's garage." His voice quavers as he speaks.

"Fuck."

I don't bother with other questions. My hand flicks the switch for full lights and sirens. I slam-reverse out of the space we were in and gun it to the highway.

I've never been to the garage. The only thing I know about it is that Cade's buddy Ford owns it, and his boyfriend Silas works there. The love-of-his-life, borderline-adorable-borderline-codependent, all-consuming, he-hurts-I-hurt boyfriend that he *just* settled down with.

This is not good. My stomach lurches at the thought of how many ways the next hour could play out for my partner.

I know better than anyone that the worst day of your life is never something you see coming.

Red tendrils of dawn are licking over the horizon as I careen across town in record time. The good thing about Possum Hollow is that it's fucking small. I can make it there in six or seven minutes if I disregard all safety protocols, and fuck safety protocols right now.

There's one corner that I take hard enough for the inside wheels to lift a little, but apart from that, the drive is clean.

As I'm pulling up to the auto shop, I debate whether to call for backup right away. I don't know how objective or functional Cade is going to be once we get inside. The kid's had a fucked-up life, and he's generally pretty good at compartmentalizing, but he's been all kinds of soft for Silas since the day they met.

There's no one else on duty right now, so I'd have to get someone from a different station, which is why I ultimately decide to take a wait-and-see approach.

We both clamber out of the ambulance at full speed. I switch my brain to maximum work mode, and I can see by the set of Cade's jaw that he's trying to do the same.

"Are you gonna be able to do this, kid?" I ask, my voice nearly drowned out by the sound of our feet crunching across the gravel parking lot.

"If you try to make me sit outside, I'll deck you. I swear to God."

Cade doesn't get serious very often, but he has a dark side buried in there. I haven't seen it a lot, but he can be ferocious when he needs to be. Blame my own lifetime of trauma, but the fact that he's getting pissed instead of weepy gives me more confidence in him.

"I'll assess the scene. You will do every single thing I say, exactly as I say, or I will bench you and deal with this myself. Understood?"

I don't get an agreement, which makes my inner sergeant chafe at the disrespect, but I also don't get a "fuck you", so I'll take it.

There's a police cruiser in the lot with its lights still flashing, but the roller door at the front of the garage is pulled down, so we can't see the situation inside. I had let myself be optimistic and didn't bother with a stretcher until we get the lay of the land. Cade walks us in through the side door like he's been here

4

a million times, which I guess he has, and my brain immediately starts breaking down everything that's going on inside.

Silas is sitting down, holding a questionably clean towel against his ribs over what I'm assuming is his injury. He looks bright and alert, though, even if he's in pain, which is a good start. Cade is thundering over to him before I get the chance to say anything, of course.

"I'm totally fine." Silas heads us both off at the pass. "The knife glanced off my ribs, it's barely a graze. Please don't freak out."

His words do nothing to eat at the worry rolling off Cade in waves, but it settles me a little. Silas is stoic, but he's rational. At least about things that aren't to do with Cade. Confident that he's probably not dying, I'm happy to let Cade handle it and turn my attention to the chaos unfolding on the other side of the shop floor.

"Full head-to-toe, make sure there aren't any injuries the adrenaline isn't letting him feel. You've got this," I call out to Cade as I walk past the pair of them.

Because my attention is on the same thing as the cops are focused on, which is the other person in the building. The two patrolmen have him penned into the corner, and the energy coming from them is that kind of crackling tension that spells trouble. He's in handcuffs and he's bleeding from a small head laceration, but the fact that he's not already in the back of their cruiser makes it unclear whether he's the perpetrator.

"What's going on?" I'm vaguely familiar with both officers. I can't remember their names, but they both look like they walked straight out of central casting for small town cops with a grudge and a power trip. "Is this the suspect?"

"He's my fucking boss!" Silas yells from across the room. I don't think I've ever seen him raise his voice before. He's normally pretty shy, but right now he looks pissed. Cade pulls his focus back to the exam, but Silas jerks away to keep yelling. "These assholes put him in cuffs because they're morons. He doesn't fucking talk. If he's cuffed, he can't type or sign, so how can he give a statement?"

They made shitty assumptions as soon as they walked in the door and haven't listened to a word I'm saying."

"That's enough attitude out of you, son," Officer Asshole Number One says. "We know it's Ford's shop, but he's acting erratic, and we just want to keep everyone safe while we ascertain the truth of the situation."

"The truth of the situation is that I got stabbed by a fucking meth head who was trying to rob us. I called the cops and because he's upset that his shop was trashed, you called him 'aggressive' and treated him like a criminal," Silas calls out.

The tension in the room is rising, but I narrow my focus on the man in question.

I've heard of Ford Novack, but we've never actually met. Apparently, he has a reputation in this town for violence, although according to Cade, it's outdated.

I can see why he would put people on the defensive. The man is ferocity in human form. I'm fucking tall at 6'3", and he's got at least an inch on me, plus a lot of muscle and bulk. Long, dark hair that was probably tied back earlier, but has come loose and is flying around his bloodied face adds drama to the image, and underneath the blood and beard I'm pretty sure I can see a big-ass scar running down one cheek. His pale skin makes all that blood and hair pop, so he looks like something out of a graphic novel.

The thing that really gets me is his eyes. He has husky eyes. Light blue and totally fucking crazed. I love it. Something about that raw, feral intensity sparks my own crazy in response.

I don't generally trust cops any more than I have to. I've seen too many who are so shit-scared in their suburban neighborhood that they can't exercise a little self-control and not open fire at random. Compared to the nineteen-year-old kids who get thrown into literal open warfare and still manage to adhere to the rules of engagement.

But even if I was going to side with the cops, crazy husky eyes here would have changed my mind.

This situation is rapidly deteriorating, and I'm too exhausted and hungry not to take charge.

"Well, if he didn't commit a crime, I'm gonna need you to remove the cuffs so I can give him medical attention. If you're too piss-scared of a random law-abiding citizen just because he's taller than you, then give me the keys and wait in your cruiser while the grown-ups work."

Watching the cop's face turn red is deeply satisfying. I'm not going to lie.

"Hey, I don't know how things work on the east coast, but around here, the law is in charge."

Jesus fucking Christ, he even talks like he walked out of a bad cop movie.

"Bitch, I wouldn't trust you to police your way out of a traffic jam. Unlock the cuffs now, or I'll be filing a report with your department for unlawful detention. You may think you're hot shit, but this is middle America and a lot of people are willing to listen to a war veteran first responder over some small-town schlub on a permanent power-trip."

Apparently, that's enough to close the issue. The cop looks pissed as hell, but he takes the cuffs off Ford before walking away. I know making enemies in a small town isn't a great idea, but I'm from South Boston. If there's anything I know how to do, it's hold a grudge.

Both cops retreat to take a statement from Silas, leaving me and Ford in a tentative little bubble of peace. The amount of tension running through his body is palpable, even from three feet away. In deference to the cops, Ford does look like he wants to crush someone's skull in his giant canned-ham hands. I still think I could take him if I had to.

"Can I take a look at your head, man? You're bleeding pretty good."

I watch as he forces his muscles to unclench, one by one. The anger slips out of his body and is replaced by a profound level of weariness. As he nods his consent, he seems to sway on his feet.

"Let's sit down." I place a hand on his elbow, which makes him scowl, but he lets me guide him gently until he's sitting on some kind of toolbox. I crouch down in front of him to take a look. I try to place my fingers on his chin to tilt his face towards me, but this time he jerks out of my grasp completely.

This guy seems like he's pretty self-contained. And if you don't talk, I imagine most people find you difficult to read. But I make my living looking at people's bodies for clues. Which means I clock that his pulse immediately starts to speed up, to the point that I can see his vein fluttering over his throat. I see his jaw clench as his nostrils flare and his eyes widen, all while he pulls away from me.

That's not anger. That's fear.

Oh, he's just getting more interesting by the minute.

I need to grab a Telfa pad from my jump bag anyway, so I turn away as slowly as I can, using the moment to give him a second to breathe. When I turn back around, his chin is tilted in a little protectively, so I take a different tack.

"You're still bleeding, so I'm gonna hold pressure for a couple of minutes, okay?"

I get the smallest possible nod, those bright blue eyes watching me with the hyperintensity of someone who's known more bad touch than good. I'm an expert at keeping patient interactions surface-level, but something about his expression hits me deep.

Avoiding touching him anywhere else, I press the pad against his forehead. From a cursory glance it doesn't look terrible, but foreheads are vascular as fuck, so I need to stop the bleeding before I can do anything else with it.

"What happened?"

Huffing, Ford shakes his head and rolls his eyes so hard it almost dislodges my hand. His hands come up in front of him, clutching uselessly at the air, and I put two and two together. He doesn't have his phone, and Silas said that's how he generally communicates.

"You sign, right? Go ahead, I know ASL."

This time when he jerks away from my hands, it's in shock, not fear. Our gazes collide, and he looks at me for longer than I expect, his expression guarded.

Intensity hangs between us like the spit-trail after a really dirty kiss.

Eventually, his hands move. Slowly at first, but with more confidence as I nod to confirm that I'm following what he's saying. My hand is still pressing the gauze to his forehead, which limits his ability to raise his eyebrows, basically hamstringing him from signing properly, but there are enough context clues for him to get his meaning across. If I miss anything, it's my fault for getting distracted by how nimble he manages to be despite the obvious strength in his hands.

"We don't usually open until later," he signs. "But Silas has a side project he wanted help with, so we came in early. When we got here, three guys were inside, ransacking the place. Meth heads, grabbing shit and breaking shit at random. I grabbed one, but his buddy got Silas with a knife, so I let him go to help. They all ended up running out before I could catch any of them, but one of them hit me with a fucking wrench in the process. Then Silas called 911 and everything just got worse."

He looks around briefly at the shop, which is definitely trashed, and the heartbreak is clearly written on his face. Then he turns back to me. Narrowed eyes tell me he still isn't convinced I understand, so I switch out my hand for his holding the pad and sign back at him instead of talking.

"My little brother was Deaf. I'm a little rusty, but I understand you." I lean in to whisper the next part, "Don't tell Thing One and Thing Two over there, though, because they're nosy and I don't like to talk about it."

He fingerspells "OK" softly, like an afterthought, still holding my gaze.

The laser focus that I normally carry into a scene stutters for a second. It's been a long night, followed by a weird end-of-night call, and saying anything personal about myself always sets me on edge. I feel like all the wheels and cogs inside my work-brain are catching slightly off, and I have to concentrate to bring my attention away from Ford's haunting, anguished eyes back to the scene.

"Cade, how's your boy?" I yell across the open space once I've rejoined the living.

"He's stable; single shallow lac, but we're taking him to hospital to get him double-checked by a trauma doc if I have to fucking sedate him to get him there."

I bite back a smile. Cade may be a golden retriever most of the time, but he's a bulldog when he's in protective mode, and it's one of the things that cemented our friendship.

"Fair," I say, turning back to Ford. He's still staring at me with an inscrutable kind of intensity. "What about you? Feel like a field trip to the ER? I can make sure you're stable, but I'd feel a lot better about your head if you got a CT."

As the words came out of my mouth, I knew the answer would be a hard *no*. Ford's face shutters. In the short time I've been there, he's been constantly expressive: despairing about the shop, angry at the cops, fearful of me, shocked that I understood him... But this is nothing. This is totally shut down, in a way that seems familiar to him.

I inhale and exhale through my nose, long and slow, weighing the pros and cons of arguing with him. In the end, I decide against it. We've built a fragile peace after he seemed ready to tear those cops apart, and it's not worth ruining that over a fight I won't win, anyway.

Instead, I let the silence fall over us. I take his vitals, checking he's okay before I touch him each time. I go through concussion protocol to see if I have cause to bring him in against his will. He sits through the whole thing like a rock, and he's as stable as I'd hoped. The head lac has stopped bleeding, so he lets me give it a rough-and-ready cleanup and a quick butterfly bandage before his patience runs out.

I go through my spiel about why he shouldn't be skipping the CT and signs of a concussion to look out for. I tell him to have someone monitor him, though I know he won't, and pull out my iPad for him to sign that he's staying Against Medical Advice.

Leaving him alone feels wrong, but I know there's no kind of logic or cajoling that's going to work against his brick wall of obstinance. By the time I'm done, Cade and Silas are out in the ambulance, ready to go.

With a last look, I watch him sit there in silence, surrounded by the trashed shop that he obviously loves, staring at the floor and already pretending I don't exist.

CHAPTER TWO

FORD

I don't know where to start.

This shop has been the center of my life since I was eight years old. My dad built it from the ground up, and I have to take care of it now that he's gone.

With the broken pieces of it strewn around me, it's pretty obvious that I've failed. Not that things were exactly perfect before today. My head throbs in time with my pulse, and the thought of getting up to start cleaning makes me want to hurl.

The paramedic that works with Cade said that could be a sign of a concussion, but I think it's more likely a sign of how fucking disastrous my day has been.

The fact that Cade and his buddy witnessed the whole thing makes me feel even more itchy and irate. This is exactly why I don't like people being around. No good can come from it, and it's just more people to witness when shit goes sideways.

I feel so dazed, I'm not exactly sure when I drag myself to my feet. I start picking shit up at random, taking a vague inventory of what they did manage to steal. The fucking asshole cops should have gotten all this in their report before they left. I need it for the insurance claim, and now I'm going to have to chase them up for it, which is a real dick punch after an already shitty morning.

After who knows how many hours, I get a text from Silas.

> Got some stitches at the ER. All fine, but they gave me the good drugs, which have made me kind of loopy, and I may or may not have puked in Cade's lap. He says I'm not allowed to come back to work today. You ok?

> I'm fine. Just cleaning up today and doing inventory. Sleep it off and if you want tomorrow off as well, that's cool.

My fingers hover over the screen, my brain flickering as I try to decide whether to send the next message.

> Thanks for trying to protect the shop. It means a lot that you care about it.

That feels way too fucking exposing, so I jab my thumb against the screen as fast as I can to erase it from the world.

> Thanks.

After that, I feel like I step out of time. My brain is a reel of images of this shop in its glory days, and all the amazing restorations Dad did here. I don't want to think about that while I stare at the mess it's become over the last year, so I do my best to shut my brain down and clean on instinct.

I have no idea how much time passes before someone knocks on the roller door. That's the first reminder that I didn't officially decide to close for the day, but I also never opened the doors.

The rattling metal is typically a soothing sound to me, but right now, the idea of communicating with anyone is exhausting. I inherited some regular clients from Dad who are easy to work with. The rest of the town at least knows me by reputation enough to be prepared to wait for me while I write shit down.

I hate using those text-to-voice app things that they have now. I'll use them if I absolutely have to make a phone call, but otherwise people can just suck it up and read what I type out. I get treated like a freak enough as it is without some disembodied robot voice dictating my thoughts to the room.

Day to day, being mute is not the crippling handicap that people make it out to be. At least, for me it's not. Especially because it discourages chit-chat, and I fucking hate chit-chat. If it's not about work, I don't want to hear it. When people are awkward about talking to you, especially if they're a little afraid of you, they're much more likely to leave you alone.

Which is exactly what I want.

But I need the money to keep this place afloat. Dad ran us at a steady profit my entire life, and as soon as he died, I started running us into the ground. Fuck knows how. I didn't change a thing. I'm beginning to think the man was using black magic. But until I crack the code, all I can do is take every possible job someone throws at me.

If there is an afterlife, I hope Dad appreciates the gargantuan effort this conversation is going to be, all in the name of keeping his shop alive.

The sun glares in, framing the person standing in front of the door and making me half-blind for a few seconds. I squint, but eventually my eyes adjust, and the figure comes into focus.

It's the paramedic. I don't know who I was expecting to see, but it wasn't him. And definitely not with a big-ass fucking Mustang sitting behind him, ugly-ing up my parking lot. It's a boat—in powder blue with a white racing stripe—and there's rust eating into half of it. Just by looking at it, I'm amazed he was able to drive it here.

"Still alive?" He hits me with a half-smile/sparkling eye combo that probably makes girls trip over themselves chasing after him. No one should be that good-looking in real life. Especially around here.

There are no movie stars in Possum Hollow.

I grunt at him. The fact that he's here so soon after seeing me falling apart makes me feel twitchy and vulnerable, and that pisses me off.

It takes a second for my brain to remind me that he knows ASL. I could sign to him in full sentences, but it feels kind of weird. In a town of less than 2,000 people, as far as I know, my dad was the only other person around who understood me. Silas has been learning a little, because he's a sweet kid, but I haven't had a real conversation with someone in over a year.

It should be exciting. Instead, the thought of it feels like a weird violation of Dad's memory. He would be the first one to tell me that's stupid, but I can't shake the thought, and the weight of it keeps my hands pinned to my sides.

The medic seems unperturbed by my lack of communication, though. Instead, he brushes past me, walking into the shop with the kind of charm and confidence that comes from being gorgeous and winning the privilege lottery in life.

He looks around for a second, taking in the pathetic amount of cleaning I've managed to get done today. And it must have been a while, because he looks like he's at least showered, if not slept, since I saw him this morning. The blue polyester uniform has been swapped out for stonewash jeans and a threadbare white t-shirt. One that he somehow manages to make look expensive, even though it's already sticking to him with sweat from the late afternoon heat. The white of the shirt somehow makes his skin look more tanned than it did before. Almost golden, like a surfer or every Australian actor ever. His thick, dark hair is a little fluffy on top, like maybe it air-dried on his way here.

Lifting one hand to run his fingers through it, I see a faded, indistinct tattoo peeking out from his sleeve, wrapping around his bicep.

"How are you feeling?" He continues to act nonchalant, but I can see the way he's studying me out of the corner of his eye. Ah. So that's why he's here. I bet Silas sent him.

"I don't need a babysitter," I sign to him. His easy confidence irritates me enough to blow past all those reservations about signing with someone who isn't Dad. At least for the sake of getting him out of the shop and the hell away from me.

He holds up his hands. The half-smile remains, but his gaze is as analytical as ever. I feel like I'm being played, and that irritation curls through my gut, twisting it tight.

"I'm just here because I need a good mechanic," he says. Gesturing to the beast sitting in front of my lot, he keeps rambling, although I'm not even pretending to pay attention. I've already turned back to cleaning up. "I had grand intentions about learning how to restore cars when I moved here. I figured I put people back together. Cars can't be that different, right? Turns out it's a lot different. I need someone who knows what they're doing, so I'm not breaking down on a weekly basis."

"I'm busy. Also, that's a stupid fucking car to own in the countryside," I sign.

He gasps dramatically, bringing one hand to his chest like a lady in a period drama clutching her pearls, and I bristle because I can tell he's making fun of me. "How very dare you? She is a classic. She's just a little rough around the edges because I haven't been able to work on her. But after this morning, I figured my new bestie would be the perfect person to help me out with that. I fixed your pretty face, you can fix my pretty car. It's the foundation of a lifelong friendship."

Standing up, I fix him with a stare that normally makes people cower. He, of course, continues to give me sparkly eyes like a jackass. I set down the pry bar I'm holding so I can give that stupidity the response it deserves. I don't know if it's his smug expression or his weird accent that makes him come across as too slick for his own good, but it's time to nip this in the bud. Whatever he thinks he can get out of me, it's not going to happen.

"Your car is fucking ugly. So is my face. You didn't save me from shit, and we are not—" I pause, because I don't know if there's a sign for besties, and I feel like an idiot spelling it out, "—friends."

"Tsk tsk tsk. That's no way to talk to your bestie," he says. If anything, his smile is getting bigger and even more smug, a wicked glint in his eye. It's all I can do not to physically growl at him, and the fact that it seems to entertain him makes me feel a little unhinged.

This man is infuriating.

"I get it. You're a feral junkyard dog who doesn't need human contact. Consider me suitably intimidated, *Cujo*," he says, throwing his hands up but not looking intimidated in the least.

He steps closer to me, his confidence not wavering for a second. He gets closer to me than most people in this town ever get, and then he keeps going.

When we're close enough that our chests are almost brushing, I try not to lose my temper. The emotion clawing at the back of my brain, begging to be let out, isn't anger. I'm not totally sure what it is, but it's strong and it's visceral and he's sparking something vicious in me.

He's almost as tall as me, which also isn't something that happens very often. I can see every detail of his face, from the sea-green color of his eyes to the notch where it looks like he broke his nose once upon a time. His skin is smooth and tanned, but with enough stubble that I know it would be rough to the touch. And though he's much leaner than me, he gives off this impression of size, or strength, or something. Like he's filling up all the space around me with his confidence. It sets me on edge.

Leaning in, he holds eye contact with me as he deliberately reaches out and presses a set of keys into my chest. My hand comes up to grab them on instinct and I'm left cursing myself, because it's too late to take it back now.

I swear, for a second it seems like he sniffs the air around me. Like a wild animal and its cornered prey. His eyes flick up and down my body once, but I can't tell what he's looking for. Only that he's looking.

17

It's kind of like the look some guys get when they take my size as a personal offense to them, and immediately decide they have to fight me or be unmanned. But not quite as aggressive.

I can't place it. And my head is throbbing too much for me to try.

"I have faith in you. Let me know whenever it's ready, bestie." His lips curl around the last word like he's savoring it.

He saunters out like someone in an old Western, turning at the last minute to yell back at me, "My name's Tristan, by the way. You should probably know that if we're going to be friends."

I'm not even sure how he leaves. Did he have a ride? By the time I've snapped my brain back into my head from whatever the fuck that was, he's gone.

Not for the first time in my life, I have no idea if he was flirting with me, making fun of me, or trying to manipulate me. Or some combination of all three. And not for the first time today, I wish Dad were here so I could ask him what to do.

No matter what Tristan wants from me, there's one thing I'm going to have to get clear.

I'm the predator here, never the prey.

Chapter Three

TRISTAN

Checking on Ford yesterday eased the tension in me a little, even if he was unnecessarily bristly about it. I'm sensing that's part of his whole vibe. Between his perma-scowl, imposing physique and the blackout tattoos that cover a large portion of the skin I could see, it's obvious he's cultivated a deliberately prickly exterior.

It's fine. I'm not afraid of a few thorns, if it means keeping him alive.

Once Silas was taken care of at the ER, I'd finally been able to take the rig back to the station and clock out. I have the next three nights off and all I wanted was to sleep for six hours, wake up, eat and then go back to sleep until I saw daylight. Tomorrow's daylight. Instead, I tossed and turned, worrying about Ford having a fucking brain bleed and slowly hemorrhaging to death on the shop floor by himself.

Something about him has set up shop in my brain and refused to leave me alone. Those psycho husky eyes got their hooks into me, I guess.

I refuse to let that beautiful kind of crazy be snuffed out of the world because of one meth head with a socket wrench.

Which is why I dragged myself out of bed after one measly REM cycle and went over there. I already felt like I knew him well enough to know he'd hate it, so I used my car as the pretense.

Not that it was a lie. My car is a piece of shit, and I haven't been working on it. My house is also a piece of shit, and I also haven't been working on it.

I'm starting to suspect I'm the piece-of-shit common denominator here.

Moving down here, I had big plans about escaping my problems and living the simple life. I was going to get away from it all. I was going to get in touch with the earth, and in a place that wasn't halfway around the world in a combat zone.

It's possible that this idea was born out of some magic mushrooms and an intense binge-watch of home renovation shows. My military discharge was unplanned and... abrupt. I'd been planning to re-up, like always.

The last thing I expected was to end up back in Boston, taking care of a mother I hadn't seen in years and never wanted to see again. I was in a bad place, walking the knife-edge of filial loyalty vs. my own mental health. All I wanted was to break free of her hold for the second time in my life and get as far away from her influence as possible.

I may have taken my escapism a little too far.

As soon as I saw that you could get whole-ass houses for like $30k, my city-boy eyes lit up. I could practically smell the pine needles and feel the soft earth under my hands. Nothing but peace and nature for miles in any direction, no one that I knew and, most importantly, fucking no one that I would be responsible for.

It's possible that the reality of it hasn't exactly panned out.

Sure, I'm in the middle of nowhere. Sure, I got a fixer-upper car and a fixer-upper house for peanuts. But I'm still a fucking paramedic, so I have no time and energy to throw into fixing the damn things. There's a reason the house cost $30k, and it wasn't because it's a beginner-friendly renovation.

It turns out there's a difference between being "handy" and having actual knowledge of construction. Plus, even though I tell myself every week I'm going to stop picking up overtime, I can't help it. If I go too long without an adrenaline fix, I get the itch.

I wanted the quiet, but sometimes it's too quiet here.

My childhood was loud. The Army was loud. After that was... Boston with my mother was soul-destroying, but still loud.

Possum Hollow feels like a whole lot of nothing, sometimes. I don't think I realized how much I always relied on having that background noise around me until it was suddenly gone. It leaves too much silence for my brain to fill, unless I preemptively fill it with some good ol' fashioned blood and guts.

Maybe that's my fault, though. It's not like I've put down roots. I basically befriended Cade against my better judgment. The combination of how much he looks like my little brother used to and the desperate need he has for someone—anyone--to look out for him was like an assault on my conscience. All I'd meant to do was help get him a decent job. I hadn't intended for the friendship to stick, but he's indefatigable when it comes to attaching himself to people.

So that's it. I have one friend. My relationship with Silas could be considered a tepid detente at best, because he thinks I tried to sabotage him and Cade when they were first getting together. As if pointing out that they were both barely adults, emotionally illiterate from their abusive childhoods and weighed down by crippling mental health issues somehow makes me an asshole.

Fuck, maybe I am the asshole. It's not like my cup of mental health spilleth over, and I've been working on it for a decade longer than they have.

At least they have somebody to go home to at night.

I shove those and all my other morbid thoughts into my mental lock box and focus on the task at hand. I may not have many things figured out in my life, but there's one thing that no one can ever take away from me: I'm a fucking excellent medic.

And I love it.

Picking up an extra shift tonight was an *excellent* idea. I can already feel those gnawing, painful thoughts fading into the background before we even make it to our first call of the night.

As soon as I jump out of the ambulance, the smell of blood and gunpowder hits me like a brick wall. It's acrid, combining with the syrupy, claustrophobic heat of the night into a substance that wants to force its way down my throat until I choke on it.

It's not a combination of smells I've experienced since moving here. The closest I've gotten is the occasional Fourth of July fireworks catastrophe.

It immediately takes the edge off the fractious energy that's always bubbling just beneath the surface of my skin. Which is a terrible thing to admit to yourself—that the scent of explosions and death makes you feel at peace. But being in control of a situation always settles me, and every time I approach a scene, I get a warm rush of endorphins from my body telling me this is a situation I've been in a thousand times before and will be a thousand times again.

Whatever situation I'm about to encounter, my brain is a Rolodex of problem-solving options. All I have to do is work through them one by one until something does the trick. If people are dying, I have the power to give them their best possible shot at survival. I can't control the outcome, but I'm 100% in control of the quality of care each patient receives.

The rest of it is out of my hands. That kind of consistency is something I've always found reassuring. Which makes sense to me, but there's no way to articulate it that doesn't sound like a supervillain origin story.

There's one body sprawled on the ground, unconscious. No blood that I can see, but that doesn't mean much. Only one patrol car beat us here, and the two cops are too busy holding back the growing crowd of rubberneckers from the bar to pay any attention to the man potentially dying in this parking lot.

As soon as I move towards him, it's like every switch and connection in my brain gets put to the correct setting. My body moves like molten metal, all muscle memory and instinct as I begin a set of actions I've done so many times they're probably etched into my soul.

The bone-deep sense of calm I only get when I'm working a trauma like this settles inside me, and the volume on the world gets turned down to a low hum.

My EMT and I do a quick assessment and then get the patient strapped to a board. Because this is an extra shift, I don't have Cade with me, which is a bitch. We need to move fast, and I don't know this guy at all, except that his name is Mathers. He's relatively new, and his eyes are bugging out like he's never seen a gunshot victim before.

Which he probably hasn't. Occasional hunting accidents, robberies gone wrong and domestic violence are the kind of violent deaths we see. And they're not that frequent.

This looks like an old-school gangland execution, if I was placing bets.

"This is going to be a rapid extraction, Mathers," I tell him as we get the patient strapped to a backboard while jostling him as little as possible. "Tell me why."

He looks at me with the same wide-eyed, overwhelmed expression as before. His mouth hangs open like he wasn't expecting to be quizzed while he works, even though it's the backbone of medical education, but at least he's keeping up. By the time we have the patient strapped up and in the back of the ambulance, he still hasn't come up with anything, so I put him out of his misery.

"Because this was a violent attack, and they don't have anyone in custody. We need to clear the scene as quickly as possible for everyone's safety. Now we can assess."

He swallows hard and nods. "Okay."

He has enough wherewithal to do his job though and gets an oral airway in the patient so he can start manually delivering oxygen. Meanwhile, I'm moving around him like an octopus, cutting off the man's clothing to assess his wounds, as well as grabbing supplies to get fluids into him.

"He's getting hard to bag, Tristan," the kid says, looking confused.

"Fuck," I say as soon as I get a good look at his chest. Placing my hand on the side of his chest, it felt like a tight balloon. Combined with the gaping chest wound and the fact that I could barely feel a pulse in his neck could only mean one thing.

The wound is letting his chest fill up with air, which is compressing his lungs and making it impossible for him to breathe.

Mathers' eyes go wide one more time when I pull out a 3", 14-gauge needle and prepare to stick it into the man's chest to release the trapped air. But this is only the beginning.

I shut down my brain. Like always, for the next thirty minutes, everything in the world seems to make perfect sense.

As we unload the patient from the ambulance, I can see there's a trauma team waiting for him under the watchful eye of my absolute favorite ER charge nurse.

"Oh, hell no!" Rebecca says the second she sees me. One disdainful look up and down lets her take in the blood covering my face and shirt, as well as the adrenaline-fueled grin on my face. She throws her hands up in the air as Mathers and I half-jog the stretcher over to the gaggle of doctors and nurses waiting to take him off my hands. "What did you do?"

"Oh, hell yes!" I'm completely out of breath but buzzing too high to let that stop me. As the trauma team takes over the stretcher and heads inside the ER, I move with them to give report. I rattle off his vitals at the scene, describe the locations and nature of his injuries and what work I did on him on the way over here.

"—and after two liters of rapid-infused saline and gaining control of the bleeding, his pressure is 108/76, pulse ox up to 96%, pulse of 112, he became responsive to light and sound, and was able to move all four extremities."

As soon as I finish, the trauma doc nods that she heard and whisks away to get to work. My part is done—apart from paperwork—so I'm left standing in the hallway, my chest heaving as I catch my breath but unable to wipe the feral smile from my face.

Rebecca is tapping something into her iPad while her team does their thing. She somehow manages to write and look at me like I'm scum on the bottom of her shoe at the same time.

She's special like that. It's why I like her.

"Did you hear that? Four fucking holes in his chest, one in his thigh, *two* needle decompressions on the way here and now his SPO2 is 96%. 96%! He has more oxygen in his blood than I do right now," I pant. "And a more normal fucking heart rate as well."

I fist-pump right there in the hallway, because nothing feels better than taking someone out of the jaws of death and ripping them back. That's the last straw for Rebecca apparently, because she drags me deeper into the nurses' station where patients are less likely to see me.

"Yeah, but you look like Carrie at the prom. Did you rub your face in his open chest wound before you slapped a dressing on it?"

I shrug. "He had a bleeder. I got it eventually. Scared the shit out of the kid, though." I snort, looking around for my partner and finding him leaning against a wall, taking deep breaths and looking a little green around the gills.

Rebecca squints. "That's not your usual mini-me, is it?"

"Nah, I picked up tonight."

I would keep talking, but she's manifested a pair of gloves from one of her twelve different pockets, as well as a pack of bath wipes, and she's scrubbing at whatever horror show is caked on my face.

To hell with boy scouts. Nurses are the ones who are always fucking prepared.

It's silent for a few minutes while she works, and I let my heart rate come down to a more appropriate zone.

There's a steely look in her eye while she continues to take me in, and the discomfort is enough to start chipping away at my elation.

"What?"

Rebecca snorts. "Nothing. I was considering giving you a lecture about taking care of yourself, but I know you're all a bunch of fucking adrenaline junkies and it would be like scolding a house plant. I'll save my breath."

"Aw, buddy, don't do me like that," I croon. "I thought we'd bonded over our mutual shady pasts."

The look of disdain she gives me should be bottled and sold as a chemical weapon. It's that powerful.

"I moved here because I was sick of gang violence and patching up gunshot victims, and I decided that dealing with quiet, insidious small-town racism was the lesser of two evils. St. Louis is one race riot away from open warfare, if you ask me. I have no idea why you moved here. Apart from bringing me fucking gunshot victims, apparently."

She sighs, finally letting go of my face like she's done as much as she can. Her hands settle on her hips just as a tension settles over the conversation. My adrenaline high is officially gone, and a hollow sense of foreboding has replaced it.

"Yeah, that was..." I'm not sure what to say. "I've never seen something like that here. Maybe a drive-by? Whoever shot the kid wanted him dead. That much was obvious. Hopefully, it's a one-off and not the start of a new crime wave, or you and I are going to have to move to an even smaller town for some peace and quiet, if we can find one."

Rebecca doesn't say anything. She doesn't need to. There's tension running through her, and I get it. I don't know the details of her background, but from the day we met, there was a kinship between us. She moved here from the murder capital of the USA, and she has the unique kind of exhaustion behind her eyes that comes from seeing more death and destruction than your average ER overnight charge. Which is really saying something.

Faded tattoos crawl over her hands, neck and the edges of her hairline. Between makeup, the natural dark umber tone of her skin and the strategic way she styles her heavy box braids, you can't make out what any of them are. But it's another small thing that indicates a complicated past.

Technically, they're a violation of hospital policy, but nurses with her skill set and expertise are difficult to find around here, so hospital admin has obviously chosen to turn a blind eye.

Eventually, she blinks a few times, like she's snapping her attention back from whatever memory briefly captured her. Warm, russet-brown eyes look me over one more time before she sighs.

"You should get some sleep, Tristan. And a shower. Don't let yourself get sucked into whatever this is. Maybe go a week without picking up overtime. Eat a hot meal. Go on a date. You're supposed to be living your life, so go live it." Her words are gentle, but there's a defeated tone to them that makes me think she's talking to herself as much as to me.

"Aw, Rebecca, I didn't know you cared. I've never been mothered by someone the same age as me." My smile doesn't reach my eyes, because the exhaustion is setting into my bones. And the fact that she genuinely does seem to care is making me feel hot and itchy all over in a way I don't want to look at too closely.

"Clearly, you've never been mothered at all. You were raised by wolves, otherwise you'd have enough sense not to go wandering around covered in blood and fist-pumping in front of sick people. Now go on. Go home. Get out of my ER before you pull more gunshot victims out of your ass."

I snort. "Kinky. One day I'll figure out if you're hitting on me or not."

Rebecca turns me around while I talk and shoves my leaden body towards the exit.

"Not. I promise. Now go home." Her tone leaves no room for argument.

I'm only kidding, and she knows it. There's never been that kind of vibe between us. Hell, maybe she only likes women. Or guys that aren't assholes. But I like to tease her, and she doesn't seem to mind.

My mind turns the thought over in a chaotic way, and I realize she's right. I do need to sleep. I'm not even making sense to myself.

The kid is quiet as we shuffle back to the ambulance and begin the long drive back to the station to close out the night. I know tonight must be weighing on him. It was a lot, especially for someone not used to seeing that kind of raw, visceral violence that normally concentrates in bigger cities. It's an unofficial part of my job to give him some words of wisdom right now, but frankly, I'm tapped out.

I can't think of anything to say. I could say it gets easier, which is partially true. It does. But only because you get better at compartmentalizing and numbing yourself to the emotional effects of it. Or you develop a progressively more unhealthy relationship with the trauma of it all until something in your life eventually explodes. Or you get so burned out that you genuinely don't give a fuck anymore who lives or dies.

For some people, it's a combination of all three. I've never been that optimistic about what's in store for me the rest of my life, but if I can hope for anything, it's that *that* never happens. I'm good at compartmentalizing. I blame my weird childhood. But hopefully that's enough to keep the burnout at bay.

Because this job and the elation that things like tonight's victory tend to bring me are about all I have left going for me.

For some unknowable twist of brain logic, thinking about the vastness of my empty life turns my thoughts towards Ford. Even though we've only interacted twice, I feel a kind of connection with him. I know isolation when I see it, and it's not often I find someone who's devoted even more energy to isolating themselves than I have.

Which makes me want to know more about why he seems to have removed himself from the world. A lot of the times I've chosen isolation were more about

28

it being easier than what I actually wanted, and if I had to guess, I'd say he knows a little something about that.

Not that I know the man.

Not that it's any of my damn business.

Apparently, some deep, primal part of my brain has decided to make it my business, though. Probably the same part of my brain that decided the best way to distract him from being pissed at me for checking up on him was to flirt as hard as humanly possible. Which probably surprised me more than it surprised him.

I'm not ashamed of being into guys. There's nothing wrong with it, and I'm not going to lie about it to anyone who asks, unless there's a genuine danger involved.

But I went from the Southie tough guy crowd to the Army, and then to butt-fuck rural America. Sure, being queer in any of those situations isn't the potential death sentence that it used to be, but it doesn't make your life any easier. I signed up six months after DADT was repealed. Just because we were officially tolerated did not mean we were welcomed with open arms.

I learned from a young age that your life is a lot easier if you keep certain things close to the chest. Especially if looking and acting like a stereotypical macho jock is comfortable for you. I guess I lucked out in that sense.

I always passed. Always. Nothing ever forced me out of the closet, and I was never in a situation where trying would improve my quality of life. After a while, being quiet about it becomes second nature.

Which is why flirting with the man-beast crazy-eyed mechanic in broad daylight was a really fucking uncharacteristic thing to do. As much as I like to think Silas wouldn't work for an asshole, there are still a lot of guys who draw their 'tolerance' line in the sand firmly in between what other people do, and what people direct at them.

Flirting with him should not have been my first line of defense. But there I was, batting my fucking eyelashes at him and draping myself over the furniture like a cat in heat, while he continued to glare at me in what I'm assuming is his default setting.

I'm not sure what it is about him that's reeled me in. He's clearly kind of an ass. He's also made it no secret that he doesn't like me and doesn't want to be my friend. But for whatever reason that I will also blame on my fucked-up childhood, my brain has taken all that prickliness and open hostility and decided *that, just that, that's what we want.*

My sex drive has taken a nosedive the last few years. I was hoping that getting away from home and my mom and all that baggage would be a fresh start. And it has. But that part of me never bounced back like I'd hoped. I nearly scoffed when Rebecca told me to go on a date a couple of minutes ago.

I've kept myself too busy to dwell on the subject. Especially because I'm allergic to introspection, with the exception of this long, depressing drive back to the station.

I told myself it was stress, and it would work itself out when I met the right girl. I assumed it would be a girl. I've always been more female-leaning, even if I'm not picky about what you've got in your pants. And when I do hook up with guys, they tend to be more femme, twinky types.

And it's not like I've been completely celibate. I just haven't had the same kind of drive that I used to.

But my body has decided to say fuck the right girl and be sucked in by someone who is the furthest thing from feminine I've ever seen. It's like my subconscious is giving a big 'fuck you' to everything I ever thought I wanted in life, while Ford gives me a big 'fuck you' to my face.

Either way, I'm pretty fucked.

CHAPTER FOUR

FORD

"I'm so sorry, baby," Mama says as she pulls me in and holds me to her chest.

Normally, I'd tell her I'm too old to be hugged like this. I'm eight years old. I'm not a little kid anymore.

But there's snot and tears mixing with the blood running down my face, and it hurts to breathe because I'm crying so hard. I feel like a little kid right now. And Mama's crying too, so if she wants to hold me, she can.

I fist my hands in her shirt, trying not to get blood on it even though it's already ruined. We sit on the kitchen floor for a long time like a couple of bawling babies. She's soft, and still smells like home, even under the metallic smell that I think must be the blood.

She rubs her hand over my hair again and again while she shushes and rocks me. One of her eyes is nearly swollen shut, but her split lip has already stopped bleeding and there's dried blood crusted on her chin.

Finally, she pulls back to look at my face. It makes her eyes get shiny with tears all over again, but she holds them back this time.

"I'm so sorry, Ford. I never thought he would do something like this. He's been so good to us, and then it seemed like he was having a rough couple of weeks with everything going so wrong for him at work. I figured he's allowed to be in a bad mood sometimes, just like anybody else. In a million years, I never thought he was the kind of person who'd hit me." Her eyes glaze over, until she's looking past me, or through me or something, instead of at me. "I never thought I was the kind of person who would let myself get hit."

She shakes her head, like maybe she can shake the thought right out of her head. I want to reach up and touch her face, but it's so swollen, I don't want to hurt her.

"Never again, Ford," she says, looking me in the eye again. "No one who hurts you gets to stay in your life, no matter what excuses or promises they give. Got it? That man is gone, and he's never coming back. I'll never let him hurt you again."

I nod. I want to tell her how sorry I am for making Tommy mad in the first place. I know she's saying it's his fault, but it feels like I'm the one who's been making him mad recently. He always says I'm too loud, or in the way, or that the way she treats me is making me soft, like a girl.

I never liked him. But I never thought he'd hit me, either.

Then today I lost my temper and told him I didn't have to do anything he said because this is my house, not his, and his eyes got dark. His fist hitting my face felt like a firecracker going off. As soon as I was on the floor, he pulled off his belt and hit me some more with that, yelling something about teaching me some manners.

I wish I'd been brave, like Mama. But it hurt so much, and I didn't know what to do. When Mama came home and saw the welts on my arms, she started yelling, too. That only made him angrier.

Now he's gone, but we're both still crying on the floor like babies and I don't like the way the world feels anymore. Everything around us feels wrong, somehow.

"I'm sorry, Mama," I say, still sniffing through the tears.

Time seems to stretch and distort, layering itself over and over until I'm living through the same scene again and again. My child-brain brushes up against my adult-brain. We both watch the moment repeat itself, like we often do, until my awareness drifts close enough to the surface that I realize I'm dreaming.

Dreaming. Remembering. It's all mixed together. Either way, it's not real anymore.

When I wake up, it's with a gasp. My throat feels tight. Too tight, like there's no air getting through, and my chest is burning with the effort of sucking oxygen into my body.

I hate that no amount of familiarity with this process makes it suck any less, or does anything to dull that initial feeling of panic before I can remind my brain and my body of where and when I am.

My skin is tingling like there are ants crawling underneath it. My body feels too light and too heavy at the same time, and all I can do is sit there, half-awake, dragging in one gasping breath after the other while I look around and fixate on all the details that tell me this is my room.

Breathe in for four. Hold for four. Breathe out for four. I squeeze my fists rhythmically, almost painfully tight, in time with the breathing. The fragmented pieces of the dream slot back into their appropriate storage spaces as I focus on the here and now.

That's the desk chair I broke the one and only time I tried to have sex in this house, before Dad got home and we had to scramble out the window to avoid getting caught. For the single hour of my life that I felt like a 'normal' teenager, whatever that means.

Wrapped around me are sheets that are rough from over-washing. I don't want to get rid of them because Dad bought them for me nearly a decade ago, and losing them would feel like another reminder that he's gone. He spent too many nights sitting on the end of my bed on these shitty sheets, trying to figure out how to talk to the busted-up child that wandered into his life.

The room smells like old wood, as well as the artificial citrus scent of the industrial, grit-filled soap I use every day to strip the motor oil from my hands. Outside, I can hear cicadas, as well as the distant sound of coyotes fighting in the scrap yard. It makes me briefly consider going downstairs and chasing them off. Maybe chasing out the nightmare by working out for a while. But the thought of it exhausts me right now.

The important thing is that none of these things were present when I was eight. Eventually, my body realizes this and unknots itself, the fear leached out of me like venom from a wound.

It's replaced by sadness, but that's not new and it's a lot easier to ignore than blind panic.

I grab my phone to check the time. 3:12a.m., which is not ideal. I need to get up in two hours, and getting back to sleep is probably not in my future.

But I also notice that I have a string of text messages from an unknown number.

> Hey it's Tristan.

> You know, your new bestie. I got your number from Cade. I want to check on my pride and joy and see how she's doing in car jail.

> The car hospital?

> That makes more sense. The car hospital. When do you think she can be discharged to her shiny new life of functionality?

I don't know whether to laugh or roll my eyes at the cascade of thoughts he's bombed me with during the night. Maybe he was drunk. I very briefly consider being polite and waiting until morning to answer him, but fuck it. I have nothing better to do right now. If his drunk ass was too stupid to forget to put his phone on silent, he deserves to be woken up.

> Your car is a hot mess. Just like that series of messages. I'm going to need at least a week and two grand if you want her to be reliable. But if you want my advice, you should get rid of her and get something that's even close to appropriate for driving around the countryside.

I'm about to put my phone down when I see three dots appear on the screen. Hmm, maybe I did wake him up.

> Bestie! You haven't forgotten me. I was getting worried.

> I was asleep, like a normal person. Like you should be.

> Nah, I'm on nights. Medicine never sleeps, and whatnot. I've only got one night off between shifts, so there's no point trying to switch my schedule.

> I can lie in bed, eating cheez-its and binging murder documentaries at 3a.m. just as easily as any other time.

I have no idea how I'm supposed to respond to that.

Before I can think of anything, he sends a picture. It's dark, like the only light is coming from a TV, but it's clear enough for me to make out his shirtless, muscular torso, lounging in a messy pile of sheets, with a box of cheez-its resting below his chin.

It should be repellent. But something about the unselfconscious way he offered it up makes me want to laugh, despite myself. The last lingering tendrils of my nightmare are chased away before I even realize what's happening, and I find myself smiling at the photo of some weird, invasive guy in the middle of the night for no reason.

Snapping my scowl back into place, even though no one can see me, I type out my response.

> See? Like owner, like car. A mess.

You're pretty sassy for a junkyard dog. I like that about you, Cujo. Keeps me on my toes.

> Yet here you are, still annoying me. You obviously like it.

True business. *winky face emoji*

Now that really makes me huff out a laugh. True business is ASL slang, and seeing it typed out in words is weird but also makes total sense. It reminds me that as annoying as Tristan is, in so many ways, at least there's one person around here I can talk to.

If I want to. Not that I ever will, because people are the worst. But it's nice to have the option.

> If you're 100% sure you don't want to scrap the rust bucket, I'll fix her for you. You can pick her up on Wednesday. Bring a check or a credit card. I don't accept bags of bloody singles, fyi, and you kind of give off that vibe.

Aww, see? You're warming up to me already. Taking care of me. Who knew you were so much nicer over the phone?

> Maybe that's what happens when people don't have to look at your smug face.

36

I've been told my face is a delight to look at.

I'm sure you have.

Is that a COMPLIMENT?

gif of a woman fanning herself

Depends on how well you understand sarcasm.

This is it. This is our meet-cute. I feel like Sandra Bullock right now. Or maybe one of the dogs that eat spaghetti. Except I'm less like a lady and more like an alley cat. Star-crossed lovers, obviously.

I didn't think medics were allowed to get high on their days off.

They're not. This is all my unfortunate, unvarnished personality. Don't pretend you don't find it charming, though. I can almost feel you glowering with adoration through the phone.

Do you want me to work on the car or not?

Do you ever get tired of giving the world the cold shoulder?

Don't worry, I'll wear you down. I'm irresistible when I put my mind to it.

2k. Yes or no.

> Any chance I can pay you in sexual favors?

> Hilarious.

> Don't worry, Cujo. I'll bring money. I'd never welch on my bestie.

I can't think of anything to say back. Irritation prickles at me, and it's made worse by the fact that he made me laugh—or at least want to laugh—more than once during that conversation.

Clearly, Tristan is like a splinter. The kind that wriggles under your skin and sits there until it gets infected, and you end up having your whole arm amputated.

Throwing my phone back onto the bedside table, I lie back down. Screw it. It's not like I can afford to say no to the work. There's a stack of bills on the dining room table that tells me I have to put up with Tristan's antics, whether I want to or not.

I just have to keep going until I figure out how Dad kept this place profitable for so long without breaking a sweat. I'll get there eventually, and then I can be as picky with jobs as I want.

Things will go back to normal, and I'll never have to speak to Tristan again.

CHAPTER FIVE

TRISTAN

We're walking into a small but nicely-kept trailer, ready for our first call of the night. Cade gives me a weird look when I check my phone for what may or may not be the tenth time.

It's dumb. It's really dumb. Like, high-schooler with a crush, dumb. But the brief conversation I had with Ford last night made me laugh more than I have in a long time, and it's allowed the flicker of attraction to him to lodge in my chest and take root.

He's prickly and rude and obviously brimming with some kind of unresolved trauma.

He's most likely extremely straight.

He's made it pretty clear that he doesn't care for me even a little bit.

None of that has stopped me from wanting to know how much of his big body all those black tattoos cover, and possibly work out the percentage with my tongue.

I want to make him growl at me again almost as much as I want to see if I could ever make him smile. The thought is as compelling as it is ridiculous.

Clearly, I need to get laid. My sexual drought has gone to my head. I shove my phone back into my pocket forcefully this time, determined not to look at it for the rest of the night. Especially considering he has absolutely no reason to text me and will probably be asleep soon.

Besides, Cade and I have something else to focus on.

"*Tita* Anika, my favorite patient," I say, coming to kneel in front of the woman with a smile that actually isn't forced. "If you keep calling us like this, I'm going to think you're trying to seduce me. What's going on?"

My demeanor is light, but even while I'm joking around with her, I'm taking in her appearance and building my assessment in the back of my brain. I've been doing this long enough that I can run on autopilot to a certain extent, and keeping things light never hurts with frequent fliers like Ms. Tanikon. She has enough to worry about.

She gives me a warm smile back, although it looks a little strained.

"I'm not the one who called this time. My grandson moved in with me a few weeks ago and he's done nothing but obsess over my health ever since." There's still a soft accent when she speaks, courtesy of her childhood in the Philippines, combined with the Ozarks twang she's picked up after spending decades in Missouri. "*Apo*, come tell them why you called."

Anika leans back in the chair, out of breath just from speaking, although she's trying to hide it. It's concerning, and I keep one eye on her while a young man emerges from somewhere else in the trailer.

He doesn't look much like his grandmother. He's much lighter-skinned; sand-colored to her tawny. They both have black hair, but his is curly and falling in his eyes, while hers is straight and always tidy. But their eyes are nearly identical. Angular, and a sort of honey-brown color, with matching angular cheekbones that make him look almost delicate.

The delicate features contrast sharply with the big, dark tattoo crawling over half his neck. I can't see it clearly, but it's something like an ornate letter—maybe a *B* or *R*—with a snake wrapped around it.

If that doesn't scream *connected*, I don't know what does.

The other difference is that while Anika always exudes calm, this boy--around Cade's age, I guess—is twitchy as all hell. He may have the trappings of a thug, but he carries himself like a scared teenager. He has one hand wrapped around his opposite elbow. His shoulders are hunched, making him seem much smaller than he actually is, and he barely flicks his eyes up to look at us before training his gaze back on the ground.

"She hasn't been eating," he says, his voice low. "And I think she's been throwing up, and everything seems to make her out of breath. She won't go to the doctor, though. She's been getting worse all night, so I called 911."

Anika rolls her eyes. "I'm fine. I'm old, I'm allowed to get tired. There's no need to get an ER bill because of it."

"There's also no need to die over an ER bill. Better safe than sorry." Cade is already taking her vitals, the furrow in his brow telling me he's noticed that she's not looking nearly as well as she's pretending. I try to keep her distracted with conversation so he can get a more accurate read on her.

The easiest way to get an inaccurate respiration rate on someone is to let them realize you're counting their breaths. It makes even the most level-headed person temporarily forget how to breathe, for whatever reason.

"You did the right thing..." I trail off.

"Tobias." He glances up at me, but quickly breaks the eye contact and shuffles like he's uncomfortable with this entire situation.

"Tobias. Good job."

The boy flushes all the way to his ears at the words, which is not the reaction I was expecting. Tell me you're a black hole of parental love without telling me... Or have a praise kink. Or both, I'm not judging.

But he's not the patient right now, and with Cade and Silas I'd say my waifs and strays roster for pseudo-parenting is currently full. I try to ignore the stupid paternal instinct that he's tripping in me and turn my attention back to Anika.

"Have you been taking your insulin consistently?"

The steely-eyed glare I get in response tells me everything I need to know, but I still need to hear the words, if possible. I arch an eyebrow at her, waiting for her to admit it or spit out whatever lie she has ready for me.

"Insulin's expensive."

I nod. "You're not wrong. But you need it to live. If you keep rationing it, which I'm assuming you've been doing, you're only going to get sicker. Cade, tell Tita Anika why she shouldn't be rationing her insulin."

He looks at me bug-eyed for a second, caught off-guard. "I don't—"

"Yeah, you do. You know what's going on. Why don't you tell her while I get an IV going, so she can get fluids on the way to the hospital."

As an EMT, he doesn't *have* to know the answer, but the kid's a lot smarter than he gives himself credit for. He absorbs information like a sponge. He's just never had anyone in his corner to push him. I know exactly how that feels, and how far you can go once you get a little help.

Which is why I broke my no friend rule and put him on the waif/stray roster in the first place. There's so much potential there, I can practically smell it.

He licks his lips nervously, before a look of focus comes over him. "Possible DKA. Diabetic Keto... acidosis. You're not getting enough insulin, so all the glucose is building up in your veins, fucking up your—I mean, messing up your electrolytes, and making you shed too much water, so you get dehydrated. And the whole thing makes your body too acidic, which is why you're out of breath, because your body is trying to blow out all the extra acid, because acid and carbon dioxide are kind of the same thing?"

Cade looks at me, the question mark obvious in his tone as well as his expression. It's hard not to let how proud I am of him show on my face. Instead, I smile at him and shrug, before looking at Anika.

"Basically, yeah. The point is, you can't live without it, and rationing it is making your entire body go out of whack. We're going to take you to the hospital so they can confirm this with tests and then fix the imbalances, but I promise you, if you continue to do this and ignore what your body is telling you, it *will* kill you. Possibly after putting you into a coma that will rack up a very big hospital bill, if that's what you're still worried about. So *please* take your insulin. But first, you're coming with us."

Her fluids are set up, so as soon as she nods—exhaustion in her eyes—we prepare to transport. Her grandson stands to the side, still looking nervous and unsettled. I feel like he wants to say something, but he's too afraid, or shy, or something.

I hope he doesn't go off the deep end while she's in hospital. She's a nice lady who doesn't deserve any of this shit, let alone the guilt of something happening to her grandson that she's most likely rescued from a bad situation.

Everyone is quiet as we get her ready for transport. The air is filled with the sound of Anika's heavy breathing. Tobias continues to linger nervously in the background until he comes out at the last minute and tells her he'll meet her at the hospital after he finishes work.

When she's in the back and I'm still standing in their front yard, he snags my arm. There's a desperate energy to him now, and it seems to have transformed him completely from the nervous kid I saw before into someone much more intense.

"Excuse me, sir?"

"Don't call me sir, I work for a living," I say out of habit. It's stupid, but I'm unfocused today and the old joke trips off my tongue.

He looks confused, which makes me feel like I'm a thousand years old, so I refocus.

"Sorry. What's up?"

"Did you mean it? That she'll die if she doesn't take her insulin regularly?" His eyes search my face like he's expecting a bullshit answer, but I don't mince words when it comes to this stuff. Or anything, really.

I don't see the point.

"100%. She needs to take the insulin at the correct dose. Every day. Missing doses or trying to ration it can kill her and can also put her more at risk for

43

other diseases that can kill her. Diabetes is a manageable disease, but you have to manage it. Which, unfortunately, can get expensive. It sucks, and it's not fair, but it's the truth."

He doesn't really respond. I'm pretty sure it's the answer he was expecting, even if it wasn't the one he wanted. Either way, his face looks set. His face is blotchy, like he's either been crying or fighting the urge, but the grim expression he carries tells me he's made up his mind about whatever it is he's thinking about.

I don't want to know anything about what internal choices he seems to be making about how to find the money for this insulin. I give him a reassuring shoulder squeeze, because it's about all I have to offer here, and then turn around to head back to the ambulance.

Not my waif. Not my stray. I cannot get involved.

The words repeat themselves in my head like a mantra the whole way to the hospital.

When we unload her at the ER, she's already looking a little better from the fluids. I lean down and whisper a few words in her ear as I hand her off, which makes her smile and answer me back in her native tongue, touching my hand in that soothing way only grandmothers can.

Not my grandmother, obviously. Like Rebecca pointed out, I was raised by wolves. But I've seen other people's grandmothers on TV, and occasionally in person, baking cookies and giving hugs and shit. I always thought it looked nice. A slight ache hits me in the chest as I take a deep breath and turn around to head back to the rig.

Except Cade is standing there, staring at me like I've grown a second head.

"What?"

He narrows his eyes, staying silent. It makes me suspicious, but I don't have the energy to deal with him right now. We both start cleaning the back of the ambulance and flipping it for the next patient, but the steady burn of Cade's eyes on me makes me snap.

"I swear I've never seen you concentrate this hard on anything that didn't involve a dirt bike or Silas' ass. What the hell are you looking at?"

Cade snorts, but still looks confused. "Since when do you speak Filipino, man?"

"If you want to get technical, that was Tagalog. Filipino is the standardized version that they made the official language of the Philippines in the 80s. They're similar, but not the same."

He mouths the word *Tagalog*, looking even more bewildered.

"I know a *little* Tagalog, because I spent some time in the Philippines." I turn my back on him to shove my jump bag back where it belongs, hoping that will bring an end to this conversation.

"When you were a Ranger?"

I try to level him with my stare, but he's not nearly as scared of me as he used to be and it's fucking irritating. "That's classified. Now do some fucking work."

Cade snorts before his bewildered expression returns. "Bullshit. And did they teach you sign language in the fucking Army, too? Because I saw you the other day chatting it up with Ford like it was nothing. Why have you never mentioned that? Like... Who even are you?"

"It's not my fault you never asked. I contain multitudes, Cade. Don't try to pigeon-hole me."

He fishmouths, like he can't decide if I'm making fun of him or genuinely pissed off. When in truth, it's a little of both.

My phone buzzes, but when I glance down, it's just a bullshit notification and I try not to let the disappointment seep into me. I have no idea why I want to hear from this guy. I flirt because it's fun. I fuck because it's good stress-release. I don't attach emotion to either of those things, because giving someone that kind of power over you is a guaranteed way to fuck yourself over.

One of my mother's more charming life lessons, but she's not wrong.

Cade notices, because he's still eyeing me like he has more shit to say. Not for the first time, I get a pang of guilt for not telling him... Not about my schoolboy infatuation with Ford, because that shit is too embarrassing for anyone to ever find out, but about the fact that I'm not technically straight, like I've let him assume I am.

Last year, he went through a whole baby-bi awakening thing when he fell in love with Silas. I debated whether telling him about myself would make him feel less alone, or just put the focus on me. In the end, I decided against it. It's not like I had any sage wisdom to share just because I've given and received a few blow jobs between bros.

I don't date, and I don't talk to people about my sex life unless I'm about to fuck them. The idea of even having a sexual identity has always seemed irrelevant to me.

But now that he's out and proud, I can't help but wonder if I missed a moment to be a more supportive friend. If I somehow betrayed him by not letting him in on this one extra thing we have in common, especially when it's something he was struggling with.

The whole situation makes me feel frustrated and vaguely guilty. Right now, he's looking at me like a kicked puppy because I didn't fax him my linguistics resume the day we met. It makes me feel even more apprehensive about how betrayed he might feel that I lied by omission about my sexuality.

This? This is why I don't have friends. Bristling with annoyance, I try to shove it anywhere other than at Cade or myself and end up slamming the door when I get in the driver's seat.

A shooting victim would really take the edge off right now. I'm not going to lie. But the radio stays silent, and Possum Hollow continues to sleep.

When Cade shakes me awake, it's such a jolt to my nervous system I go from lying on a stretcher to on my feet in half a second.

I'm looking around for a non-existent threat, my body on high alert, but it's just Cade. He's crouched like I am, because there isn't enough room back here to fully stand, but his hands are up in a wary gesture and he's looking at me with wide eyes.

I remember the shift being slow as hell. I remember going into the back to catch some shuteye so I wouldn't have to fight the dual urges to stare at my phone like an idiot or bicker with Cade. Also like an idiot.

I remember...

"Sorry, dude. It sounded like you were having a nightmare."

Cade's using the voice he uses on patients with me, which is annoying, but I can't focus on it. My brain is still spinning through the remnants of my dream, trying to piece back together what it was.

My mom was there. Conor was there too, back when he was little. One of my mom's interchangeable boyfriends and/or marks was there, and we were all on a drug run over state lines. The time she locked Conor in a hot car by accident, and I had to break the window to get him out.

That was when she was self-medicating for what would later be diagnosed as Bipolar I, before she was even trying to be a real mother. She never had much success, but at least that incident woke her up enough to try.

It's not like it made a difference. Conor still ended up dying young, even if it was a decade later. And it was still her fucking fault.

I think the rest of the nightmare was about his death. That's where most of my dreams tend to lead. I didn't see it happen because I was on the other side of the world at the time, but I've seen plenty of people get shot. My brain has no problem constructing vivid images of how it must have looked. It plays like a movie reel over the top of my real memories; always in slightly different incarnations, but always ending the same way.

This isn't the first time I've had that nightmare this week. So why is there unease sitting in my stomach like a lead weight?

What day is it?

The anniversary has been coming up, but I was trying not to think about it. It's possible my subconscious has betrayed me.

"Was it military shit?" Cade asks when I don't say anything for a suspiciously long time, too caught up in my own thoughts.

I blink, trying to shake the cobwebs from my mind. "Yeah, sure."

It's a lie. It's a lie I've told a thousand times, and probably will a thousand more.

It's just easier. People expect you to have nightmares about combat. It's almost more weird that I don't, possibly because my brain is too full of images of a death I didn't witness to relive the ones I was actually there for. I can't explain it to myself, let alone someone else, and I'm not in the mood to try.

"Come on," Cade says softly. "It's almost the end of our shift. B crew are ready to take over."

That's it. That's what day it is. I really did let myself get so caught up in this twisted angry-flirt thing with Ford that I lost track of time, and now the anniversary has snuck up from behind to backhand me.

Fuck my brain. I almost would have preferred to keep forgetting. It's not like remembering ever does me any good.

CHAPTER SIX

FORD

The blue monstrosity is sitting in the middle of my workspace, staring at me. Old cars have a way of being more expressive than new ones. Even ugly bitches like this one.

She looks like one of those dogs lying on her owner's grave because she doesn't understand he's never coming home.

Tristan was supposed to collect the thing hours ago, and he's not answering his phone. I'm not worried about him, but it does confirm my first impression that he's a cocky, self-centered asshole. I text Silas to see if I can get any traction on his whereabouts.

> Hey, any chance you know where Tristan is? He was supposed to pick up his dump truck this morning and never showed. I texted him and Cade, but no answer.

I wait for a response, staring at the screen. I have other work I should be focusing on right now, but this is like an itch at the back of my brain that I can't scratch.

The guy's an asshole, but if I know anything about him, it's that he loves this stupid hunk of metal. He's paying me so much to keep it drivable that he would be better off getting a better restoration from the same era. And in a color that doesn't look like an Easter egg.

> That's weird. Cade just said he was supposed to be at work two hours ago, but he no-call-no-showed and isn't answering for them either. Cade's all freaked out about it.

> Do you think he's okay?

> I mean, you met him. If anyone can take care of themselves, it's Tristan. I'm sure he's fine. He probably just slept through his alarm or something. Cade's not happy unless he has someone to mother-hen. He'll turn up, eventually. He survived armed conflict. He's not going to disappear into the woods.

I get what Silas is trying to say, but if anything, it makes me even more unsettled. Vets can be predictably unpredictable. My dad was the strongest, most put-together person I ever met. He was always the one you'd want in your corner during a zombie apocalypse. I've seen him build fire and shelter out of basically fairy dust and tree branches.

But I've also seen him so zonked from nightmares and flashbacks that he couldn't tell reality from memory. I've seen him build a shelter in our backyard because he thought he had to, because he'd temporarily lost his grip on where and when he was. As far as I can tell, no matter how long it's been since you served, those switches in your brain never get totally deactivated.

I spend a couple more minutes finishing the oil change I was working on, telling myself I'm not responsible for a man I barely know and have only met twice. And don't fucking like.

I don't get involved in other people's drama. It's my number one rule. I've had enough drama for one lifetime.

But the images of where he could be and what could be happening are inserting them into my mind's eye in relentless waves, and I feel compelled by basic human decency to follow up.

> Are you going to check on him?

Is my last-ditch effort for this to not be my problem.

> I can't. I've got Sky for the day. She's got the flu and Kris and Cade are both working. Cade will probably swing by at the end of his shift if no one hears from him.

That's in like ten hours.

Already cursing myself for being a soft-hearted idiot, I head to the office so I can look up this damn fool's address from his invoice.

Well, this is a dump.

His house is even more of a shit heap than his car. It's also in the middle of fucking nowhere, which is a saying a lot by Possum Hollow standards.

It's a little clapboard thing, falling apart, sitting on a plot of land outside town and so overgrown, it's like the woods are threatening to swallow it back up. Like a fixer-upper that's twenty years past its fix-up date.

The only indicator that someone lives here is the '68 Triumph sitting in the driveway, which looks completely out of place because it's in pristine condition and clearly the only thing Tristan owns that isn't about to be condemned.

The other sign someone lives here is the music throbbing from inside the house.

I'm not really a music person, but it sounds kind of familiar. Something chaotic and surreal from the seventies, or maybe the eighties, played at maximum volume, vibrating through the walls of the house so hard I'm surprised it hasn't collapsed.

Walking up, I can see the front door is open and the screen door is ajar. He's too far out of town to worry much about crime, but there's still a million critters in these woods you don't want to let in your house. Even someone from the city would have picked that up the first time he found a garter snake at the foot of his bed and learned to keep his shit shut.

The heat beats down against my back as I move slowly towards the door. By the time I'm pushing it open and peering into the house, the music is so loud I can barely hear myself think.

For once, I wish I could shout to announce my arrival. But I'm not convinced he could hear me over the racket, anyway.

There's no movement inside. It looks just as run-down inside as out, and the sliver of living room that I can see from the doorway sends a ripple of concern through me. There's an old sofa that's been upended, and a few more things strewn around the space.

I flash back to how my shop looked after those guys tossed it during the robbery, and my heart clenches in fear. Panicked, I let go of my hesitation and take a few big steps into the house, looking for Tristan. Maybe crime is a problem out here, after all.

The sound of the gun cocking is close enough that I can hear it over the music. It stops me in my tracks.

"Don't move. Hands where I can see them, turn around slowly and tell me what the fuck you're doing in my house."

Following his instructions, I keep my hands out to either side and pivot until he can see my face. Tristan is a few feet away, holding a camo-painted hunting rifle with the easy confidence of someone using muscle memory.

Despite the fact that he's shirtless and barefoot, wearing nothing but a pair of gym shorts, everything about him commands attention. All that defined muscle that I suspected he had is on full display, and he's more muscular than I would have guessed. His stance is confident, and I have no doubt he's willing and able to shoot me on the spot, given the proper motivation.

Then he sways.

His whole body shifts, like the world is lurching beneath him. That, combined with the cloudiness in his normally bright green eyes, tells me he's stoned, shit-faced or both.

He squints at me as he looks at my face, and I can see the wheels turning slower than normal to remind him he knows who I am. Or maybe blink me into focus.

"Ford?"

I raise my eyebrows and look pointedly at the gun he's still aiming at me.

"Oh," he says, releasing the butt to let it swing in a loose arc until he rests it against the wall, pointed up and away from both of us. Somehow the movement manages to be incredibly graceful, at odds with the way the rest of his body is jerky and looks on the verge of a drunken collapse.

"Whoops. Sorry. I only bought the damn thing in case there were bears out here, but this," he gestures at me, "isn't the kind I was worried about."

Jesus Christ, he's lit.

He smiles at me, a sloppier version of the charming side-smile he gave me the other day, and then attempts to wink but doesn't quite make it. He'd somehow managed to circle around behind me without being noticed before he told me to freeze, but now that the tension is released from the room, he moves past me with the loose, stumbling gait of any other drunk person.

Tristan miscalculates the distance, and his bare chest brushes against me as he moves into the living room. His skin is practically radiating warmth, and I can smell he's already sweating vodka. Still, the sensation of his firm body against mine distracts me for a minute.

I blame my general lack of human contact for it. I normally don't like it when people touch me, but there's something about Tristan's deep-seated casual attitude towards everything that makes him seem somehow... softer than other people. Not gentle, but like touching him is less offensive to my senses.

The same song restarts, and I'm pretty sure it's been playing on a loop since I got here.

"How can I assist you on this glorious summer day?" he asks, as he roots around his destroyed living room, searching for something. He doesn't bother to turn around and look at me for an answer, though, so I have to snap to get his attention.

"Ah ha!"

He keeps ignoring me because he found what he was looking for, which is apparently a grimy-looking mason jar filled with some liquid that's a nauseatingly radioactive shade of green.

"Gotcha," he says, smiling to himself before taking a swig.

I snap my fingers a couple of times until he catches on, turning to look at me. When I glare at him, the pieces fall into place and he shakes his head like he's pulling me into focus.

"Shit, sorry. Go ahead," he says, actually watching me so I can sign to him.

"You never came to get your piece of shit this morning. And you didn't show up to work. Cade is freaking out. Did you get robbed?" I gesture to the disaster that is his living room, but he just shrugs like it's no big deal.

"I'm having a bad day. I called out, don't those assholes check their text messages?"

He scrambles in the mess until he finds his phone and holds it at a weird enough angle that I'm pretty sure he's seeing two of it. Thumbing through the screen, he eventually finds what he's looking for and laughs.

"Oh shit, it looks like it never sent. Service is shit out here, I'll tell you. My bad."

I don't know what to do other than shake my head and sigh.

Tristan is laughing to himself, because apparently this situation is hilarious to him, but there's an undercurrent of darkness to it that reinforces my concern. I may not know this guy, and I definitely don't like him, but I've spent enough time around loose cannons to be concerned.

He swigs from his gross jar again before holding it up and raising his eyebrows at me.

"Do you want a redneck dirty martini?"

My fists clench as I push back on the frustration beginning to build in me.

"What the fuck is a redneck dirty martini?" I sign at him while he continues to grin, running one hand through his dark hair and making it stick up in every direction.

"I invented it when I moved here. It's vodka and pickle juice, and I give it five stars."

Jesus, fuck.

"Can you please turn off the endless loop of the Rolling Stones so I can think?" I sign once I can get his attention.

There's a twenty-second delay while his sluggish brain works out what I'm saying, but then I'm rewarded with another melodramatic gasp.

"This is the Pixies, you fucking cretin. Just how young are you?"

When I don't dignify that with a response, he continues to move around the space, throwing things for no discernible reason. It's starting to make more sense why it looks like he got robbed in here. Along with the books and papers scattered everywhere, there's a well-loved Gerber folding knife on the coffee table and at least two other utility knives that I can easily spot, which does nothing to make me less antsy.

It's starting to feel like the chaos of Tristan's house and mind is crawling under my skin, making me itch.

I watch him for a while. He looks like a German Shepherd that's been left alone all day and started shredding the sofa cushions for the sake of it. He's acting casual, but the whole thing has a tone of *wrongness* that is obvious to anyone who's sober.

I don't know what's going on, but I can see him winding himself up to something worse.

Is that an *acetylene torch* under his coffee table? Oh, absolutely fuck this.

Hard pass on death by accidental immolation today.

When I grab him by the shoulder to stop his movement, the look he gives me is deadly. That's the same guy that had a rifle pointed at me a minute ago even though he could barely stand, instead of the smarmy, kind of flirty guy that I've seen all the other times.

"What's wrong?" I move my hands slowly, looking him in the eye as I do it.

A smile breaks out on his face, and the tension leaves his body again, but it feels false.

"I'm good, big guy. I'm an adult, and if I feel like getting drunk at home one afternoon, that's my damn business. So, if you're not here to drink with me or show me the rest of your tattoos, then you can leave."

His fingertip grazes the cuff of the coveralls I'm still wearing, and he tilts his head like he's trying to peer up my sleeve. It sets off a little flare of panic in me, so I slap his hand away on instinct.

Possibly harder than I needed to, but he took me by surprise. What also surprises me is that he pouts fiercely about it. His lower lip juts out and everything.

It is *not* adorable. I tell myself this firmly.

Even shit-faced, this guy manages to press every button I have for being irritated. Someone needs to bring him in line before he hurts himself or anyone else.

"People are worried about you," I sign. "Cade is worried about you right now, and you're supposed to be his friend. Either something is wrong, or you're just a selfish piece of shit. Which is it?"

"Something *is* wrong." His eyes darken, and anger clouds his face, abruptly erasing the pout. "What's wrong is that there's a stranger in my house right now, giving me shit for what I want to do with my day. Cade is not the fucking boss of me. You are not the fucking boss of me. I ask for one day a year where I'm allowed to be a selfish asshole and fall apart without anyone giving me shit, and I fucking deserve it. I earned this day. So, you and your judgment can escort yourselves off the premises or I'll get my rifle and do it for you, Cujo."

He's pissed, and it's making him seem more unsteady on his feet, but I still don't want to test his temper. Even if I could take him, nothing good would come from it.

I don't think he realizes how much information he just gave me in that little rant.

"What's today?" I sign. "Why today?"

It was a high-risk, high-reward question, and it definitely sparks a reaction.

"Get out!" Tristan reaches for the stack of medical textbooks nearby and sends them flying to the floor to punctuate his outrage. "Get the fuck out!"

This time he rounds on me, his hands coming up and giving me a hard shove to the chest.

He's strong, I'll give him that. But I'm stronger, and I'm sober, so it doesn't move me back more than a few inches.

"People are worried," I repeat, staring him down. "You don't seem okay."

"Get out!" Another shove. "Get out!" More crap sprays across the floor. "Get out!"

The level of raw anguish in his face right now isn't what I expected when I came over here. I don't know what I expected, but it wasn't this. I don't know what today is for him, but it's clear that he's at the end of his rope and his coping mechanism is to crawl into the bottom of a bottle until he passes out in a pile of garbage and miscellaneous weaponry.

He goes to shove me again, but this time he staggers and falls against me instead. I grab his elbows to keep him upright, and he tugs away from me, but there's not a lot of heart in it.

His breathing is ragged, and I can feel his chest heave against mine as he sags his weight into me. His eyelids flutter, and for a second, I think he's about to pass out. All that rage dissipates so quickly, it leaves a hollowed-out husk in its wake.

Trying to get him to stand on his own feet is a fruitless exercise. He groans, bringing one hand to his head. I've been here for fifteen minutes, and he's ping-ponged from fierce to flirty to violent so hard he seems to have jump-started his hangover.

Fuck my life.

I don't want to drag this guy home with me, but I'm not staying in the middle of the woods and letting the shop get raided again. I also can't leave him to choke to death on his own vomit and break Cade's fragile little heart.

Also, all the weapons he has lying around are making my skin crawl.

The decision is made already, even if my brain wants to rail against it for a minute. I awkwardly shuffle his big-ass body until he's got one arm over my shoulders, half-conscious enough to support some of his weight, but still leaning a lot of it into me.

"Whe' we goin'?" he mumbles into my ear when I maneuver us towards the door.

My hands are busy, and I think he's too out of it to follow me at this point, anyway. Instead, I turn my head and try to catch his eye. Our faces are inches apart, and I can see just how bloodshot and wrecked his eyes are.

I have the urge to speak to him out loud, which hasn't hit me in a very long time. Maybe because he won't remember anyway, or maybe because it's Tristan, and he doesn't seem to care about anything, so he wouldn't care if my voice failed me.

Not that it matters. He's fading too fast, right in front of my eyes.

I toss my head in a "come on" gesture, and he sags into me a little more. That's as close to a yes as I'm going to get at this point, I think. And for all my noble efforts, dragging him bodily to my car is my reward.

CHAPTER SEVEN

TRISTAN

When I wake up, I have no idea where I am or what time it is. Or kind of who I am. None of which is a new experience for me, but the way my body is screaming at me with aches and pains and my stomach roils in revolt makes me think I'm probably getting too old for this.

Dignity has never been my strong suit. My mom always taught me that thinking you're too good for anything is a great way to screw yourself out of opportunities. When Kaitlyn O'Brien says "opportunities" of course, she really means "crime"; but in the larger sense I think her point still holds up.

The light coming through the blinds is pink-hued and cool, which my shift worker brain automatically clocks as dawn. My smartwatch is long-dead, obviously, so I'm telling time on instinct. The room also has that kind of lingering early morning heat. Like so much heat got sucked up by the ground yesterday and then slowly released overnight that it still hasn't quite dissipated in time for the whole cycle to start again.

My entire body is slick with sweat. Not the cleansing sweat of a good workout or a fuck, but the tacky kind of sweat that comes from trying to purge alcohol and sleeping in one semi-comatose position for too long. By the smell wafting off me, I'm almost 100% sure that no one would have been willing to get close enough to fuck me yesterday, and I definitely wasn't working out.

Which brings me back to my primary question: where the fuck am I?

There are distorted memories of yesterday in my brain, but their jagged edges are only exacerbating my pounding headache, so I shove them back into my subconscious and decide to get up and be surprised.

The house I'm in is modest, but kind of cozy. It's all dark wood and soft gray fabrics, kind of like what I was picturing for my "renovation" before I realized I don't know the first fucking thing about renovation. I follow the hallway to some stairs that lead down and hear just enough to confirm I'm not alone in the house.

I move noiselessly out of pure muscle-memory. In an unfamiliar space, not feeling on the top of my game, the idea of letting someone know I'm coming makes my nausea worse, even if I know I'm probably somewhere normal and safe. Although this isn't Cade's place, and I don't exactly have a long list of buddies. Unless I really did find a hookup with no fucking standards, I have no idea who would have wanted to mop my drunk ass up off my living room floor.

Unless I went wandering? That's a sobering thought.

Walking into the kitchen immediately reveals my... rescuer? Something like that. Tall, impossibly broad shoulders, and a stiffness that seems like it has permanent residence. Or at least it does when I'm around.

Ford.

I was supposed to pick up the car yesterday; I realize with a slamming tidal wave of guilt. Whoops. Add that to my thriving list of failures.

The rest of the dots aren't difficult to connect, although it only exacerbates the creeping sense of shame that's been building since I woke up. People aren't supposed to see me when I'm wallowing in self-pity. And for whatever reason, I wanted Ford to see me, least of all.

My only option is to try to make a joke of it, and hope that Ford hasn't completely seen through my mask into what a walking, talking disaster-human I am.

I look like an adult. I sound like an adult. But I missed out on all the life experiences that were designed to build you into a real adult. Instead, I'm just a collection of excellent life anecdotes wrapped up in a polyester jump-suit.

But no one's supposed to *know* that.

"I thought you were a junkyard dog, Cujo, not a St. Bernard," I finally say, forcing my tone to be light. I expect him to jump, because most people do when I'm creeping around. But instead, he just turns, slowly and calmly, and gives me a head to toe once-over that makes me feel more exposed than if he had x-ray vision.

"What?" he signs, his brows furrowed at me.

"Y'know, because St. Bernards rescue people?" Which makes him sigh, as if the existence of that joke is a heavy burden on his soul, and I bristle a little in return. "You know you're allowed to have a sense of humor. It doesn't detract from how scary you are to most people, I'm sure."

"And you're allowed to make jokes that are actually funny, yet here we are," he signs, still giving me that piercing stare.

"Ouch. All you do is wound me, Cujo. Death by a thousand dog bites. It's really going to put a damper on our love story when you finally murder me with your quick wit."

Flirting my way out of an uncomfortable situation has been a tried-and-true method for a long time. Especially with men, because most of the time it will make them uncomfortable enough to leave you alone, and on the rare times that they're into it, you can almost immediately parlay that conversation into sex.

Right now, either of those outcomes would be a win. Instead, Ford keeps staring at me like all my feeble devices are beneath him.

Thankfully, my stomach makes a painfully hollow sound and saves me from having to process where that conversation was going.

"Do you have any food?" I ask, pretending I haven't already inconvenienced him enough. I'm in the narrow hangover window where I need to eat through the nausea. If I leave it long enough for the sickness to get its claws into me, anything I eat will immediately be puked. But as long as I inhale some carbs in the next fifteen minutes, I should be able to absorb some of the acid churning inside me and head that off at the pass.

Ford nods, tossing his head towards the fridge. He watches me move around his space with a carefully neutral expression, which is fucking irritating because it makes it that much harder to get a read on him.

Is he pissed about yesterday? Or does he feel sorry for me? I'll pick anger over pity if I have to, but neither would be ideal.

I open the fridge, and the chill air hits me like a slap in the face. It knocks my hangover down by at least half a percent all on its own. There's a big Rubbermaid container in there that looks like it's full of spaghetti, and my body practically throws an internal temper-tantrum demanding it.

It only takes a little scrabbling before I find the right drawer for a fork, and then I pull off the lid, kick the fridge door closed and dig in. The salt-acid-sugar-carb combination is exactly what I needed, and I end up leaning back against the counter with a practically orgasmic moan.

Ford is staring at me. He's the master of blank expressions when he wants to be, but this one's a little extra expressionless. Like the absence of an expression is supposed to tell me something.

"Don't worry, I don't have cooties," I say, continuing to dig into his food straight out of the container. "I'd be happy to lick you in several key areas if you need further proof."

He completely ignores the cheesy come on, just like he has every other time I've tried to get a rise out of him. It's getting to the point that the fact that he's not acknowledging me flirting with him is almost pissing me off more than a rude refusal would. Not that he seems like he'd be rude, but still.

We stare each other down for a minute before he starts to sign.

"I have other food if you want something more... breakfast-ey," he signs, watching me shovel cold spaghetti in my face with an aura of mild horror.

"Pssht." I try not to spray spaghetti sauce as I talk. I would shoot for at least a little dignity, but I'm still racing against the nausea clock. "Capitalism already ruins all our lives. Why would I let it dictate what time of day I'm allowed to eat delicious pasta as well?"

"Capitalism?" He fingerspells the word, because if there is a sign for it, I definitely don't know it and he might not either. Then he raises one eyebrow at me, which is a lot harder to do than most people think. It also makes him look unreasonably sexy. Possibly because of how the rest of his giant, bulky body stays completely, profoundly still.

I take a deep breath. I have a love-hate relationship with this spiel, but he asked, so I'm physically incapable of stopping myself from answering. My mouth refuses to be muzzled.

"Everything we think of as 'normal' about how we structure our day is actually artificial. When the Industrial Revolution happened, human labor shifted from fields to factories and our corporate overlords had to figure out how to bleed as much out of us as possible. So, they made new standardized work hours and meals based on what the factory needed, instead of the eons-old ones that had actually evolved with us over time.

"I'm a grown-ass man. I've marched and slept and eaten exactly how the US government wanted me to for the better part of a decade. I'll be damned if I got out just so I could force myself to eat cereal for breakfast, because Old Man Kellogg had the world's biggest stick up his ass and thought bran flakes would keep people from masturbating, so they were more productive. Fuck that. I want spaghetti."

Ford blows out a breath, and the silence goes on for a smidge too long, like it often does after I let myself get caught up in a tangent. I shove more noodles into my mouth to pass the time.

Finally, he looks at me again and picks up his hands to sign.

"Who the fuck are you?"

I can't help but grin around my mouthful of food. Hopefully, it makes me look like a very sexy chipmunk.

When most people clock that I'm not quite normal, it encourages them to leave me alone. Which I'm a big fan of. But Ford looks intrigued. He's leaning in, looking like he wants to puzzle me out just as much as I want to get to the bottom of all his quirks and foibles. Whether he's willing to admit it or not.

I shrug. "Jury's out. But I am your new bestie. Especially since you took such good care of my baby and all."

Ford sighs and shrugs back. I'm wearing him down, I can tell. Soon we'll be real friends. I can figure out whatever the hell his deal is and put my weird fascination with him to rest.

The thought makes me happy enough that it holds back the tide of my hangover, and I finish off the spaghetti in record time. But then Ford catches my eye, and his expression is serious.

"Are you going to tell me what happened yesterday?"

Well, there goes my good mood. All the darkness that crowded into my mind yesterday comes screaming back with a vengeance, and I feel like I've snapped into someone else's body, the change is so abrupt.

"Nothing happened yesterday," I snarl.

Ford gives me a derisive look, like he doesn't buy that for a minute, and it's condescending enough to get on my nerves. Anger bubbles up inside me, filling my brain with vapor. My body feels strung out and rubbed dry like a husk. I've become something fragile that would be easy to snap, and the food is a ball of weight in my stomach.

I take a step towards him. Not threatening, per se, but filling the air with an aggressive energy in the human equivalent of a warning growl. It's served me very well in situations like these before for getting people to back the fuck down, but Ford remains as unimpressed as he always is.

This is night and day from the unhinged, feral guy that I first met at the shop. Right now, he is a brick wall of impassivity, and it's pissing me off so much more than a fight would.

The silence of the house feels like it's taking big, Pac-Man-sized bites out of my brain while we stare each other down.

Inappropriate flirting and inappropriate aggression are the only real weapons I have. How the fuck else are you supposed to interact with other men?

If fucking and fighting are off the table, what's left?

I feel like if he continues to just sit there calmly and stare at me, I'm a hair's breadth from throwing an actual temper tantrum. Over nothing. I hate that feeling. I'm not exactly the poster child of stability, but I'm normally able to control myself and act like a rational human being.

Ford unsettles me, in both good and bad ways. But right now, it's all bad.

"What? Why are you staring at me like a gargoyle?"

After a beat, Ford lets out a long breath and looks at me with soft eyes that make me squirm.

"We're still not friends, but if you need to talk to someone, you can talk to me. Don't bottle up whatever it is until you end up hurting yourself."

He looks so fucking sincere I might throw up. Eighteen protective layers of my various personas have been scraped back without me even noticing, and Ford is staring straight at my soul. Every cell in my body vibrates with panic. I extricate myself from the situation before I do something even crazier, like punch him. Or kiss him. Or start crying.

I throw the empty Tupperware on the counter and march my ass straight out of his house without another word. I don't bother to put my boots on, just grab them from their resting place by the door and run.

I'll come back for my car later. For now, all I need to do is leave.

"What the fuck happened to you yesterday?" Cade doesn't even have the decency to let me pour myself a cup of coffee before getting in my face. It took me forever to get a taxi to pick me up from the side of the road and take me home. I only had time to take a whore's bath and brush my teeth before riding my bike to work, and now I'm facing twelve hours of Cade's invasive questioning with a pounding headache and a pissy attitude.

In the blazing heat, because we've been rotated back to days, which I hate. It also means my uniform has to be tucked in and shit because daytime equals management loitering around. I've never been less in the mood to tuck my shit in. Please, please, can the world let me be a mess for once?

Or at least give me the decency of caffeinating before dealing with Cade.

I expected him to be annoyed about yesterday. I did mean to call out, but I guess the text didn't go through. I get it, it's annoying. But when I turn around and take in his face, he looks *stricken*. Like he's legitimately upset.

Which should make me feel even more guilty, but instead something about it seems to choke me. Like the walls of the room are closing in. Having someone genuinely give a shit about whether I live or die is like a wet rag over my mouth, and I'm on the cusp of suffocating.

My brain riffle-shuffles through emotions before pulling out the easiest card to play: irritation. It's simple and accessible, and right now I'm too fucking hungover to be introspective.

"I called out. I'm sorry the message didn't come through, but you're not my mother, so you really need to take all of this," I wave a hand in his general direction, "down a little."

I can see Cade fighting with himself to get control of his temper, and any other time, I'd be fucking proud of him for how much he's grown lately. But right now, I feel raw and eaten away by all Ford's silence, and I kind of want him to fucking scream at me. I deserve to be screamed at. I'm aware of this, and something inside of me is just itching to get it over with so all the creeping, crawling guilt and doubt can come to an end.

So, when he doesn't, and swallows it all down instead, my frustration stays trapped inside me. Instead of being released in a confrontation, it turns itself inwards and shreds itself into coarse pieces that continue to rub my organs raw.

I'm aware that I'm acting like a child, but I can't seem to control myself. It's as if everything about the past twenty-four hours has been designed specifically to make me feel unhinged. And all with the constant thoughts of Conor's death—and all the guilt that eats away at me about it--acting as backing vocals to the crazy chorus in my brain.

Nothing makes sense anymore. I moved here to be alone with my guilt and grief. I wanted it to slowly fade away into numbness. Instead, I've ended up with an unnecessary crush on a man who won't give me the time of day, but also saves me from myself and looks at me like it was worth it, and a friendship with a 23-year-old that I'm completely ill-equipped to maintain, because having people care about me is a fucking foreign concept.

Maybe I should go back to chasing a bullet. It was more overtly self-destructive, but also simpler. And I could leave all these painful, convoluted feelings in the trash, where they belong.

CHAPTER EIGHT

FORD

Tristan left my house yesterday in the same swirl of chaos as he entered. I didn't mean to piss him off so much, but he kind of deserved it. His lone-wolf, I'm-too-tough-for-feelings schtick is already getting old, and I've known him for like a week and a half.

Everything I know about him has been garnered from a handful of interactions and the information on his paperwork in the shop.

In my opinion, no one has ever needed to be taken in hand quite as much as Tristan O'Brien. But that's also not my problem.

He's not my problem. I'll remind myself as many times as it takes until I stop worrying about it in the back of my mind.

He still needs to pick up his goddamn car, though. So, I'm not surprised when he shows up the next day. I'm a little surprised that he saunters in with a big smile on his face, all expensive sunglasses, perfect white teeth and golden tan, looking like he's never been hungover a day in his life.

It's infuriating.

"Good," I sign, trying not to look at him more than I have to. "If you took any longer to show up, I was going to start charging you for storage. This isn't a marina."

Tristan slides his aviators on to the top of his head like he's in a commercial for something summery and then squints at me. His fingers sort of twitch as he tries to figure out what I meant, because the sign for "marina" obviously isn't in his mental dictionary, which makes sense. His eyes narrow when he gets it.

"Oh, because she's a boat," he deadpans while copying the gesture. "I see. Ha ha. You're hilarious. Thank fuck you don't talk, or no one in this town would ever get anything done. They'd be too busy cracking up at your jokes all day and basking in that sunny disposition you've got going."

I manage to not actually laugh, but it's close. Maybe it's the East Coast in him or maybe it's just a Tristan thing, but whenever he speaks it's so unapologetically blunt it almost swings back around to charming.

Almost. He's still an asshole, and I don't like him.

But I'll take him cracking jokes at me for not talking while treating me like a normal person over someone walking on eggshells around me any day. He keeps smiling at me all goofy and pleased with himself, like he knows he almost made me laugh. It makes the tiniest hint of a smile threaten to creep out, no matter how hard I try to keep my face on lockdown.

I will not give him the satisfaction.

We both stay quiet while I charge him out for the car and let him read over the invoice. It's peaceful, in stark contrast to the tense, frigid silence that stretched between us yesterday before he stormed out of my house in a hissy fit.

I don't even realize that we've basically been standing there half-smiling at each other for thirty seconds until Silas comes over. At first, I only glance at him, but then he has my full attention when I notice there's anger practically vibrating off him.

Silas isn't angry. Ever. Cade has a temper sometimes, but Silas is like a touch-starved baby deer, following around in his wake.

"What the fuck is your problem?" He bites the words out as both hands come up to shove Tristan in the chest. He must have pushed him hard, because Tristan steps back into me, and I have to catch him by his arms before we both end up toppling to the floor.

Tristan looks around with a baffled expression on his face while I put one hand on Silas' chest to hold him back. I'm sure he has a good reason for being pissed, but I'm not actually letting him get in a fistfight at the front desk.

"What the hell?" Tristan says, sputtering.

"What's wrong with you? You blow off work, blow up at Cade, then show up here looking like you're having the best day of your life. I gave you the benefit of the doubt that you were maybe having a bad week or something, but now it seems like you just enjoy being a self-involved dickbag to my boyfriend for no reason."

I see the pieces fall into place as Tristan sighs. "Look, it wasn't—"

"Spare me. I don't need to hear some excuse. I need Cade to stop coming home upset because you decided to take your bad mood out on him. He's not your punching bag."

I've never seen Silas with this kind of fire before, but he's clearly not backing down.

Tristan visibly bristles. All that good mood from before was as artificial as I suspected, because it's gone in a flash. The hard-eyed expression he had before he stormed out yesterday is back, and he seems to pull himself up and loom over Silas, despite hardly being taller than him.

"No, he's my partner. Does he know you're out here fighting his battles for him? Because if this is some territorial dick-swinging bullshit, you can give it to me without the self-righteous candy-coating. Just warn me to stay away from your boyfriend like you've been dying to since day one."

Silas pulls up short a little. They hold each other's gaze, and for a second, I think they're about to blow up into a full-on high school-style bitch fight. But after a minute, Silas seems to deliberately let out a breath, taking the edge of his anger with it. When he speaks again, his voice is still terse, but he's quiet and controlled.

It's a series of actions I'm intimately familiar with. Reining yourself in even when you don't want to. The tension in the room dissipates like a popped balloon.

"No, it's not... that," Silas says, looking deflated. "But every time you're in a crappy mood and snap at him for no reason, he carries it with him for days. Aren't you the one always lecturing him about his mental health? He has fucking damage. He has abandonment issues. You know this. You can't do the same push-pull shit with him that his parents did.

"Half the time you treat him like you're some benevolent older brother, doling out wisdom and getting involved in our shit. Which would be fine, if you actually cared. But whenever he worries about you, you act like you're barely even coworkers and push him away. He doesn't say anything, but I can see the toll it takes. It triggers the shit out of him."

Tristan is standing there with such a stony expression, I wonder if he's ignoring Silas or just trying to process.

"I'll talk to him."

It's all he says, but it's obvious that's the best we're going to get right now. Silas' shoulders are still up around his ears as he nods and goes back to work, but at least they're not scrapping on the shop floor.

I look at Tristan's blank expression as he stares into space, so different from the flirty, attention-seeking guy that walked in here. My brain continues to argue with me that I want to understand more about whatever the hell is going on with him. For all that I don't know about him, it's obvious that no one else is around to try to help him. At least no one that he can't intimidate or bitch out into backing off.

He stands slouched, like a small child that's still soaking in their own anger but is right on the cusp of switching to bawling after they've gotten in trouble. Exhaustion seems to seep out of his pores.

Once again, he's fucking crying out for someone to take him in hand.

"Silas is right, you know." I cross my arms over my chest for a second and stare him down before I continue to sign. "Cade is fragile. A lot more than he lets on. If you can't be a decent friend to him, you should leave him alone."

For a second, I think that anger is about to ignite in him all over again. But then he sags and runs a weary hand over his face.

"I know. I'm an asshole, okay? I just can't seem to get anything together right now. Everything feels out of whack. I don't know why."

I can feel my eyebrows climb up my forehead. That's probably the most honest thing he's said to me since the day we met. He finally looks at me, and I feel like I'm actually looking *at* him. Not some constructed version of him.

It's only for a moment, though, before he shakes it off.

"Are you going to tell anyone why you pissed off the only people in this town who care about you to get shit-faced by yourself in the woods?" I sign, preparing to get bitched out again.

But all the fight seems to have gone out of him. His skin pales and he rubs at his forehead, as if his hangover is creeping back in real time.

"Listen, can we just... Thank you. For mopping me up."—It looked like that hurt to say—"But I don't want to talk about it. I promise I will make it up to Cade for being a piece of shit."

"Good."

"I am a piece of shit though, right?" he asks, almost like he wants it to be true.

"I mean, I'm not exactly the person to ask. I've turned pushing people away into an Olympic sport. But if you want to isolate yourself, there are nicer ways to do it."

There's a pause while we both try to figure out how our simple conversation somehow ended up here.

"May I suggest shutting the fuck up once in a while?" I add.

That makes him huff out a laugh, and a ghost of a smile creeps back onto his face. Not the fake movie star smile he likes to flash at me when he's being a dick, but a real one.

I hate how much I like that I put it there.

Tristan scrubs a hand through his hair, and I'm a little jealous of the way it falls perfectly back into place. I can almost see him pulling his normal-person face back on and changing the tone of the conversation.

He points to a picture of my dad with his most prized possession—a 1965 Mustang restoration he did from the ground up, worth well over $100,000 at completion.

"Is that your dad? I wasn't expecting him to be so blond, but I see why you're built like a linebacker now. So, exactly how much was he obsessed with vintage Mustangs? And how did his love skip a generation if you hate my baby so much? I mean, he literally named you Ford, which is kind of on the nose, if you ask me..."

"He didn't." I shake my head, because everyone thinks this, and it's annoying. "My dad didn't know I existed until I was eight years old. My mom named me, and she didn't give a shit about cars. The whole mechanic thing was just a hilarious coincidence because the universe couldn't think of enough reasons for kids to make fun of me in high school."

Tristan eyes me, clearly surprised by the fact that I actually answered him with details about my life. But he's not as fucking surprised as I am. It was like the information spilled out of me before I had the chance to realize what was happening.

"That's okay, Cujo. I think my name suits you better, anyway." That sly smile of his is back, and for the four-hundredth time I can't tell if he's flirting with me, making fun of me or just being aggressively friendly.

"He loved that car, though," I continue. "It was stolen just before he died."

My face twitches, and I have to work harder than usual not to let any emotion slip through.

74

"You never got any leads on who took it? I feel like such a rare car would be easier to track down, right?"

"As you saw the other day, the cops around here aren't exactly SEAL Team Six. And I'm also not their favorite person. I don't think they tried, to be honest, and then Dad was gone and the whole thing seemed too exhausting to deal with."

Once again, I catch myself off-guard by vomiting up all this personal shit. I'm not someone who shares. But something about Tristan makes my brain open itself up to him without my permission. Or maybe he really is that pushy.

There's a look on his face I can't quite place. But it looks like he's up to something. I get the feeling he looks like that a lot, considering he never seems to be out of trouble for long. Whatever. If he wants to concoct a scheme, I don't give a fuck. As long as he leaves me out of it.

Finally, I remember why he was here in the first place and pass him his car keys.

"So sad that we'll never have to interact again. Please feel free to lose my number," I sign with an obviously fake smile.

"There's no need to pretend, Cujo. I can see the heartbreak in your eyes. Don't worry though, I'm not going anywhere. I'm like a penguin. I bond for life. I'll be back."

With another unfairly handsome smile, he pulls his sunglasses back down, turns and leaves me feeling like a tornado passed through.

Tornado Tristan. I was just starting to get used to it.

CHAPTER NINE

TRISTAN

I have no idea why I said half of what I said to Ford yesterday.

Bond for life? I don't bond with anyone. If there's one thing I excel at, it's running away from anything resembling a human relationship.

I also didn't mean to spill my guts about how guilty I felt about Cade. But everything Silas said had hit me right in the conscience. I'd told myself all along the reason I was getting involved in Cade's life was some kind of do-over. Emotional penance for abandoning my little brother to run away and join the Army, and not being there for him when he needed me.

Instead, I've ended up doing exactly the same thing all over again. Giving him just enough of myself that he depends on me and then bailing when I get distracted by my own bullshit.

That thought is enough to have a black hole of self-loathing threatening to swallow me up. But I've done enough wallowing for one week. I need to snap out of this shame-spiral before it gets its claws into me any deeper.

Besides, admitting my faults out loud to Ford made them feel more manageable somehow. Like the fact that he heard me say the words and didn't run screaming in disgust was a positive sign. He maintained the same stiff, detached body language that he always does around me, but his normally icy eyes were warm.

I thought that the memory of it would give me the push I needed to talk to Cade today and apologize, but of course this has to be the first balls-to-the-wall shift we've had in forever.

"Motherfucker." I wince as Cade presses the freshly cracked ice-pack against my eye a little harder than necessary.

He hasn't said anything to me that wasn't about work, so I still have no idea if he knows about Silas fighting for his honor yesterday or not. He's been a little less chatty than usual, but that could also be my paranoia getting to me.

That was my favorite thing about the Army. Feelings were strongly discouraged. Show up, follow orders, just add hot water, minimal emotional intelligence required.

Okay, that's an oversimplification, but still.

Realistically, we've been too busy to have any Kodak moments. From the second our shift started, it's been one long string of overdoses and bar fights, and the last one ended with me catching a very sharp elbow with my eye socket, unfortunately.

Hence the ice pack. I grunt my thanks and press it to my face, trying to let the cold chase away the ache while ignoring the pain in the rest of my body from all the hours of running around, hauling fentanyl addicts back from the brink of death.

"I'm getting too old for this shit," I mutter to myself.

Cade snorts as he collapses next to me. We're both perched on the back of the ambulance with the doors swung open, taking a minute to catch our breath before the next call inevitably comes in. And, more importantly, trying to waft out the scent of all the piss and vomit that's been spilled in there today.

It's evening now, red licking across the horizon as the heat seems to settle in for the night. Just like it has been the last million summer nights, my cheap polyester uniform is sticking to me in the worst possible ways. The temperature is making the swelling in my face feel worse, and a low throb settles in my cheekbone, keeping time with my pulse.

"You should report that so you can go home and ice it, instead of doing another two hours of this shit," Cade says. He's looking out at the sunset, and this time I'm sure the tension in his voice isn't something I'm imagining.

"Pfft, I am not doing that much paperwork over a glorified bruise," I say. "Also, Verne is an okay guy when he's not lit up like the fourth of July. You know how much cops love to throw the book at any incident involving emergency services. I know it was an accident. I shouldn't have gotten so close until they were done fighting. But that won't stop him from getting thrown in the can for a trumped-up felony assault charge just to satisfy some cop's desire to dick-swing."

Cade doesn't say anything. He just watches me, a frown on his face and a weird look in his eye.

"What?" I ask when I can't take the silence anymore.

"Sometimes I can't tell if you're an asshole wearing a person-suit or a person wearing an asshole-suit."

I stare at Cade, trying to filter through what the hell he means by that.

"I beg your fucking pardon?"

Cade shakes his head, biting his bottom lip and looking away from me like he can't make up his mind if it's worth saying more or not. I give him a second, and eventually, he breaks the silence.

"Like... Most of the time, you act like you couldn't give two shits about the rest of humanity. Then you come out with these things that are deeply considerate, or make it seem like you really, really care about people, and I can't tell which one is the real you and which one is the illusion."

Cade pauses. I can see the tension as he clenches his jaw, and it hits home again just how much I've failed at keeping myself out of emotional entanglements with the people around me, no matter what I told myself.

"Look, kid," I can see his shoulders rising, but I plow through my sentence before he has the chance to get defensive. "I'm sorry I was so short with you the other day. I'm having a shitty week, and I think that you're always the one who's around to catch the brunt of it whenever I'm in a bad mood. It's not fair. I'm sorry."

That's the most apology I've apologized to anyone out loud in a long time. I hope it works, because I don't know any other ways to say it other than acknowledging that I'm an emotionally-stunted asshole a million times.

"I'm going to assume Silas said something to you?" Cade asks, still staring straight ahead.

"The words 'self-involved dickbag' may have come up."

Cade huffs a laugh, and a little of the tension eases as we both smile at the image.

"I honestly don't think I've ever seen him say so many words in one conversation," I continue. Bumping Cade's shoulder with mine, I let my tone get serious again for just a second. "He really loves you. You guys are doing good. I'm proud of you."

Cade blinks a little too quickly for my taste. I didn't mean for this to get so heavy, but maybe we both needed it. Hell, I know exactly how it feels to grow up in a vacuum of praise. In that moment, I make a concrete decision to set my own shit aside and do a better job with Cade. And Silas.

And maybe Tobias. If I'm going to give myself arbitrary emotional redemption side-quests, I need to actually commit.

Conor deserves that.

Cade blows out a breath and changes the subject before either of us is forced to emote more than we have to. "Is it weird if I admit that I feel more relaxed now, though? Like that super violent call took the edge off?"

That thought of it makes me chuckle, even though I know it's not what he means.

"You mean watching me get a black eye made you feel better because you were pissed at me?"

Cade barks out a laugh but shakes his head. "No, not that. I mean like... It's good to get this excess energy or adrenaline or whatever out sometimes. It's like I've spent my entire life being on high alert, functioning on caffeine and adrenaline. Now I live with Silas and things are chill. He's turned me into some kind of pampered house cat. He makes me eat fucking salad, I swear to God. There's nothing to be scared of, and nothing to fight against, and it makes my body constantly feel like it's about to short-circuit."

"Believe it or not, I know exactly what you mean. I get that a lot here, I think. Since I left all that," I wave vaguely, "behind."

Cade looks at me with wide eyes. "How do you deal with it?"

"Not very well, I'm sure. Fucking and fighting are time-honored traditions, of course. Getting myself into dangerous situations that I shouldn't. Doing this." I jut my chin in the direction of the chaos we just left behind. "You have motocross, right? Doesn't that burn off some of that need?"

Cade scrubs a hand over his face. "It used to, but I haven't been riding very much, especially not in competitions. Silas thinks I'm going to get hurt. His anxiety gets so bad sometimes, then I get worried about him, and then the whole thing turns into some perpetual feedback loop of anxiety that makes everything worse."

I watch him for a while. Normally, I would try to dole out some kind of sage wisdom here, but with my eye throbbing and my entire body still holding onto the ghost of my hangover from Wednesday, I don't feel particularly sage right now. Just old and tired.

It makes me think of Ford, and the placid way he looked at me while I basically had a tantrum in his kitchen for no reason.

In a crisis, I'm the steadiest one around. When shit gets incredibly real, everything inside me gets calm. But I couldn't imagine being that stable outside of a situation where you have a life or death need to be.

Once again, my mind is pulled back to how attached I've gotten to Ford in such a short amount of time. I still don't know if my flirting is pissing him off or if he secretly likes it, because he refuses to give me even a hint of what's going on in his head, but at this point I feel like he's done me several solids in a row.

He didn't need to come to my house and pick up the pieces of my meltdown when I didn't show up on Wednesday. And he definitely didn't need to talk my shit out with me yesterday after me and Silas basically caused a scene in the middle of his business. I've done nothing but bring him drama since we met.

I get the impression that Ford is allergic to drama. It seems like he's going out of his way to help me out, whether he'll admit it or not.

The least I can do is find a way to help him in return. And unless he injures himself, I don't have a huge amount of (legal) marketable skills to work with. But I am pretty fucking good at sticking my nose where it doesn't belong. I can't get the image of how heartbroken he looked when he told me about his dad's car out of my head. It doesn't seem right.

A car that unique? In a town this small? I doubt it would have been chopped for parts. It would be worth too much in one piece. There was a chance it would still be sitting around in an off-books junkyard somewhere, waiting for the right illicit buyer to come along and pay what it's really worth.

If I can find the right elbows to twist, I bet I can track it down.

Maybe looping Cade in will be an olive branch, too. It sounds like he's itching for a little more chaos in his life.

"Hey, when the shift finishes, any chance you wanna help me with a project? It may or may not involve beating some information out of people."

Cade looks confused for a second, but then he smiles, looking only slightly psychotic. "Sure. Sounds like fun."

The first hour of asking around was deeply unsatisfying. Small towns are tight-knit, and anyone who has even tangential knowledge of a chop-shop operation generally knows to keep their mouth shut.

But the later it got, the drunker people got, and gradually people's lips started to loosen. There has to be someone running low-level crime around here. Meth doesn't deal itself. All we needed was one or two names of someone we could potentially peel some information out of to work our way up the chain and find out where the car would have gone after it was lifted.

Beyond that, I don't really have a plan for getting it back. But that's a later problem. Right now, I just need a name.

And after an exhausting amount of shooting the shit with drunk-ass locals, a couple of names started to come up repeatedly as being affiliated with local gang-crime. Most of them were unfamiliar, but one of them was surprisingly familiar and accessible.

Tobias.

I knew just from looking at that kid he was mixed up in some shady shit, so it's not a huge surprise. But it is a shame. His grandmother is a sweet woman, and he seems like a delicate kid to be fucking around with gangs.

By the look of the tattoo I caught a glimpse of before, he's possibly already in way, way too deep. I know how hard it is to pull yourself out of organizations like this, and if he's taking care of his grandmother and can't flee the state the way I did, he's basically fucked.

Either way, he's our first stop for information.

Cade and I march up to Anika's trailer in a weird echo of the other day, only this time we're both in street clothes and have a much less honorable mission in mind. As far as I know, Anika is still in the hospital, so we should at least be able to ask Tobias openly about what the hell he's mixed up in.

It was barely a few hours ago I was wondering if I should make some effort to look out for this kid as well, and now he's being basically put in my lap. It seems like fate.

The door opens a crack when we knock. I expect him to be surprised to see us, but that surprise quickly morphs into fear. Naked, unfiltered terror. Tobias blanches, slams the door shut in our faces and all I can hear is the sound of footsteps running to the other side of the trailer like the cops are about to bust in.

Cade and I look at each other, both equally confused. There's only one way to figure out what's going on, I guess, and when Cade shrugs at me, I can tell we're on the same page.

Splitting up, we run in opposite directions to circle the trailer. I vault over a low fence, my eyes already adjusted to the dark, and get to the back just in time to find my favorite patient's grandson crawling out of the fucking bathroom window like he's about to go on the lam.

He's slim, but not small enough to get through that little window without a struggle. When he sees me coming, he seems to panic and redouble his efforts. He flails like an animal caught in a trap to the point that I'm worried he's going to hurt himself.

As soon as I reach him, I grab his hoody and use it as leverage to haul him the rest of the way out of the window. Cade catches up just in time to help, and soon we have him standing between us unharmed, but looking like he's in full fight-or-flight.

I hold up my hands and take a step back. As much as I was down to beat the information out of someone if I needed to, I meant an asshole criminal, not a terrified kid. We were just going to talk to him, and his knee-jerk reaction has given me even more questions.

"Will you calm the fuck down," I say, being careful not to raise my voice. "We're not here to hurt you. You looked like you were about to lose a limb hurling yourself out of that window. What the hell?"

Tobias' gaze flicks between me and Cade, the whites of his eyes shining bright in the darkness. When he eventually answers, he faces Cade, not me.

"Look, I'm sorry about your boyfriend. It wasn't supposed to go down like that, I swear." He looks desperate, and his body is shaking just as hard as his voice.

There are a few seconds while the words sink in, and then the energy around us shifts. Cade's expression goes from confused to murderous, and the next thing I know he has Tobias' smaller frame shoved up against the wall of the trailer, his arm pressing across his throat and lifting him high enough that Tobias' toes are barely touching the ground.

Choked noises slip out of Tobias as Cade asks him, "What about my boyfriend?"

But I think we've both put the pieces together.

"You were one of the thieves," I say, because Cade is pressing down too hard on Tobias' throat for him to answer. He nods, still wide-eyed with terror like a rabbit in a snare. "Were you the one who stabbed him?"

This time, he shakes his head fervently. Cade relaxes his grip just a fraction.

I put a hand on Cade's shoulder. "Put him down. You're hurting the kid. Come on. Take a breath."

Cade looks at me. There's murder in his eyes still, but I hold his gaze and after a long, tense moment he relents. Tobias' feet hit the ground, and he takes a rough, gasping breath. Cade talks while Tobias wheezes.

"You knew who I was this whole time?"

Tobias rolls his eyes, and I see a lot more fire in him than I had suspected before. "Please. I may have just moved back, but everybody in the tri-state area knows about the pro-motocross player who ditched his career to suck trailer park dick."

In a heartbeat, Cade has him slammed back against the trailer wall, gasping for air again. "I'd watch your fucking tone," he says in a quiet, deadly voice, his mouth right by Tobias' ear as the boy's face begins to turn purple.

Tobias struggles to talk through the wheezing.

"Look, I'm sorry. It wasn't supposed to happen. The shop was supposed to be empty. I don't even know those guys. I was just doing what I was told. No one was supposed to get hurt."

I feel my eyebrows climb up my forehead as another avalanche of questions is unleashed in my brain. Who does Tobias work for? Was Ford targeted specifically, or are they just robbing businesses at random? I thought crime here was all low-level gang and motorcycle club shit, but is it actually more organized than I assumed?

The image of the gunshot victim I brought into the ER the other day pops into my mind. The one that screamed *gangland execution*.

I'm still not willing to beat information out of this kid, but it's becoming apparent that he's more deeply involved in the criminal underbelly of this town than I suspected. And I want some answers. I'm not above intimidating him in a hands-off sense, at least.

I tug at Cade's shoulder until he's eased off enough that Tobias can catch his breath. Drawing myself up to my full height, I lean into Tobias' space and speak in a low, threatening voice.

"You're going to tell us everything. Starting with who the fuck you work for."

CHAPTER TEN

FORD

It's past 11p.m. when I hear a knock at the door. It's too late for creditors, and I don't have fucking friends, so I don't know who it could possibly be. I open the shop early tomorrow, so I was already in bed, but curiosity compels me to answer.

I grab today's jeans out of the hamper and pull them on over my boxer-briefs. Muggy evening heat is hanging in the air like a shroud, so I almost don't bother with a shirt. But I don't like anyone seeing my scars if I can help it, even if they're strangers. I tug on the first flannel I found in the dresser as I pad to the front of the house.

Peering through the peephole gives me more questions than answers, but at least it's not repo guys.

"What the fuck do you want, Tristan?" I sign as soon as I've opened the door.

"Damn," he says with a salacious smirk. "I was hoping to catch you in your jim-jams. I'm loving this, though." He reaches out to trail his fingers over my hair, which I didn't bother to tie back like I normally do, until I shrug his hand away.

"T-R-I-S-T-A-N," I fingerspell his name again, letting my frustration show in every movement.

"I have a name sign, y'know, if you were ever polite enough to ask."

He demonstrates, making the sign for tall—an open palm facing sideways with his right hand sliding up it—but instead of pointing upwards with his index finger like normal, his thumb is tucked between his first two fingers for the letter "T".

"Because my name starts with a T and I'm tall," he says with a shrug, giving me that smug expression that seems to be permanently etched onto his face.

"You're really not," I interrupt. He is, but I'm taller, and the temptation to fuck with him is too strong to resist. When he gives me a startled look, the amount of satisfaction I get from it is unreasonable. If he's going to invest so much energy into curating this too-cool-to-give-a-fuck persona, I can't help but enjoy knocking him down a peg from time to time. I have to bite the inside of my cheek to keep from smiling.

"Bullshit I'm not tall. You're just—" he flaps his hands at me, "unnecessary. No one needs all that. Unless you're trying to reach the top shelf in outer space. Besides, my brother was like four years old when he came up with it, so everybody seemed tall to him."

He softens at the mention of his brother, and I don't have the heart to tease him anymore. I haven't gotten a good read on the details, but the way he talks about him on those rare occasions it comes up makes me think his brother isn't around anymore. Or at least that Tristan doesn't get to see him.

Either way, it doesn't seem like a story with a happy ending.

I copy the movements of his name sign before I forget, and it makes the smile slip from his face. He's usually so animated, but for once a still sort of sadness settles over him.

When he catches me watching him with concern, he shakes it off.

"Sorry," he says. "I just haven't seen that in a long time. Anyway, that's not the point. Get some shoes on. And do you have any clothes that are a little stealthier?"

I look at his outfit—black tactical pants tucked into black tactical boots, topped with a light-weight black henley that seems like he must have deliberately bought one size too small, because his muscles are busting out of it. He looks like he just walked off the set of an action movie. I'm immediately irrationally pissed that the bastard is somehow pulling it off and looking suave as shit instead of ridiculous.

"I'm not helping you rob a bank," I sign, arching a judgmental eyebrow at him. "Plus, it's like an hour's drive to the nearest bank."

Tristan ignores me and keeps running his mouth with a fevered excitement, as usual.

"I have a surprise for you. It'll be an adventure, and if I'm right, you might get something awesome at the end of it." He pauses as I continue to stare at him, not bothering to hide my disgruntled expression.

Tristan takes a half step towards me. Not enough to be dramatic, but just enough that he's invading my space. His face seems to take up more of my field of vision than is reasonable, and the sly smile he's wearing is difficult to say no to.

"Please? Just trust me?"

Against all my better judgment, curiosity is winning out.

With a small huff, I turn around so I can get his stupid face out of my sight for a minute.

"Wait here," I quickly sign to him, before heading to change into whatever I can find that might count as *stealthy*.

By the time we're outside, I'm ready to refuse to get in his boat for this ridiculous excursion. But it's not where I expect to see it. Instead, his beautiful, sleek Triumph is sitting there in all its glory.

Tristan passes me a helmet, but I look him up and down, using all my self-control to not let my mouth hang open like an idiot.

"What? This is quieter than my car or your truck. Like I said, the name of the game is stealth. Hop on."

"You really think the both of us are going to fit on that thing?"

Now he unleashes a full-sized, salacious smirk that I remind myself to hate before he leans in close to answer. The air around us is already hot, but I can still practically feel the warmth rolling off his skin as he stops himself barely an inch away from me.

There's a tension in my gut that I can't quite explain, and I hold myself impossibly still.

"I guess you'll have to sit close, then. And hold on tight, because I don't plan on going slow. Come on, we're wasting perfectly good night cover."

Not for the first time, I wonder why I keep letting Tristan suck me in like this. I tell myself it's curiosity about his endgame, even though that's not entirely true. It's clear that he's used to using his looks to get what he wants, and flirting his way both into and out of every situation is second-nature to him.

Someone that looks like him would never hit on someone like me just for the sake of it. He can't really be into men. He's too... Army-looking. The whole thing has the flavor of an elaborate prank. So, the question still sits, uneasy in my gut... What does Tristan want from me?

And what about me makes him think I'm an easy mark?

The thought makes me uneasy. I've spent a lifetime honing my internalized life and impassive face. The idea that this strange, boundaryless man could stumble past me and start reading into things—let alone use them to manipulate me towards some unknown goal—is disconcerting.

This is a terrible idea. Not only do I feel ridiculous riding bitch, to his obvious amusement, but I'm convinced we're going to tip over on the first sharp corner.

It is a beautiful bike, though.

The rumble of an engine has always settled my nerves. Of all my go-to sensory anchors, that's been one of the top ten for a long time. So being surrounded and flushed with something that normally settles me, while pressed up against a man who seems to have made it his personal mission to unsettle me at every turn, is making my stomach twist and my brain do weird emotion algebra to try to figure out what's going on right now.

I guess I'm along for the ride.

I spend half the journey wondering if Tristan's taking me into the woods to murder me, and the other half thinking this is some kind of elaborate prank. By the time we've driven miles out of town, ditched his bike off the road in a copse thick enough no one will see it, and then hiked another half mile on foot, still with no more explanation from him, I don't really care if he kills me.

It's dark, it's still hot and so muggy I feel like I'm suffocating, and Tristan is stalking through the underbrush like we're in a scene from *Apocalypse Now*. He moves with a grace like he was born to do this, all of which makes me feel even more ungainly and too-big than usual.

Eventually, I snap. Grabbing his shoulder, I turn him towards me. He shushes me immediately, but I smack his hand away from his mouth because that's a stupid thing to do to someone who doesn't talk.

"What the fuck are we doing here?" I sign, huffing with exasperation.

Instead of answering me, he gives me another one of his feral grins that make his eyes light up, greener than the trees surrounding us, and sucking me in despite all my efforts to avoid it.

For the sake of being silent, he signs back to me instead of speaking. It's weird to see, because normally I sign to him and he just speaks back to me, for the sake of expediency. His long fingers move with an elegance that I didn't expect, even if he doesn't have the fluency of a native speaker. He's graceful. I get so caught up in being surprised by how... delicate his hands are, despite their obvious strength, that I almost miss what he's saying.

"You're no fun. Just wait. I promise it will be worth your time if we find what I think we're going to find."

Still grinning, he reaches out to ruffle my hair. I slap his hand away for what must be the millionth time in the weeks since I met him, but he remains undeterred.

After another ten minutes of walking—well, Tristan prowling like a jungle cat, me stumbling like an elephant—we find whatever he's looking for. It's a barn, apparently. A huge barn on a property that's set at least a mile back from the road and surrounded by dense woods.

"What is this?" I ask Tristan when we stop moving.

"This," he leans in closer than he needs to so he can whisper in my ear, his hot breath ghosting over my sweaty neck and leaving goosebumps in its wake, "is the local headquarters of an Irish mafia family called *The Banna*. Bet you didn't know *this* was sitting just outside town, did you?"

My eyes widen, because I definitely fucking didn't. How is that possible? All small towns love to gossip, and with a population of barely 2,000 people, a mob hideout sitting thirty miles outside the town limits seems pretty difficult to hide.

"I know. I was surprised, too. It's a new development," Tristan whispers. "Apparently, there's a gang war between them and the Aryan Nation in Oklahoma, and a bunch of them are retreating to satellite locations and beefing them up. Either way, this whole thing has been going on for months, but before that the property was owned by the motorcycle club that buys their drugs from the Banna. They used it as a chop shop slash location for whatever illegal shit they were up to. Which means it very well might contain stolen goods they haven't moved. Especially, say, fancy restored classic cars that are worth more in one piece than chopped up and farmed for parts."

I gape at Tristan. It's too much information to sink in, and my brain feels like it's trying to read computer code.

"We're looking for Dad's car?" I sign at last, my mouth still hanging open like an idiot.

Tristan nods, and his smile gets smaller but more warm. Something sits in his eyes when he looks at me, but I can't name it. I almost want to say it's like he's actually looking *at* me, instead of his eyes quickly moving past the way most people do. Like someone's seeing me. But that thought is more discomfiting than anything else, so I shove it aside.

"Unless you don't want to?" He quirks an eyebrow at me, and once again looks unfairly handsome, to the point where it's distracting. I'm jealous. Some people got all the luck when they were born, and I have no idea what that might feel like.

And this is the man that took an off-hand comment about my dad's stolen car, managed to infer how much it meant to me, and then showed up in the middle of the night after concocting a half-baked scheme to get it back.

For me. A guy he met barely two weeks ago, who's been nothing but dismissive of him.

I was suspicious of Tristan's motives before. I couldn't figure out why he's been pursuing this flirtatious friendship thing so aggressively or what he wanted to get out of me for it. This makes it even more impossible to wrap my head around.

Why would Tristan do all this for me?

I force myself to focus. I can ruminate later. The shop may be a disaster and threatening to fall through my fingers, but if I could get Dad's car back, at least I'd have one piece of him that couldn't be taken away.

Instead of replying, I walk towards the barn, hearing Tristan's quiet laughter float behind me before he hurries to catch up.

I feel ridiculous creeping up on this place. Also, the knowledge that this is mob property sinks in over the next few minutes, and I realize that this is actually a colossally stupid idea. But it's too late. By the time my heart is pounding in my throat and my palms are slick with sweat, we're standing at the side door of the barn and Tristan is pulling what looks like an honest-to-God lock pick kit out of one of his millions of pockets.

He whips it open and gets to work, picking two implements and working them into the keyhole. I'm partially focused on wondering how the fuck he knows how to do that, while the other half of me is distracted by how mind-numbingly hot it is.

In the all black outfit, crouched down and skillfully picking the lock, he looks like a cat burglar.

I've been fighting my attraction to Tristan for a while. It's normal to notice when someone is objectively drop-dead-fucking gorgeous. Especially when they shove themselves in your face all the time. It's also normal when you're low-key jealous of it, and being around him always seems to make me feel that little bit more scarred and ungainly than I normally do.

But right now, this isn't just noticing that he's hot. I'm sucked in. Watching him bite at his plush lower lip in concentration while his fingers work is making arousal bubble in my gut and my entire body is honing in on him like a missile.

My brain still thinks he's a cocky asshole, but it's clear by the tightness in my pants that my dick doesn't care.

When the lock finally opens with a satisfying click, Tristan smiles up at me from his knees, his bottom lip still pinched between his teeth, and a wave of arousal washes over me in response. The urge to dirty up that perfect movie star face is almost uncontrollable.

"Who the fuck are you?" I ask instead. "How do you know how to do that? I'm pretty sure the Army teaches you how to blow doors up, not pick locks."

He just shrugs, an infuriating twinkle in his eye. "Some moms teach their kids to bake or sew or whatever. My mom had a different skill set."

I raise an eyebrow at him, but he doesn't give me any more than that. This might not be the time, but I need to know more. There's too much about him that doesn't make sense. It's like a scab. I can't resist the urge to pick at it and pick at it until eventually it comes off and all his secrets will finally spill out.

CHAPTER ELEVEN

TRISTAN

I barely get a *glimpse* of the inside of the barn when we hear a noise.

It sounds like someone coming towards us. I have a split second to decide whether to try hiding inside the barn or running for it, and all my senses tell me that getting pinned down here is a terrible idea. I grab Ford's warm, insanely oversized hand and pull him along with me.

We stay low and attempt to keep quiet as we run through the underbrush to the tree line. When we hit it, I straighten up and take advantage of the cover to run faster. Ford keeps up with me. He can really move for such a big guy, and we make it to the edge of the property fast enough that we weren't noticed.

I think.

Fuck, maybe this was a stupid idea. Going up against the mob over a single stolen car is probably not a great alignment of priorities. Even if I thought we could be sneaky about it. This was meant to be a scouting mission, so we could point the cops in the right direction. I wasn't trying to drag Ford into a firefight with the crime lords of Possum Hollow.

By the time we get back to where we stashed my bike, we're both out of breath. Ford is running his hands through his hair. It was tied back in a sort of messy bun before that I dug way too much, but it must have come loose at some point because now it's fluttering around his face like a dark halo.

He tugs at the strands, stress and fear clear on his face. Which I put there. Guilt creeps up on me, twisting my gut. This project was supposed to make him feel better, not freak him out. I was trying to do something nice after he's been so helpful to me all this time.

"This was a stupid idea," he signs at me, his face twisted into an angry grimace and his movements sharp. "I should never have let you talk me into it. It's not worth the risk even if the car is still here, which it almost definitely isn't. You're reckless."

The word hits me harder than it should. I shouldn't care what he thinks of me. I am reckless, after all. But having that pointed out, the one time I go out of my way to try to do something nice feels like a real kick in the balls.

Shake it off, Tristan. It's been well-established that I piss him off. This isn't news. There's no need to get all worked up over it.

I force a smile and keep my tone upbeat. "Come on, Cujo. At least we're making progress. If you scowl any harder, your pretty face is gonna freeze that way."

My intention was to lighten the mood. Maybe even make him crack a smile, if that's physically possible. Instead, I end up with my back against a tree, coughing out all the air in my lungs as a walking wall of muscle slams into me before wrapping his thick fingers around my throat.

He doesn't squeeze, and without meaning to, I tilt my chin up a little in invitation. The pain is bright and real, and I feel my fingers tingle with a surge of being alive.

Blood also rushes to my cock without my permission, but I don't think he's leaning close enough to feel it.

Those crazy blue eyes bore into me like he's debating whether he should rip my head from my shoulders, and after a long, suspended moment, he huffs out a breath and shoves himself off me.

"Stop fucking saying that," he signs, his movements jerky with anger.

"What? Cujo? I've been calling you that all week. I promise you it's a compliment. I love a junkyard dog. You need a name that fits your level of ferocity. Unless you'd rather I start calling you Princess or something. I can roll with that."

"No." An audible growl emphasizes this, and it's the first vocal noise I've ever heard him make. "Stop calling me pretty."

I frown. This seems like an overreaction, even for someone who supposedly has a temper.

"I know I haven't exactly been subtle in my flirting, but I figured you're buddies with Silas, so you can't be that much of a homophobe. Chill the fuck out. Just because I appreciate the view doesn't mean I'm going to do anything about it."

His eyes flick from side to side, and he looks lost for a second. His hands hang in the air, his fingers frozen like he's not sure what he wants to say.

"I'm not homophobic." Is what he settles on.

"Then what's your problem?"

"You know I'm not pretty, I know I'm not pretty, and I've been made fun of enough to know when it's happening."

That's not what I was expecting. I don't like to stereotype, but he never came off as the kind of guy that would be sensitive about his looks.

Especially when he looks like *that*.

Sincere isn't exactly my comfort zone, but I think it's the only appropriate response in this situation. I do my best.

"I don't know who's been filling your head with garbage, but Cujo, you are a very tall, very broody drink of water." I inhale before I continue, peeling myself off the tree he shoved me against and chasing him as he retreats from me. "Look,

I went from the projects to the Army, then back to the projects, then to here. I'm not ashamed of liking men, but I've never been in a position to be front and center in a Pride parade, if you take my meaning. It's possible I haven't been as upfront as I thought I was. But I can tell you that I think you're very fucking pretty, scars and all. And just being around you gets my dick hard."

Ford's breath catches. I'm nearly overwhelmed by the urge to add in a joke, or some other layer of double-speak and plausible deniability, so I can play this conversation off if it goes sideways. That's what I'm used to. But I don't let myself this time.

It's glaringly obvious that no one has ever told this man how gorgeous he is. Whether he's interested in me or not, maybe the decent thing I can do for him today isn't anything to do with this half-assed mafia break-in. Maybe it's just telling him to his face that I think he's fucking stunning. He deserves to hear it, however he feels about me.

The space between us continues to narrow, like rogue planets about to collide. I don't know which one of us is doing it, but it all feels suddenly inevitable.

I don't normally need to do much seducing, when it comes to this part, but I'll do my best. Going for sultry, I look up at him through my eyelashes and lean in further.

"If you don't believe what I'm saying—" his mouth is hanging open, his lips parted slightly and his breath coming quick, "—then believe this."

I take the hand that was squeezing my throat a minute ago and bring it to my crotch. I've been rock hard since he slammed me into the tree, and I can see his pulse fluttering in his throat as he feels it.

Arching my back, a sigh slips out of me as the gentle pressure of his hand sends tingles up my spine. My stomach swoops like I just jumped out of an airplane instead of touching a man I've been relentlessly hitting on for weeks.

Covering his hand with mine, I use it to grind his palm into me, rubbing up and down and creating friction through my jeans that's just on the right side of painful. When I feel those thick fingers wrap themselves around my length and squeeze, the ground seems to fall out from under me.

Panting softly, I keep whispering filthy things in his ear while he seems suspended in time.

I don't want to push him if he's not into this. But every part of his body is reading like this is someone who's enthusiastically on board, only hesitating, instead of the other way around.

I lean back to look at him, but stay close enough that our lips brush when I speak.

"If you've never done this before, I'm happy to steer you around the curves."

Something unshutters in his eyes. I get another growl out of him, but this one sounds predatory, rather than angry. Then I'm getting shoved into the tree a second time. This time, the wall of muscle drapes himself over my body in a way that sets me on fire down to my toes.

We're pressed together everywhere, and Ford buries his face in my neck. He mouths over my pulse point, his tongue hot and wet, catching me with his teeth enough to make me hiss and my dick throb even more. He works his way up my neck, over my jaw, where he licks and bites at the stubble, before kissing me like my mouth is something he already owns.

This isn't a kiss. This is my mouth getting fucked by his tongue, and I have absolutely no desire to stop it.

When we part, he pulls back just enough to bring his hands between us. I whimper at the loss of pressure on my cock, but I want to know what he has to say.

"I'm not a homophobe, or a virgin. I'm fucking gay. I just don't spread my business around because I don't like people and they don't like me. I didn't like you hitting on me because of your obnoxious personality, not the fact that you're a guy. But you had to keep pushing, because you're a brat. And now I need to put you in your place."

Nine times out of ten, when I'm with a guy, I'm a top. It's not a fragile masculinity thing, it's just my personality. I like being in control. But something about those words, even signed instead of spoken, makes me fucking shiver.

The idea of this big, broad, badass man bending me over his knee suddenly pops into my head and my stomach drops out at the thought in the best possible way.

Caught off guard by my internal rush to submit, I don't know what to say. Instead, I just nod, blushing like a virgin bride. I see him watch the way my Adam's apple bobs as I swallow hard.

"Yes, please," is all I eventually manage to get out.

Ford takes my hand and pulls me towards my own bike without another word.

CHAPTER TWELVE

FORD

The entire ride back, it's hard to tell what is the vibration of the Triumph's engine and what is the frantic vibrating energy building between me and Tristan right now.

I've been fighting this. I've avoided getting involved with anyone in town since I finished high school. I don't do relationships, and I don't get close to people. It's a lot easier to scratch the itch by going into the city for Grindr hookups from time to time and keep my privacy around this gossip factory. That's the way I've always done it.

Sometimes, seeing Cade and Silas make their relationship work without getting nearly as much shit for it as I expected, I wonder if I've been overly cautious. But then I picture Dad potentially spending even more of his time having to come to my defense, and I think I made the right choice. It was easier for everyone this way. Quieter.

I wasn't planning on Tristan crashing through the walls of my carefully constructed defenses like the Kool-Aid man. He's mouthy and bratty and mutters filth in my ear like a porn star, and you can only have that throw itself at you so many times before you give in.

It doesn't mean I like him. He's still a cocky asshole. I just need to get it out of my system. I need to know what those lips feel like wrapped around my cock, just once.

He was taken by surprise when I took charge earlier and seeing him fall apart under me was absolutely delicious. It makes me want to rip him apart, metaphorically speaking. I want him to be turned inside out by what I do to him until the only thing he can see or hear or breathe is me.

Just for tonight.

Pressing myself up against him, I make sure he's enveloped in my bulk. I keep one arm wrapped around his chest to pin him to me, while the other reaches down to keep a firm, possessive grip on his cock.

I briefly consider jerking him off, but it's dark out here and I can already feel his body turning into liquid in my arms. I don't want to crash and die before I get the chance to fuck the sass out of him.

He pulls up to my place and parks the bike in between the garage and the house. Both of us are moving fast, controlled enough to maintain the illusion that we're not scrambling for it, but well past the need for bullshit small talk.

Once we're inside, all bets are off. He squares up to me there in the entryway, and the energy crackling between us is electric. The fact that he's almost as big as me makes it more exciting that I can see the challenge in his eyes.

I reach out to shove him against the wall again, because it made him melt for me before. He stops me this time, although it's with a sloppy, self-satisfied smile that makes me want to beat his ass pink until he comes so hard he cries.

"Y'know, I'm generally a top. Just because you're a teeny-tiny bit taller, you think I'm automatically going to bend over for you?" He's putting up a fight, but that stupid smirk makes it feel like lip service.

I stand back, removing my hands from him completely. He sways towards me, like he misses my touch already, and I know he's putty in front of me.

"You can leave any time you want if you've changed your mind," I sign, keeping my expression neutral and my body relaxed. "But we both know topping has nothing to do with your size. From where I'm standing, you look like an overgrown twink playing dress-up. A bratty bottom, desperate to be put in his place. I see a hole standing in my entryway. So, are you going to leave, or are you going to get on your knees for me, hole?"

I can see him quiver from here.

There's a moment where he battles with himself, and I watch him trying to decide how much of a fight to put up.

When he sinks to his knees, but still with defiance in his eyes, I can't help but smile. He goes the extra mile and pulls his shirt over his head, and the miles of tan muscle and dark ink make my mouth flood with saliva.

I want to eat him alive.

"Good hole," I sign before stepping closer and wrapping my fingers around his skull.

Encouraged by the hungry look on his face, I bring my free hand to his mouth and push two fingers between his lips. I push slowly but with unrelenting pressure. I didn't consciously mean to test how obedient he's going to be for me, but a wave of pleasure unfurls inside me when he puts up no resistance.

Tristan's hands reach up to grab me, his fingers digging into the flesh of my hips. He clings to me while I continue to explore his mouth. His tongue is soft and warm, laving over my fingertips, and it makes my blood flush with desperate arousal.

Thankfully, he only seems interested in clutching at me, and doesn't have the wherewithal to try to get my shirt off. Because that's not happening, and not having to answer stupid invasive questions about it is yet another reason I normally stick to anonymous hook-ups.

I need to distract him before he gets any ideas about taking this further than it's going to go. When I pull my fingers out of his mouth, he practically chases them. They're slick with his spit, and all I want to do is see my cock sitting between those pretty lips.

I let go of his head for a second to unzip my pants and pull out my cock. It hangs right in front of his face with his eyes focused on it, looking just as swollen and desperate as the rest of me feels right now. When I move my hands into his field of vision, I catch Tristan's eyes for a second to quickly sign.

"I finally figured out how to shut you up."

I don't give him even a second to respond, immediately grabbing my shaft and feeding it into his mouth. My other hand finds the back of his head again, cupping it so I can hold him right where I want him.

Tristan takes one deep breath through his nose, and that's all the time I give him to adjust. If there's anything I know about this man, it's that he doesn't shy away from a challenge. And he needs to be put in his place. My cock is long, thick, and uncut.

I want to see him choke on it.

My hips move, starting gently but soon picking up the pace. The sounds that pour out of him are intense: choking and gurgling. Wet, raspy sounds, combined with the harsh rasp of his breath coming through his nose.

When I push into the tight heat of the back of his throat and feel him swallow convulsively around me, I almost snap.

Before I lose control, I pull out of his mouth. Tristan's face is already slack and there's a hazy look of pleasure in his eyes. When I reach down to pull him to his feet, he comes easily, but he's almost as unsteady as he was the day I found him drunk at home.

With my cock still hanging out, I ignore the throb of my own arousal for a minute to focus on holding a boneless Tristan upright and undoing his pants at the same time. He's about to punch through his fly, and when I free his cock, he sighs and sinks even more heavily into my arms.

He's fucking heavy, so it's not easy, but the feeling of him pressed against me from head to toe is comforting in a way I've never experienced before.

When I wrap my hand around his cock and give it a loose stroke, he sighs. His fingers grip me by the shoulders, digging in tight. I rest my forehead against his, but there's not enough coordination left after everything else for us to kiss, so we settle for sharing breath, lips occasionally brushing as we lean into each other's space.

I wish I had something to slick my hand as I work him over, but my own cock is still practically dripping with his saliva. An idea occurs to me that I've never tried before, but always thought about.

I finally pull Tristan into a kiss with one hand on the back of his neck. It's messy and uncoordinated, but something about this moment feels too intense to continue without having some kind of physical connection. As if my body needs evidence that this is actually happening. My tongue presses greedily into his mouth, and he opens wide for me like I belong there. I have to push down on the feeling rising in my chest that's already asking me for more.

This is only going to happen once. I better make it count.

When I pull our mouths apart, I lean my forehead against his again before reaching down to take him in one hand and myself in the other. His body is still soft and pliable for me, even though his cock is painfully hard, and he watches, entranced, as I roll back my foreskin to reveal the angry, swollen crown.

We're both begging for release, and I'm running out of patience to draw this out. Even if it's never going to happen again. I need to see what he looks like when he comes more than I need to breathe right now.

I'm glistening with spit and precum, and even just the friction of pressing Tristan's cockhead against mine makes me hiss. Slowly, luxuriating in every moment and tingle of sensation, I roll my foreskin back down until his cock is engulfed in it as well as mine.

It feels like we're being gripped tight, held together, and my body refuses to let him go.

There's an uptick in Tristan's breathing. He's leaning against me hard, his forehead boring into mine, and staring down at the place where our bodies are joined. I can see his chest heave and flush with arousal as I wrap my hand around us both and stroke the soft skin gliding over us under the pressure of my palm.

"Oh fuck," he whispers, sounding utterly wrecked.

I reach my free hand back up to grip his neck again and force him to look at me. Inches apart, I hold his gaze, both of us trembling and panting. Both on the verge of being overwhelmed, holding each other's gaze like a lifeline.

"Fuck, Ford," he whispers again. "Fuck, fuck." His lower lip trembles, and I know what he's trying to say.

I squeeze the back of his neck hard and nod. I want him to come for me. While I'm wrapped around him.

As soon as my hand squeezes his cock a little tighter, his breathing gets pitchy. It's almost a delicate sound, and it should look comical coming out of someone so masculine, but in the heat of the moment, it's one of the hottest things I've ever heard. With a breathy moan, his muscles clench, and I can feel his cock pulse its release over mine.

The place where we're connected gets even more wet and sloppy. Arousal has an iron grip on my gut, so I speed up my hand, jerking us both hard and fast for a second, milking the last of his release forcefully enough to make Tristan whimper and sending me flying over the finish with him.

"Fuck," he says one more time, still breathless as he comes down from his orgasm.

I can't help but huff out a voiceless chuckle. Everybody thinks not talking is such a tragedy, but they use their power of speech to say nothing but stupid shit, over and over and over.

"You okay?" I sign, bring my hand between our faces. Once it's there, I don't realize what I'm doing before I sweep my thumb over his cheek, trying to still the faint tremor I can still see there.

He nods, still looking a little stunned.

I kiss him one more time. It's soft, just lips pressing together in a lazy slide, but there's an unspoken intensity to it.

106

It feels like there's a ticking clock before I have to push him away and put that space between us again, and for once I don't necessarily want to. As soon as the thought becomes concrete in my head, though, a spike of fear jolts through me.

I always want to leave. Whether it's porn or a casual hookup, as soon as I've come, I want all that as far away from me as possible and to go back to my life. People are problems. Always.

I've never stroked someone's cheek in my life. But seeing this strong, cocky guy brought to his knees for me, both literally and figuratively, is making me loopy. He looks like a work of art, all sketched out right here in front of me. The urge to pull him close to me is still there, throbbing inside my body, but it feels dangerous.

I take a deliberate step back. The air between us is cold, and I fill my lungs with a deep breath of it to bring myself back to my senses. Tristan watches me, his red, kiss-swollen lips still parted. I can practically see the moment he shutters away all that vulnerability that just unexpectedly poured out of him.

His eyes flick to the floor. That cocky smile of his I'm quickly getting used to appears on his face. It seems forced, but I'm not going to call him on it. We both need to snap ourselves back to reality a little bit.

"Thanks, Cujo."

I can tell he's trying to sound nonchalant, but the hoarseness of his voice ruins the illusion.

As the cold continues to sink further into me, Tristan rights his clothes, gives me a half-smile and then turns to go.

I regret not saying anything else before the door is even closed behind him. But it's for the best. It's not like I have anything else to offer him than what we just did.

Chapter Thirteen

TRISTAN

"*T*ake your brother in with you. Buy some candy, then go out the back door when no one's looking. And whatever you do, make sure no one looks inside your backpack. Got it?*"

Ma shoves a crumpled wad of ones into my hand while I try not to roll my eyes. Of course I've got it. I've done this a hundred times before.

"Yeah, I got it."

As soon as Conor and I turn towards the store, she heads in the opposite direction. She has a cigarette in one hand and that kind of twitchy, nervous energy that tells me one of her moods is coming on. Maybe if we get enough money from this job, I can convince her to take a break for a couple of days and leave the two of us alone while she gets it out of her system.

Sometimes she just needs to let loose, and she always comes back better. I kind of get it. I'm seventeen, and I go fucking stir-crazy if I spend too long trapped inside. I can't imagine what it must have been like for her to already be saddled with a toddler at this age.

It makes sense, but it sucks for Conor. He's still just a kid.

"How long is this going to take?" he signs to me once we're alone. "I want to got to the park."

"Sure buddy," I sign back while talking. I've been trying to get him to practice lip-reading more, so he's more independent. The worse things get at home, the more obvious it is that I might have to leave him with her. At least for a little while, before I can come back for him. He needs to be able to take care of himself in the meantime. "We'll go to the park after this. And maybe then we can see if one of your friends wants to have a sleepover. I think Kaitlyn's in a mood."

He snorts, looking so much like a little version of me when he does it. I don't know how we came out looking so similar with two different dads, but I guess Kaitlyn's genes are strong. The only difference is that his eyes are brown.

"She's always in a mood. Fuck her."

I'm laughing to myself while we walk up and down the candy aisle, letting him pick out whatever he wants. I've got one eye on the back exit, and the rest of my brain is looking for security cameras. We just needs to get out back and make the drop without being caught on tape.

"Yeah buddy. Fuck her. At least we get to spend her money, though. Now, what do you want?"

The constant vibrations of my phone are setting my teeth on edge. I'm considering turning the damn thing off. Or maybe throwing it at the wall. But there's a slim chance that work will call, or Cade will have an emergency, and I'm scared to go completely off-grid literally twenty-four hours after I resolved to stop being such a selfish, self-isolating dickbag.

Maybe I should finally block her. Is blocking your mother an automatic entry to Hell, or something?

I'm probably Hell-bound, anyway. Not that I'm religious, but when you grow up in an Irish-Catholic neighborhood, all that guilt sinks into you and never really leaves, whether you consciously buy into the premise or not.

I just can't spend another minute of my life listening to her sob about Conor.

She did fuck all to take care of him while he was alive. Sometimes she actively put him in danger, if there was a payday on the line. I raised both of us while she was out running cons and running from one mafia sugar daddy to the next. When she wasn't making me actively participate in her little schemes, that is.

The only reason I left him alone was because I knew when I turned eighteen I had a choice: get out, or be sucked into the life for good. The organization she worked for had given me a lot of latitude, but they weren't going to allow me to keep hanging around the fringes as an adult. I'd have to join them or get out. And no mother of mine was going to let me live a legal, minimum wage life under her roof.

I thought Conor was old enough to survive her laissez-faire parenting style. I figured I'd join the Army, get some distance, save up some money, and then when he turned eighteen, I could get him out of there as well. I made a hard play to be a medic, so I would have a decent civilian career afterwards. The only reason I went for my ranger tab was because I know it impresses people, and I thought it would help me get a better job back at home.

I had a plan. My whole plan revolved around how to save us both.

It never occurred to me he might not see his eighteenth birthday. I never thought she'd be that reckless, even though I had a lifetime of evidence to the contrary. And maybe this is a shitty way to look at it, but I thought being deaf would give him more of an out. The guys she ran with were old school.

I thought they'd see his deafness as a fatal flaw. That it would mean he was no use to them. Instead, they thought that between that and being underage;

he was untouchable. No one could blame a poor deaf teenager for being in the wrong place at the wrong time.

Every time I rotated stateside, I'd come check on him, and he made it sound like they were doing so well. Ma was diagnosed by then, and on her meds. He was in school. They painted the perfect picture. By our standards, at least. When the whole time, she was using him to run drugs and fuck knows what else on the side, to keep them afloat, and convincing him to lie to me about it.

She's lucky I didn't let her drown herself in her own guilt after he died. I did my fucking time. I cleaned her up, stayed until she was stable and had a support system outside of her shitty criminal circle, and then I bounced.

It was more than she deserved, and now I'm done.

I didn't want to talk to her on the anniversary of Conor's death when I was busy making a fool of myself in front of Ford, and I don't want to talk to her now.

Especially when I feel like I'm still mostly making a fool of myself in front of Ford.

Last night was... intense.

I've never gone to my knees like that for anyone. I've never had my whole body trembling and begging to become soft and compliant. Something about his calm, steady demeanor and the way he refuses to put up with my shit makes me immediately fall to pieces for him whenever he asks, apparently. It was embarrassing. I know exactly why he put distance between us as soon as we'd both come.

I was embarrassed for myself, too. I'm sure he had no idea what to say after watching a grown-ass man—one who's supposed to be able to take care of himself—whining and whimpering like a desperate child.

I shiver a little; not for the first time today. It's boiling hot in my house, with the A/C losing its fight against the late summer heat, but there's a chill inside me that I can't seem to shake. Maybe I'm getting the flu. That could explain why I felt so weak the whole way home after I fled from Ford's sight.

Pacing my living room and getting progressively agitated over Mom's relentless calls isn't the most productive use of my time, but my head feels too fogged for anything else. It's like I'm swimming in a sea of my own humiliation, and flashes of last night keep assaulting me. And each time, I'm hit by arousal even harder than I'm hit by shame.

Which makes it all worse.

The heady, salty taste of Ford on my tongue. The undeniably powerful, masculine body I clung to while he fucked my mouth. The way I felt delicate when he cradled my face, even while he pulled inhuman sounds out of me.

It's too quiet. I turn the volume up on the music, but it's not helping. My brain feels like it's slowly unraveling, each gray fold trying to flatten itself and wiggle free from my ear. Maybe my brain is just as embarrassed and ashamed of myself as I am.

I need to... Fuck, I need to hurt someone. Or something. The idea of literally picking up a cushion and ripping it in half is suddenly appealing, which isn't a great sign.

I already worked out until my muscles screamed, and I'm not on shift again for two more days. There's nothing I can do except continue to work myself up and try not to think about Ford.

Ford. God, he tasted good. I wonder what the rest of him tastes like. I wonder what it would feel like to be pinned underneath him, and if it would be just as satisfying as it was to have him tower over me.

Would he be disgusted by how easily I seem to give in to him? Or does he secretly love it, even if it's humiliating for me?

I don't care. As soon as I start to picture his hands on me, it's all I can think about. I'm not normally one for physical contact, but right now the idea of him wrapping me up in his thick arms and squeezing me until my eyes pop out of my skull sounds really fucking appealing.

The shivering continues, because I'm still so fucking cold. Goddammit. I put on a hoody, even though it's nearly one hundred degrees outside. It's as if the heat can't break through my insulating shell of humiliation and shame.

Shiver. Pace. Shiver. Pace.

Continue to ignore the phone.

This desperate urge I have to see Ford, less than twelve hours after I left him, is pathetic. I don't know what I'm even expecting. For him to look at me without shame in his eyes? For him to invite me in and fuck me sideways?

It doesn't matter. As the shivering gets worse, not better, I decide to give in to my pathetic cravings. I'll blame it on the flu later, and say I was hallucinating or something.

I need to go back. There's no logic to it; only endless, vast, aching quantities of *want* that I've never experienced before, and would never like to again.

CHAPTER FOURTEEN

FORD

The sound of a wrench hitting the shop floor echoes through the room like a gong, making me wince. It's not the first clumsy or careless thing I've done today—not even close—and the raised eyebrows I'm getting from where Silas is shuffling through a stack of invoices in the office tell me it hasn't gone unnoticed.

"You okay, boss?"

He doesn't specify that he means in the greater existential sense, but I think the implication is there. I'm bone-tired from spending all night with Tristan getting into pointless shenanigans. Ending the adventure with my dick in his perfect fucking mouth was only the icing on the very confusing cake.

All day I haven't been able to get the image of him on his knees out of my head. The moment I saw his pride break, and he gave in to his desire to be... used. It was palpable. Like a living thing in the room with us.

I've never had any interest in a relationship. And between my desire to stay off the small-town gossip circuit and the wavering attitudes towards non-hetero sexualities, it was always easier to get my itch scratched outside the town limits.

There are plenty of places around here with people looking to get railed by a beefy top and willing to skip the conversation part of the equation. It's quick and dirty and suits me just fine.

I've never shit where I eat before. Which means I've never even contemplated the idea of a second round with the same person. It's never been an option, and no part of my brain has ever sent me looking for it.

Now, in the space of twelve hours, I feel like I've broken all the rules I've created in my life to keep myself safe.

People bring problems.

Relationships are distracting at best, and downright dangerous more often than not.

My neck feels tight, and I scratch absently at the scar running under my beard. Swallowing takes more effort than it should, and I can feel the wall inside my brain, the one that holds back the memories I need it to, waver under an onslaught.

Suddenly, there's an acrid smell of blood and urine and death in the air, although I know it's really in my head. I try to shake it off, but the smell persists. It burns the inside of my nose and makes the choking sensation even worse. I take a deep breath to even myself out, but it gets stuck somewhere in my tightening throat and I have to cough to shake the feeling loose.

I don't realize that I'm rubbing at my neck until Silas touches my elbow. It's gentle, but still makes me jump. He steps back, his hands up in the air and concern clear in his eyes.

"What's wrong?" he asks, not bothering to pretend like everything might be fine.

Forcing myself to settle, I blow out all the air in my lungs and try to force all the shivery, twitchy sensations crawling through my body with it.

"I'm sorry," I sign, once I've collected myself. I pull out my phone to tap out a message for him.

I didn't get any sleep last night and I'm not feeling it today. Pick-ups are done for the day. Let's just close. You can get an early night. You're still injured.

Silas continues to frown at me, looking like he's debating prodding me for more details. He's laconic, which is what I like about him, and he generally stays out of other people's business. But I also don't normally act this frazzled on the shop floor in the middle of the afternoon, so I can see why he'd be confused.

"Ok," he says eventually, relenting. He wipes his hands off with a rag and takes a step back. "It was more of a cut than a stab wound. It's almost healed. I'm all good. I'll see you tomorrow. Text me if you need anything, okay?"

I nod, but he keeps staring at me.

"I'm fine," I sign, and this finally has him giving in and getting ready to head out.

Once Silas is gone, I have no reason to try to maintain a mask of sanity. But I also don't like to let my demons get the better of me, whether I have an audience or not, because I know exactly where that road leads and how dangerous it can be.

There's no reason for me to be this off-kilter. I had a hook-up with someone I kind of know. It's fine. It's not going to happen again, and Tristan and I will go back to being two people who never see each other.

I do the bare minimum to shut up the shop, slamming the roller door with more force than necessary and leaving all the tools around in a mess that is probably making Dad roll over in his grave.

With a familiar cocktail of shame and anxiety and grief crawling under my skin like a parasite, begging for me to let it out, I head out to the yard between the shop and the house.

There's nothing much out here. It used to be storage, I think, but Dad converted it back when I was a teenager. Once he realized that my ability to turn my grief and anger inwards and take them out on myself was really fucking literal, he tried a lot of things to get me to channel that energy.

Teaching me to bulk up and fight seemed like a good idea at the time. He was a soldier. It was an outlet he was familiar with. He fought in the Gulf War, and PTSD had its claws in him deep until the day he died. He knew exactly how it felt to be so angry at the world you didn't know what to do with it.

Even though he did a lot of stupid shit sometimes, his anger always poured outward, never in. He thought I was going to get into fights no matter what he did, so he might as well teach me to win. But in reality, he just taught me a more socially acceptable way to abuse my body and ground my mind in pain.

Scars on your arms are pretty difficult to make up excuses for, especially after the first few. But cuts and bruises from fights? That's just 'boys being boys'. Pick enough fights with enough guys that are bigger than you, and you can be a walking ball of injuries every single day.

It still makes my heart twinge that he cared enough to try. I know a fuck-ton of dads around here that wouldn't, and didn't, and that's for kids they *wanted* to have. Dad got me like a surprise FedEx delivery, already half-baked and full of trauma, and he did his best with the situation.

He cleaned up this patch of weeds and rusted junk and turned it into a little outdoor gym for me. It's still exactly the way he put it together, even though some of it's a little worse for wear. A bunch of bars at different heights for resistance training, all of which he welded together from scrap. Barbells and free weights cobbled together from old tires and other car parts. And my personal favorite, a giant-ass tractor tire sitting on the side of it all.

I spent years building up the strength to be able to flip that fucker. It turned into a challenge. I needed to conquer it. And eventually, the scream of my muscles burning was almost as satisfying as taking a fist to the face, and yet another step up the ladder of social acceptability.

I keep Dad firmly in my mind as I head out there now. I lose myself in the familiar rhythm, moving from one area to the next, grounding myself in the ache and strain of my body and shutting out all the intrusive thoughts my mind keeps trying to throw at me. I even let myself play back the memory of Tristan's mouth on me last night, as it's vastly preferable to whatever horror show memory is trying to poke through my defenses right now.

By the time I'm pouring sweat and down to flipping the tractor tire with a single-minded intensity, too emotionally burned out to concentrate on anything else, the world has gone blissfully quiet.

Until something interrupts me.

"Goddamn, you really are a junkyard dog. How did I not know you had this out here?"

Tristan's voice floats through the air, pulling me out of my thoughts and back to reality. Although my thoughts were so focused on him, I almost think his voice is a figment of my imagination and I've finally cracked under the stress for a minute.

Until I look up and see him standing there. He's standing in the grass about ten feet away from me, looking as casual as he always does. His arms are crossed over his chest, which is probably making all his muscles pop deliciously, but I can't see because he's wearing a beat-up hoody, despite the sweltering early-evening heat.

It makes me quirk my head at him for a second. He's smiling, but it's not the full-body smile that he normally gives me. It's not something I can exactly put my finger on, there's just something about him that's less *Tristan* than usual. Even if his face is as hypnotically pretty as always.

Not my problem, I remind myself. I'm supposed to be distancing myself from him, not fretting about him like an overbearing grandmother.

"You didn't know because we are not friends. What are you doing here?" I sign at him. I've spent all day trying to chase him out of my mind, and him showing up here looking like sex on a stick isn't fucking helping.

"I'm bored. I get destructive when I'm bored. I thought you might be a more appropriate outlet for all that energy."

How he manages to make the word 'energy' sound so dirty, I'll never know.

"Well, go bother someone else. I'm busy."

I don't bother to wait for a response before turning around and heading towards my house. I have no idea whether I want him to follow me, even if I'm being honest with myself, but I'm not at all surprised when he does.

"Pay attention to meeeee," he whines in the background, his footsteps chasing mine. "I'll put out. I just need something to do."

"Do a puzzle. Get a hobby. Stop using me like your own personal sex toy."

We're inside my house now, Tristan closing the door behind us to make it clear he has no intention of leaving until he gets the attention he seems to so desperately desire. When I kick off my shoes, he does the same, as if he's an invited houseguest.

I'm not sure if he really wants the attention, or if he's just trying to prove some kind of point. Either way, I'm sick of his games. A line needs to be drawn before this gets even messier. I don't do repeats and I don't do whatever this whiny, needy thing he's doing is, even if it is clearly put on for a joke.

He's practically grinning as he moves towards me, all sultry, reaching for my sweat-soaked shirt.

"I have a hobby. It's annoying you. I'll let you pretend to hate it, I swear."

I roll my eyes, because there's no arguing with him when he's like this. And it doesn't help that whenever he gets close to me, the reasonable part of my brain seems to go offline while my base instincts–the ones telling me to *fuckbreedpossess*–take over.

Distance. I'll keep moving further away from him. He can't chase me forever. He's bound to get distracted by a butterfly or a car chase or something, eventually.

I shrug off his touch and jog up the stairs as fast as I can, hoping he takes the hint.

Like always, Tristan does whatever the fuck he wants anyway, and follows me upstairs.

Chapter Fifteen

TRISTAN

F ord scowls and turns away from me, a series of movements that I've become intimately familiar with, even though we've known each other for barely a week.

He throws a hand behind him, not looking at me, pinching his two forefingers against his thumb.

No.

"What's up your ass, dude? Because it ain't me, and frankly, it should be."

I stalk forward, refusing to let him walk away from me again.

Yanking on his shoulder is like yanking on a hunk of cement. Being around him makes me feel fluttery and girlish in a way that's crazy disconcerting, but also kind of fun. It's definitely nothing I've ever felt before, and it brings back all the memories of how good it felt to go to my knees for him. Even if it was weird.

When he looks at me with his signature irritated expression, I bat my eyelashes at him. Annoy him until he cracks. That's what always seems to work here. I have to do something to get under his prickly exterior before he'll tell me what he really wants.

If he does want me to leave, I'll go, obviously. But I've gotten too many mixed signals from him so far to take him at his word the first time. I'm not going to jump him until he wants me to, but I will linger here like a parasite until I get an honest answer, one way or another.

I shiver again, still cold despite the heat. The truth is that the thought of going back to my empty house is a lot more unappealing than it normally is. I get bored easily, yeah, but I don't actually have a problem spending time alone. I'm good at keeping myself occupied with something.

Today I feel wrong, somehow. Like my body is made up of grooves and joints that are all slightly incorrect, so nothing is sitting right.

For some reason, I feel like he's the one who made me feel this way. Him, with his stupid giant hands and magical dick and filthy fucking eyes. He's clearly the right person to put me back together.

I'm so lost in thought, I don't notice Ford watching me closely. I'd accidentally let the teasing smile slip from my face and my shoulders hunched in on themselves because of the cold that's still penetrating me. Nothing about me is projecting the confident, teasing persona that I've carefully cultivated, and I can see that Ford's clocked that.

Whoops. This isn't how any of this is supposed to go down.

"What's wrong?" His brow furrows with concern as he looks me up and down.

"Nothing," I say with a tight smile.

"This is how I know you were never a spy, even though you act like it sometimes. You're a terrible fucking liar," he signs, taking a step closer.

The proximity of his big, warm body to mine makes my resolve weaken, and I suddenly care 30% less whether he thinks I'm being pathetic or not. I close the rest of the distance between us and press myself against him like a cat rubbing up against a radiator.

Warmth immediately sinks into me, right to my core, and the creeping unease that's been bothering me all day begins to retreat.

I can see Ford frown out of the corner of my eye. I ignore it though, content to keep rubbing myself against him like the pathetic creature that he's managed to turn me into. Eventually, with a lot of hesitation, he brings his arms up and wraps them around me.

"Mmmm, perfect," I mumble into his neck. He's practically radiating heat from his workout, and the smell of clean, fresh sweat is making the whole thing feel distinctly more sexual than it would if I had a less dirty mind.

After a minute—too soon, in my opinion—Ford leans back and looks me in the eye as he signs.

"Seriously, Tristan. Why are you here?"

I don't know how to explain it, really. I don't even know the answer. But I have a deep-seated feeling that getting him naked will go a long way towards offsetting all the malaise I've been feeling lately. I've found exactly one thing that gets my blood up since moving here, and this weird, grumpy asshole is it.

I can't put it to him in those words, obviously.

"Look, you're private, I get it. I was in the Army, I can do private sex. I'm not asking you to go steady, I'm not even asking you to talk to me. I just wanna get in your pants."

He stares at me for a few seconds, like he's trying to dissect my brain with a mental laser beam. It makes me squirm.

"I don't do relationships."

I snort, because he took the words right out of my mouth.

"Come on, do I look remotely stable enough to not have a chronic fear of commitment? Bitch, please. I promise I'm not asking for hearts and flowers here."

At least that part is totally honest. I don't want a relationship, even if I'm not being forthcoming about how strong my feelings are. I can't very well tell him about feelings that I can't articulate to myself, can I?

Exactly. That's how I justify it.

"If we do this, we can't tell anyone because they'll get the wrong idea. And I don't want to hear Cade bitching at me about it. Got it?"

"You read my mind. Now, can someone please take their pants off? I promise I don't even have feelings to hurt." Or at least I didn't used to. And the ones I have now aren't really feelings, so much as a constant, unnamable ache in my chest that I desperately want to get rid of.

There's only one more moment of hesitation before his mind shutters and he throws himself towards me.

When he kisses me, it's just as ferocious as every touch we shared last night. He walks me backwards towards what I assume is a bedroom, and against my better judgment, I go soft and allow myself to be led.

But when he tries to toss my ass onto the mattress like some skinny bitch, I stand my ground. Giving in to him was fucking fun, but I'm sure it's going to be even better if I put up a fight first.

Instead of going down, I grab him by the belt loops and jerk our hips together. I can feel that thick cock is already hard for me, betraying any attempt he makes to pretend he hasn't wanted this since I walked in the door. I deepen the kiss, licking into all 360 degrees of his mouth and then sucking his bottom lip into my mouth.

When I bite down on his lip, I don't go easy on him. He hisses in a breath but doesn't pull away. Instead, one big hand cups the back of my head, his fingers tangling in my hair, the other pressed into the small of my back and holding me close.

Eventually, he does break away, but it's only to look me up and down like he wants to eat me alive.

Bringing his thumb up to his lip, he finds a trace of blood where I bit him. It sparks something in those ice-blue eyes, and I see his chest heave with a breath.

This time when he pushes me, I go down to the bed, hard enough to bounce. There's no time to get my bearings before he's all over me.

His hands run up my chest, rucking up my shirt until it's tangled around my neck. I shrug out of it clumsily while he's sucking hickies into my abs and then biting my pec hard enough to leave a bruise.

"Oh, God." The moan slips out of my mouth before I can stop it. I bring one hand to his head and grabbing a hank of that long hair is just as satisfying as I imagined it would be.

He moves lower, kissing and biting his way down my body until I'm stretched out in front of him like a meal on a platter, my skin slowly turning red from the scratch of his beard and his vicious mouth. When he gets to my pants, he makes quick work of getting them off me. Before I know it, he's shucked them off with my underwear in tow and I'm bare-ass naked and spread out before him, with Ford sucking more hickies into the crease of my thigh in a way that makes me tremble.

The first time he sucks my cock into the perfect heat of his mouth, my eyes nearly roll back in my skull.

But after a minute, my awareness of the world creeps back in. I feel stripped and vulnerable in a way that I'm not used to. And Ford feels very far away.

With my fingers threaded through that beautiful hair, I want to tug him to me. I want to ask him to stay closer to me, where I can see him. I want to ask him to fucking hold me, and all of those urges are so unnatural for me, it only makes my discomfort worse.

Taking what I want is what I'm comfortable with. Dominating. It's time to flip the switch and shut out the harsh voice of this alien anxiety.

Instead of tugging, I yank Ford towards me with a growl.

My cock slips out of his mouth. I catch him off-guard enough that he moves easily, and soon I'm pinned under his bulk, his bright eyes peering at me like I'm a code he has to crack.

Yeah, we're done with all that.

I swivel my legs, using momentum to leverage my body until I've rolled over and pinned Ford under me. To keep him off-balance, I kiss him ferociously, biting and sucking his lips hard enough to make him wince.

His hands are pinned under mine, and I lean all my weight and strength into it to keep him there. He tolerates this for a minute, but when I let go of his wrists with one hand and reach for the hem of his shirt to level the playing field a little, he growls at me again and bucks his hips.

Before I know it, I'm flat on my back again, so close to the edge of the mattress we're both in danger of slipping off.

Ford holds me down with an ease that pisses me off. He keeps studying me with those fucking eyes of his, and it makes me feel more naked than my actual nudity does.

Not willing to risk letting me go, he clearly mouths to me, "What's wrong?"

I shimmy underneath him, uncomfortable in my own skin and unable to articulate the disjointed thoughts that are tearing me in a million directions right now.

Without an actual explanation, I fall back on my trusty side-kick: snark.

"Who elected you the Stone Top of Possum Hollow?" I wiggle my eyebrows at him, going for charming and salacious, but feeling too off-kilter to really sell it.

I punctuate this with a roll of my hips, but it makes him smile in a feral, humorless, predatory way.

Leaning back, looking like a man with all the time and power in the world, Ford slowly clicks his tongue to *tut tut tut* me, like I'm a naughty child about to be punished. It makes something deep inside of me pulse warm.

When he lets go of my wrists, I don't try to flip us again. Something about the way he's looking at me holds me pinned all on its own.

"Like I said before, you can leave anytime you want. But you don't look like a big bad top to me. You look like a needy hole, begging to be filled. Now, are you going to keep pretending to put up a fight? Or are you going to be a good hole and let me give you what you need? What you came here specifically to beg me for?"

His words run through my veins like melted butter, and I have no control over the way my body melts into him.

Yes, please, I think, but manage not to say.

I want to silence all the voices competing for my attention with their shitty fucking attitudes until there's nothing left surrounding me but him.

Instead of saying that, I nod.

"Good hole," he signs, looking so pleased he might be about to purr. He uses gentle hands to flip me over onto my stomach, and I go willingly.

With one massive paw wrapped around my skull, pushing me face-first into the mattress, I can hear him undoing his pants with the other hand, barely audible over the sound of his harsh breath.

The weight of him leaning into me should probably feel demeaning or dehumanizing somehow. But we seem to be past that. Instead, his hand on me is like an anchor, allowing my brain to flutter itself away to an empty, hazy place where I'm not in charge of shit.

He strips me out of the rest of my clothes while he leaves his on, keeping me face-down on the mattress the whole time. Even that weird power imbalance seems to be doing it for me because I'm still painfully hard and smearing precum onto his sheets.

A pleasant emptiness spreads through me while Ford preps me with thick, steady fingers. I'm not worrying about being bent over and exposed for him, because he's got me. The stretch of his fingers burns at first, but he moves into me slowly, with a gentleness that contrasts sharply against the firm grip his other hand has on my head. The rest of his body is laid out on top of me, pinning me to the mattress, which also helps.

He's more thorough than I think is warranted, but I guess I'm not the expert here. And it's not like he's rocking a starter cock, which is one of the many reasons I didn't want to tell him I've never done this before. I've had fingers in my ass a few times, but I've never had the opportunity to go quite this far.

It's not worth bringing it up. It's no big deal. I'm hardly a blushing virgin. He's already been peering at me like I might be hiding something, and I had to convince him that this was a 100% string-free situation. If I add more complications into the mix, it's only going to give him more excuses to back away from what we both obviously want.

I can take him. As long as he keeps holding me down like this and keeping my mind blissfully empty, I can take anything he wants to throw at me.

I'm just his hole. There's a freedom in that thought that I never expected to feel.

My hips are grinding into the mattress, my cock hard and leaking, and I'm already halfway to floating by the time I hear the snap of a condom being put on. Warmth covers me again, and this time it's the broad, blunt head of Ford's cock pressing into me instead of his fingers.

He presses in unrelentingly. I feel my body stretch and stretch and stretch around him until I feel like there's no more space to give, but then he pushes another fraction of an inch and I soften a little more to let him in.

My breath is coming in quick, shallow pants. I'm trying to relax into it, but the more he pushes, the more I realize we have to go, and the more those voices fight their way back into my head.

Ford must be able to feel me clenching around him because eventually he stops. A trickle of disappointment runs through my chest as I'm afraid he's about to pull out and give up on me altogether, but instead he leans forward, putting his lips against the ear that isn't smushed into the mattress.

Shh.

The noise is so soft, I can barely hear it over my pulse roaring in my ears. But it settles me. Then he does something else unexpected. He places a featherlight kiss on the arch of my cheekbone before trailing more down the line of my jaw. Each one seems to release some thread of tension that was tugging at my body.

Before I realize what's happened, I've relaxed enough to suck Ford into me until his hips hit my ass.

After the interruption of his uncharacteristically gentle kisses, the first hard thrust he gives is such a shock it sets every one of my nerves alight with pleasure.

I gasp in shock, my toes curling and my fingers digging into the mattress. Ford thrusts again, and then again, each time seeming to sink into me even deeper than before. The drag of his shaft against my rim is just the right side of painful, and I feel impossibly full. That fullness is spreading outwards, replacing the sense of emptiness from before with a weird feeling of possession that I can hardly articulate to myself, and don't really want to try.

The sounds of Ford's soft grunts fill the room, making me feel even more enveloped by him. It's like he's slowly turning me inside out, getting me ready to wear as a second skin.

I've never wanted anyone to see me vulnerable before, let alone have the upper hand. But now that I've given into the sensation, it comes with an overwhelming sense of freedom that I've never experienced before.

I realize that I'm making noises as well—high-pitched, keening noises that spill directly from my open mouth into the mattress he's pushing my face into. His other hand is next to me for leverage, and the entire length of his large, powerful body is rolling with every snap of his hips, gaining momentum and force, until each thrust is driving into me hard enough to jolt me further up the bed, inch by delicious inch.

"Uh-uh-uh-uh," is the closest thing to words that I can get out.

Ford takes it as the encouragement it was intended to be. Leaning back, he moves his other hand from the mattress to wrap it around my hip, holding me tightly in place while he drives into me. My thighs are shaking and it feels like every inch of my body is clenched against the pounding it's taking, even while my nervous system shoots sparks of pleasure all the way to my fingertips.

My cock is dragging over the sheet in time with his cock dragging over my prostate, and I can feel that I'm leaving a wet mess with every rough movement. I want to reach down and jerk myself, but my arms feel too boneless to cooperate.

I hear Ford's breath start to catch, while my own noises are getting impossibly high-pitched. I couldn't stop them even if I wanted to. There's a tightening of something building deep inside me. It's different from a normal orgasm, and it's hard to tell if my body wants to come or if it's threatening to tear itself in half from being impaled on Ford's monster cock.

Either way, I could think of much worse ways to die.

I'm twitching under his grip, although there's no purpose to it. I can't figure out what to do with this twisting, curling pleasure-pain. Ford keeps holding me tight, though. Always. He leans over me, so his face is close enough to the back of my head that I can feel his breath, even if I can't see him.

There's something incredibly intimate about it. Like we've created our own arousal echo chamber with nothing more than the sound of our breath: his raspy, throaty panting and grunts, and my hoarse, pitchy gasps that he punches out, one after the other, with every thrust.

I can feel the moment he begins to lose control. His fingers dig into my hip, tight enough to bruise. His thrusts become faster and more uncoordinated, and more of his bodyweight ends up pressing me into the mattress.

My cock is enveloped between that and my own stomach, and the friction combined with that twisting pleasure building inside of me sparks a chain reaction. Ford's face finds the side of mine, our open mouths catching aimlessly. I let out a high-pitched whine as I spill my release all over the bed.

Heat sinks into me directly from Ford's sweat-slick skin, and he pumps into me a few more times before he's shuddering and emptying himself into the condom. I wonder what it would feel like without it. To have him fill me up even more than he already has. But this is still incredible, the feeling of his thick length pulsing inside me, combined with my instinct to clench and milk him for everything he's worth.

It seems to go on forever, but it's probably just my endorphin-addled brain stepping outside the constraints of time. Not that it matters. The only thing that matters to me in that moment is the feeling of Ford weighing me down and the sound of his breath in my ear, while a breathless, sated sensation sinks into every one of my limbs.

We lie there in silence for a long time. Long enough for both of our breathing to return to normal, and Ford to soften inside of me. When he pulls out of me with a grunt, I still wish he wouldn't, but the words are so far from coming out, my mouth might as well be sewed shut.

Chapter Sixteen

FORD

Words are impossible for me at the best of the times, but right now I feel like I'm choking on the very thought of them. It's not just my throat that's closed, it's also whatever part of my brain takes my thoughts and feelings and turns them into sentences.

All I'm getting is an overwhelming sense of *fuck, what did I just do?* descending into my mind like a shroud.

I don't do this. I don't have sex in a bed. Or in Dad's house. Tristan already knows more about me than 99% of the men I've ever hooked up with, and he's more pushy and bratty than anyone I've ever met. That seems like a dangerous combination, and setting this precedent is a bad way to make sure he doesn't end up with any expectations.

There's no way I could ever give him more than what we just did. I'm not built for intimacy. Being able to rely on myself and no one else has been at the core of who I am for too long for that to ever change.

But everything about what just happened was also intoxicating. The way he fronted up to me before bending and softening into my hands so beautifully.

Like he's been waiting for someone to put him in his place all these years, but he's such a little shit that no one's ever bothered to try.

The way his eyes went hazy and distant while I fucked him like a nameless object... I've never seen him seem peaceful until that moment. The power he gave me was like a drug to me too, and I'm already craving another hit before I've even come down from this one. Tristan lies next to me, spread out in his naked glory.

He's all muscle and sweaty skin, his tan highlighting every curve and line of muscle in the low light in a way that keeps tugging my gaze back to him. Dark hair covers his chest in all the right places, and now I know from experience that all of him is so much softer to the touch than I would have expected.

When he moves I almost startle, like I've been caught staring at something forbidden. But he doesn't look at me, instead stretching out his long torso, arching his back with the same indulgent feline grace he does everything else. As if the rest of the world is waiting on him to get up.

Something about that level of confidence has drawn me in. I hate to admit it, but it's true. I'm confident, but in a very different way. I keep myself to myself. Tristan just has this energy that tells the world it's operating on his timetable and somehow manages to do it without coming across as an asshole.

Most of the time.

Finishing his luxurious stretch, he rolls his shoulders and then finally looks up at me, green eyes glinting in the lamplight.

The thought that he's going to want to talk about what any of this means practically paralyzes me.

"Bathroom?" he asks.

He looks relaxed, although there's still a flush to his face and chest from being fucked into the mattress, and red fingerprints running up and down his flank where I was holding him. The sight makes me feel savage. It helps roll back the tide of apprehension that was threatening to pull me under.

132

I focus on the memory of how his flesh felt under my fingers a few minutes ago, warm and strong. How he squeezed my cock when he came, and how the vibrations of his slutty moans practically ran through my entire body.

That's it. That's what brings my brain back to the real world.

I realize Tristan is still looking at me expectantly because I haven't answered. Shaking myself out of my trance, I gesture to direct him to the bathroom downstairs. Partially because the one upstairs doesn't have a shower, which he probably needs after what we just did, and partially to put as much distance between the two of us as possible until I can get my head together.

He gets up without any further ado, picking up his discarded boxers from the floor but not bothering to put them on yet, looking completely at home as he saunters out of my room. His spent dick and stomach are still shiny with his cum, and the way he walks flashes me another view of the world's tightest ass.

Which is also still throbbing red with my fingerprints.

My dick tries to rally at the thought, but now is definitely not the time.

Before I can get derailed again, I get up and focus on anything tangible I can grasp.

Pants. I only got them unzipped and pushed down a little before I was fucking into him, so I look like a mess, but it only takes a second to right myself. I let the rough cotton run between my fingertips in the process and concentrate on the way the waistband digs into the fleshy part of my hip when I zip them back up.

The wooden floor is cool under my feet, so I work my toes into it to anchor myself as I try to decide what to do next.

The decision is taken out of my hands, though, when I hear a knock at the door. Now I really have no idea who it is. It's late, I still don't get visitors and the one person who's decided to fling themselves into my life like a crash-test dummy is already in my bathroom, probably washing lube out of his ass.

If only it was my cum that he was full of.

Don't get distracted.

I'm saved from having to figure out how to kick Tristan out without A) pissing him off and B) getting distracted by putting more fingerprints all over him by going down to answer the door.

As fortuitous as the interruption is, it's still an unwelcome presence on my property, so I swing the door open with more force than needed. I guess in all the years I've spent managing my internal fear of the world around me, a part of me has gotten used to the fact that I intimidate most people without actually realizing it. Somewhere along the way, I must have stopped taking a lot of the more real-world precautions that my paranoia encouraged me to.

Checking who was at the door before opening it is one of them, apparently.

A hard slap fills the air, and before I know what's happening, the door is slamming back hard enough to bounce against the wall next to me. Three large men pour themselves through the open doorway without hesitation, the one in front grabbing me by my shirtfront before my brain can even process what's going on.

After a mental record scratch, all I know is that there are strange hands on me, and fear is crawling through me like a poison. Acting on pure animal instinct, I headbutt the man holding me hard enough to send a spray of blood arcing from his face over mine. He curses, leaning back, but it's obviously not the first time he's been head-butted because he doesn't come close to letting me go.

I'm taller than him and roughly the same build, but he manages to pull me up on my tiptoes, shaking me like an unruly kitten before letting go of me with one hand and using it to backhand me across the face.

My brain rattles in my skull when he shoves me hard enough to hit the floor, and the warmth on my lips tells me that now both our noses are bleeding.

What the fuck is happening?

An angry rumble begins deep in my chest. There are men in my house, slapping me around like a rag doll, and I will not fucking tolerate it. I scrabble to get my limbs underneath me and push off the floor, ready to tackle the slapper to the ground and show him he stormed into the wrong house.

But by the time my legs are straight, I hear a familiar *click* and realize there's a gun pressed against my forehead. The haze of fear and rage recedes enough for me to look around before I do anything stupid, and I take in the picture in front of me.

It's not three men, it's four.

The first three look like classic biker thugs, and the one lurking behind them is smaller, huddling in the shadows.

But my attention is on the thug in the middle, because he's the one pointing a gun at me.

"I'll put this away, but only if you can behave like a civilized human being instead of a rodeo bull. I'm here to talk. Deal?"

Tension ripples through me, but it's not like I have a choice. I nod slowly and force myself to unclench my limbs one by one.

Silence sits between all of us, and I realize that I don't have anything to write with, so they'd better not be expecting me to start this conversation. Unless they magically pull some ASL fluency out of their asses, like Tristan did that day at the garage.

Tristan.

Fuck.

He's still in the house. I hope he snuck out a window or something, but that's probably too much to ask. He's definitely going to do something stupid. Like fight them all off with a knife he's currently whittling out of toilet paper or setting the house on fire or something.

Who the fuck knows?

The ringleader slips his gun into the back of his pants as he starts to talk, pulling my attention back to the people invading my living room.

He's just as thuggish-looking as the other two, with light blond hair buzzed short and tattoos crawling all over him that read like gang affiliations. Actually, they all have similar tattoos, the most noticeable of which is a big-ass, ornate letter *B* with a snake wrapped around it on each of their necks.

I don't recognize it, but I'm beginning to think that maybe I should. I didn't exactly grow up in Beverly Hills. I've spent plenty of time around shady biker types, and my dad had a history with the local motorcycle club between getting discharged from the Army and me showing up on his doorstep. I'm hardly a wilting flower. But these guys seem very organized by Possum Hollow standards, and I immediately wish I knew more about whatever I've stumbled into.

The thing that's creeping me out the most, though, is the ringleader. His eyes are bright blue, not unlike mine, but looking at his, it's like no one's home. I have no doubts this man will kill us if he wants to and not miss a wink of sleep over it, which sets every cell in my body on red alert.

"My name is Eamon. And this," he reaches behind him to grab the smaller figure, jerking it forward into the light, "is Tobias. Tobias, tell Ford why we're here."

Without giving the kid the chance to answer, Eamon yanks his hood down with enough force to snap his head back. Tobias winces, but stays silent in the way that you do when you know making a noise will make your situation much worse. As much as this kid is dead-eyed and still, when I see his face, I'm almost shocked enough to make another move for these fuckers.

The kid, who couldn't be older than 22 or 23 and 160 lbs. soaking wet, is sporting a face that's more bruise than skin. Blues and purples run down the length of one side, from temple to chin, and there's a shiner on the other side that's swollen enough he probably can't see out of that eye. There's something about him that's familiar, but he's too beat up to place him.

A busted lip completes the image and makes his words come out a little slurred when he speaks.

"Your paramedic friend beat the shit out of me until I told him where the Banna headquarters are," he mumbles, his eyes trained on the ground.

Eamon grabs the kid by the hair, yanking him until his toes barely touch the ground and his body twists in pain. Not dissimilar to what his henchman tried to do to me before, but with a lot more success considering he's twice the kid's size.

"And what else?" When he speaks, his voice is low and threatening. He leans in closer to Tobias' face than necessary, and the kid can't seem to help but flinch away.

I know gangs have a clear-cut pecking order and a rough way of maintaining it, but the energy between these two is... *off*. I don't like the way the kid's shaking in Eamon's hands, and I don't like the sadistic pleasure that he's not bothering to hide in his expression.

It's all a little too familiar for my taste. I wiggle my toes, pressing my bare feet into the wood once again, and focus on the throbbing in my still-bleeding nose to keep myself from getting caught in a memory.

"And if you trespass on Banna property again, it'll be more than just your shop that gets torn up."

The kid's voice goes up high at the end because Eamon gives him a shake before releasing his hair and dropping him back to the ground, panting and scared. But that's when something clicks.

It was him. He was one of the fucking junky gangsters that robbed the shop. The one that I had in my hand until I had to let him go when the other one *stabbed* Silas.

Rage slaps into me like a tidal wave, and I take a step towards him before I even realize it. But Eamon looks at me, *tsking* at me like I'm an unruly child, and lifting up his shirt to flash his gun in his waistband and remind me who's in charge here.

Not that I would hurt this kid, anyway. He's clearly been beaten enough. But it leaves me throbbing with an anger that I have nowhere to put, bubbling inside me like hot tar, leaving me to clench and unclench my fists impotently while I wait for them to make their point or leave.

But that thought reminds me: he said it was *Tristan* that did that to his face, which makes something twist deep in my gut. I know he's a loose cannon, but would he really beat the shit out of someone so vulnerable?

Just for information about a car? Just for me?

The thought makes me feel a lot of weird, conflicting things that cycle through my brain too quickly to pick any one thing out. But the overarching vibe is bad. I broke all my rules for Tristan, against my better judgment. Have I let a person into my life only to find out that he's exactly the kind of hyper-aggressive asshole I've been trying to avoid?

The thought is cut off though by a sudden noise of thumps and grunts.

He really knows how to pick his moments.

One of the biker-thugs had moved around behind me, leaning against the wall, and apparently Tristan thought he could jump him. To be fair, he does look fucking hardcore, doing some kind of military hand-to-hand combat shit that makes him look badass even though he's still in his underwear because all of his clothes are trapped upstairs.

I have a split-second to react, and then I bull-charge Eamon, hitting him low and hard and sending us both flailing to the ground. I manage to keep him pinned under me, though, grabbing for his hands so he can't reach for the gun.

Tristan managed to knock out the first guy quickly enough that he's grappling with the third over another gun, but I still don't like our odds. It's obvious these guys don't want to murder us, or we would have been dead already. It's only their reluctance to create a body count that seems to be working in our favor right now.

I reach for Eamon's gun regardless, elbowing him in the face in the process. All while Tobias huddles in the corner, flinching at every sound.

I'm stronger, but this fucker has long arms, and he manages to snatch it from my grasp right at the last second. Once he has the cold muzzle pressed against my forehead, my stomach drops and everything gets cold.

Tristan sees the position we're in and freezes. Thug number two is groaning on the ground behind him, while Thug number three is able to dust himself off, pick up his own weapon and point it at Tristan with a smug expression.

Eamon's voice is still light, like this whole thing is a joke, but there's an undeniable undercurrent of menace to it when he speaks.

"I'm not going to repeat myself again. Stay away from our property. The only reason you're getting this warning without a broken kneecap right now is out of respect for your old man."

My blood runs even colder, and the world seems to slow down.

I have no idea how this guy knew Dad, let alone well enough to owe him respect. But it can't be because of anything good.

There's no time to process that now though, because Eamon finally gets his gun out of my face, letting me take a breath, and they all head towards the front door.

Tobias catches Tristan's eye as he heads towards the exit, and an unspoken communication seems to go between them. Tristan nods at him and mouths something, which makes me think he must have met the kid before, although I don't want to believe he's capable of being the one to rough him up like this.

Whatever he was mouthing, Eamon catches it. He's been in control this whole time, but something about it makes a switch flip in him. Rage takes over his face and his whole demeanor shifts. He takes a couple of large steps to cross the distance over to Tristan and grabs him roughly by the jaw.

It's like a sick, twisted parody of the way I grabbed him last night, and I hate watching it. Tristan stares at him with defiant eyes, but otherwise holds still.

"I said stay away from my fucking property. That includes the boy."

He shoves Tristan hard enough to make him stumble, landing on one knee on the hardwood floor.

The silence around us is tense, the room vibrating with it as we wait to see what will happen next. Eamon turns around again to leave, hustling Tobias out of my house with the others.

139

But at the last second, his posture shifts. He seems to change his mind, and he moves so fast I can't think or act or even breathe before it happens.

Eamon lifts up his gun and fires one bullet at Tristan, catching him in the shoulder and filling the room with the bitter scent of gunpowder. Tristan makes a noise and doubles over, slowly falling to the floor in shock and pain.

"If you ever look at my property again, the next bullet goes in your skull."

Then they leave, and my panic finally takes over.

CHAPTER SEVENTEEN

TRISTAN

*G*od-*fucking-shit-damn-jizz-cock.*

Apparently, I've gotten complacent in my safe little life out here in the woods, because I completely forgot how much getting shot fucking *hurts*.

My heart is pounding like it's trying to rattle my chest until it falls apart, and every breath I take feels like it's ripping through my lungs.

That's just the adrenaline talking. It's okay. Get it together.

I mentally reach inside myself to grab the feral, instinctual part of me that's panicking and squeeze it into submission. Deep breath in, hold, deep breath out. The throb from my arm continues to reverberate through my entire body with my pulse, but the rest of me quickly settles as I remind my various body parts that we've survived worse than this before.

With a groan, I push myself into a sitting position from wherever I fell to the floor when the bullet hit me. There are warm, large hands clutching at me, helping me up, and when I blink open my eyes enough to turn my focus outward, my field of vision is entirely filled with Ford.

Ford, who's staring at me with the widest of wide eyes, his already-pale skin looking bloodless as he helps me sit up.

"I'm okay," I say to reassure him, although my voice comes out raspy and strained. "I'm okay."

Ford's hands hover over my arm like it's a bomb about to go off. Looking down, I can see that it's bleeding sluggishly, so at least I know my artery wasn't hit and I'm not seconds from death.

That's a plus.

Other than that, I can't get a good visual. Even though I've got my initial adrenaline surge under control, the pain is making me nauseous enough that it's hard to kick my paramedic brain into full-gear.

"Fuck, um..." What do I need? Of all the shitty things to happen today, I really wasn't expecting getting shot to be one of them. At least a quick glance around confirms that those redneck mafioso wannabes are gone. They left the door wide open though, so the hot evening air and mosquitos are pouring in here to further choke the life out of me.

"Get a towel or something to put pressure on it," I say to Ford. His gaze snaps up to mine. There's a hazy look in his eyes, like he's not quite present, and it makes me see past the fog of my own pain for a second to be worried about what's going on in his head.

He gets up, though, running to the kitchen to grab a towel before looking at me again with that same lost expression. Blood and guts are not his thing, clearly.

"Okay, just wrap it around and tie it tight enough to put pressure, but not so tight that it cuts off the circulation. I still need to be able to wiggle my fingers. And then call Cade and tell him to grab the secret stash of medical supplies that we both pretend he doesn't steal from work and get his ass over here."

"What about the hospital?" Ford signs, his hands trembling so hard it's difficult to follow the movements.

I shake my head. "Gunshots mean paperwork, which means cops. I don't want to give those assholes another reason to be pissed at us. I think it's just a flesh wound, so let's stay off the grid with this if we can."

Ford nods, but now his whole body is shaking while he uses what must be a text-to-speech app to call Cade. Their conversation is brief. He only tells Cade to come to the house with his med kit. I'm guessing Cade gets that it must be important for Ford to call him out of the blue like this.

It seems so incongruous for this huge, hulking man to be trembling like a leaf in the wind, but the second that thought crosses my mind, it's followed by the thought that I'm an asshole. The idea that muscles mean you're never afraid is the Army talking, and it was also in the Army when I saw men piss themselves with terror on more than one occasion. And justifiably so.

Taking another deep breath, I try to rattle out the conflicting toxic thoughts that constantly dog my inner monologue and focus on what's important. Ford's breathing is quick and shallow, and the tendons in his neck are straining, like crouching down in front of me has his body on high alert.

"Hey," I say, speaking softly. I use the fingers of my good hand to tilt his chin until he looks me in the eye. He flinches at first, but doesn't move away.

Holding eye contact while both our pulses race and I drip blood onto his floor somehow feels more intimate than the way he railed me into his mattress twenty minutes ago. A part of me wants to squirm away from it. This isn't something I do with girls *or* guys.

But the thought is quickly squashed when I consider the idea that Ford is scared enough right now that he can barely catch his breath. That's fucking intolerable. It needs to be rectified immediately.

"Look at me," I murmur, still holding his chin with two fingers. His beard is softer than I would have imagined, and I press my fingers into his flesh a little harder so he can feel that I'm there. "I'm okay. We're okay. It's going to be fine. Those assholes made their point, and I'm gonna be patched up before you know it. And you can go back to pretending you hate me. And I'll go back to pretending I believe you."

I give him the sexiest smirk I can manage under the circumstances, and while it doesn't get a smile, I see a fraction of the tension fall away from him. He nods and takes a deep, if shuddering breath, and I'm calling that a win.

I was expecting him to sit back, but instead he hovers. His gaze runs over my face like a searchlight, and I stay still as the surprising intimacy from before continues to drip over us like warm honey.

"We're okay," I whisper again, although I'm not sure if I'm reassuring him or myself at this point. His hand is still shaking, but when he brings it up to cup my cheek and swipes his thumb over my clammy skin, it stills a little.

God, even his fingers are fucking huge. How am I getting turned on right now?

For a second I think he might kiss me, and my lips part like a virgin on prom night without my permission. But he doesn't. Instead, he presses his forehead against mine, while moving that big hand around to hold the back of my neck. My good hand finds the front of his shirt and hangs on, because I have a sudden, overwhelming need for this to not end.

I've had a lot of intense, masculine bro hugs, including the kind where you thunk your foreheads together like morons. And I've had a few intimate caresses with lovers, although mostly with girls, and not for a very long time. This is the weirdest combination of the two, and it fills me with a stomach-swooping, toe-tingling sensation that's strong enough to dull the pain in my arm for a second.

With Ford's big body caging mine in and his face pressed against mine, I feel contained. Both of us stay still, filling our lungs with shared oxygen over and over, and letting the stress and fear of the past few minutes slowly filter out of us as we anchor to one another.

I'm not sure how long we sit like that, but it's long enough to get Ford's shaking under control and to turn my pain into a dull, draining throb instead of the sharp burn from before.

It's also long enough for Cade to get here with Silas in tow, because their house is barely ten minutes from here. And because the front door is still wide open, we get no warning other than the thunder of feet rushing through the doorway before abruptly stopping at what they see inside.

Ford jerks away from me. I get the sense he's not closeted in a shame-spiral kind of way, but he's definitely a very private person. I'm sure being seen as vulnerable in any circumstances isn't going to sit well with him. He gets up from the floor, his movements stiff and jerky, while Cade and Silas stare at both of us like wide-eyed baby deer.

"What. The. Fuck." Cade is the first to break the silence.

Ford exhales, sounding like a bull that's about to charge, before turning and stomping back to the kitchen.

"Get water!" I call after him. "And more towels! And some fucking whiskey!" Because this day has become too taxing to face sober.

Cade and Silas are looking at each other, doing that thing couples do where they have a silent conversation entirely in facial expressions. I can guess what they're thinking, and I don't want to hear it.

"Are you here to help or are you here to gossip? I'd really like to not bleed out here."

That snaps their attention back to me and Cade moves forward, dropping to the floor and opening his jump bag. He slips on a pair of gloves while he eyes my arm, but I can still see him eyeing the mostly naked rest of me as the wheels in his head continue to turn.

"So, was this like a kink accident, or–ow!" Cade jolts forward, nearly dropping the gauze pack he was opening, when Silas knees him from behind while looking down with a stern expression.

"What? My boss is bleeding and half-naked at your boss's house at night and we're just not allowed to acknowledge that it's fucking weird?"

Cade's tone is petulant, but Silas manages to shut him up with a raised eyebrow. I'm a little impressed. I didn't know he had it in him, to be honest, but I see more and more why they work.

"It's none of our business," he says, looking up as Ford comes back into the room with an armful of supplies and a thunderous expression.

Cade rolls his eyes, and I'm running out of patience for him turning this into a joke when I'm still bleeding. But while Silas is frowning in his concerned way at Ford and Ford is devotedly not making eye-contact with anyone, I catch a flicker of something else on Cade's face as he looks at me. Something that looks a lot more like hurt.

Ah, hell. Maybe I do owe him an apology. I thought it was enough to be supportive through his whole bisexual awakening without specifically outing myself, but maybe I was wrong.

I touch his arm with my good hand to draw his attention before he unties the bloody towel. "Look, I'll explain later. Can you check for an exit wound first? It's a gunshot."

His eyebrows shoot up and he looks between me and Ford.

"Who the fuck shot you?"

I sigh. "Remember how we shook down Tobias for information? Well, apparently he's more connected than I thought, and we pissed off a lot of people who wanted to make it patently clear that I need to stay out of their business."

Ford grunts, holding out the thumb and pinky on one hand and using it to point between the two of us with a pointed expression.

"Sorry, 'we'. We need to stay out of their business." I was hoping to ease his guilt in this, since he already seemed so freaked out by the situation. Apparently, he's not letting himself off the hook for the shenanigans that I single-handedly pulled him into.

Cade still looks stunned by this information, though. When he speaks, the only word that comes out of him is "Whoops."

I almost laugh. "Yeah, whoops. Now, how does it look?"

"Shit," he turns back to my arm, which he'd forgotten about for the thousandth time since he got here. He slowly unknots the towel and passes the bloody rag to Silas, who grimaces and throws it away somewhere. When Cade presses a wad of gauze against the wound, it feels like he's punching me in the throat and my whole body tenses, but I keep breathing through it.

"Silas, can you pass me the thing?" Cade asks, pointing at his bag.

Silas just looks bewildered. "Uh, like, hydrogen peroxide?"

Cade opens his mouth to reply, but I cut him off.

"No, because this isn't the fucking 80s. Hydrogen peroxide destroys your healthy cells along with the bacteria. It should be banned from all first aid kits. For the love of God, Cade, what do you two talk about after he's finished spanking you into submission for the night? Have you taught him nothing?"

Silas has the decency to look sheepish, while Cade only glares at me. He decides to switch their places instead of asking for things and risking my wrath again.

It's not my fault. The children have to learn somehow, and hydrogen peroxide is a public health menace.

Directing Silas to put on some gloves and hold pressure on the wound, Cade starts soaking some gauze in saline to clean up around it so he can get a better look. "Ford, this is the second time I've had to clean up your attempt at first aid and you have got to stop wrapping things with dirty towels. Please buy a first aid kit. I'm begging you."

Ford scowls in response, but I can still see the way his chest is rising and falling faster than it should be. He's hiding it well, but he's still panicked. I catch his eye and take a slow breath. The urge to reach out and touch him hits me by surprise. I have no idea where it came from, but it's almost overwhelming.

But once my hand is in the air, a part of me panics. I don't do this. I don't do casual intimacy in times of stress. That's not no-strings hookup stuff. So I swerve, reaching for the mostly full bottle of whiskey he put on the floor next to me.

Ford shakes his head like I'm being ridiculous, but opens it for me, anyway. I take a swig. The first one burns, the second one almost chokes me, but the third hits my stomach like water. After a couple of minutes, I can feel the pain in my arm dulling, and the confusing thoughts about Ford becoming more distant.

Thank you not eating today, I guess.

We all sit in tense silence while I drink and Cade pokes and prods at my arm.

"You realize you're just thinning your blood by drinking that, right? Aren't you supposed to be setting a good example?"

"This is one of those 'do as I say' scenarios," I say, a hint of slur already hitting my words as the whiskey goes straight to my head. I sway a little, feeling more light-headed than I probably should, although whether it's from the alcohol or the blood loss, I can't tell. "Plus, this makes me care so much less about whether I die."

This time when I sway, there's a hand stopping me. Ford's palm is on my back, holding me still and radiating warmth into my skin. Flashes of how his hands felt on me before and how his fingerprints are probably still all over my hips and ass run through my brain, and I can't muster the energy to be embarrassed about them.

I push my weight into his hand, wanting to see if he'll keep holding me up. It's a weird sensation, and one that I'm enjoying in my current blurry, alcohol-softened state.

I must have leaned too hard, because he takes his hand away. Disappointment swoops through my stomach and I almost topple backwards, but then something larger than a hand catches me. Ford has folded his big body up to sit on the floor behind me and is pulling me into his chest. It's less intimate than it is stabilizing me so Cade can work, but something about it still feels unlike anything I've ever experienced.

This is a lot of intimacy for one day. I really did only come over for sex and snark. I'm not emotionally wired to handle whatever this is.

But I'm getting drunk, so I let myself relax and worry about figuring out what it means tomorrow. My eyelids fall closed as someone plucks the whiskey bottle out of my hand. I make a grab for it, but it's half-hearted.

"Jesus, did he really drink that much that fast? Was no one watching?" Cade's voice cuts through the fog of my thoughts, and I open my eyes again.

There's a bandage around my arm, so I'm guessing we're done here.

"All good?"

Cade gives me a serious look he usually reserves for patients. "Sorry, but you're going to the ER whether you want to or not. I know you wanted this off-book, but you'll have to make something up. Hunting accident, or... fuck, how many people do we see who shoot themselves cleaning their guns? Anything. There's an exit wound, but there's also a lot of damage. You've got decreased reflexes in your fourth and fifth finger and the bleeding is still not totally under control. I packed it, but it's just a temporary fix. You need an adult." When I don't move or say anything, he waves his hands at me. "Now! Come on. Non-optional, let's go."

"All right, all right," I grumble. I try to get my legs under me, but someone seems to have replaced them with Jell-O while I was sitting here, and my head is swimming even worse than before. "It's gonna be embarrassing as fuck to tell people I'm stupid enough to clean a loaded gun."

"More embarrassing than telling people you're stupid enough to try to steal from the Banna?" Silas says, staring me down.

"Hey!" I point at him, but then pause. "Okay, that's fair. That was pretty stupid." I take another deep breath and try to stand, but my body still isn't cooperating. "I feel dizzy as fuck, Cujo. You might have to carry me."

Ford wraps his arms around my torso and lifts me like I'm a lot lighter than I am, which is dizzying in and of itself. But I don't miss Cade and Silas turning to each other, Cade mouthing the word "Cujo?" and both of them sharing yet another *look*.

Whatever. I can worry about it tomorrow. Right now, Ford is warm and steady as he throws my good arm over his broad shoulders and starts walking me to the car.

CHAPTER EIGHTEEN

FORD

I fucking hate hospitals.

Everything about them. The second we stepped inside, the familiar choking sensation had me wanting to claw at my throat. Memories of the weeks I spent in a pediatric ICU bed regaining the ability to breathe on my own again crowd into my mind, trying to choke me in their own way.

Every time my memories get triggered and my body starts to think it's back in that hospital bed or back on the floor of that house being choked to death, I ground myself in my senses. I have to remind my body that it's just a memory. I smell the air; I touch the ground; I see and hear the things surrounding me and let those senses drag my body back to the present moment.

Only right now it's not working, because all of my senses are giving me things that overlap with those memories. The fluorescent lights that feel like they're leeching the life from your body. The smell of disinfectant, with a faint undercurrent of bedsores and feces that always manages to linger. The constant hum of conversation that's somehow distinct from any other busy building, because nearly every conversation being had is tense or sad, and it gives that hum a flavor. The weird heat that builds up at shift change when there's double the amount of nurses in the building for half an hour and the building's A/C can't handle it.

I'm half expecting to see Dad's shocked and weathered face as he shows up to find out his entire world has been turned upside down.

This is the first time I've been in a hospital since the day Dad took me home, and it sucks exactly as much as I expected it to.

The only thing that's different this time—apart from the obvious, that I'm neither a child nor a patient anymore—is Tristan. He's not just here; he's in his element. All the things that are clutching at my mind and dragging me down remind him that he's at home. This is the place where he feels the most powerful.

So, if my sense of smell and touch and everything else can't help me, I can at least focus on that.

Tristan. Drunk off his ass, apparently. Surrounded by ER nurses who all seem to know him, already turning into his "gun cleaning accident" into an epic, hilarious misadventure that's captivating their attention.

He's dazzling them all with his perfect smile and endless charisma, animated and chaotic despite his serious injury and the significant amount of whiskey he pounded before we got in the car. I flash back to how he looked when he came into my house earlier tonight. He started out with that same false bravado he always carries, but underneath I caught a glimpse of a very different face of him.

I realize more and more that it's not a side of him I think many other people ever get to see. That warms me up a little, as much as I don't want it to. It's getting to the point of absurdity if I keep trying to deny how drawn to him I am.

The nurses all eye me warily, which I get. There's no hospital in Possum Hollow, so we're out in Mission Flats, and it's far enough from home that no one knows me here. My silence probably seems like an intimidation tactic instead of a disability. I must look weird, some giant guy standing in the corner, staring at Tristan like my life depends on it, but not saying anything.

But not only is Tristan's pale but smiling face currently my lone tether to this psychic dimension, I also can't seem to tear my eyes away from how much everyone keeps touching him.

Most of them are only passing by to check on him, but every one of them seems to do it with a lingering touch to his knee or shoulder. Which is normal, I guess. But it's setting itself up like an itch beneath my skin that I can't quite get to.

Barely an hour ago, I had my hands on him. I got to feel how he shivered while I buried myself in the perfect heat of him and told myself it was the first and last time this would happen. Which is why it shouldn't be bothering me whether people want to touch him or not.

Everyone probably wants to touch him. He's fucking stunning. It's only logical. And he's normal—more or less—so he doesn't flinch away from their casual contact the way I would.

This is good, I tell myself. This is yet another reminder of why this thing with me and Tristan needs to stop as soon as he's patched up and safe.

The nurse taking his vitals seems to be a particularly good friend, and has no problems letting his hands linger on every single part of Tristan's body. He gets him into a patient gown that's absolutely indecent and has nothing but long, tanned, muscular, naked limbs spilling out of it in every direction. And it's the ER, so there's only a whisper of a curtain between us and all the other beds for privacy.

It doesn't make my blood boil. It really doesn't. I have no claim over him. He can touch the little twink to his heart's content.

Really.

"Hey, Ford," Tristan's slightly slurred voice snaps me out of my trance. "This is Micah. He works a lot of the same shifts as me, so we're report buddies sometimes. His don't-give-a-fuck attitude is possibly even more powerful than yours, and it's the root of our friendship."

I look at Micah, who's giving me an appraising once-over. My face stays the same as it always is, and if that happens to be gruff and intimidating, so be it. It has nothing to do with the fact that his hand is still on Tristan's arm, even though he's clearly finished taking his blood pressure.

Tristan continues talking without any prompting, as usual. "This is Ford. He's my new bestie."

I really wish he'd stop saying 'bestie'.

Tristan's good hand shoots out clumsily towards me, making a grabby motion like a toddler who wants a sippy cup. I raise my eyebrows at him, because I have no idea what he wants. Then it sinks in.

He wants me.

That settles the itch under my skin more than I want to admit.

Any other time, I'd think about the repercussions of being seen touching another man in a questionably intimate way. Not that I'm buried deep in the closet, but it does just make things easier. It's not like I have a lot of people I care about enough to give a shit whether they know anything about me.

But right now, getting rid of Micah's hand on Tristan's bicep seems like the single most important thing I can focus on. Without hesitation, I step forward. Tristan's strong hand slides over my forearm like warm butter. He uses the leverage to tug me closer, until my chest is pressed against his back, and I decide I can stand here like a sentry if that makes him feel better.

He lets go of my wrist to lean his weight into me, and without meaning to, my fingers find his hip and rest there. Just barely. So lightly that most people would probably think I was just leaning on the thin mattress, but there are enough points of contact between us to send electricity through my body in a way that continues to flush out my discomfort and grounds me in the present moment.

Micah tilts his head, and a sly smile spreads across his face.

"Oh, well, it's very nice to meet you, Ford," he purrs in a tone that tells me this is the best gossip he's gotten all week. But when he looks back at Tristan, his smile turns warm and he finally drops his fucking hand away, so I decide I can stop worrying about it.

I'm interrupted from any more excruciating self-reflection by the rasp of metal on metal as the bay curtains are jerked apart.

Yet another nurse stands there, this one already wearing a *what am I going to do with you* expression that Tristan seems to pull out of everyone he meets. She's beautiful, about Tristan's age, with dark skin and intricate braids. She also carries that air of someone who's unquestionably in charge.

I wonder briefly if Tristan's ever hooked up with her, then I do my best to banish that useless thought with all the other intrusive ones. I curl my fingers a little harder into Tristan's hip, and he leans even further into me.

"Tristan, when I told you to get a hobby or go on a date or something, this is not what I meant," she says with a scowl.

He just grins at her with that permanently unhinged sunshiney expression that says he doesn't give a fuck.

I can feel his good shoulder shrug. "It's not my fault I've forgotten how to do social things properly. How was I supposed to know that William Tell isn't an appropriate first date game?"

Micah snorts, but the other nurse looks like she wants to smack Tristan.

"Boy, you'd better be kidding. I do not have the energy to 5150 the most experienced paramedic in the county right now."

But Tristan keeps smiling. "Of course I'm kidding, Rebecca. Don't get your stethoscope in a twist. I was cleaning my gun, and I forgot to clear the chamber. Clearly retirement has made me soft, and public humiliation is my punishment. Which is not my kink, fyi."

"Is he on morphine?" Rebecca turns to Micah.

He holds up a handful of medical supplies. "I was just about to put an IV in. Doc hasn't even been in yet, I swear. He showed up hammered with an at-home patch-up job. Don't even pretend to be surprised by this."

The sigh that comes out of Rebecca is bone deep. I can feel it in my own joints.

"Of fucking course. I'll send someone over. Tristan, be a good boy and do whatever the doctor tells you without arguing, okay? It's too busy tonight for me to come back here and argue with you."

He nods so enthusiastically that he bounces a little in place. "Yes, ma'am."

Only when she's turning to leave does Rebecca seem to notice me standing behind him. She gives me the same assessing look that Micah did, but hers has a little more warmth behind it.

"You look like you have some sense," she says to me. "You're in charge of making sure he doesn't cause trouble in my ER. I'd tell Micah to do it, but they're both as bad as each other."

When she walks away, the two idiots in question both laugh like high-schoolers who just got scolded by a teacher, so it looks like she has a point.

The next twenty minutes are occupied by a lot of waiting and progressive rounds of paperwork. They all blur together for me, but Tristan seems to understand what's going on better than I do, even in his state. At least I don't have to help him with that part.

All I do is stand behind him and keep holding him up. And pretend that I don't love the way he pouts whenever I try to move a few inches away.

He gets fluids, pain meds and antibiotics. At some point we get moved into a slightly larger procedure room, where a harried-looking resident stitches up his arm and tells him he's an idiot multiple times. She asks him if he wants to be admitted for the night just to sleep it off, but he turns to me with sleepy, hooded eyes and says he's got it covered, and fuck if that doesn't wake up every protective instinct I never knew I had.

Freshly bandaged and on the verge of collapse, Tristan leans into my arm in one slow, liquid movement after he says it. The doctor gives me a long look, but by this point, I've gotten used to being evaluated by everyone. She seems satisfied by whatever she sees though, because she goes over his care instructions, sends

156

a few prescriptions to the pharmacy, and then tells us we're good to bounce as soon as Micah comes back to pull his IV.

"Fuck that," Tristan mumbles into my shoulder as soon as she's gone. Before I know what's happening, he reaches down and pulls the little piece of plastic out of his hand, dumping the dirty tubing and saline bag into the trash with a very sloppy lay-up.

"Boo-yah. Let's go home, Cujo." The stupid motherfucker has the audacity to grin at me while I scramble through drawers until I find some gauze to put over the blood trickling from where his IV just was. Placing his hand over it to hold it there, I give him the most scornful look I can muster.

"You really are an idiot. Come on, we need to get your prescriptions," I sign with a sigh.

The grin he gives me is beatific, although he wobbles slightly as he leans back and forces me to reach out and steady him.

"Can't be too much of an idiot. I tricked you into taking care of me, didn't I? I think that makes me pretty fucking smart, Cujo. One point to Tristan. Let's bounce."

CHAPTER NINETEEN

TRISTAN

"Carry me, bestie."

It's not the first time I've said it tonight, and a little piece of me is waiting to see how far I can push Ford before he finally flips and leaves me on a fire station doorstep in a cardboard box or something.

I'm aware that it's self-destructive, but that doesn't help me curtail the impulse. Everyone has their breaking point, and the one thing I excel at is helping people find theirs. I've been told I'm exhausting to be around by more people than I can count. In a variety of ways. Ford already has a basement-bargain tolerance for noise and human contact. I can only imagine I'm grating on his last nerve.

This is the push he might need to kick my ass to the curb.

Instead, he looks at me with the same weary but tolerant expression he's held all night. Well, apart from the times that he just looked panicked. That was less fun.

Whenever I'm in a hospital, I feel at ease. Even as a patient. I know what's going on, how things are going to play out and even in the worst possible scenarios,

I know I'll have the understanding and the ability to compartmentalize to deal with whatever happens. It's easy to forget that most people don't feel that way.

I spend a lot of time giving people platitudes as I pass them off to the ER staff for treatment, but it's another thing entirely to watch someone that you know—someone who is so fundamentally strong—slowly vibrate apart with a latent, unspoken fear. Just because of where we were standing.

At least, that's what I assume. The only other reason for Ford to be upset would be that I was hurt, which would make even less sense. Especially because he still barely tolerates me, and it really is just a flesh wound.

I'm so caught up in this train of thought--and pleasantly coasting on the morphine train—that I forgot I said anything to Ford. So, when he reaches down and grabs me, I practically squawk with surprise.

I've already been shocked by how it feels when Ford manhandles me, but so far that's been in a sexual context. Which is brutal and glorious and makes sense in my brain in a convoluted way. He wants something from me; I want to give it to him; he takes it.

This... this makes all sorts of things inside me go offline in a way I don't understand.

Ford scoops one arm under my butt like you would do to an unruly toddler, hoisting me up the side of his body until I'm perched on his hip, my feet are dangling in the air and my good arm is clinging to his shoulders, and then continues his steadfast march towards the car.

Holy *fuckballs,* he's strong.

And I'm being carted home like groceries.

There's the barest flicker of an urge to protest, but it's quickly extinguished by the cocktail of meds, liquor and exhaustion that's swimming through my veins right now. I've never been one to seek comfort when I was sick or injured. I mostly have jobs where you don't have that luxury, and before that I was busy taking care of Conor and Ma.

Even before Conor was born, it's not like my mother had a lot of empathy to spare on kissing scraped knees better. She was still trying to raise herself, I guess.

It's never bothered me. Of all the things I regret about my life, missing out on the touchy-feely childhood stuff is not one of them. But right now, cradled in Ford's ridiculous arms and lugged to the truck like a small child, I kind of see the appeal.

My mind drifts away, just like it did when he bent me over before and fucked me so hard I couldn't have formed a cohesive thought if the world was on fire.

It's nice. Empty. But in a warm, fluffy sort of way. Not the cold way that emptiness normally feels.

Or maybe it really is the morphine getting to me.

I don't care either way, because when he gently slides me down his big body and into the passenger seat, then leans over me to *literally buckle me in*, I almost swoon. I'm way past self-respect or integrity. I don't care. My shoulder hurts, and so does my head. I'm tired, and this is fucking excellent.

Carry me around all day for the rest of my life. I'm yours to baby. Please.

Ford gives me a weird look when he gets into the driver's seat, and it's possible I may have said some of those things out loud. I level my most ferocious glare at him to counter-balance the neediness, but I must miss the mark because he almost laughs.

Nothing more gets said once he turns on the engine, and I let myself drift the whole way back to Possum Hollow.

I didn't think I fell all the way asleep, but I must have, because when I drift back to reality, Ford is dragging my heavy ass out of the car. It's nice, but it's got to be difficult because of my size. Once I've blinked a little awareness back into my body, I try to get my own feet under me.

"It's okay, I got it."

Ford doesn't say anything, but he watches me with an intense expression and keeps his hands on me as I climb out of the cab unsteadily and head towards his house.

Wait.

"Why am I not at home?"

Ford makes that bull-snort-exhale he seems to always make when I'm annoying him. Releasing me slowly, as if I might topple over any minute, he eventually pulls up his hands to sign carefully in front of me.

"Please. The doctor said you shouldn't be alone. And you look like you're going to pass out any minute. You can sleep here."

It shouldn't get to me. It's not a big deal. Most people would let someone crash at their place in a situation like this. But for whatever reason, it hits me like a lawnmower to the heart.

Just chunks of viscera and cardiac muscle splattering the inside of my thoracic cavity, all because this grumpy asshole showed the slightest hint of human warmth towards me. Something about him has turned me soft.

I'm too tired to care about it now. I don't even pretend to put up a fight as he takes me inside. I'm wearing sweatpants of his that are way too big that he threw on me before we left, my own boots, and no shirt, because the idea of getting one over my brand-new sling was exhausting. It's a warm night, but my body is drained beyond measure and a chill is settling into me.

Ford helps me kick off the boots and guides me upstairs before basically dumping me into his bed. As soon as I'm horizontal, it's like the last bit of adrenaline leaves my body. Whatever duct tape and optimism were holding me together finally let go. The world around me dims, and all I'm aware of is my battered body sprawled across Ford's bed.

I'm cold. So fucking cold. I start to shiver so violently I can hear my teeth chatter, and I clutch haphazardly at the blanket with my good hand to try to warm myself up.

I never get cold like this. Not even before I came over, when I had that weird, achy chill I couldn't shake. Fuck, maybe I really was getting sick, and it wasn't all in my head.

Maybe I'm going septic.

Maybe I'm having a psychotic break.

All I know is that nothing feels real anymore, and all I can concentrate on is the unbearable, bone-shattering cold that seems to have settled over Ford's bedroom on this balmy summer night.

He must have stepped out to get something, because he walks back in with some orange pill bottles in his hand, but stops short as soon as he sees me. Ford shoves the pill bottles somewhere and rushes towards me, but then pulls up short right before he touches me, looking side to side with his hands slightly outstretched, like he's not sure what to do.

I kind of thought I would feel better when he came back, because he's been comforting me more than I should have needed all night. But this time it doesn't help. I squeeze my eyes shut while my body continues to be racked with shivers and my shoulder throbs. I feel nauseous and dizzy, and it's like every discomfort I've ignored all night is swooping down on me all at once.

Ford shakes my good shoulder, forcing me to open my eyes a sliver. He's signing at me with sharp, frantic movements, but my brain feels too blurry to piece together the meaning right now. A haze has come over every inch of me, and all I can think is *cold*.

He looks scared. I don't like it when he looks scared; it seems so out of place on his normally dispassionate, adorably grumpy face. But more and more, I seem to be the common denominator for all the fear that's entered into his life.

Ugh, now I feel a sliver of guilt and self-hatred creeping in alongside the cold.

When he pulls his phone out of his pocket, I reach for him. I don't know if he's planning to call Cade or 911, but it's not necessary. It's just an adrenaline crash. A harder adrenaline crash than I've ever experienced in my life, which is really saying something, but still.

God, I have gone soft. I grab for his hand and shake my head, speaking through chattering teeth.

"It's fine. I think my body's crashing a little. I'm just cold, it'll pass. Don't worry, Cujo."

Ford hesitates. I can practically see the wheels turning. The skin of his wrist feels softer than I expected in my hand, and practically radiator-hot.

"Come warm me up."

More hesitation. He looks lost, and I don't blame him. This isn't what we do. Either of us, as individuals, or what we do together. But right now it's the only thing I want, and I feel pathetic enough to ranger up and ask for it.

"Please," I say, my voice soft. That must get to him, because he finally moves. More gently than a person of his size should be able to, he climbs over my body and slides himself under the blanket behind me. He's still fully dressed, but even so, I can feel warmth running off in waves that penetrate the cold shell around me when he lays against my back.

I curl in on myself as he wraps himself around me. I feel smaller and smaller, letting his heat sink into my core. His big arm lays over my side, his chest to my back, and he delicately avoids my injured shoulder as he places his hand on my chest and uses it to press me even closer to him.

The urge to turn around and burrow even deeper into the warmth of him is strong. But this will do for now. Already, the chattering and shivering is starting to subside. It's less dramatic, anyway, with my body trembling slightly as he holds me tight. His warm breath puffs on the back of my neck, and the world goes back to swimming pleasantly around me as the tension leaves my body once again.

In my entire life, I don't think I've ever been held like this. It's intoxicating. I kind of want to drown in it.

We drift together for a while, not moving or speaking, just breathing in a matched, even rhythm as my limbs remember how to function.

I think I must sleep a little, because I have no idea how much time has passed when my awareness comes back to me. It's still dark out, so it can't have been more than a few hours, but my mouth is sandpaper dry and my stomach is cramping painfully after being fed nothing but booze and painkillers for so long.

It feels like I have to peel my eyelids apart, they're so tacky. Eventually, I shimmy until I'm on my back and take in my surroundings. I'm still in bed, illuminated by the soft moonlight from outside. I can feel Ford's heavy body depressing the mattress next to me. His eyes are closed, but I can tell from the sound of his breathing that he's not asleep.

I don't know why he would pretend, but I'm too exhausted to bullshit with him.

"I know you're awake, bro. You don't have to pretend."

His eyes flick open immediately, and his gaze rakes over my body with a predatory intensity that never fails to make my heart beat a little faster. But I can't read his expression. His face is back to its trademark blankness, and for once I don't want to have to pester the truth out of him.

Ford's arm is still draped over my stomach like an anchor, and the warmth of him is wrapped around me like a shroud. So he can't be that annoyed with me. But there's not even a hint of warmth on his face. I know I was a handful last night—always, really—and the idea that I've finally worn out my welcome with him is more distressing than I was expecting.

"What?"

There's a long pause while we stare at each other. His eyes are so pale, they look practically white in the low light. They bore into me, and I suspect I'm just weak enough right now to spill all my secrets, if he asked me the right combination of questions.

164

Instead, he asks me something I wasn't expecting.

When he lifts his arm away from me to sign, I feel untethered, but try not to let myself show it. I concentrate on following his graceful movements, even in the darkness.

"Did you really beat up that kid?" he asks, his expression grim.

"What?" My brain screeches to a halt. I have no idea what he's talking about, and every part of me feels too sticky and worn out to work properly.

"The kid. Tobias. That asshole said you were the one who marked him up when you were looking for information. It's not... It's not true, right?"

Again, the darkness hampers my ability to tell, but I can sense a tension in him that isn't normally there. I'm used to him insulting me, or screwing around and calling me names, but this seems serious.

"I know we don't know each other that well, but do you think I would?" My voice is a whisper into the darkness between us.

Ford's hands hover in the air and he can't seem to quite look at me. I can see that he's turning something over in his mind. I'm trying not to take offense, which isn't something I often struggle with, but the idea that he thinks I might have beaten that poor kid makes me ache.

"People are capable of a lot of things you wouldn't expect," he signs at last.

Ahh. My brain may still be fogged by exhaustion and painkillers, but the pieces of everything he's not saying are starting to fall into place.

"I'm not a good person, Ford, in the grand scheme of things. I've killed people and let a lot of people down. But I promise I've never hurt someone... vulnerable. Not like that. I hope I never would." Ford exhales slowly, so I keep talking, keeping my tone low and even, forcing myself not to reach out and touch him, even though I want to. "I know the kid's grandmother. She's one of my patients. I've seen that he's gotten mixed up in some heavy shit. I did ask him about the Banna and he told me where to find their headquarters, but we just talked. I'm 99% sure that creep Eamon beat the tar out of him as a punishment and then blamed it on me for shits and giggles."

Ford finally turns and looks at me.

"I do not like that guy, FYI," I add for good measure.

He nods solemnly, pointing between the two of us to tell me he agrees.

I feel like he believes me, and the tension in the room seems to lose its edge. A quiet sadness takes its place, though, which is almost worse. It's obvious Ford's been through some shit, but the more I get to know him, the more I can fill in the blanks and figure out it's probably worse than whatever I first pictured.

He rolls his big body over until he's facing me. I can't turn to face him completely because I can't put pressure on that arm, but I turn my head until our faces are inches apart. Without overthinking it, I reach out with my right hand and run my fingertips over his beard. The scarring that I've never asked about is impossible to see in the darkness, but it's as if our combined unspoken awareness of it is louder than anything else right now.

The quiet continues for a long time. I don't know how long. My eyelids grow heavy again, but I don't want to push him to talk.

Eventually, his fingers twitch, and he looks like he's going to sign to me. Instead, he reaches for his phone. With a detached expression, he taps out a message quickly and then hands me the phone, avoiding eye contact.

I squint at the screen, adjusting to the light so I can read what he wrote quickly.

My mom's boyfriend beat her up once. And me. She left him, because that's what you're supposed to do. He came back and killed her. Almost killed me too. That's how I ended up with Dad. And lost my voice.

"Is that where all this is from?" I ask, my thumb still sweeping gently over his scarred cheek.

I feel him nod more than I see it.

The tension is coming back to him now, and I get it. This is the point where most people jump up and down to say how sorry they are, and how awful it is,

166

and somehow end up making *you* feel worse for how bad they feel for you. Like you feel bad for exposing them to something so horrific, even tangentially.

Or they're so distressed by it that your ability to distance and numb yourself to your own fucked up traumatic memories somehow makes you seem like a bad person. As if it didn't affect you as much as it would have done a normal person, because you're able to walk and talk and breathe and move on with your life, which some stranger who knows nothing about it finds incomprehensible.

Instead, I swallow and sigh. What happened to Ford was colossally fucked up, and more fucked up than anything that's ever happened to me. But there's a flavor to it that I'm very familiar with.

I don't get upset on his behalf. It's not helpful. But I do feel his exhaustion.

The painful familiarity of it all settles in my bones like a cancer, and my chest aches.

"That sucks," I say. Ford nods again, and we both know that nothing else needs to be said. The feeling of mutual understanding is something thick and viscous between us, and more palpable and real than a million "I'm sorry's" spoken out loud.

Neither of us needs to explain ourselves. We get it.

I move my thumb to gently press his eyelids closed, one by one. He accepts the gesture with a huff, but settles in to sleep some. I close my own eyes, and as soon as his arm snakes back out to pull me into him again, I allow myself to drift off.

CHAPTER TWENTY

FORD

I can't stop screaming.

I know I should be small and quiet, but there's too much blood coming from Mama's head and the part of me that's smart enough to know she's dead is too busy to do anything else, so the rest of my brain tells me to scream.

Besides, my face hurts so much. Screaming isn't helping, but I can't seem to stop.

The world is full of sound. Not just the sounds that I'm making, but the sounds of Tommy throwing things and cursing. There's a dog barking outside, and I think I hear sirens in the distance. Although I already know they can't be coming for me. I'm not that lucky. If I had any luck, they would have come before he killed her, so nothing really matters now.

There's broken glass everywhere, and my face is sticky with blood from where he shoved me into the floor and it cut me up. My hands are cut up too, so I don't want to reach for Mama in case I get my blood on her.

Even though that's stupid. She's already covered in her own blood, and she ain't moving.

Tommy shatters something else.

I jump, and finally my scream turns into a sob. I start to choke on something, maybe just the air, as I cry. I don't know what to do. I just want Tommy to leave so I can lie down next to Mama and wait for all the noise to stop, but he keeps yelling and breaking things and rattling the house like a cage.

"Shut up!" he yells in my face, spit flying, when he notices me.

I try to stop crying, but it's too late. He grabs me again. But instead of throwing me at the ground and hitting me like before, this time he grabs my throat in his hand. It's so big he only needs one, and he squeezes me so hard I can't breathe.

I can't see Mama anymore. I can't feel the blood on my face, or hear anything. I thought I knew how much I could hurt, but I was wrong. This hurts so much I wish I could keep screaming, but the sound can't squeeze past his fist; it's squeezing me too tight.

The world gets darker and smaller, until all I see is a tiny circle of Tommy's angry face in front of me, and everything else is black and quiet. But fuzzy, like the TV when it's not working right. Static.

Then it feels like all the air really is gone. My throat is so crushed in his hand it feels like it must be mush, and everything around me goes dark.

Finally.

Normally, when I wake up from a nightmare, I'm gasping for air. This time, I can't even get that close. My body is still so convinced it's in the dream that my throat won't remember it's not being crushed.

Air isn't moving in or out. My muscles strain and my chest feels like it's collapsing in on itself in slow-motion.

I try to force my lungs to move. A breath doesn't come, but instead, I do something I haven't done in a very long time: I make a sound. A garbled, choked, horrific sound.

It rasps out of my throat like a sort of cry, ripped from my chest by sheer terror. But it's enough to kick-start the movement in my lungs again, and afterwards I take a huge, gasping breath, throwing myself on my back.

I'm in my room.

It was a nightmare.

He's not here, and I can breathe.

I focus on the air, in and out. Which is why it takes me so long to realize I'm still making noises. Raw, wounded animal noises that escape from my chest with every breath. I have no control over them. It's not even worth trying, I think, when I realize there are also tears running down my face.

Just focus on the room.

Then Tristan comes into view. He looks concerned, but with this kind of laser focus, instead of the panic that most people get when this shit happens. He goes from asleep to awake in an instant and instead of rolling over, he straight-up launches himself onto me, straddling my lap and pulling me into a half-seated position.

I reach around haphazardly, trying to find the sheets or something to rub and focus on their texture. Instead, Tristan's good hand finds one of mine, and our fingers tangle together.

My senses are on high alert, and every detail of him gets swallowed up whole by my brain. The slight callous to his fingertips. The warmth of our combined body heat escaping the sheets where they're thrown off us. The sound of his mumbled words that I can't make out, but have the calm, even tone of someone trying to soothe a panicked animal or talk someone off a ledge.

He brings my hands one at a time to his naked waist, and I let myself dig my fingers into the flesh there hard enough to bruise. Then he shrugs off his sling with a wince and cups my face in both his hands until I'm forced to meet his gaze.

His hands are impossibly steady. His eyes are calm, and he nods at me slowly, taking one breath after another.

"It's just a nightmare," he says. I can't stop myself from whimpering.

My voice croaks from disuse. I can see how surprised Tristan is, even though he quickly smooths the expression over.

I don't want to talk about it. I don't want to think about it. I want to chase away the vestiges of the worst nightmare I've had in the last ten years and remind my stupid malfunctioning brain once and for all that we're in the present.

Tristan's skin is hot and sweaty under my hands. Without letting myself second guess anything, I flip us, so he's on his back with me in between his legs.

He looks shocked, but I don't give him the chance to be rational and object. I want to touch, and taste, and feel. He's still shirtless, and my hands move over every inch of his torso, grabbing and tugging at whatever skin I can, only being careful enough to avoid his shoulder.

I bend over to suck one nipple into my mouth hard enough to make him gasp, then tear away to claim his open mouth in a kiss. There's no time for pleasantries. I need to taste him. I need to be inside him.

Tristan kisses me back after a moment of hesitation. His hips grind against mine on instinct, his legs wrapping around me to hold me closer as I feel his length thicken against mine.

I tug off the sweats that he borrowed from me, and satisfaction pours through me when I see how close he is to hard already. Tristan bites back a moan when I take him in hand and stroke.

I already feel better. The dream is being chased away as I fill my world with the feel and scent and sound of Tristan, and do everything I can to make him writhe underneath me like the needy thing he is.

The only thing that makes me pause is when his hands reach for the hem of my shirt and tug.

I should say something. Explain, like an adult. But even just the idea of words makes me want to choke right now. I just want to *feel*.

I give in to my inner demons and roughly flip Tristan over until he's face down on the bed. He goes without complaint, though. He lets me pin his working hand over his head, and the way he pushes his round ass into me when I scrape my teeth over his neck tells me he's happy to play along for now. It's almost too easy to slip off the baggy sweats of mine that I'd dressed him in for the trip to the hospital.

In an instant, he's bare for me. His back is arched in invitation.

We shouldn't fuck. He's injured and strung out on booze and meds, and I'm basically one deep-fried trauma response in a human shell right now.

But I need to feel him against me.

Instead of going for his hole, even though he's offering it up to me on a silver platter, I shove down my own sweats, grab my leaking erection and shove it in between his thighs. It doesn't take much maneuvering until my body is bracketing him in, his thighs pinned together and giving me delicious, sweaty friction to slide between.

I use my free hand to reach underneath him and jerk him off. I don't bother to be gentle. I want him to feel everything as intensely as I do right now, and when I squeeze his length a little harder than I should, he lets out a deep, guttural moan.

He's every bit the pain slut I knew he would be.

"Fuck," he bites out, but it's breathy and desperate. "Fuck, more."

I jerk him aggressively as I fuck his thighs. The whole thing is dirty and aggressive. We're both desperate. I paw at him, trying to pull more savage sounds from his throat, and growl in his ear when I feel my orgasm begin to build.

It only takes a few more thrusts before I'm spilling in between his strong thighs, and he quickly follows me, making a fucking mess of the sheets. I blanket his body with mine, weighing him down into the mattress as we sink into one another and catch our breath.

No one speaks for a long time.

Eventually, slowly, Tristan rolls over. I keep him underneath me, but I do feel a little relief when he doesn't look unhappy at the rough treatment that I just gave him. It wasn't exactly the most thought-out moment of my entire life.

Tristan plucks at my shirt, and then at my pants that I've already pulled back up. I know what he's saying without having to say it out loud. He's noticed that I won't let him take my clothes off, but he's choosing not to push me on it.

The wave of relief it makes me feel is so powerful that I let my face fall against his neck and take a deep breath, filling my lungs with the scent of him.

If he pushed me, I'd have to get rid of him. I know I would. I've never let anyone get even half as close to me as he is right now, and even that thin layer of fabric's difference would be enough to push me over the edge and run.

But I don't want to.

I want him to not push.

Instead, he wraps his good arm around me and traces absent patterns on my back for a while as we both settle into this weird thing that we've stumbled into between us.

"I guess we should admit that it wasn't a onetime thing, huh?" he says, eventually. His voice is husky in my ear, and it makes me think of how hoarse he sounded after I fucked his throat.

Goddamn, that was barely a couple of days ago.

How are things able to shift in my life so quickly?

I squeeze him to me a little tighter, even though I won't even admit to myself that I'm doing it.

"I've never really had a fuckbuddy before," he adds, mischief in his eyes as he gives me a sloppy half-smile. "Wanna pop my cherry?"

I grunt at him, but I don't let him go. That's all the answer he's going to get from me right now. I can tell from the contented sigh that slips out of his mouth that it's all he was looking for.

CHAPTER TWENTY-ONE

TRISTAN

I'm so bored, I'm considering chewing off my own arm if it'll get me out of here.

After Ford and I decided to become off-books fuckbuddies in the most awkward, uncomfortable conversation I've ever participated in, I think we both shrank back a little bit. The sleeping part was amazing. I've never been a cuddler, but after all that cold and stress, being wrapped up in his warmth and bulk grounded me in a way I hadn't known was possible.

Then we woke up, and shit got even more awkward. He had to work, and I am strictly on bedrest for a week until I get some mobility back, and even then, I can only go back to work with restrictions.

This gunshot is lame as hell.

Ford drove me home in silence. Then there was the moment where neither of us knew how to say goodbye. How do you say goodbye to someone who went from being a total stranger to giving you the most incredible orgasm of your life with only a hand job and some thigh-fucking in the matter of two weeks?

I don't fucking know. This is not the kind of thing I'm good at. So, I made a few lame-ass jokes to annoy him—so at least one thing felt normal—and then bailed out of the car so hard it made me dizzy.

Since then, I've been on my couch for days, slowly rotting. I am become one with the couch. The couch and I are fused together, and nothing can tear us apart.

I can't watch my normal shitty home renovation shows, because they make me feel guilty about how much I've neglected this beast. I can't watch any other shows, because they always end up with lights and sirens at some point that makes me miss work.

And I can't talk to Ford, because that would imply that I *need* him. Or even *want* him.

Which isn't true.

There's nothing between us. We're just experimenting with some fuckbuddy shenanigans because the universe has forced us together, and I seem to find him inhumanly sexy. I just need to keep going until I've fucked him out of my system—or until he's fucked the needy, whiny version of myself that he's created out of me—and then things will go back to normal.

Maybe I should get a pet or something.

He's texted me a couple times to make sure I'm okay, but that's it. No banter, no flirting. I'm keeping my distance, so he doesn't get the wrong idea and assume I'm desperate for his company. I'm also discouraging myself from getting the wrong idea.

The only other thing that's invaded my quiet, boring little couch-land is the constant buzzing of my mother's unanswered calls.

I still don't know what the fuck she wants. I'm not coming home to clean her up if she's off the rails again. I don't care. I've done my time, and I have too much shit here to take care of. She can take her own ass back to the psych ward. She knows where it is.

I don't care. I don't.

It's not like she ever did anything to raise me. I raised myself, and my little brother, while tolerating an endless train of her shitty con artist boyfriends who treated us like shit, along with her endless manic mood swings.

And my reward was a dead brother and the abrupt end to my military career, so I could go home and drag her out of the gutter when the guilt got to be too much.

Worthless.

I don't care what happens to her.

She can go fuck herself.

I roll over on the couch, bury my face in the sweaty fabric and close my eyes, trying to let the constant vibrations lull me to sleep.

On my fifth day of bedrest, I can't stop thinking about Ford. And his magic dick. If I don't do something to snap out of it soon, I'm going to go crawling to him for some crumbs of affection, and he's going to see what a needy, whiny little bitch he managed to turn me into.

This isn't me. I don't *do* depending on anyone. Self-sufficiency is really the only thing I've ever had going for me.

To stave off the urge, I give in to the only other self-destructive urge I have, as the lesser of two evils, and answer the phone the next time she calls.

"Kaitlyn," I say, trying to keep my voice even as I immediately regret choosing to answer. "What do you want?"

"Jesus, fuck, Tristan. I thought you were dead. Why weren't you answering the phone?"

She doesn't sound like she's calling me from a locked ward or tied to a chair in a cartel's basement, but first impressions can be deceiving.

"I have a job. And a life, none of which involves you. What do you need?"

"Why can't I call to check on my son? You left Boston so fast it made my head spin. I know you wanted to go play back to the wilderness or whatever. I thought if I gave you time you'd get it out of your system and stop being so petulant. But I'm worried about you. It's been over a year. Come home."

"It's been more than two, not that you've been paying attention. So, no. Negative on ever coming home. Is that everything?"

This was a mistake. I don't have the energy to listen to her pretend to care for half an hour until I get to the bedrock of what the fuck she wants.

"I promise, Tristan, I really don't have an agenda here," she says. She sounds sincere, but my mother has been a professional con artist since she was a teenager, so that doesn't carry a lot of weight. "I'm worried about you. I know I was kind of a mess when you were here—" I don't even try to hide the snort that comes out of me, "but I appreciate you taking care of me and I feel like I should repay the favor. Come home. You shouldn't be alone like this. Conor wouldn't want that."

For whatever reason, hearing his name in her mouth flips my switch from irritated to enraged in a heartbeat.

"Fuck you, Kaitlyn. You never gave a shit about him when he was alive, and you only started to do this whole self-indulgent song and dance once he died. Which was only because you dragged him into your shitty fucking life of crime. You don't know shit about what he would have wanted, and as far as I'm concerned, you're the reason he's dead. I took care of you until I felt like you weren't on the brink of total meltdown anymore, but now I'm done. I'm living my own life."

Stony silence answers me from the other end of the line. I can hear her breathing, choppy and harsh, but I can't tell if it's because she's trying not to cry, or because she's gearing up to yell at me.

It could go either way.

When she starts to speak, it's with a sort of half-sob, and the exhaustion that floods my body at the sound is instantaneous.

"Tristan—" she says, but I cut her off.

"No. I'm done. Take your meds, stop dating criminals, get a real job and leave me the fuck alone."

I wish I had an old-fashioned receiver so I could slam it into the cradle when I hang up on her. That would be so much more satisfying than viciously tapping a screen. I would probably still have this hollow feeling either way, though.

I don't even notice where my body is leading me until I'm getting up and heading out to my car. My beautiful working car that Ford fixed for me.

I tried to use Ma as a distraction, and it just made me feel so wound up I'm like taut, frayed piano wire that's about to snap. And I can't keep lying around all day or I'll crawl into the painful silence of my own brain and never come out again.

That only leaves one distraction left. As much as I was trying to avoid him.

It's a short drive to Ford's shop, thankfully, because I've only got one useable hand and very little focus left. I briefly consider turning around and going back as soon as I pull into the parking lot, but I know I can't keep doing this. I'm going to start banging my head against the wall if I can't get something better to focus on.

As soon as I let myself in, Ford's head snaps up. His gaze finds me like a searchlight in a storm, and he frowns. Abandoning the engine he was bent over, he quickly moves towards me and starts to sign.

"What's wrong? Are you okay?"

And fuck if that doesn't hit me in whatever raw, shriveled part of my heart still has feeling.

I can't tell him the truth, obviously. So instead, I put a big smile on my face and try to draw him into my orbit with a charming expression.

"I'm bored."

Ford rolls his eyes at that, but he still moves closer to me without seeming to realize it.

I can tell that Silas is watching us from the corner of his eye, even though he's trying to be subtle about it. So, I toss my head in the direction of the hallway that has some storage rooms; I think. Anything with four walls, a door, and no windows will do right now.

Ford continues to frown, but when I move, he follows me like there's an invisible string between our chests, and being apart from each other for too long causes the skin there to tear away. Whether we like it or not.

The first closet I find is small, but I don't care. In fact, I kind of love it. The cramped quarters make Ford feel even bigger than normal, and the more space he takes up, the less space there is in the world for all of my shitty thoughts and feelings that I've been desperately trying to silence.

I don't bother with subtlety, because what's the point?

As soon as the door closes behind us, I stick my hand down his pants and wrap my fingers around his thick cock. He sucks in a breath, his eyes going dark, but otherwise stays still. I realize that for all we've done together, this is the first time I've deliberately touched his cock. Normally, he's so aggressive, he just throws me down and fucks whatever orifice of mine his sadistic little heart desires, while I slut-moan and beg him for more.

I love the feel of him in my hand. He's velvety smooth, and there's an easy glide from his foreskin that lets me work him over until he's achingly hard in just a few minutes. He continues to stand there and take it for so long that I get kind of frustrated, though. As delicious as this is, I wanted him to fuck the sense out of me right now.

"Are you just going to stand there like you're stoically tolerating the world's shittiest hand job?" I ask, trying to get some kind of reaction from him.

"I wasn't sure where you were going with this. It's the middle of the day and you show up to grope me. I thought maybe you wanted to... take charge, or something."

The expression he's making is genuine, which feels unnatural. The only thing worse than being a desperate bitch on my knees for him is having to admit out loud that I actually want to be a desperate bitch on my knees for him, but I'm so stressed and horny right now that I'm passed caring.

"Nope," I say, popping the 'p' as I shake my head. "I want you to fuck all the thoughts out of my brain, please and thank you. I'm having a shitty day."

He cocks his head and looks me up and down, his icy eyes calculating. Then, without warning, he pushes me. Hard enough that I stumble, but not hard enough to risk fucking with my injury.

There's a stack of boxes behind me that I stumble-crash into, and before I know it, I've got an arm across my chest pinning me to them, while his other hand works open my pants. Ford leans in close like he's going to kiss me, but stops just short. I chase his lips with a barely contained whine, but he still doesn't let me have anything.

When he licks his lips, I follow the movement of his pink, wet tongue, but still, he doesn't kiss me.

Instead, he pulls out my cock, kneels down and swallows me in one fluid movement.

It's a fucking surprise, to say the least.

Before I know what's happening, one of his hands is wrapped around my throat, not squeezing hard, but continuing to hold me at his mercy. He has to stretch, but his arms are long and having him laid over me like that makes me feel utterly pinned. The other hand is pushing my shirt up and pawing at my waist while his head bobs on my cock and sucks at a ferocious, relentless pace.

Fuck, it's been so long since someone's given me head. It's been even longer since someone's given me earth-shattering, dizzying, out-of-control head like this. The world seems to spin as all the blood rushes to my cock, and I immediately know this is going to be embarrassingly fast.

"Christ, Ford, fuck," I groan. "I'm not gonna... I'm gonna—"

He ignores my babbling and only works harder to get me to come in record time. It's less than two minutes before I'm spilling into his mouth with a strangled sound of relief. Bliss is already sinking into my limbs, making them heavy, and I feel 1000% better than I did when I walked in here a few minutes ago.

But Ford isn't done.

He stands up and manhandles me to my knees. He's careful of my shoulder, but that's about all the consideration I get. Without any idea of what's coming, he plunges two of his thick fingers into my mouth and pries it open. I feel soft and compliant, so I open readily, expecting his cock.

Instead, he leans over and spits. My mouth is filled with my own release, hot and wet, some of it spilling down my chin.

There's no time to think, because then Ford follows it up with his hard cock. He slides into the wetness he's created, fucking my face relentlessly right from the start. He holds my head in place as he bruises my throat. The room is filled with the sound of his soft grunts, as well as the slick, obscene sounds of my own cum lubricating his fucking cock.

He's quick too, spilling into me with a rough, audible groan that surprises me. My mouth is impossibly full, so I have to swallow quickly to get it all down. When he finally pulls his softening cock out of me, I'm gasping for air.

My head and body feel weightless. There's nothing in me but the load he just poured down my throat. Nothing else exists, and it's perfect.

CHAPTER TWENTY-TWO

FORD

I 've been staring at the numbers on the screen for so long I feel like they've turned into hieroglyphics. Nothing makes sense anymore.

No matter how much work I take on, we're still hemorrhaging money. Well, maybe not hemorrhaging, but not turning the kind of profit that's kept us so comfortable all these years. It was only Dad and me before, so even though Silas is still learning, it feels like we're turning over roughly the same amount of business. Sure, I don't have his head for restorations, but I don't remember them ever being common enough to make this big of a difference in the bottom line.

Why the fuck did I never bother to learn about the financial side of things until it was too late for Dad to answer my questions?

Maybe because I wasn't expecting him to stroke out at fifty-two and leave me all alone.

I growl in frustration and shuffle through some more papers. Yet another problem: Dad's lackadaisical approach to accounting means everything is spread between a shitty, under-utilized QuickBooks account and little scraps of paper stuffed into his desk drawer. And I'm convinced he must have been doing cash jobs that he didn't keep a record of.

I know he was involved in some less-than-legal stuff before I moved in with him. Mama always warned me about him. He was a biker veteran with off the wall PTSD and no legal job at the time. She told me she never should have gotten involved with him. That's why she didn't bother to tell him when she got pregnant.

But he cleaned up his act when I got dumped on his doorstep. He was a good dad, and he ran a good business. Everyone in Possum Hollow would agree.

So why am I failing so fantastically at following in his footsteps?

The thought grips my spine and shakes me hard enough to rattle my brain, making me feel even more off-balance than I did before. The idea that he was never honest with me about exactly how he kept this place successful, possibly because it was something less-than-legal, is dogging at my mind. But I can't begin to picture him as the kind of person who would lie to my face for all those years. It doesn't make sense.

And the fact that Tristan is constantly here now, wandering around the shop and touching everything with his stupid sexy hands, isn't helping. Well, it is, actually. It's about the only thing that makes me feel better about any of this, but that fact is fucking terrifying, which keeps sending me into catastrophizing cycles about how I could possibly have let myself come to rely on this damaged, ridiculous man-child to improve my mood.

I hear something expensive-sounding crash to the floor and pick up my phone to text him. The only reason I agreed to let him hang out here was because I thought he was on the cusp of losing it if he stayed in his house, and at least if he's here I can make sure he's wearing the stupid sling and not using his arm.

> Stop touching things. If you break anything, I'm taking it out on your ass.

There's a pause, then I see through the open doorway as Tristan reaches for his phone, reads the message and then laughs. It's a full-body laugh, warm and husky, coating me like honey. He tips his head back and the late afternoon sunlight hits his hair in a way that looks like little licks of flames.

"Don't threaten me with a good time!" He calls over to me, wandering towards the office at the same lazy pace he does almost everything, like he's completely at home in every situation. "Besides, I was in the military. I'm very familiar with gizmos and gadgets. All the machines and whatnot."

"The fact that you call them 'gizmos' makes me think that can't possibly be true," I sign to him. "You fix people, which is a much squishier set-up. Don't forget, I know what your car looked like. I think if the Army could have seen that engine, they never would have given you a gun."

Tristan snorts, but doesn't take the bait. Instead, he leans back, swaying his body and reaching for me with grabby hands like a petulant child, something I've noticed him doing more and more often, but I don't think he's even aware of.

"Come play with me. Or fuck me over the hood of that Deville. I'm boooooored."

I pin him with a stare. "You're a child. And you're welcome to be bored somewhere else. Also, why aren't you wearing your sling?"

Tristan huffs. "It's driving me nuts. If I can't work, the least you can do is let me play with your toys. And there's no point in going somewhere else. I'll only be back here for a booty call in an hour once you finally give up on whatever you're pretending to do. So, hurry up. I need enrichment or I become destructive."

"You're a person, not a German Shepherd. Find something to do that doesn't involve damaging my shop or you won't come for a week, I swear to Christ."

He pouts at full force, which is actually adorable, but I'm careful not to let my face show that I think that, or he'll realize he has all the power here and I'll never get anything done ever again.

Tristan throws himself into the chair on the other side of my desk with a dramatic exhalation, kicking his legs over the arm and leaning back. He pulls out his phone to start scrolling, and I turn my attention back to these insane books.

I pause for a second and rap my knuckles on the table to get his attention. He looks up at me, so I slowly and deliberately fingerspell at him, like he's a toddler.

S-L-I-N-G.

He huffs, rolling his eyes, but gets up and retrieves it from wherever he threw it before returning to the desk and his doomscrolling.

Barely a few minutes pass before the phone gets thrown on my desk with another dramatic sigh. I pretend I'm not watching him as he picks at the things sitting on my desk, fishing out a blank pad of paper I use for writing notes to clients and a pencil.

Blissful quiet falls over the room as Tristan seems captivated by whatever he's scratching away into the pad, and I keep going through the numbers until I feel like my eyes are burning.

It's strange. There are more and more of these moments recently. Where we're not interacting, but we're sharing space while doing separate things in silence. It's nice. I don't think I've ever experienced it outside of work or school, and if you'd asked me before, I would have assumed it would be annoying. Especially because Tristan can only keep his trap shut for so long.

Instead, his presence makes everything feel just a little steadier. Even though I'm still sweating over the same math problem I've been looking at all day, it somehow seems less intimidating with him sitting across the table from me. It's like having the option to talk to him about it soothes my brain, even if I know I'm not going to bring it up.

It's weird. I want to ask him if this is what normal people do with their time, but I don't think he'll have an answer for me either. He keeps drawing, and I keep clicking, and the silence stretches out at a comfortable, meandering pace.

Eventually, my curiosity gets the better of me.

I wave my hand in Tristan's eyeline until he looks at me.

"What are you drawing?"

A sly grin spreads across his face. He turns the pad around, and it takes me a long time to figure out what I'm looking at.

It looks like a possum, but Frankensteined out of auto-parts, with bolts on its neck and wire whiskers. The words "Possum Hollow Auto Shop" are scrawled underneath.

I give him my best *what the fuck?* face and wait for him to explain.

"His name is Cyborg Possum," Tristan explains with a feral grin. "And he's your new mascot. Honestly, what kind of business doesn't have a logo? All you have out there is that faded ass sign that says 'Auto Shop'."

My brain is still processing *Cyborg Possum*, so I answer slowly.

"It's a small town. Everyone knows we're here. It's not like we need to advertise. I guess Dad never saw the point."

"Well, no offense to your dad, but that seems like a missed opportunity. Besides, possums are badass. Who wouldn't want their car fixed somewhere with a robotic marsupial as their logo?"

"Ummm... lots of people?"

"It's America's only native marsupial," he says, so deadpan, I think he might actually consider this as important and not be fucking with me.

When I don't reply because I'm too busy trying to figure out what's happening right now, Tristan just shakes his head and sighs with an unearned amount of confidence for what he's trying to sell me on.

"I swear. This is my gift to you. He's your mascot. You can make a big sign and everyone driving past will be so captivated by my artistic ability, they'll be willing to overlook how unbearably friendly you are and keep bringing you business." He takes a breath and then gives me another winning smile, just a hint of his tongue pinched between his teeth as a tease, as if everything we're doing right now is totally normal. "Now let's fuck."

"You're intolerable," I sign. Meanwhile, my brain is telling me the exact opposite. Whatever part of me was resisting him gave up pretending a long time ago and wants to bathe in that ridiculous movie star grin.

But it seems dangerous. And like something that would end badly for both of us. It would be better to end everything now, before either of us gets even more sucked in than we are. It's not like we're capable of or interested in having a real relationship, so all this is destined to be is a fuckbuddy situation that ends up with too many strings attached and someone getting hurt.

Of course, thinking about ending it isn't the same as wanting to end it. Instead, I take him into that storage closet and put him on his knees for me for the second day in a row, pushing all those anxious thoughts to the back of my mind.

When Tristan comes, I feel him moan my name even though my hand is clasped across his mouth, and something inside me is set even more at ease.

CHAPTER TWENTY-THREE

TRISTAN

"**F**ucking finally!"

I fist pump in the warm evening air, even though it still causes a twinge in my shoulder. I may have fudged my physical a tad so I could go back to work sooner rather than later, but I maintain that it was the right choice. It was critical for my mental health that I do something other than lying on my couch or loitering around Ford's shop all day.

Plus, the longer I spend there, the more often I catch him looking at me with this inscrutable expression. I can't decide if I've worn out my welcome and he's about to kick me out of his life, or if he's secretly falling in love with me.

I also can't figure out which one would be worse, which is utterly fucking terrifying.

So, my arm is fine, the sling is gone, and any-and-all inappropriate feelings I'm definitely not having about that stupid giant silent man can be shoved back into a drawer in my head where they belong, never to be examined again.

He can continue to bang me like a screen door in a hurricane without ever making eye contact, and nothing will ever change.

It's perfect.

Cade is giving me The Look, but I have no idea why, because there's nothing wrong with celebrating a little blood and guts on a Saturday night. We just finished transferring our most recent shooting victim into the ER. We got there fast enough that he stands a good chance of making it, so that's a successful night in my books.

"You seem pretty fucking perky," he says, and I don't bother to hide my smile when I turn towards him, grabbing him by both arms with both of my *functioning* ones and shaking him.

"I'm fucking free, Cade. Free! I can operate like a human being in the world again. Do you have any idea how useless I've felt while I've been banned from work? God. You can't take work away from a workaholic. It's the cornerstone of my identity. This entire psychological house of cards crumbles without it."

I gesture to my head. I'm kind of poking fun at myself, but there's a kernel of truth there. Okay, maybe more than a kernel. If I can't save lives, then there's literally nothing else I'm good at in this world, and where the fuck am I supposed to get self-esteem from then?

Apart from my good looks, obviously. But that only goes so far.

Cade chuckles at me and gives me a playful punch in the arm.

"And here I thought you were so happy because you were getting laid." He's playing it light, but there's an edge to his tone, and my good mood immediately takes a dip. I was hoping we could get away with never, ever talking about this.

"Shit, do you hear that?" I ask, making fake mouth static as if the radio is going off. "Sounds like the entire town just exploded. We better go. That'll keep us occupied all night, for sure."

I dive into the driver's seat of the ambulance. He's been driving tonight while I catch up on paperwork, but I want a distraction right now. Or at least an excuse to not look him in the eye.

Cade follows me into the cab, clearly not amused by what I thought was a pretty funny diversion.

"Come on, are we really never going to talk about it? Between you and Silas, I feel like I'm going fucking insane and I dreamed the whole thing. But I didn't make this up. You were in your underwear... with a gunshot wound... on Ford's floor. Ford, who I thought you'd met once for about a minute and a half on a job. There's no way we're going the rest of our lives without you giving me some kind of explanation."

There's a long beat where I struggle for words. Why is no one ever dying when you need them to be? I suck at this stuff.

"I thought we were friends," Cade finally says in a small voice, and fuck me. He really went there.

I was about to head out from the hospital, but I pull us off to the side so we're not blocking anything. I put the ambulance into park with a sigh before turning to look at him.

"Fine. You can ask me three questions. I will give you yes or no answers, and then we're never talking about this again. Go."

The look on Cade's face tells me he was definitely expecting to get stonewalled again, which makes me feel another twinge of guilt. He fishmouths for a minute before he figures out what he wants to say.

"Are you and Ford dating?" he asks carefully.

The nuance of the question makes my stomach twist. "Fuck no," is all I say, though.

"But you've had sex?"

"Yes."

There's a long pause while he thinks about his next question.

"Are you queer?"

I take a long breath in through my nose and take a second to gather my thoughts. The obvious answer here is 'yes', but I feel like he deserves a little more than that.

"I guess I never thought about it that way. I've never really dated anyone, to be honest, just hooked up with whoever I could. And I always lived in situations where a lot of guys were open to hooking up with each other, but you never talked about it. And no one considered it gay. It was more... opportunistic. I never planned to do more than that, so I figured it wasn't worth thinking about." I shrug and look him in the eye. "I don't know. Honestly. And I genuinely don't care. I'm sorry I didn't tell you before, but I promise I wasn't deliberately holding out on you. I just didn't have anything helpful to say."

He thinks for a minute, chewing on his lip and looking at the floor. Then he seems to accept it, and then the tension eases between us.

I'm about to change the subject anyway when I see a familiar figure walking through the parking lot.

"Wait, is that—?"

There's no time to finish my sentence or my thought. I dive out of the ambulance and run up to that smug shit to find out what he's doing here.

It only takes me a few seconds to jog across the parking lot, and Cade is hot on my heels. When I catch up to Eamon, the man turns slowly, almost like he was expecting me.

Even in the evening dusk, his hair is too blond. Everything about him seems slightly wrong, like he's designed to be unsettling.

I do not like this guy. Vibes are off.

"I see you survived your injury. Congratulations," he says dryly.

"Hilarious. What the fuck are you doing here?"

"Visiting a friend. One of my boys ran into some trouble. I'm here to check on him."

His tone is more serious than I expected. I can only assume he means the gunshot victim we just brought in, because who else would be mixed up in this asshole's business?

I consider my next words carefully, because I don't want to get involved any deeper than I have to with this situation, but the uptick in violent crime has been noticeable, to say the least.

"If you're looking for who I think you are, he's doing okay. I know you told me to stay out of your business and I am, but bodies seem to keep dropping in my lap, so I'm going to ask you one thing against my better judgment. Is this the beginning of it or the end?"

The smile that Eamon gives me is predatory. And not in the sexy way Ford does before he throws me against something. The cold, soulless way that makes me suspect he spent his childhood setting fires and torturing small animals.

"I guess we'll find out, won't we?"

He doesn't bother giving me more than that before turning and heading inside, leaving me with more questions than answers.

I know I shouldn't get involved. I only have to treat these people after the fact. But the whole thing makes me nervous. Ford's shop has already been targeted once, and Silas got stabbed because of it. Between that and the cryptic shit that Eamon said about knowing Ford's dad... This is a small town. It feels like the people I care about are already too close to it to escape from whatever organized crime shitshow is about to descend upon us unscathed.

The thought comes screeching to a halt in my brain as I realize how I phrased it.

The people I care about.

Cade. Silas. Ford.

I guess I've made connections with people, whether I wanted to or not.

If that thought isn't terrifying, I don't know what is. And the fact that it isn't sending me running is even more disconcerting.

I definitely can't let it slip to Ford, though. All his lingering looks aside, I'm pretty sure if he suspected I might have a feeling buried deep inside me, he'd kick my ass to the curb so fast I'd get road rash.

"Fuck!" I shout, at no one in particular.

Cade looks at me, eyes wide.

"What's happening?"

"Honestly?" I bend over and lean on my knees for a second, catching my breath even though I've done nothing to wind myself except *feel* things. "I have no idea, kid."

After our shift, Cade has to pick up Silas and I'm too keyed up to go home, so we both head to the garage. When we walk in, Cade freezes, and I immediately look around for some source of danger. Until I realize that he's staring at Silas like he wants to eat him.

"Baby, why do I immediately want to jump you?" He doesn't even bother to hide the rasp in his voice, despite the fact that they are very much not alone in the room. Fucking kids.

Silas just smirks to himself and continues what he's doing, not even looking up from the engine he's working on.

"Because I'm wearing a trucker cap and you have a blue-collar fetish, you freak."

"Oh yeah, that must be it. The trucker cap and coveralls combo is my kryptonite." Cade bites his bottom lip, continuing to appreciate the view, until I smack him on the back of the head. "Hey!"

"You two have a home you can do that in, y'know," I say, eyeing him down.

Ford wanders over and upnods me by way of greeting. "They already defiled the shop floor. Less than a month after Silas got hired, and I had to walk in on them trading hand jobs over their fucking dirt bikes like animals," he signs at me.

I couldn't stop myself from cackling, even if I wanted to. Watching Ford mime hand jobs while looking at me with a completely placid expression is one of the funniest things I've ever seen. Especially considering Silas is turning so red I'm worried he might self-immolate, and Cade is darting his eyes between the three of us with his mouth open, trying to figure out what's going on.

"Just take your man home, kid," I say, still chuckling as I push him towards Silas.

That's enough for Cade, apparently. He winks at me, because he's a little shit, then closes the few feet between them and launches himself at Silas. It forces him to catch Cade as he wraps long legs around his waist like a spider monkey.

I wince, because it wasn't that long ago that Silas was injured, even if it was minor. But I forget sometimes just how resilient you can be at that age. Silas seems completely unfazed, mesmerized by the six-foot-tall boy who's leaped into his arms.

Cade tips back the trucker hat to kiss Silas, much more enthusiastically than I wanted to witness, but at least it distracts Silas from dying of embarrassment from Ford's story.

"Byyyyyyyye," I say, because my fingers are itching with how much I need to touch Ford. I'm not going to do it in front of them though, because I still have a scrap of self-respect. They both wave, still caught up in each other, and then Silas finally carries Cade's ass out the door.

When I turn back around, Ford is looking at me with a small, peaceful smile. It catches me off-guard, and for a second I feel like all the air has been sucked out of the room.

I don't think I've ever seen him look peaceful before. Stoic, sure. Placid. Empty. But not happy. And the way his eyes are shining tells me it's all for me.

It unleashes a feral hunger in my chest. The kind that says maybe this man is mine, whether either of us is ready to accept it or not. I can have another meltdown about it later. In the meantime, he looks too delicious to let myself get distracted.

I move towards him like a jungle cat on the prowl, unable to keep the smile from my own face. Ford raises that damn eyebrow at me at first, but then he seems to guess what I'm about to do.

"Don't you dare jump on me, T," he signs, looking serious. "We are not horny 22-year-olds and you weigh 200lbs. Don't do it."

But he can't hide that the ghost of that smile is still there, tugging at the corner of his mouth.

When I jump on him, he catches me with a grunt, but doesn't stumble. This giant oak tree slab of man.

His hands slip under my ass to hold me up, and I wrap my thighs tightly around his abdomen. If I squeeze tightly enough, he'll never put me down, and all the rest of the shit in my head can go to hell.

Right?

CHAPTER TWENTY-FOUR

FORD

W e've been making out for so long that my lips are tingly and swollen, but I don't care. I feel like a teenager.

Actually, I feel like what I imagine you're supposed to feel like as a teenager, which is way, way better than what my actual experience was. I had a handful of awkward make-out sessions and spent most of my time wallowing in anger and self-loathing.

This is fucking great. I should have been doing this the whole time instead. The ground could crack open underneath us right now, and I wouldn't notice as long as Tristan was still in my arms.

Tristan's body is warm and firm, half underneath me as we're both sprawled across my too-small bed. He's been keyed up since the second he walked in the door after his first day back at work. All of his sparkle that was dulled by pain and frustration is back, and it's like Tristan times a thousand has been delivered into my lap.

We immediately traded hand jobs as soon as I closed the shop, but that barely even slowed him down. All it did was take the edge off. We've been rolling around like idiots ever since, and we're both well past the point of being ready to go again.

I've been hard and aching for so long I can hardly even feel it anymore. My entire body is alive with sparks that won't stop, and every inch of me is like a firecracker about to go off.

Tristan's no better. As well as writhing around underneath me like a wanton thing, he's really let go of whatever inhibitions he had initially about being 'submissive'. He moans like a whore, groaning and whining, threading his hands through my hair as he holds me close to him and begging me for more whenever I pull away.

He's obsessed with my hair, which makes me glad I never gave in and cut it. Every time we fool around, his fingers find their way there and he slides them through the strands. Nearly every time I make him come, he's pulling on it desperately while he groans.

It's like a drug. I never want to stop. The sensations are so overwhelming that the fear I would normally feel at that idea is getting drowned out by all this pleasure.

"Let's fuck," Tristan croons directly into my mouth, before plunging his tongue back in.

I let him wiggle against me for a few more minutes, his legs wrapping around my waist, until I pull back far enough to sign.

"I thought that's what we were already doing?"

Tristan huffs. "No, I mean *fuck* fuck. Your dick in my ass fuck. Or my dick in yours. I'm not picky." He illustrates by making an exaggerated humping movement against my hips with his, which has no business being cute, but somehow is.

"Charming." I scrunch up my face to show I'm being sarcastic.

He bites his lip. There's a flicker of insecurity there that I'm not used to seeing from him. It seems unnatural, and I'm not sure what to do about it or how it got there.

We haven't done *that* since the first time; the night he got shot. Not because it wasn't good. It was epic. I'll probably die dreaming about how it felt to tunnel into his impossibly tight, perfect ass, having him laid out beneath me like something to devour.

We've done a lot of other stuff. Basically, every combination of hand jobs, blow jobs, docking and thigh-fucking I could come up with, all of which end with him on his knees for me in one way or another. He seemed to love it. I thought I was getting away with not bringing it up.

Because that one time we fucked, it was the heat of the moment. It was fast and dirty, with no questions or conversation. It made sense for me to throw him down, strip him and fuck him senseless without taking my own clothes off, and at the time it was meant to be the end of this thing between us, so I wasn't worried about setting any kind of precedent.

Now our boundaries have softened. We're just fuckbuddies, but that's already more intimacy than I've ever had before. There's conversation. Tristan-conversation, so it's mostly him making stupid jokes and teasing me until I threaten to spank the snot out of him, which is what he wants anyway, but still.

There's no way I can get away with it this time.

Sudden nerves grip my gut and twist hard. My throat tightens, and the air seems to suction out of the room.

I'm so used to this, I'm good at not letting any change show on my face. But Tristan cocks his head at me all the same.

"What's wrong?" His voice is soft and full of empathy, which is also so unlike him I feel like I've fallen through the looking glass into some kind of alternate dimension. Which I basically have. The one tablespoon of empathy that this man contains has been allocated to me.

Tristan and I, two essentially closeted people who don't even do regular hook ups, let alone more than that, have been fucking consistently enough that we're having a somewhat honest and emotional conversation about sex. Or my feelings. Or whatever.

At least, we would be if I would fucking say something.

But the words aren't coming to me at all.

So, I do what I always do. I pull him back into a kiss, cupping the back of his head and holding him close to me as I kiss him with an intensity I've never felt before.

I don't want him to go. But I can't let him get any closer than he is right now, and I also can't explain that to him. I need him to just know.

I can feel Tristan frown into the kiss, but eventually he softens and responds. His arms wrap around my neck and his fingers tangle in my hair again. We kiss and kiss and kiss, like before. He doesn't make any move to escalate things, so I guess he's taken some kind of hint. But that only makes me ache for him even more.

If he can read between the lines well enough to come this far, maybe he'll let me keep setting the rules the rest of the way without asking any questions.

That idea plants itself in my head and takes root. Soon, I feel fevered with how much I need to have him. I've been denying myself all this time because there are so many things I didn't want to have to talk about, but if there's one thing Tristan has shown me so far, it's that he's loving his newfound hobby of shutting up and taking it like a good hole.

My hands get rough. I sit up but keep him flat on his back so I can loom over him, the way that always seems to make his pupils dilate. Soon, Tristan is gasping as I pull his clothes off him as quickly as possible. Any time he reaches for me, I bat his hands away with a growl until he turns it into a game.

Like a brat, he tugs at my shirt and pants. He's not even actually trying to get them off. He just wants to see if he can wriggle his hands away from my grip, grinning like a thief every time he succeeds.

"You may be bigger than me, but I've got nimble hands, Cujo. Surgeon's hands. Don't think I won't beat you after a while," he says with a something approaching a giggle.

He's having so much fun with it, I almost laugh. But it's outweighed by how desperately I need to be inside him right now. The next time he makes a grab for me, I snatch up both his wrists in one hand and pin them to the mattress behind his head, stretching his naked body out like a work of art.

Slowly, keeping an eye on him, I let go and lean back. He stays put, but he's biting his lip like he's fighting the urge to laugh, so I don't know how long it'll last.

Now that I have both hands free, I can sign to him.

"Bad hole. Being disobedient. I think this hole needs to be punished until he learns his place."

Tristan's eyes widen in shock, and a beautiful flush colors his cheeks, making him look so much younger for a minute. I want to take the time to kiss over every inch of his body until he's flushed like that everywhere, but not right now.

Later. Right now, he needs to know who's in charge.

Still leaning over him, I grab his hips and wrestle him over until he's on his stomach. He's heavy, but a lifetime of training with that stupid tractor tire feels like it was all meant to prepare me to manhandle Tristan any way I wanted. In the end, he goes easily.

He gasps when I jerk his hips upwards and push his face down into the mattress at the same time. I spread his cheeks to reveal his pink hole and don't hesitate before dropping a gob of spit onto it. I rub the wetness around before blowing on it, and Tristan shivers at the sensation.

Then, without warning, I give him a hard slap to each cheek. Hard enough to make his entire body jerk forward. I end it with a slap of my fingers directly onto his hole. It's not very hard, but I imagine he's already so keyed up from the competing sensations that it feels like an assault on every sense, and the strangled noise he makes in response while he instinctively tries to crawl away from me is my reward.

I grab his hips to steady him while he settles. He's panting like he ran a marathon, but he stays still. He looks back at me, his face bright red already, and my desire to wreck this man only increases. But I don't want to push too hard. I trust Tristan to let me know if I go too far, but we both have a tendency to jump into things without thinking or talking beforehand.

When he sticks his tongue out at me, I know for sure he's fine, and reward him with several more smacks to his ass that make him moan.

Brat.

His ass is as red as his face, eventually. He's writhing into the mattress, desperate for some release, but I've got an iron grip on him so he can't get his hips low enough to get any friction on his aching cock. All I can see is the trail of precum leaking from it, slowly seeping into the sheets as it hangs, looking almost painfully swollen.

One more slap, and I'm rewarded with a few drops of precum splattering onto the sheet and another hoarse shout from my brat.

I think he's had enough. Without warning, I change tactics and cover his hole with my mouth. He jumps at the sensation, but I still won't let him get away. Just as he was writhing a second ago to try to get to the mattress, now he's writhing to get back to me, trying to fuck himself on my tongue as I lick over and into his hole.

He's wet and shiny with my spit, loosening easily for me. I work my fingers in with my tongue gradually until he's stretched. I don't know how long it takes, because time seems to have stopped for me, but it's been long enough that Tristan sounds like he's nearly lost his voice from being such a vocal bitch.

Not that it's stopping him from continuing to moan, his body practically vibrating around me with pleasure.

When I pull back, letting him go has him slumping into the mattress in a messy, breathless pile. I grab lube and a condom, pushing my pants down enough to free my cock and getting suited and slicked up as quickly as I can.

I need to be inside him more than I need to breathe right now.

Pushing into him slowly, I listen for the sound of Tristan's breathing to make sure he's adjusting. I can feel him clench around me, and all I want to do is pound into him until we both find release.

But another part of me wants to drag this out. The part of me that says there's inevitably an expiration date on whatever we're doing together, and I should squeeze as much out of the experience while I still have the chance.

I listen to that voice for a while. I keep pushing in, letting Tristan catch his breath until I'm fully seated. And when I start to thrust, it's slow and shallow, rocking him into the mattress. I drink in every whimper and whine that I pull out of him. Watching his hard cock continue to leak and his sweaty limbs contort themselves as he tries to be good for me and not fuck the mattress in desperation.

Chapter Twenty-Five

TRISTAN

I'm dying.

This is how I will die. Killed by Ford's perfect, magical dick.

I feel like he's been edging me for hours, even though it probably hasn't been that long. I've never been spanked in my life, but the raw, swollen heat of my ass cheeks is making everything feel a thousand times more real somehow, making my entire body seem like a channel designed for his pleasure.

I want to curl into him and never come out.

Once he was inside me, I expected him to fuck me roughly into the bed until I came screaming, like he did last time. But this is different. He's moving slowly, rocking my body as he fills me up, letting me feel each agonizingly delicious inch of him piston in and out of my oversensitive hole.

None of this is what I was expecting from him, but I'm not complaining.

Ford stops, and for a minute I think he's going to freak out or call the whole thing off. I still don't know what it was that pulled him up short earlier. And although I'm dying from curiosity, I figured all I could do was try to distract him, make him laugh, and fuck him in whatever configuration he was comfortable with, if that's what he wanted.

So, I'm fucking stunned when instead of pulling away entirely, he actually pulls out, manhandles me again until I'm lying on my back, then drapes his big, beautiful body over me and pushes right back in without hesitation.

I gasp. I've never been fucked in this position before. Mostly because I've only been fucked once, by Ford, and it was about as brutal and impersonal as you can get (in the most delightful possible way).

I'm so fucking full I feel like I'm choking on his cock. It's turning me inside out and he hasn't even started to move yet.

And best... or worst... of all, his face is hovering right over mine. His bright, icy eyes are staring at me, like he's looking for something. I'm looking back, and I know we're saying something to each other without saying it right now. I'm just not sure what it is.

Whatever it is, it's making my stomach bottom out, my ass clench around his dick and my face feel tight. Ford starts to move, still slow, and the drag of his thick length over my prostate pulls a high-pitched whine out of me that I'm way beyond feeling embarrassed about.

After that, Ford doesn't move a lot faster, but it feels like the world does. Maybe everything just gets more intense.

He stays close to me, his arms bracketing me in and blocking out the world until all I can see is him. His eyes continue to study me, and I can't look away. My mouth is dry, but I'm too breathless to close it. He dips in a few times to taste me in sloppy, open-mouthed kisses, but neither of us can focus on them.

My legs are clamped around his hips like I'm afraid he'll run away, and my whole body rocks with him every time he thrusts. Every inch of me feels impossibly stretched, impaled on him, but I still want him to get deeper and my hips open wider and wider of their own accord.

I flick out my tongue to wet my lips, and he traces the movement with his eyes. I don't know where to touch him, because I get the feeling that's part of the problem he had earlier, but my brain is too fried now to process it. All it knows is that my hands feel empty, and without him in them, he feels so close, but still too far away.

Giving in to my instincts, I let my hands run up under the back of his shirt. I don't explore. I just grab onto the flesh and hard muscle of his back and cling. I need something to anchor myself to.

He stiffens for a second, but apparently he's too far gone to care as well, because then the moment passes and everything goes back to normal.

Soon, we're just two bodies connected at every possible point, sweating into each other, panting our sticky breath onto each other's skin, and filling the room with the feel and sound and scent of us.

I'd forgotten about my weeping cock until Ford snakes a hand between us and grabs it. He doesn't jack me off. I don't think he has the coordination. He just makes a loose fist, and then fucks my body forward in a way that thrusts my cock into his hand.

It only takes a few seconds of this before I'm spilling into his hand. My body draws bowstring-tight, my hands flying to tug on Ford's hair, and I can feel myself clamp down on his cock where it's splitting me in two. It's so tight, it pulls a noise out of him.

A harsh, guttural, choked noise, but a real voiced noise, nonetheless.

I work hard not to let my surprise show on my face, and it helps that I'm distracted by the slow-boil orgasm that feels like it's shredding my body into tiny pieces and then pumping them all out of my dick in a hazy endorphin waterfall.

Instead, I keep clenching around him as much as I can. His rough groan continues as he buries his face in my neck. I can feel the vibrations of the sound as well as hear it, and then he's making more noises, like a desperate animal, as he starts to pump himself into me. He keeps his movements shallow but fast, practically bending me in half and working himself through my tight hole so frantically it almost hurts, but not quite.

It wouldn't matter if it did. Watching him chase his own pleasure with this single-minded intensity, while he clutches my body to his, is one of the most mesmerizing things I've ever experienced. I'd go through a lot more than pain to see it again.

Ford pounds his hips into me hard and fast. I can feel his teeth bite down on my neck, right over my pulse, and a sound like a sob rips out of him as he finally tenses and unloads inside of me.

For a second, I wish there wasn't a condom between us so I could feel him filling me up. But for now, I settle for trying to squeeze and milk him for everything he's worth.

His hips jerk and he trembles through the aftershocks, continuing to unleash what feels like a lot of pent-up *something* into my body along with his cum.

Eventually, we collapse together. He doesn't pull out of my ass, and he also doesn't pull his face out of where it's buried in my neck. He continues to mouth over the bite mark he just gave me, sucking and worrying at the skin there like he's trying to mark me. I keep myself wrapped around him as tightly as I can and focus all my energy into not letting my stupid thoughts and doubts creep back in and ruin this moment for either of us.

One of us should say something. I... I should say something. That was intense, and I need to make sure he's okay.

I'm desperate to make sure he's okay, but the words and concepts of how to do that tangle themselves in my head like a knot until I don't know what to do except continue to hold him, or panic and run.

And I'm tired of running. I'm trying to stop.

When Ford gradually, slowly draws his face out from the crook of my neck, it's blotchy, and his cheeks are rubbed raw from my stubble. His expression is completely shuttered. I can see I'm not the only one who's not quite sure how to proceed from here.

I try to keep a casual expression on my face. Running my hands over his, I wipe off whatever spit and other bodily fluids have been smeared there to try to clean him up a little, which makes him pause. He holds my gaze, and for the longest time, we continue to stare at each other.

I've never been more aware of how collectively broken the two of us are until this moment.

"Water," I say. My voice is raspy as fuck from moaning, which proves my point, but my heart sinks a little in self-hatred because it's a copout.

Fuck it. Maybe we both just need a second to pull our shit together.

I quickly pull on my boxers, because I'm never walking around naked in his house again. Not when there are criminals who could burst in and hypothetically shoot me at any time. Then I head to the kitchen and rummage. I find two ancient-looking maroon cups that remind me of Pizza Hut in the nineties, and very possibly came from there, and fill them up from a pitcher in the fridge.

When I get back to the bed, Ford is even more shuttered. Every inch of him screams *don't touch me*. He's not looking at me, his shoulders are hunched, and he's leaning back against the headboard with his legs tucked in tight against his body. He nods when I hand him the water, but that's about all I get.

Fuck.

I feel like I've already fucked this up, and I'm not even sure how.

The urge to go over and plant myself in his lap is overwhelming, but I don't think I could take it if he shoved me away. My brain feels too frayed, and everything that's going on is about a million light-years removed from what I'm comfortable with in terms of sex-related interactions.

Instead, I settle for sitting cross-legged opposite him. I move close enough that my knees are almost touching, but not quite, and I drink my water.

Which was an excellent idea. My throat is burning from all the fucking noise I've been making.

When Ford doesn't say anything or really look at me, I decide to change the subject.

"I saw that Hitler Youth-looking motherfucker at the hospital tonight. Eamon. One of his boys got shot. I'm worried that whatever situation these guys have with the Aryan Nation is spilling over into Possum Hollow. There's been a lot of violent crime lately that feels out of place."

That gets Ford's attention. He looks up at me, his hand tight around the plastic cup.

"Did you ever figure out what he meant when he was talking about your dad?"

Ford shakes his head and shrugs. There's a long pause, but eventually he drinks some more of his water, then puts the cup down on the bedside table and lifts his hands to sign.

"I have no idea. My dad was kind of a biker before I moved in with him, I think. I know he used to be involved in shady stuff, but he cut all that out when he started the shop. That was almost twenty years ago. Eamon would have been the same age as me. There's no way they could have known each other. The whole thing is weird."

I feel a little better now that I know he's not completely ignoring me. Bouncing my eyebrows, I paint a more playful expression on my face than I'm feeling to try to reel him in.

"Wanna do some investigating? I bet I can help you ferret out some information."

Ford gives me a sharp look. Sharper than the slaps he gave my ass before, which are still making it hurt to sit down.

"Absolutely not. The last time you decided to play fuck around and find out with this Irish Mafia Brotherhood... Banna, whatever, you found out. By getting shot. We are 100% closed for shenanigans, T."

My smile gets smaller, but a hell of a lot more genuine. It still makes my heart twinge a little whenever Ford uses my name sign. It reminds me of Conor, which hurts, but also just knowing someone who uses my name often enough to need it is kind of nice. Or heartwarming. Or something.

I don't know the word. My vocabulary for positive, healthy emotions is as limited as my capacity for them.

Feeling awkward and uncomfortable all over again, that urge to run is back and stronger than ever. Ford is watching me, his entire body tense. It almost seems like me being here is making things worse for him. Which is the opposite of what this little fuckbuddy experiment is supposed to be about.

Maybe I need some fresh air and a good night's sleep to clear my head. I can never think straight when he's around. Everything gets twisted because my body and my brain are always screaming at me for things they've never wanted before and that I don't know how to give them.

I'll come back tomorrow, when we're both rested. We can have an adult conversation then.

Yeah.

Perfect.

When I explain that I have to be up early tomorrow, so I need to head home, I tell myself he looks relieved. I tell myself I feel relieved. I won't admit that leaving feels like the worst possible thing to do right now, because that would mean I'm making yet more bad decisions on top of all my other bad decisions, and I'm tapped out for one day.

My ass hurts, and so does my pride.

I need to sleep it off until something in the world feels as easy as it used to before I met Ford fucking Novack.

CHAPTER TWENTY-SIX

FORD

I 've been on edge all day. I tell myself it's not about Tristan, because it's not.

He's just a fuckbuddy. He's not supposed to sit around and hold my hand because I'm having feelings I can't process. I'm an adult, and he's not my babysitter. Of course, it makes sense that he left last night so he could get to work this morning.

Maybe a teeny-tiny part of me wanted him to stay, but that part of me is weak.

What I'm actually upset about is this shit with Eamon and Dad. I've spent my entire life being so proud of how Dad turned his life around and left all his bad habits in the past when he took me in. I built my identity around it. Sometimes, when shit got really bad, it was the only thing that kept me going.

If Dad could pick himself up and build a life for both of us, even though his PTSD stayed so bad until the day he died, and he never had any kind of role model to work with, the least I could do was not slit my wrists myself over a few nightmares and some paranoid dissociation.

I told myself that for years, and it worked. Dad built us a life, and we both spent every day choosing to set aside our demons and continue to live it. Every time I felt like I could feel Tommy lurking in our house, coming to finish me off, even though I knew that wasn't possible, I focused on Dad.

If all that was a lie, and he was still doing his old shit behind my back, I don't know what that means. I don't even know what his old shit was. He never talked about it, and all I know from Mama is that it was criminal.

I remember a few shady biker types hanging around the shop when I was younger, but it all drifted away after a while. Especially once Dad realized how bad my self-hatred and anger spiral was getting and threw himself into trying to save me from it.

There were no more bikers or nights at the bar for him. We both accepted that I was never going to talk again, even after my throat was mostly healed. It just... didn't work. I tried, I swear. But every time I thought about it, it started with hoarse, raspy noises and I could feel Tommy's fist wrapping around my neck all over again.

It wasn't worth it. So, Dad got us both an ASL tutor online, when that was only just becoming a thing and expensive as all hell. He made the gym in the back to distract me, and all his shifty friends stopped coming around.

It was just me and him. Or so I thought.

These are the thoughts that dog me as I plow through the workday without ever really noticing what I'm doing. It's one of Silas' days off, so I have the shop open for limited hours and take fewer jobs. Which is a fucking relief, because even that limited amount of work has exhausted me by the time I finish up.

Tristan is still out saving lives or whatever. And what happened between us last night has left things awkward. I didn't want him to see me or hear me being so intense. Everything just escalated.

And then he ran.

Asking him for help to track down information about my dad doesn't feel like something you would ask a fuckbuddy at this point. There are too many emotions swirling around. It feels like something you would ask a partner, and I'm not fucking doing that.

So, I can take advantage of the fact that he's distracted for the next few hours, and use this time to hunt down the information myself. And if I get shot in the process, at least he'll know it was my own stupidity to blame.

Getting to the Banna property is easy. It's getting back alive that I'm worried about.

I drive right up to the front gate. I'm pretty sure any hint of secrecy will only make things worse, so I don't bother with it. Instead, I pull up, get out of my truck with my hands in the air and walk up to the gate while two guys with gun-shaped bulges under their shirts walk towards me.

I recognize one of them from the shitshow at my house. He's the one that speaks.

"I'm pretty sure Eamon told you and your little butt-buddy to stay the fuck off our property. Unless you're looking for that kneecapping."

Adrenaline floods my system, and I'm once again reminded that this was a stupid fucking idea. But it's too late to turn around now.

Moving slowly, I reach down to my pocket and pull out my phone very carefully, making it obvious that's what I'm getting. These guys look more amused than afraid at least, so I'm not that worried about them shooting me by mistake.

When I hold up the screen, they both lean in and squint to read the message I typed up in advance.

I want to ask Eamon a question. Can you please check if he'll see me?
If he says no, I'll leave and pretend I was never here. That's all.

The guys both make faces at each other, like they're almost amused by my ballsiness. I'll take it.

One of them pulls out his phone and wanders away to make a call. And before I know it, I'm being ushered past the gate on foot. I'm inside the compound, which is technically a success, but also makes me feel like I'm much more likely to get murdered.

I make sure to keep my eyes on the ground and not see anything other than where they're taking me. I'm so focused on the ground that I almost crash into the guard in front of me when he stops.

Looking up, I realize Eamon is out here. We're standing in front of one of their little satellite buildings, still a ways from the main house. And he's grinning at me like I'm a rabbit in a snare, which makes my skin crawl.

"I've never had someone deliver themselves to me to get executed. I gotta say, I like the convenience. I should suggest it to DoorDash as a new feature or something. If they release a gangsters-only account type."

Why do all bad guys love to monologue? God, I really do fucking hate most people. Especially the ones who are in love with the sound of their own voice.

Except maybe Tristan. But only because he's too dumb to hate. It would be like hating a puppy for barking and peeing on the furniture. They can't help themselves.

I pull my focus back to the present and pull up another pre-written message on my phone, holding it up for Eamon to read.

You said you knew my dad. I just want to know how. Everything I've found since he died seems kind of weird, and I need to know the truth. Then I'll leave you alone.
Please.

Eamon's eyebrows run for his hairline. I guess maybe it is a ballsy request for someone who he's already threatened, but I'm desperate. I can't spend the rest of my life wondering if the foundations of my existence are a lie.

214

I already spend most days fighting to bring my brain back to reality. If that 'reality' isn't even real because Dad was lying to me all this time... I don't know what I'll do. That's a question for quantum physicists, because it can't be possible.

But I have to know.

The asshole studies me for a second, then asks me in a cold, calculating voice, "What do I get for it?"

What do you want? I'm fucking broke, so don't bother asking.

I type it out quickly and shove the phone back under his nose. He snorts, but continues to act like he's pondering the mysteries of the universe, milking this conversation for all the drama and amusement he can get out of it.

"Any chance you have the same skill set as your father?"

My eyes narrow. So, he really did know him. Although I'm not sure what skill set he means.

I'm a mechanic. That's about it. And I don't want to do anything illegal.

"Yeah, we're not haggling here. Either you do what I ask you to, or you don't. But if you can't provide the same services he could, I can't continue the same arrangement. You're just not worth it."

I want to growl in frustration, but I hold it in. He's not even listening to me. He's so busy trying to make quips and admire his own criminal mastermind excellence.

"I'm surprised to hear you cling so desperately to the idea of good and evil," he continues. "Your old man was very pragmatic. I always assumed you'd take after him. I was kind of hoping you'd see the light and come into the fold at some point. It's practically your birthright, after all. And we can always use some extra brawn. Guys your size aren't always easy to find, especially not ones with half a brain."

All I want is to know what my dad did for you. When it started, how long it went on for, all the details. In exchange, you guys can bring all your shit to my shop and get it fixed for free for a year. Legally. That's all I have to offer you. After that, I want nothing to do with you.

I'm desperate, and it's showing. This is already a ridiculous deal, but I'm feeling fucking unhinged and the more he hints that my fears about Dad were founded, the more I feel my grip on reality slipping out of my fingers.

Eventually, Eamon shrugs.

"Alright. Do you know what your old man did during the Gulf War?"

Why does this conversation involve so much talking in circles?

He was in the infantry.

"Bzzzz, incorrect. Looks like I wasn't the only thing he lied to you about. He was a CBRN Specialist. Chemical, biological, radiological and nuclear weapons. I'll let your imagination fill in the gaps about how that kind of specialist knowledge might have been helpful to an organization like the Banna. Needless to say, he was well compensated for his services. He's been around longer than I have. He was never a full member, but sort of a well-trusted contractor. Friends with all the old guard around here. I knew he had a kid to pay for, and I knew he had a job he wanted us to do that he was saving up for as well. He was desperate for that job, I remember. He even sold me his sweet Mustang to pay some more money towards it."

My mouth hangs open, and the smug shit looks so happy that he's undone the threads of my existence in about forty-five seconds. I don't know why, but the fact that Dad lied to my face about his car being stolen is the biggest twist of the knife out of everything Eamon has revealed so far. He looked so distraught when he told me. I lived with that man for nearly twenty years, and I never knew he was such a good liar.

Who knows what else he was lying to me about?

I'm focusing on everything in the moment that I can to keep myself from losing it. The temptation to let rage take over instead of everything else is strong, and if it were anyone else, I'd say to hell with personal growth and pound this asshole into the dirt.

But that would definitely get me shot.

My hands are already shaking as I sign to him, then realize what I'm doing and type out the next message.

What job?

He shrugs, still showing off his casual attitude towards my world falling apart. With an over-the-top, fake level of nonchalance, he says, "Some dude just got out of prison that he wanted us to take care of for him. Tommy something?" He looks me dead in the eye and shrugs again, a hint of a smile tugging at his mouth. "I guess whatever the guy did, it must have been pretty bad for your old man to spend his life savings on getting rid of him. But he died before he paid us, so Tommy whatever is walking around free."

My vision blurs as a wave of memories and images assault me. I think I'm going to throw up. I can't let Eamon see that he's getting to me.

Everything turns into a blur after that. I think I sign thank you to him, although whether he understood or not is anyone's guess. Asshole doesn't deserve to be thanked, I just needed to leave.

The rest of my energy is spent getting back to the fence, getting in my truck and going home. The entire time, the world seems to twist and distort around me. Shadows get longer and darker, and every corner seems like it contains unknowable horrors, waiting to pounce.

The memories from my past coil around me like a snake trying to strangle its prey.

Adult me is long gone, buried inside. He's still trying to cope with Dad's betrayal. My eight-year-old self is in charge, and together we stumble into the house, slam the door shut behind us and lock it every possible way.

If only either of us knew what to do next.

Chapter Twenty-Seven

TRISTAN

"Seriously, what crawled up your ass and died?"

Cade is glaring at me because I just asked him to redo the sloppy restock job he did of the back of the ambulance while we're in between calls.

Okay, I might have told him to do it, instead of asking. Snapped would possibly be an appropriate word. I've been in a funk all day, and I can't seem to shake it.

"Can you just do what I tell you without giving me attitude, for once?" My words come out as a grumble and I'm barely looking at him because I'm still distracted by my own inner monologue. I was hoping that would put an end to the conversation, but it seems to have the opposite effect.

Cade freezes, and it looks a little like he's counting to ten in his head. Then he puts down the roll-gauze he's holding and turns his body until he's fully facing me.

"No. You've been weird all day. And you promised you were going to stop taking it out on me when you were in a shitty mood because it's convenient, so your options are to either magically make your bad mood go away, or talk to me about whatever's going on. Emote. Like a human. I promise it'll only hurt a little."

I must make a face, because he smiles at me like this situation is hilarious, sits down on the stretcher and pats his lap.

"Come, tell Daddy Cade all about it."

That actually makes me laugh, the little shit.

"You're ridiculous. And don't pretend for one minute I don't know you're the bottom in your relationship."

He picks the gauze up and throws it at me, but I duck.

The whole interaction makes me feel a little lighter, and when I sit down with a sigh, I decide he has a point. I did promise to stop being a moody asshole and forge real friendships or whatever. *Blah blah blah.*

Just because I actually *care* about the people around me.

"You're right, I'm sorry. I shouldn't have snapped at you. I'm having some sort of internal crisis and it's distracting the fuck out of me, which makes me feel like I'm bad at my job, and that's about the only thing I have going for me so without it, I don't know what to hang on to."

Cade nods. "What's your crisis about?"

I bite at the skin around my thumbnail; a very old, gross habit that I've never been able to completely break.

"Let me guess," he continues. "6'4", broods a lot and if I had to guess, fucks like a freight train."

I glare at him again, but apparently I've overused the expression because at some point he stopped being afraid of me and all he does is grin back.

"Shut up. But yeah."

"So, what did you do to fuck up?" He looks at me expectantly, but I bristle.

"What makes you think I fucked up?"

"Because I know you, and I've known Ford since high school, and out of the two of you, I think it's a safe bet that you were the one who fucked up. Even after

220

Noah died and Ford was a wreck, he still kept it together, more or less, and his dad was his whole fucking world. You're a problem-child at the best of times."

"Hey, I—" I start to protest, but then I trail off as his words sink in. "Wait, what? You went to high school with him? What the... How fucking old is he?"

Cade just stares at me like I'm an alien for a minute, and then he shakes his head and starts to huff.

"Jesus Christ, Tristan. You've been sleeping with him in secret for what, weeks? Months? And you never asked his age? I know you said you weren't dating, but you can still be polite with the person whose dick you put in your mouth. He was a senior when I was a freshman. I think he's 26 or 27."

Relief washes through me. Ford is huge and the epitome of manliness, not just in how he looks physically, but also in how he moves through the world. He carries himself with a huge amount of confidence, even with the assorted traumas that I know haunt him. It never occurred to me that he would be younger than me.

Six years younger is fine. If he was Cade's age and I never noticed, I'd be a little freaked out.

But it does put some things in perspective. I already knew Ford carried an ass-load of trauma with him, even more than me, but he's so much younger than I expected. Between that and losing his dad so recently...

Fuck, I really am the world's biggest asshole.

I've been running around having commitment issues and not thinking about how he's dealing with any of this at all. I knew he was struggling with it like I was, but he's always been kind of in charge of the dynamic between us. I've let him do his thing, while I continued to push and pull at him like he's a chew toy, depending on my mood.

He can be in charge of me all he wants when I'm naked, but I should have stepped up outside of that. I should have talked to him.

Fuck.

I'm in the middle of processing this when I hear a call come through. I'll have to put this existential crisis on hold until after the shift is over, when I can go find Ford and force him to talk to me until we figure out what the fuck we mean to each other, and how we can stop repeating this pattern where one of us spins out until the other gets hurt.

My heart sank as soon as I heard the address. When Cade pulls us up to a familiar trailer, Tobias is standing outside, looking panicked and waving us inside. His face is still a mess of bruises, although they've faded to ugly yellows and greens and the swelling seems to have gone down.

I absently wonder how he explained that to his *lola*, but I get the feeling he's had some practice.

There's no time to address all the weird shit that's happened between us outside of work. Like the fact that the last time I saw him, his boss fucking shot me. I shutter the part of my brain that controls Tristan the person and narrow my focus to the scene. Cade lets a brief expression of anger flicker over his face, then I can practically feel the energy around us shift as he does the same thing.

"What happened?" I ask as he leads us inside.

"I'm not sure." Tobias has been crying, obviously, and his words are coming out choked. But he's more focused than I expected him to be. He explains how he just got back and found Anika having chest pains. They seem to be getting worse, but she's still conscious.

She insisted she couldn't be having a heart attack because she was still awake, but he called 911 anyway.

"I don't understand. She's been taking her insulin, I made sure of it." He looks me in the eye when he says it, which isn't something that happens often, and everything about him has an intensity I've never seen before. Like he's right on the edge of... something.

I don't want to know what he might have done to pay for that insulin. Instead, I nod to him and focus on his grandmother, asking her the same questions I asked him while Cade takes her vitals.

The whole time we work, Tobias continues to linger around us like a dark cloud of misery. I want to hate him, but I don't have it in me. I've never met anyone who has pain rolling off them so profoundly. I can practically see it.

When we finally load her up in the ambulance to go, he declines the offer to come with us. He has something to take care of, he tells us.

I make a mental note to come and check on him later, if he'll let me. Work first. Then Ford. Then maybe I can fish this kid out of whatever hole he might have dug himself in, as long as I can stay below Eamon's radar and not get myself shot again in the process.

One step at a time.

Anika is not having a heart attack, thank fuck. She is having very acute hypertension and some abnormalities on her EKG though, so by the time I hand her over to the ER, there's a cardiology consult on the way and telemetry ready to monitor her heart consistently while they run some tests.

I don't get the chance to say goodbye to her before she gets whisked away. Which isn't unusual, but in this case it kind of stings. I've gotten attached to the old girl, even without my concerns about her grandson.

Instead of rushing back to clean up, Cade and I lean against the nurses' station for a minute. We're at the very tail end of our shift, so if our luck holds out and no more calls come through, we can head from here straight back to the station to clock out.

I'm tired. Bone deep exhaustion, sitting in my body like lead, dragging me towards the floor. It wasn't even that busy a shift. I'm just beat.

"What's wrong with you?"

Rebecca leans against the counter on the opposite side of me from Cade, her warm eyes peering at me.

I open my mouth, but no words come out.

"I don't even know, to be honest."

"He's having relationship drama," Cade supplies in a less-than-helpful tone.

Rebecca's eyes harden for a second. "You're not fucking one of my nurses, are you? Because I don't have the energy to deal with that."

"Fuck no. Do I look like I have a death wish? I have no interest in getting involved with someone who would literally ruin my life if shit went sideways."

"Good. Then what's your problem?"

Once again, when I don't know what to say, Cade answers for me.

"He accidentally flirted his way into a situationship and now he's having feelings he doesn't know how to process. But he won't give me any of the details, so that's all based on speculation and having Silas low-key spy on them."

I feel trapped right now. A large part of me is telling me to just run out of the hospital so I can escape these two and their knowing, judging stares, but constantly running is what got me into this situation in the first place.

Instead, I take a deep breath and bite the bullet. I turn to Rebecca and make the most pathetic *help me, I'm a dumbass* expression I can, which isn't difficult.

"He's kind of right. I don't know what to do. There are feelings involved now when there were never meant to be, which has made everything super awkward and we both keep avoiding the subject and finding excuses to leave the room whenever the vibe starts to get too real. I'm hard-wired to handle crises. I'm not emotionally equipped to cope with something that might be a calm and functional relationship. Please help. What do I do?"

She sighs. "Tristan, I'm tired. I am not your therapist and I am not your mother. So, please don't stand there all doe-eyed, like a big, dumb oversexed baby, and act like you need me to tell you that all your flirting is a defense mechanism and you need to make better choices."

There's another long, slow sigh before she continues, while I slowly feel more and more like an idiot. "You had a fucked-up childhood. I get it. So did I, so did this one," she waves long, elegant fingers in Cade's face. "I don't even know him and I can smell it on him. You're emotionally handicapped. It's not fair, but it is what it is. If you want to have a functioning relationship, whatever that is, you need to choose to grow the fuck up and figure out how to have one. I don't know what your deal is, but you're a smart guy. I'm pretty sure you could get there if you stop making excuses for yourself and leaning into this whole Peter Pan persona you've created as a cop-out."

"Wow," I say, my mouth hanging slightly open. "That was a lot of information. With a lot of shade woven in. I'm impressed, and a little turned on."

Now I know I've crossed the line, because her expression goes from tolerant to annoyed, and she smacks me lightly on the back of the head, while Cade watches the whole thing as if the only thing he's missing is a bucket of popcorn.

"Tristan, what did I just say?"

Oops. Something about flirting being a defense mechanism, I think.

"Sorry, sorry," I say, grimacing because this is all such a weird and uncomfortable conversation. I feel like I've apologized to more people in the past month than I have in the rest of my life combined. "You're right. It's not your job to fix my problems. Even though you told me you're not my therapist and then immediately gave me excellent advice, basically in the same breath."

She moves like she's going to hit me again, but she's smirking as I hold up my hands in surrender. "Yeah, well, you're not the only one who's fucked up. Also, don't think I won't be cashing in this favor. The shitty deck around my house is about to collapse and I'm sure it would be the perfect distraction from all your problems to come fix it for me. You can bring your situationship and your little assistant here to help, as a sign of appreciation for all the bullshit I tolerate from you. Now, what are you going to do?"

"I will fix my problems. Somehow. Once I figure out what they are."

Cade raises his hand, making me scowl in his direction.

"You pissed off your boyfriend. Go back, apologize, grovel, then figure out how to not do whatever it was again. You're welcome."

"He's not—" It's on the tip of my tongue to say he's not my boyfriend, because he's not. But the rest of Cade's point still stands, so there's no point in arguing over semantics. "When did you get smart?" I ask instead.

"I was always smart. But now I have emotional depth, or whatever. I don't know. Silas literally has worksheets. Therapy is weird, man, but it beats offing yourself or turning into your parents." He shrugs like it's no big deal, and then huffs. "Can we go get food yet, or do you need to whine some more?" He gives me a pointed look when I don't respond quickly enough. "Was I this intolerable last year? I'm hungry, bro. You can bitch me out all you want as long as we go to Sonic first. I need a chili cheese dog and a cherry limeade. Wait, fuck, is it Tuesday? I bet we can get half-priced cheeseburgers. Or maybe a burger *and* a chili cheese dog."

Cade's mind has wandered to food now, because he looks dreamy instead of impatient. It makes me laugh, but he still has a point. Also, we should probably let Rebecca get back to her real job.

"Fine. Food, because you still eat like a teenager, and then end of shift as long as our luck holds out."

226

"Dude, I have to eat before I go home. Silas is on a health kick and has basically banned everything edible from the house. Whatever there is for dinner is either fermented or some kind of leaf. Or a fermented leaf. Save me, please."

He looks at me imploringly before we stand up and start to head down the long corridor towards the exit.

"And after that you're going to..." Rebecca calls after us.

"And then I will clean up my own mess, because I am an adult," I yell back with a grin, louder than I need to for the small space. "And possibly also eat a vegetable!"

She pretends she isn't laughing, but I can see it. The laughter is in there, buried deep down.

CHAPTER TWENTY-EIGHT

FORD

When I first moved in with Dad, this place seemed huge. It's not, it's just a small family home on a lot of scrubland that he inherited when his folks died. But Mama and I always lived in trailers, so this two-floor home with lots of rooms seemed enormous.

And to my fucked-up little kid brain, that also means that it seemed unnaturally dark and full of shadows. Ones that got larger and more threatening the longer I was here.

Dad tried, but he was struggling. He barely slept, and when he did, he had nightmares. He spent a lot of time knocking around the house, doing odd jobs to distract himself, so it was always filled with the echoing sounds of tools and small crashes at all hours. Like a horror show version of a carnival funhouse.

I remember spending a lot of time in bed. I was still injured, and I was supposed to be resting. Instead, I would lie there, terrified, while the sounds and shadows amplified themselves in my mind until they became scarier and larger than they could possibly be in real life.

And at the end of it all, I would finally drop into a fitful sleep, where they would turn into the same things. Mama dead and bleeding. Tommy with his hands around my throat or pushing me into a floor full of broken glass. Police sirens and shouting and gunshots.

This happened constantly for months, while Dad and I worked out how to co-exist. I got stronger and spent less time lying in bed, but nothing about the shadows and nightmares changed.

Even when I went to school. I was the weird kid covered in scars who didn't speak. I was either tormented or ignored, so it's not like that was a healthy distraction from how I felt at home.

I don't know if it was a conscious choice to copy Dad's 'ignore it and hope for the best' approach to mental health, but it's what I did. I assumed it would go away with time. But it just got worse.

Tommy's figure seemed to haunt me everywhere, leaping out of every shadow at night and in the day, until I could hardly tell the difference between reality and my own fears.

That was when I started to find ways to ground myself. By focusing on the things around me, I could force my brain to acknowledge that he wasn't there and draw myself back from the brink. But the more serious the fear was in a given moment, the harder it was to anchor myself.

I started using pain, because it cuts through the fog of emotional bullshit in a way that nothing else can.

Physical pain is like emotional napalm. Sure, it'll scorch the earth and turn everything into a wasteland long term. But in that moment, whatever you're trying to run away from gets incinerated.

First, it was digging my nails into my palms, the way little kids sometimes do when they get stressed. Then, as I got older, I figured out ways to escalate it to match my body's increasing need for that endorphin hit, as well as the sweet, numbing distraction from my hallucinatory fears.

It's been fourteen years since the first time I deliberately cut myself, and seven years since I stopped. It's been years since I've even had the urge.

I'd let myself believe that all I had left to deal with was the lingering embarrassment of it. All that shit in my head was childhood crap, covered over with thick enough scar tissue that the buttons in my brain couldn't get pressed anymore.

As I pace around the home I shared with my father, who I idolized but apparently didn't even know, I realize that I was lying to myself. Those urges were just dormant, not dead. They were tucked away in the deepest, darkest corners of my mind, soaking in gasoline and waiting patiently for someone to come along and strike a match.

Today, I've gotten a barrage of information that I can't even sort through. The betrayal of what Dad did hasn't even sunk in yet. I don't know how long it'll take to get there. Because the one overwhelming thing I can't stop thinking about is that Eamon told me that Tommy is *free*.

My own personal boogeyman. The man who murdered my mother in front of me and tried to kill me with his bare hands is out of prison and walking around on this earth like he has a right to share oxygen with the rest of us.

That's the fact that licks through my brain like a trail of fire, lighting up all those old thoughts and feelings until my teenage brain is turned back on and begging me to take a blade to any exposed skin so all the screaming fear will die away.

Hurt. Bleed. Breathe.

I hate it. I hate that I'm walking around, jumping at shadows and not anywhere near thinking about a logical solution to my problem. I should call someone. Or do something. But all those thoughts feel so distant and intangible, while I can picture the pain and blood and immediate relief it would bring me more clearly than anything else.

Maybe none of it's true. Maybe Eamon was lying.

I cling to that thought as a desperate wall between me and my last resort. I don't know how much more I can do to find out, but there's one place I haven't looked.

Dad's room has remained untouched since he died. All the business paperwork was in the garage, and he kept his room pretty spartan. There was no need for me to go rummaging in there, and I didn't have the heart to clean it up. I kept telling myself I would one day.

If there's any physical evidence of his secrets, that's the only place they could be.

By the time I get in there, I already feel like I'm standing outside myself, watching my body as it tears through the room. The same rage that used to fuel me when it was a choice between fighting other people or fighting myself is throwing itself against inanimate objects now, tearing at Dad's last possessions like the bars of a cage.

There's no order to it. I rip the sheets off the bed, pull out drawers and empty them and pull clothes out of the closet until it's empty, but the floor is littered. At some point I must have started crying because my face is wet, but I can't feel the emotion of it.

I feel like there's barbed wire in my throat, and everything else is choked underneath it. The rage vibrates beneath my skin, further helping to contain it all.

Maybe my body is the cage.

When I get desperate enough to get down on my knees and tear through the piles of things I've unearthed, I finally see it. There are boxes under the bed. I've never seen them before, and they can't contain work stuff, or I'd know about them. Or at least notice that something was missing.

I pull them out with the same savage, reckless grip that I used on everything else. Lids go flying and I empty the contents onto the floor with everything else.

I don't know what I'm looking for. It's not like his illegal dealings with the Irish Mafia will have a written contract.

I'll know it when I see it.

When my fingers find the envelope, the shift in my emotional state is so abrupt I nearly throw up. It feels like the world is dropping out from under me, like tipping over the hill of a rollercoaster, and all the anger drains out of me in an instant.

My mouth dries as every emotion churning inside of me is instantly replaced by fear.

I'm holding an envelope from the Missouri Department of Corrections Victim Services Department. It's been opened, and I know what it says before I even pull out the letter, but I do it anyway.

Victim Services Notification of Prisoner Release

It's a notice that Tommy was scheduled for release in one year, dated fourteen months ago.

So, he's been out for two months.

I get out of the room as quickly as I can, although the letter stays fisted in my hand. My foot tangles in one of the shirts I've strewn across the floor, though, and I fall to my knees hard enough to make me hiss and wince.

The pain of it surges up my leg and gives me a few seconds of relief from the image of Tommy creeping into this house and choking me in my sleep, but it's not enough. It's not going to be enough.

All my half-assed objections are worthless. I already know I'm going to lose this fight with myself, even though I insist on having it.

I shouldn't do it. I'm a grown-ass man. That shit is embarrassing enough when you're a kid, but it's one thing to be an angsty, overwhelmed teenager pouring your anger into your own skin because you lack any other outlet. As an adult, I should know better.

A normal person would be able to control themselves. The thought of having to cover it up or make up a shitty lie to tell people is *mortifying*. But the part of my brain that can't see past right now is reminding me of how much better it will make me feel. It's reminding me that even though those days when I was younger were so much more painful, they were also a fuck-ton simpler.

I never had to try to pick through my emotions and understand them. Or find a healthy outlet for them so I didn't destroy the fragile ecosystem of my life. I never had to choose between allowing myself the indulgence of an emotional reaction or forcing myself to swallow it so I could continue paying bills and eating food.

All I did was suffer and continue to exist. It was painful, but pure. And whenever I felt anything, I didn't even come close to looking at that emotion or thinking about it. I just unleashed it on the nearest target, whether that was someone else or myself.

Everything that's happened lately is suddenly crowding around the edges of my brain, all screaming for attention at once. Tommy. Dad. All the bills I can't pay at the shop. Whatever the fuck me and Tristan are doing to each other. It's all so loud and every single thing is so fucking complicated.

My right-now brain is telling me that I have the ability to make that all quiet, and pretend things are as simple as they used to be. Even if it's only for a little while. I can lounge around and bleed and feel sorry for myself in an abstract way instead of having to engage and problem solve like a real person.

The humiliation will come later, but it can join all the other problems that will be waiting at the door.

It's like a pressure-release valve. I just need to let a little out so I don't explode. Because as humiliating as it will be to walk around as a grown-ass adult lying about having cut myself for sport, it would be so much worse to be thrown in the drunk tank for getting in a bar brawl. In terms of real-life consequences, at least.

It's not like I can find some asshole jock to goad into a fistfight after school anymore. And if there's no one else to take the pressure out on, it looks like it's going to be me. Because if I don't do it somehow, I feel like I might genuinely tear in half and ooze the black and putrid stress contained within my body onto the shop floor.

I try to take a deep breath to steady myself, but there's no need. While I was having an echoey debate in the front of my mind, the part of my brain that's in control had already made its decision. I knew I would go through with it as soon as the thought popped into my head.

Just once. No one has to know, and I can go back to pretending to be a functional adult as soon as it's over.

I know I made the right choice because my hands aren't shaking. They're more steady than ever. I don't even feel like I'm controlling them as I go through the old, familiar motions. They know what to do. My brain is practically pumping out endorphins just in anticipation of the sharp pain, and all that noise fades to a dull roar in the back of my mind while my body falls into a lull.

I used to use an old pocketknife that I kept squirreled away under my mattress for exactly this purpose. I'm an adult now though, and that's the one benefit of living alone, I guess. I have to hide from the outside world, but in here, I don't even have to pretend. That blade was little and dull as hell, and I would have to saw away to the point that sometimes the irritation was what eventually dispelled my black mood.

That knife is long gone. I threw it out in a symbolic gesture to Dad. Something about being honest and accountable, which seems ironic now, considering. He was building bombs for the mafia that whole time, saving up to have someone fucking murdered, while lecturing me about honesty.

I laugh. I honest-to-God laugh out loud. It comes out as a raw croak, because my voice is atrophied from disuse as well as permanently damaged, but I don't care right now. Everything's fine, because I'm giving in to the worst possible side of myself, and I've chosen to stop feeling guilty about it for a while.

The first blade I find is a folding knife that Dad bought before he died, but probably never used for anything. It's been sitting on the counter next to keys and a bunch of other shit for over a year. It's small, sharp, and perfect.

It unfolds with a satisfying thunk of metal falling into place. I study my left arm, looking for a gap in between my ink. My tattoos are big black sheets that cover most of my skin, because the point of them was to cover the scars. You can still see them if you look closely, and you can definitely feel them, but it's something. When this one heals, I'll just get the gap filled in and it can hide away with all the rest of them.

There's a sliver of space on the inside edge. Not over my artery, so it's safe, but also off the bone enough that it won't be in danger of going too deep. It looks fleshy.

I'll heal. Once all this is done, I'll heal and pretend it never happened, and move on with my life.

Because my old knife was so dull, I got in the habit of pressing the point into the skin and then pulling it quickly, so I could press through the tough outer layers with one swift motion. In a calm sort of daze, I watch my hands as they continue to do everything they still have the muscle memory of doing, even after all these years.

The point presses in, and then a swift, sharp movement of my hand cuts the blade across. There's a long, drawn out second before the pain hits where I feel like time is suspended. The flesh of my arm parts under the knife like ripe fruit, and for a second, all I see is the meat beneath my skin.

That's when I know I've gone too far. Right after I see the damage, but right before the pain hits. Instead of a thin line of blood, it's an open wound, and it pricks and dots with blood for a long time before the gaping maw of it starts to fill.

Then the pain hits. The pain is exactly what I was looking for. It washes over me as the smell of copper fills the room, making my body tingle and pulse and everything that was clamoring for attention in my brain gets drowned out by the white noise of it.

The pain is deep and drugging, and I want to let it pull me under. But normally there would be a slow trickle of blood to clean up later. Right now, it's something just short of gushing. Like a sink turned halfway on.

Blood quickly spills down my arm and onto my leg, then splatters onto the floor. It doesn't show any sign of stopping, and the very real fear of that—that *I fucked up*—is the only thing that draws my rational self back to the surface.

Fuck.

I've had broken bones and real injuries that fucking hurt. And that sucks. That pain is tedious and exhausting. This is like being slowly crushed in a hydraulic press, with somebody easing up on the pressure a little at a time, only to slam it back down just when you think they're done.

Endorphins and relaxation are quickly replaced by adrenaline. Which still silences all the bullshit, but in a much less fun way. I don't know what to do. I don't want to stand up and get blood everywhere, so I reach behind my head and tug at my t-shirt, shimmying it off until it's hanging around the injured arm and then knotting it over the wound as tightly as I can with only one hand and my teeth.

That slows the bleeding enough to let me take a breath. But the more the fear ebbs and I realize I'm not going to immediately, accidentally bleed out on my living room floor, the worse things get in my mind.

Now there are consequences. Real-world, adult consequences. All the things I was running away from are still there, except instead of having a small cut that I could slap a band-aid over and explain away, now I have something I need help with.

I make my living with my hands. If I've cost myself that by my own self-indulgent stupidity...

I've always wondered what it's like to be swallowed whole by shame. It's possible I'm about to find out.

Maybe I'll wait for a while and see if the bleeding stops. It might not look so bad once I've caught my breath and calmed down a little. I'll give a minute before I completely panic and call someone. If I close my eyes and breathe, I'll gradually calm down and all of this will feel more manageable.

There has to be a way to deal with this without letting anyone find out what I've done.

CHAPTER TWENTY-NINE

TRISTAN

I 'm just about to pull out of the parking lot after my shift when my phone rings. My plan was to go home, eat something and shower so I can present myself like a mostly functioning human, and then show up at Ford's house and force the both of us to have an adult conversation. No matter how much I don't want to.

When I see Silas' name on the screen, it makes my nerves flare. We might be friends, but we're not call-each-other friends. If he's calling me, it's because he needs something, and the only situations that I'm useful for are ones where something bad has happened.

I'm the guy you call when you hit a hobo and need help to bury the body, not planning your niece's quinceañera. Or whatever normal people do on their days off.

"What's wrong?"

There's a pause at the other end, which doesn't give me confidence. I can hear Silas breathing, though.

"Can you come to Ford's house, please? And don't tell Cade?" He's speaking quietly, like he's trying to keep himself on an even keel, but he doesn't sound like he's being held at gunpoint, so that's a plus. Hopefully.

"What happened? Is he okay?"

"You'll see when you get here. You have a med kit in your car, right?"

My pulse spikes, and about a thousand different scenarios run through my head, with Ford getting shot or stabbed by those redneck mafia assholes being at the top of the pile.

"Silas, what the fuck happened?"

"Look, it's not that bad. He's hurt, but I don't think he needs an ambulance or the hospital, and I don't want to tell Cade because he'll come too and make it all seem more dramatic than it is. I think the best thing for Ford is to deal with whatever's going on quietly, and you're probably the right person to do that. So please just try to stay calm. Don't break any traffic laws getting here, and I'll explain everything when you do. Okay? Everything's going to be fine."

There's enough confidence in his little speech that it takes the edge off my panic and lets me focus. I'm already on my way, and it's a short drive at the speed I plan to go.

"Fine," I tell Silas before hanging up so I can focus on the road.

It wouldn't be a gunshot. He would have called an ambulance for that.

Right?

Maybe he had an accident in the shop. There's a shit-ton of ways you could hurt yourself in there, and most of them are probably not life-and-death serious.

My mind continues to spin out possibilities—while I do my best to ignore them—for the rest of the drive.

The shop is completely locked up when I arrive, so I grab my personal jump bag out of the trunk and head to the house. The front door is ajar, and before I even get to it, I see Silas waiting for me.

He steps outside and watches me with an intensity I'm not sure how to interpret. Holding out one hand, he stops me from going inside, like he's somehow become the boss of me.

"You need to be chill," he says.

"What's going on?" Frustration bleeds into every word, I'm sure, because I can't take much more of this cryptic shit. "Where is Ford?"

"I'm just reminding you, charging in there like it's a five-alarm fire isn't going to help. So, chill the fuck out, take a deep breath, and remember that if you make me regret calling you by making him feel worse about this, I will fucking end you. Understand?"

Every instinct I have is telling me to get on the defensive with all the attitude Silas is giving me right now. But if I know anything about him, it's that he wouldn't be doing it without a good reason. It makes me more worried about what happened, if anything, and I'm more than happy to set aside my pride if it means he'll let me the fuck inside.

I nod, looking him in the eye so he can see I mean it. "Okay. I'm calm. But I can't help him out here, so let me in."

After one more moment of hesitation, Silas steps aside so I can pass.

What I find isn't any of the scenarios that I had considered, but as my senses process all the information being shoved in my face, I realize I should have known better.

Of course.

It makes so much sense.

I exhale through my nose, letting my insides settle into that deep peace that only happens when I'm working. Now that I know what the situation is, I know it's something I can handle, and all the fretting and fear drains out of me like a sink with its plug pulled.

Ford is sitting on the floor in the corner of the living room. He's wedged between the couch and the wall, which means it's a safe bet he was panicking whenever he went down there. His knees are drawn up to his chest, his shoulders are hunched in, and his eyes are on the ground.

It looks like he's taken off his shirt and wrapped it around one arm before tucking that arm in protectively behind the other, which I'm guessing is the source of all the dried blood spattered around him. Not enough to be truly concerned, but enough that he's got a lot more than a paper-cut under there.

There's a folding knife lying to the side that I can assume is the culprit. And I'm guessing Silas is the one who found a blanket and wrapped it around his shoulders.

Ford doesn't acknowledge me when I come in. He just keeps staring at the floor, looking like he'd turn himself inside out if he could. His eyes are dry but red, and the exhaustion that's evident in the way he's holding himself makes me wonder how long he's been here.

There's a gentle touch to my shoulder that almost makes me jump, because I was already completely sucked into planning my approach with Ford. But when I turn around, Silas is looking at me, his big brown eyes full of warmth and genuine empathy in a way I've only ever been able to imitate.

When he speaks, he doesn't try to whisper or hide what he's saying from Ford, which I appreciate. It's shitty enough being trapped in a situation like this. Being infantilized by the people around you isn't going to make it better.

"He didn't want me to look at his arm, so I let him be until you got here because it didn't look like it was still bleeding. I came to get the keys to the shop so I could get Cade's bike and the door was open. I was worried there's been another break in. I promise I wasn't snooping. I'm going to take the keys so I can open tomorrow and you don't need to come down if you don't want to."

He directs the last sentence to Ford, who still doesn't look up, but nods slightly, his expression soft.

Silas is a good kid.

"Thanks," I say with a grim smile. "I appreciate you calling me and not making it a big scene. You were right."

"Of course, if you just want to sit your ass down in the shop and make sure I don't fuck anything up while you rest, that's cool, too. Sometimes taking the day off helps and sometimes it makes everything worse."

Silas says this with a grimace, looking at Ford with understanding eyes. Neither of us knows Silas' whole story in detail, but we know enough to be sure that it's not pretty. He's had his own struggles with mental health and possibly suicidal impulses, if I've read between the lines correctly. He gets it.

When Silas reaches out a fist, Ford uses his good hand to bump it. It's a barely there movement, but it's a response, which makes me feel like he's already warming up to the idea of us coming in to help.

Good.

Silas leaves quietly, and then it's just me and Ford and whatever tension and defensiveness is left. But as ineffectual as I've been all the times we've had tension because of whatever there is between us, this is the kind of tension I was born to deal with.

I slide into the situation like a second skin.

Moving calmly and telegraphing all my movements, I dump my bag next to us before joining Ford on the floor. I sit cross-legged catty-corner to him, so I'm not staring him down, but we're close enough to reach out and touch. My fingers itch to pull him to me, but I know I need to give him a second.

I'd figured out that he had a reason he didn't want to take his clothes off around me. I'd guessed more scars from the accident when he was a kid, and it's probably true, but not in the way I was picturing.

"If you wanted my attention, there are easier ways to get it, Cujo. You've already seen how easy I am. You could have just texted 'come here, hole,' and I probably would have come running," I say in a teasing tone. It's stupid, but it draws a glare out of him on instinct, which is what I was going for.

As soon as he looks at me, I smile. Not teasing, something real. Something just for him.

Because no one else belongs in this moment—or any other moment like it—than the two of us. That's what I've realized today. As much as we are a shit-show and have a bunch of the same flaws, we also complement each other in the weirdest possible way.

We're supposed to be a shit-show together.

"I'm kidding," I continue, my voice soft. I knock his leg with my knee, rocking my body a little closer to him to give him the option to reach out. "I take it you had a shitty day."

Ford snorts. It's humorless, but the more I talk, the more I can see the tension easing from him. Not completely, but enough. I need him to accept that I'm not about to flip out and cause a scene, or shame him or something, and then we should be able to deal with it and move on.

"Can I look at your arm?"

He's slow to respond, but eventually gives me a fraction of a nod. Then I can see him trying to make his big body unfurl. He's stiff, like he's been sitting in this position for hours and hours.

"Is there just the one cut?"

Another nod.

"Were you trying to kill yourself?" I ask, because no one was ever helped by beating around the bush.

Ford looks straight at me, surprised for a second. Then he shakes his head with enough confidence that I believe him.

"Are you thinking about killing yourself now?"

Another confident shake of the head.

"Would you tell me if you were?"

That makes him pause again. I can see him thinking about it. It's possible he never considered it before, but he's taking the time now to turn it over in his mind and try the concept on for size.

When he nods *yes*, it's the most romantic fucking thing anyone's ever said to me.

It feels a hell of a lot more meaningful than most of the romantic shit you're supposed to say to your partner, at least.

"Okay, let me see what we're working with."

Finally, Ford holds out his arm. The first time I touch him, he flinches on instinct. It's such a weird echo of the day we met—him sitting on the floor, bloody and battered while I clean him up against his will—that I want to say something, but I can't quite find the right words.

I slowly unknot the mess of t-shirt and tacky blood until the wound is exposed, and it's bad, for sure, but not as bad as I was afraid of. And it's a long way from anywhere that you would pick if you were really trying to bleed out.

Neither of us talk while I clean it up. It's still bleeding sluggishly, but I'm confident it'll stop once I close it properly. It's a straight cut, so the edges approximate nicely, and it should heal well if he doesn't fuck with it.

"Do you want sutures or staples?"

I'm still holding his left arm hostage, but he's able to use his right hand to sign a version of *fastest*, so I grab a surgical stapler out of the bag. The cut is about four inches long, so it takes a decent amount, but he sits there stoically, only flinching slightly for each puncture.

Once it's closed and I've slapped a dressing on it, he lets me fuck around with his hand for a while, testing his mobility and nerve function as well as I'm able to. I'm pretty confident that he's gotten away with no permanent damage other than another big ass scar, but I want to check everything I can check without dragging him somewhere that would include other people in this situation.

By the end of it all, Ford seems much more relaxed. He's acting more like himself, scowling at me and huffing over every bad joke I make. It gives me the confidence to finish my exam by very professionally crawling into his lap.

I lean back enough that we can look at each other.

"You can give me the cliff notes, but I need to know what happened today to make you feel like this."

Ford huffs again and rolls his eyes at me, looking like a petulant teenager.

"Go on. Spill."

He gropes around the floor for a minute until he finds what he's looking for and hands me an official-looking letter from the Department of Corrections. It's freshly creased, like maybe he thought about crumpling it up. I read through it, and it doesn't take long for me to put the threads of it all together. By the time I get to the end of it, Ford is signing at me with a detached expression on his face.

"And I found out the truth about Dad. He was working for those guys this whole time. Making bombs or something awful, something he learned in the army. Whatever it was, it was shitty, and he did it for years. Maybe decades. He was going to use the money to pay for a hit on—" he hesitates, then gestures at the paper instead of spelling out his name. "How fucked up is that?"

When he turns his eyes on me, I can see how much this news has wrecked him. His irises are normally so pale they look ice blue, but his eyes are so bloodshot right now they look almost pink. It would be pretty if it weren't super fucked up.

But all my concern is almost outweighed by how fucking angry I am when I think about what's going on. Not at his dad, although I get why Ford would be hurt that he was lied to all his life.

This guy murdered his mom in cold blood and nearly strangled an eight-year-old to death, and what? Now he just gets to walk around like it never happened?

All it takes is one look at Ford, his face drawn with exhaustion and his body still covered in dry blood, to know that this will haunt him forever. He will spend the rest of his life jumping at shadows and wondering if this fucking shitty asshole is around the corner, waiting to finish him off.

Because trauma like that isn't rational. There's nothing I can ever do to reassure him enough that he'll feel safe. And if it keeps going like this, he runs a serious risk of hurting himself again, or worse.

Nope. Not happening.

Ford's old man had the right idea. Noah, Cade called him. Well, Noah knew that this world would be much better minus one scumbag. If only he had lived long enough to take care of it, Ford would never have had to think about any of this.

"T?" Ford signs at me, pulling my attention back to him.

"Yeah? Sorry, Cujo. I got distracted. Let's get you to bed. It sounds like it's been a day."

Ford nods, but we both hesitate before moving. I'm tangled up in him in a way that feels right, and I like the feeling of his chest expanding and contracting against my ribs with each breath he takes.

Slowly, hesitantly, he leans in. Once I know what he's going for, I help him out and close the distance.

So far, all the kisses I've shared with Ford have either been ferocious or languidly sexy. This is neither. This is passionate, but in a low-key way. In a way that makes me feel fuzzy-headed and a little lighter, like he needs to wrap his arms around me or my body might float away into the ether.

It feels sweet. And needed.

When we finally part, Ford's eyelids dip like he's succumbing to exhaustion, and I pulse with the usual satisfaction of a job well done taking care of someone.

Only this time it's different. I didn't just fix a person; I fixed *my* person.

If it's going to feel this good every time, then all the agonizing and hand-wringing it took for me to get here was totally worth it. Because Ford is my person, and I'll start dropping bodies before I let this happen to him again.

CHAPTER THIRTY

FORD

When Silas first found me, half-asleep and thoroughly enmeshed in denial, I thought my body was going to collapse in on itself from shame. But he didn't make a big deal about it, thank fuck. Which is more than I can say for Dad when he found out, even though I know it was just because he cared.

Silas was calm, and I let my brain drift off back into denial-land and pretended that none of this was happening while he made his calls. I was trying to emotionally fortify myself for the shitshow of an ambulance showing up.

Instead, it was just Tristan.

As soon as he walked in, I could breathe a little easier. Which is fucking terrifying. I barely know him. We've been hooking up for a while and watching him sweep into the situation like he had everything under control shouldn't be able to quiet all the rage and fear that were clashing with each other where I'd caged them inside my chest.

But it did. He was calm and made his stupid jokes to try to get me laughing. And it almost worked. After a while, it felt like just the two of us in the world.

Which is how it's always felt when we fuck, but more and more it's also how it feels whenever we're together, no matter what we're doing.

The smart part of my brain—the part that checked out during all of my previous decision-making today—is telling me to hang on to something that makes me feel this way. And all the paranoia and trepidation that normally fuels me has been so exhausted that it's not able to put up a fight.

Everything inside me is blissfully quiet as I let Tristan lead me to the bathroom and strip me down, throwing my bloody clothes into a pile on the floor. He looks me up and down for a minute while I perch on the edge of the counter like a small child, and his expression is a weird mixture of professional detachment and personal affection.

I should feel vulnerable being naked in front of him under the bright bathroom light. It's not something I've ever experienced before. Not really, at least. Not like this, with someone who knows me. But that's another old fear that tries to wind itself up inside me but doesn't seem to have the fuel to get itself in gear.

I'm just not. I'm not embarrassed anymore, I'm not scared. Not of Tristan, at least. The threat of Tommy is still lurking in every shadow and crevice of my brain, but that's settled to a low hum. But the last shreds of resistance I had to whatever has been building between me and Tristan has been burned out by the gentle, confident care he's shown me today.

No one's ever taken care of me like this. Dad took care of me in his own way, but this kind of tenderness is something new. Fuck it. I'm going to let myself indulge a little.

Tristan makes a series of complicated expressions before he seems to reach a decision. He holds up a finger and then steps out for a second, returning with a bunch of stuff in his hand. He takes a clear, two-gallon trash bag that he must have dug out from somewhere and starts cutting off the sealed end of it.

I don't ask questions.

I trust him.

Before I know it, the small trash bag is slid over my arm, the plastic wrapped around and taped very fucking tightly to my skin. I frown at him because it pinches, but he only gives me a soft laugh.

"I think you'll live, tough guy. Come on, time to clean up."

He gets the shower running and then ushers me in before shedding his clothes and joining me. It's kind of weird that I've made it to the age of twenty-six without ever showering with someone else. Or being naked with someone else as an adult. The shower feels too small for us, and our bodies constantly knock together, but it's nice.

Tristan's skin is warm, and he's still emanating that paramedic-emergency-zen that he's had since he walked inside.

He starts to wash me. His movements are brisk; not sexual, but also not clinical. Some kind of happy medium. I'm too fucking tired to clean up anyway, so it works for me. I stand there and let myself get posed like a doll while he does his thing. His fingertips caress my skin here and there, lingering every once in a while on an old scar, and I feel like he's trying to pour affection into me through touch alone.

I'm half-asleep by the time he turns the water off. He's watching me with a soft expression. I think he's about to turn away, but instead he hesitates for a moment, then leans up and kisses me gently. A PG kiss, like something made for daytime TV.

It's different from anything I've experienced before, and I don't hate it.

The next few minutes pass in a haze. I'm about to fall asleep on my feet, while Tristan dries me off, unwraps the stupid tape from my arm and takes me to bed. He honest-to-God tucks me in, and I mostly doze for a while as he disappears to do whatever. From the sounds I can hear, I think he's cleaning.

My fear is still lingering, but every time I hear Tristan banging around my living room, I remind myself that it can't be that bad. If there's anyone who could keep me safe, it would be him. I believe that with even more conviction than I believed in Dad when I was a kid, although I'm not sure why. They have a lot in common, actually.

But Tristan has a steadiness to him that Dad never had. He's chaotic and impulsive, sure. But it's always in a rational, playful kind of way. Not like Dad, who could be unpredictable in a way that kept me on edge. I knew he would never hurt me, but his exhaustion and nightmares kept him ragged, and his mood swings, even though he tried to internalize them, could be draining just to be around.

When Tristan eventually returns, he has a bottle of water in one hand and a sad-looking sandwich in the other. I peer at him through heavy-lidded eyes, and he shrugs at me.

"You have no food in your house, by the way. Terrible. I wanted more of that spaghetti."

He perches at the edge of the bed, hitching his leg up high enough that it bumps against where my body is sprawled under the covers. I'm still naked from the shower, but I'm warm now, with every blanket Tristan could find piled on top of me like a tower.

"Come on," he says, handing me the plate and bottle. "Eat, drink, replenish. Then you can sleep."

Turning off my brain and doing what he tells me to is easy. Blissful, almost.

Normally, I love bossing Tristan around and watching him gradually stop putting up a fight until he melts for me. When I'm feeling a little more like myself, I look forward to doing it again. But right now everything feels like we're in upside-down world, and the best thing to come out of it is this confident, in-charge version of Tristan taking all the responsibility and decision-making off my shoulders.

I made shitty choices today. If he could make the rest of my choices for tonight, I'm sure I can kick-start my adult brain and get back to making good decisions for myself again tomorrow.

Right now, I just need a break.

So, I eat the sandwich and drink the water, all under his watchful eye. He's calm, but it's almost unnatural to see him quiet, not coiled with unspent energy, doing his best to irritate me into submission.

Once I've completed my assigned task and set aside the plate, I knock his knee with my fist to get his attention.

"Are you okay?" I sign. It stings a little to use my injured arm, but not to the point where I can't sign, as long as I go slow and don't over-exaggerate my movements.

He nods, but there's an exhaustion to him that I'm only just noticing, now that my own emotions are leveling out.

I'm not good at any words, and Tristan speaks constantly but rarely says anything of substance. It's possible that words aren't the way forward right now. All I know is that I feel an overwhelming amount of affection and gratitude towards him right now, and it's successfully drowned out all the reservations that I've been wrestling with, to the point that everything I've been agonizing over seems petty and childish.

I hold up the corner of my giant mound of blankets and toss my head, telling him to get in. Tristan smirks, but doesn't hesitate. Until I hold up a hand, that is. He put on his clothes at some point after we showered, so I tug at his sleeve and shake my head with the most ferocious, over-the-top scowl I can make my exhausted face produce.

It's enough to make him laugh, and just that sound lightens me a lot. Without hesitation, he reaches over his shoulder to grab his shirt and whip it off before shimmying out of his pants and boxers in one movement. Before I know it, he's slipping under the covers next to me and wrapping all his limbs around my body with a slight shudder.

His face gets mushed into my shoulder, where I can't see his eyes. That's okay, though. I wrap my arms around him, careful not to disturb the bandage he just did, and squeeze him as tightly as I can.

We spend a while just existing together. It feels like a new normal that we both need to settle into. Tristan's spent a lot of time running away from whatever this is, and I've spent a lot of time encouraging him to get out, but I feel like as of right now we've both kind of settled.

"You scared me today, Cujo," he says. The words are quiet and muffled by my skin, but I still hear them.

I don't want to pull us apart to sign to him. There's nothing I can say that will make it better, anyway.

I scared myself, too.

Instead, I hold him tighter, and let my fingers trace abstract patterns over the soft skin of his back. I find little scars and imperfections and feel them out. I study the pathways of his muscles and tendons. It feels like this part of him belongs to me now, along with so many other parts, and I should commit it to memory.

We stay like that for a long time. I don't sleep, but a deep sense of calm settles into me. I think about it. It seems unnatural to feel so calm after how I felt just a few hours ago, and I'm trying to figure out if this is like the eye of the hurricane, or some false, temporary calm brought on by Tristan's presence, or if it's something real.

The more I try to pick apart the knot of emotion in my mind, the more obvious the answer becomes.

It's not that I feel calm specifically because Tristan is here. If he had to leave right now for something important, I don't think he'd take my tranquil mood with him.

I feel like I'm happier now that I've stopped fighting myself over him. Letting myself admit that I wanted him to help me felt like a relief. It was more of a relief than it was to cut, and it's lasting for longer, too.

It was the constant fight between what I wanted and what I told myself I wanted that was destroying me.

When I realize that, it helps as well. Because even if sex and snark with Tristan seems healthier on the surface, I didn't want to trade one self-destructive emotional crutch for another.

Another surge of affection hits me, and I sweep all the thoughts and desires to deconstruct everything out of my head.

This is a good thing.

I know it is.

I tug at Tristan until he unpeels himself from where he was burrowed in my neck to look up at me.

"What's wrong?" he asks, his eyes searching my face for trouble.

Instead of speaking, I place two fingers under his chin and use them to tilt his face up to mine.

He seems startled, but quickly sinks into it. Our bodies slowly meld together, and time seems to slow down as our kiss turns into a lazy, languorous slide.

After a while, I break it off just enough to sign to him.

"Will you fuck me?"

Tristan cocks his head. His eyes flick up and down, and he bites his bottom lip unconsciously as he works out an answer.

"I mean, yes. A thousand times, yes. But do you mean right now? That feels like the kind of thing normal, healthy people would discourage us from doing."

He is an adorable idiot sometimes.

I keep signing, to explain to him that this isn't as serious as it seems.

"I've bottomed before, just not since I was young. I didn't hate it, it just felt more intimate than I wanted to get with anyone I was hooking up with. I promise I'm not being dramatic. I feel better with you here. I feel more like myself. I'd like to feel more of you."

Double-entendres are Tristan's Achilles' heel. He can't resist.

He smiles, but I can tell he's still apprehensive.

"Okay. If you promise you'll tell me if you change your mind? There's no rush, I can show you my magical prowess at topping any time."

With a quick nod, I swoop in for another kiss.

We're both naked already, so once everyone's on board, it doesn't take long for things to escalate. We keep everything slow and steady, though, which feels a little unnatural for us.

Tristan gives me deep, drugging kisses while he slowly preps me, until I'm so relaxed I feel practically boneless. Although my body is relaxed, the sparks of arousal are consistently bringing my brain back into the present moment. I feel rooted in the here and now, and more awake than I've felt in the past two days.

At some point, with Tristan's warm body hovering over me, I become more acutely aware of the fact that I'm naked. It's a weird feeling, like shame and my resentment of that shame are wrestling for dominance. I'm not actually body-shy, I just like to hide the scars because it leads to questions I don't want to answer. It makes sense that if Tristan knows all my dark secrets, there's no reason to hide myself from him.

But after decades of hiding, it's become such a deeply engrained habit. Exposing myself in front of him feels frightening and makes me prickle with awareness of how this must be some kind of watershed moment in my life. I snatch at the covers and pull them up over Tristan's shoulders as he hovers over me. It doesn't change how much of me either of us can see, but something about it makes me feel more like I'm hidden from the rest of the world.

Tristan quirks his head. But then, like I always wanted him to, he seems to understand what I need without me having to ask for it. I doubt it'll happen very often because he's dense at the best of times, but right now it feels like we're attuned to one another, and I'm beyond grateful for it.

He shrugs his shoulders in a way that bunches up the blanket and huddles us even more deeply into the darkness before plunging his fingers back inside me, making me gasp.

When he finally pushes inside me, my legs wrap around his hips to hold him tight, like he might float away if I let go. All the buildup has the both of us so on edge, this isn't going to take long. He lets out a low, long moan while he sinks in, and when he's finally fully seated, it feels like an electrical current that was closed.

Sweat drips from Tristan's hair onto my neck while he reaches for my cock, trapped between us and aching hard. He jerks me while whispering filth in my ear about how good I feel, and when I come, it's as if all the pent-up tension from the day has drained out of me.

Tristan stares at the mess between us for a minute, his pupils blown out and his breath hitched with arousal. Then his fingers dig into my hip and he starts fucking into me with purpose. It barely takes him a minute until he finds his own release.

Soon, we're back in the same position as before, except now we're sweaty and spent. Neither of us has the energy for more than a cursory cleanup at this point.

Everything that we need to deal with can wait until tomorrow. Right now, I've found a little fragment of peace, and I want to cling to it while I still can.

It's Tristan that wakes me up.

He's twitching and mumbling in his sleep. Nothing earth-shattering, but distressed enough to make it obvious that he's having a nightmare.

Shit.

He's begging someone, although his words are too garbled for me to understand. There's so much heartbreak in it... I want to wake him up more than anything. But I know the risks that carries.

If he's having some kind of combat PTSD episode, he could wake up violent. That happened with Dad on more than one occasion, and I learned to keep my distance. Although Dad was always okay if I was in exactly the same place I was when he fell asleep. That was the key.

It was only a shift in the environment that his body would clock as a threat. If that happened, I had to be out of arm's reach, and preferably several paces away, so he had time to fully wake up before I could catch a flailing limb by mistake.

We made it work then, and I never got seriously hurt. And now I'm bigger and stronger, I can make it work again. We're in the same spot we fell asleep in, with me on my back and Tristan still curled into my side. The only difference now is that he's covered in sweat and twitching against me like an animal in a trap.

I shake him, but it doesn't have any effect. Even shaking him harder doesn't do anything. I'm holding his arms, but he's too deep in whatever rat trap his mind has him in.

"Please, help–"

Hs words come more clearly now, but he's still asleep and I can't watch him like this anymore.

I try to clear my throat and use muscles that are stiff and atrophied from disuse.

"Tristan."

The sound is quiet and raspy, barely more than a whisper. I say it again, and then again, getting a little louder and a little more like a real sound each time, still shaking him gently as I try to drag his mind back to the land of the living.

"Tristan!"

Finally, his eyes snap awake. He looks straight at me, unblinking, for a moment, before shaking his head and looking around. I can see him readjusting as he realizes where he is, but he doesn't try to hit me. That's a plus.

"Do you know where you are?" I sign slowly, right in front of his face.

He nods. "Did you say my name?"

His voice is also hoarse, but his is from sleep and a little crying, while I sound like something out of a horror movie any time I open my mouth.

"It works a little. But I don't like to. Sorry."

I keep signing, because the thought of saying that many words at once is daunting. I'm briefly distracted by a thought that comes out of nowhere, but immediately spins out on itself into something huge.

What if Tristan wants me to talk? All the doctors gave me so much shit about it. Once my throat was physically healed, they pushed and pushed and pushed for me to do the rehab and speech therapy until I could talk mostly normally again, and it only stopped when Dad told them all to shove it, that I didn't have to do anything I didn't want to, and stopped taking me to appointments.

I want to get to a place where I know I'll never cut again. That feels right. And I worked hard to deal with the anger and the fighting and all the rest of the toxic bullshit.

But the talking doesn't haunt me the way all the other things do. Yeah, it's not something that would probably happen to the version of me that had lived a picture-perfect childhood, but it's not something I feel a drive to 'fix', like I do with the other stuff.

Will Tristan feel like I'm never making enough progress if I don't eventually talk to him, at the very least?

He touches my face, bringing me out of my catastrophizing trance.

"Hey," he murmurs. "What are you thinking about?"

Maybe I should just come out with it.

"Do you wish I talked to you?" I sign.

Tristan smiles at me, and he looks so goddamn handsome in that moment, even with his face still blotchy from crying in his sleep and a pillow crease over one cheek, that I get filled with a syrupy sensation that slows my whole heart down to practically nothing.

"What did I tell you? If you talked more, no one would ever get anything done because of all your hilarious jokes. It would just be joke-joke-joke, 24/7, and then your business would go under. You never take anything seriously. Goddamn comedian."

257

I huff at him because he's being obnoxious, but pull him tighter to me at the same time before I extricate my hands to sign again.

"Are you sure it doesn't bother you?"

He shakes his head.

"You talk to me in all the ways that matter. And I talk enough for the both of us. That's balance, or something. Right? I'll fill all your brooding silences for as long as you'll let me."

Wow. That's about as close to a heartfelt third-act declaration of love as I think Tristan is capable of giving.

"What was your nightmare about?" I'm changing the subject before either of us gets too freaked out, sure. But I also want to know. "My Dad had nightmares about the war all the time. All the way until he died."

All the mushy feelings stuff didn't make Tristan uncomfortable like I thought it would, but this is the moment he tenses up and withdraws from me. Just a little, but enough that I notice the difference. Eventually, he takes a deep breath and flops onto his back, throwing one hand over his eyes. I can practically see the wheels turning in his head as he decides how much he wants to tell me about whatever's going on.

"Promise you won't think I'm a horrible person, okay?"

He looks at me as he says it, vulnerability shining in his verdant eyes. I don't know what he's about to tell me, but he has my full attention.

Chapter Thirty-One

TRISTAN

"God, there's no way for this to not sound shitty," I start. "So, a lot of times when people get to know me, especially if they know me well enough to see the nightmares and whatever, they assume I have combat PTSD. I mean, on paper it's a stereotype that I completely fit. But it's not actually true."

Ford is waiting patiently for me to continue. I can practically smell the shame rolling off myself as I try to pick the right words to explain this very abstract issue.

"I don't correct them, because it's something that everyone expects and understands. The truth is more complicated and super fucking personal, so there's never been anyone who I knew well enough that it was worth getting into it with them. I swear I don't lie about anything. I just don't correct people when they make their own half-assed assumptions about stuff."

He looks confused, and I get it. It doesn't seem that bad at first. But the more I think about it, even though it's just a lie of omission, the shittier I always feel by allowing people to mislead themselves in whatever assumptions they make.

"Yeah, but..." he signs. "People are nosy. Fuck what they think. It's not like you lied about being in the Army, right?"

I feel my eyes widen.

"Fuck no. I don't have a lot of morals and I definitely don't put the military on a pedestal the way some people do, but that would be a disgusting thing to lie about. I just... People make such a big deal about it. And even though it's true, it doesn't feel like I earned it. Have you seen us getting into a lot of wars in the past ten years? I spent like half my career doing fucking field exercises. Even when I was down range, the times we saw combat were few and far between.

"It's not the same now as it was when your dad served. But you can't say that out loud without sounding like a callous asshole, especially because there are still people serving whose experiences are fucking traumatic. I was just lucky."

I shake my head, sitting up in the bed. My body language is becoming more withdrawn, but Ford follows me and pulls me in closer to him, even if I'm struggling to look him in the eye right now.

"Even when I saw violence, or lost patients, it was the same as when it happens out here. It never *haunts* me. From day one as a medic, I've always focused on macro over micro. I can't control whether people are going to live or die. All I can control is whether I give them the best possible care, so they get the best possible chance to survive. As long as I do that, it's a win, no matter what the outcome. It's legitimately easy for me to look at it that way and always has been, but every time I see someone else crying and losing sleep over the ones they couldn't save, even though they never had a chance to begin with, it makes me wonder."

When I go silent, he nudges me to continue.

I turn to look at him. My chin rests on my shoulder, and I feel very small, all curled in on myself, shivering a little in the cold air blasting out of Ford's A/C. The moment stretches out between us like melted caramel as Ford studies me.

"Wonder what?" he asks me aloud. His voice is rough. It sounds like it's painful to talk, which makes sense if he's barely tried in twenty years. It comes out as little more than a whisper, and there's obvious hesitation in his eyes when he does it.

But right now it feels like we're the only two people in the world, sitting outside time and space. Whatever normally stops him from wanting to speak might not have the same power here. I'm not going to draw attention to it, because I don't want to set it up like I expect him to try for me. If I praise him for it, that only increases the chance that he'll feel guilty if he never wants to try again.

He doesn't ever need to talk for me. Not if he doesn't want to. But it's fucking hard not to let it show on my face how much it means that in this moment, he does.

I let myself give him a small smile, but nothing else, before blowing out a breath and turning back to my own myopic rambling.

"If there's something wrong with me. If I'm fundamentally unfixable because I don't lose sleep over things I had no control over. If maybe I'm a psychopath masquerading as a person with a normal empathy response."

I keep my affect flat as I say it, like it's not a big deal. But it feels like I ripped those words out from some deep, dark place inside myself that doesn't typically get to see the light of day.

I can see Ford struggling to find the right words to say. I don't know if he's horrified or if he's going to disagree with me, or maybe trying to decide whether to speak or sign. I know that this is a lot to wrap your head around when you've just woken up.

Instead of saying anything, he reaches out. His thumb swipes over the arch of my cheekbone, and he pushes back some of my hair where it's mussed from sleep and sex. It's getting longer than it's ever been. I've been too distracted to get it cut. But I don't hate the feeling of him running his fingers through it.

After a few seconds, he pulls his hand back and signs to me, his expression fond.

261

"I think if you grew your hair out another few inches, you would start looking like a Disney Prince."

It's not what I was expecting him to say, but after a moment of shock, I laugh.

"Okay, Cujo, you're on."

"And for what it's worth, I don't think you're a psychopath. You take really good care of me, even when I'm mean to you. If you didn't care about people, you never would have followed me around, humping my leg and forcing me to accept your care and affection all this time," he signs with a smile.

I'm not completely convinced, but I'm still smiling. And I can't stop myself from leaning into his hand where he's back to stroking my hair, which he doesn't stop. He works his fingers in deeper, scraping over my scalp in a way that makes me want to purr. I feel my body soften until I slump into his shoulder, then he wraps his arm around me and maneuvers me until my back is against his broad, warm chest.

In my entire life, no one has touched me with this kind of tenderness. It seems to strip back my layers of armor and deception until there's nothing left but soft, vulnerable flesh. But instead of that flesh being open to attack, it's swept up in Ford's hands and tucked away somewhere secret, where he can keep me safe.

We breathe in time with each other for a while, and it feels peaceful. Until Ford's breath hitches like he just remembered something.

He doesn't move me so he can sign, but I feel him reach out and grab his phone from the side table. Holding it in front of me, he types out a message.

If you don't have PTSD, what are the nightmares about then?

I exhale slowly, and another shiver runs through me, despite the warmth of being wrapped up in Ford.

"Bruh, this is the really embarrassing part."

He interrupts me by typing another message quickly.

You shouldn't call me 'bruh' within twelve hours of fucking me. It's weird.

I snort. "Sorry, it's an old habit. I don't know if I can do normal pet names though. That sounds weird. You're still Cujo to me. My little junkyard dog."

Not little, but sure. Now stop deflecting.

"Fine. I've honestly had nightmares and shit on and off since I was a kid. My childhood was not amazing. Not the worst. Nothing like what happened to you, so I don't like to whine about it too much. But my mom was a mess. She was bipolar but didn't get diagnosed until after I joined the Army to get away from her. She was always dating low-rent mafia types and getting caught up in shit. She grifted a lot. Made me and Conor get involved, that kind of shit. Not exactly a pie-baking, apron-wearing kind of mom."

I take another deep breath, but I can't make my voice come out any louder when I speak again.

"I dunno. It feels stupid. I got slapped around by her and her boyfriends a little, but nothing serious. She definitely took advantage of my looks when I was a teenager to use for cons, but it's not like she actually pimped me out or let anything go anywhere. I was just a lure. And even though it sucked that she couldn't raise her own kids properly, I loved being the one to take care of Conor. He was such a good kid. I didn't want to leave him, but once I turned eighteen, I knew I had to get out of there or I'd end up involved in that shit for life, no matter what.

"I had a plan. He was old enough to deal with her by the time I left. I was going to come back when he turned eighteen and get him out, too. Then we could both say goodbye to all her criminal ties and just live our lives. But while I was deployed, I stopped keeping close enough tabs on him. I believed them when I'd visit and they pretended everything was fine. She got him involved in some serious shit when he was still just seventeen. I think they wanted to use a minor to reduce the risk of jail time, or something. But it all went sideways, and he got shot. Rival gangsters or something.

"So, I got out, but he paid the price for it. If I'd stayed, I could have looked out for him. I have nightmares about a lot of little shit from when I was a kid, which is embarrassing, really. Like I said, it wasn't that bad. But mostly I just have nightmares about Conor dying. I didn't see it, but my mind doesn't believe me. It has no problem making me watch his death like a movie reel any time I close my eyes. I guess it's what I deserve."

It's a long time before Ford says anything in response.

I don't think it's fair to feel guilty for not wanting to become a criminal.

I shrug. I know how it seems that way, but it doesn't feel like it to me.

I also don't think it's fair to not let yourself be fucked up about the shit your mom did, just because you didn't get molested or attacked. Or at least not as badly as other people. Cut yourself some slack. I'm the one who had a meltdown yesterday over finding out that my dad was doing criminal shit, even though it sounds like the only reason he was doing it was so he could take care of me. It was fucked up, but it was the best way he knew how, I guess. And you weren't telling me to get over it.

I arch my neck to look up at him. He's peering down at me, his light eyes calculating, but it reminds me that we still need to talk more about what happened yesterday.

"Let's get some food, and then you can tell me how you're doing today."

"So, do you want to go to work or stay here?" I ask Ford once we've showered, dressed, and scavenged toast from his empty kitchen. We're loitering in the living room, a little unsure of how to address the parade of elephants sharing the room with us.

"I don't feel like working, but I think lying around here all day jumping at shadows and freaking myself out might be worse," he signs. We're back to a more normal vibe, instead of that stepped-out-of-time sensation from before, and I don't expect he'll be opening his mouth to talk to me again anytime soon.

Not that it matters. This way, I get more of him to myself. Sometimes when Conor and I would sign to each other in public, it felt like we were in our own secret club. Like we were special, rather than him being excluded from anything. I get the same thing with Ford sometimes. Or maybe it's more that everything I do with Ford feels kind of special.

I have no idea when I turned into such a sap, but I don't really care.

Ford looks around. He gets the same here-but-not-here expression I've seen on him a few times before, like he's not looking at the same room as I am. I know more about him than almost anyone else in the world at this point, because he keeps his secrets close, but I'm still desperate to have a better understanding of how his mind works.

I'm not in a position to fix anyone's problems, but I'd like to at least know what's going on with him when he gets like this.

I move a little closer to him. The way he's perched on the arm of the couch makes him a full head shorter than me, and it lets me run my fingers through his hair with ease. I love this hair. It's thick and glossy, with just a hint of a wave to it, enough to keep it messy whenever he doesn't pull it back.

The fact that he has it in the first place might be why I like it the most. Ford seems to deny himself almost every pleasure or indulgence in life. He works, he exists, that's it. But he gives enough of a shit to let himself have beautiful, long-ass hair that's probably a pain in the ass, because for whatever reason, he likes it.

I love that for him.

Leaning down, I press a kiss to the top of his head. It's an unfamiliar gesture, but it's amazing how quickly I feel things falling into place now that we're settling into these roles with each other.

"What does it feel like?" I ask him. "When you're scared, I mean. Is it like a distant fear, or like a panic attack, or what?"

Ford cocks his head, looking up at me with his brow furrowed. Not angry, but more like he's confused by the question I guess he never expected me to ask.

Slowly at first, and then more easily, he turns his body to me and signs an explanation.

"It's kind of like he's here. Like... I know he's not. I know he's not here, and I'm not a kid, but I can't totally convince myself of that at the same time. So, I see the house, but I also see my old house superimposed on top of it. The worse it gets, the harder it is to pull the two realities apart. It helps to find things to focus on that are real. Sounds, smells, feelings. The pain used to help, but y'know."

Without meaning to, I dig my fingers into his shoulder a little when I'm reminded of everything that happened yesterday.

I can't let myself get caught up in histrionics, though. That's not helpful. Instead, I let myself sift through the information he just gave me.

"Do you want to go to the shop, then? I don't want you to work with your hands for at least a couple of days, but that doesn't mean you can't do invoicing and boss Silas around and whatever else business owners do."

The side of Ford's mouth lifts in a half-smile as he keeps looking up at me.

"Yeah," he nods. "That might be good."

"It'll be loud. Silas is there if you need anything. And you text me if you need me to come back. For any reason, even if it's stupid, okay? Deal?"

Ford nods, but then his face twists.

"Wait, where are you going? I thought you didn't work today?"

I hate lying to him, so I very casually sidestep the truth instead.

266

"I have something to take care of. I don't know how long it'll take, but not all day, probably. I'll come back as soon as I'm done."

Ford continues to stare me down, clearly not satisfied by my vague answer, but he doesn't press the issue.

"You know, you don't actually have to babysit me. I feel better. I'm okay."

"I don't have to babysit you. I *get* to babysit you. In exchange for getting dicked out. That's how these relationship contraptions work, right? Or whatever we're calling this?"

I grin at him, because I can tell he's trying not to laugh. One day he's going to give up fighting it. He finds me hilarious. I know it; he knows it, and eventually he'll admit it to the world.

Instead, he shrugs at me, affecting nonchalance. We walk outside together in a comfortable silence, and I kiss him goodbye before I head to my car. I sit behind the wheel and watch him the whole time as he lumbers down to the shop. Not because I don't trust him, but because I'm not quite ready to leave.

It's all sickeningly domestic. I kind of love it.

As peaceful as this morning has been compared to yesterday, I'm very aware that it could all be temporary. If life has taught me anything, it's that happiness is fragile and inherently transient. I want to give Ford the best chance he has at fighting his demons, and that's not going to happen if he has to face the possibility of literally fighting his demons.

No matter how slim the chances that Tommy could come looking for him, I'm not taking that risk. Even if he doesn't, he will in Ford's mind. Ford's fucked-up, traumatized subconscious will create the illusion of a threat every day until Tommy finally kicks it. Every day he survives will chip away at Ford's sanity, no matter how hard he fights. I'm sure of it.

The cops won't help me. He could never get a protection order unless Tommy started coming around first, by which point it could be too late for his fragile mental health. And I've already seen first-hand how little the cops in this town think of Ford and his family.

Fuck doing this the legal way. If I want anything to get done, I'm going to have to take things into my own hands.

It sounds like Noah was maybe a little crazier than Ford's idealized stories of him let on. But he died while he was still fighting to protect his son, and the least I can do is finish what he started.

It takes hours before I find anyone with even a tangential connection to the Banna. This town knows how to keep its mouth shut when it wants to, and even though I know where their headquarters are, I'm not willing to risk charging in there after that blond fucker shot me.

I need to get him to come to me. Somewhere public enough, I can hopefully keep all my limbs intact.

It takes a whistle-stop tour of every shithole in Possum Hollow and the surrounding area before I stumble on Tobias, drinking at the Feral Possum at three o'clock in the afternoon.

The Feral Possum is not actually a shithole. In fact, it's probably my favorite place to drink apart from my own living room, which is why it's the last place I looked. Apparently, I underestimated the little shit.

I grab the barstool next to him, and as soon as I see him tense up like he's about to run, I put my hand on his shoulder to discourage it. I'm not going to manhandle him if he really wants to run. The still-fading bruises on his face remind me that he's probably seen enough shit for one lifetime, but hopefully I can persuade him to help me out without too much of a fight.

"Chill out. I'm not gonna hurt you. How's your *lola*?"

Tobias's eyes dart from side to side, then he relaxes back onto the stool. Or slumps, more like. I can see all the fight-or-flight disappear in the blink of an eye, like the reflex has been worn thin from overuse.

He goes back to picking at the napkin in front of him, surrounded by confetti shreds of other napkins that have fallen victim to his nervous fingers.

"She's back home. They said she has diabetic hypertension and... an arrhythmia. She needs even more meds. And Medicare barely covers anything. So, we're both fucked, but thank you for asking."

My eyebrows raise, but I smile at him. I like it when he shows a little teeth. He's so little and angelic-looking, it's kind of like getting snapped at by an angry kitten.

"I need to talk to your boss. Can you call him and see if he'll come here? Promise I'll make it worth his time. I'd go to him, but I don't feel like getting shot and then devoured by hogs today."

Tobias stares at me like I've grown a second head.

"You don't want to do that, man. Seriously. Whatever you're planning, just drop it. No one ever wins when they get involved with him, and when you lose, he'll take it out of your hide."

I'm about to respond when the bartender interrupts us.

"Tristan, it's been so long since you've come here to day-drink. I was worried you'd magically healed your wounded soul. That's bad for business," he says.

I try to remember his name, but I'm drawing a blank. He's served me plenty of times, though, and he's always chill. The kind of bartender that knows everyone's business in town but always manages to keep shit to himself.

"Yeah, but progress is overrated." I smile at him and order a draft, which he brings without another word. Tobias stares at the bar the entire time, avoiding the bartender's gaze, and for a second, I wonder if he's even old enough to be in here.

Probably.

It's not my problem.

Or at least it's a problem I can deal with later, once Ford is in a better place.

"Look, I promise I know what I'm getting into. I wouldn't ask if it wasn't worth the risk. Okay?"

Tobias hesitates, but eventually acquiesces. He steps away to make the call, and after a few minutes rejoins me, telling me that Eamon is on his way. I expect him to flee the building, but he sits in silence next to me, both of us nursing our drinks.

"You can get out, you know," I say when I can't bite my tongue any longer. "There are people who can help. Professional organizations and stuff. I can help, if you want."

Tobias snorts and gives me a world-weary expression that's out of place on his delicate, almost-angelic face.

"You're literally about to get in. Don't try to sell me on something you can't even do for yourself."

That's fair, I guess.

Nothing else gets said until Eamon arrives. He saunters in like he's the king of the castle, and everything around him is already his property. The bartender—Gunnar, I remember—throws a brief glare in his direction before occupying himself on the other end of the bar.

"Boston. My pet told me you requested my presence. You'd better have something pretty fucking special to offer me, or I'll be taking this audacity out on your ass."

Fuck, he's going to ruin that phrase for me. It's so much more fun when Ford says it.

Doing my best to ignore his theatrics, I let the man take a seat. He insists on squeezing between me and Tobias, moving Tobias down a stool, and I don't miss the body language between them. Tobias flinches away from him constantly, but also works hard to mask it, moving his body with an unnatural level of stiffness and control.

Once everyone is settled, I lay out my offer. It's simple, really: I want him to leave Ford the fuck alone. Forever. I don't want any imaginary debts of his father's ending up haunting him. And I want that shitbag that killed his mom erased from this earth, just like his dad was working towards.

In exchange, Eamon can have whatever the fuck he wants from me.

"What makes you think I want anything from you?" Eamon's response is cold, his gaze unflinching.

"I'm useful. I can basically do field surgery off-book. And I grew up around an organization similar to yours, so this isn't my first rodeo. Are you telling me you don't want free, paper trail-less medical care in your back pocket? It's a good deal. All I want is for you to leave some random mechanic—who has nothing to offer you and no criminal background—alone, and do a job that his dad had probably 90% paid off, anyway."

Eamon pretends to think about it, but he looks more like a cat toying with its food. This whole supervillain routine is already getting old. I'm regretting offering to involve myself further with this guy.

But the thought of him dogging Ford's heels or worse, Tommy showing up at random and sending Ford into a downward spiral, makes it worthwhile.

"That's where you're wrong. I like Ford. He belongs here. He's smart, he keeps his mouth shut, and he was basically born into this family, even if he doesn't realize it. Why do you think I had his shop rolled in the first place? It's easy to parlay an offer of protection into a work contract and get him into the fold where he belongs." Eamon says.

I'm shocked by this revelation, although I feel stupid for not putting the pieces together sooner. Eamon doesn't give me the chance to say anything though before he continues.

"I don't like you. I don't know you, and I wouldn't be surprised if you left Possum Hollow as soon as you realized that nobody else around here wants your presence either."

I'm trying to formulate an argument, while also reminding myself what a terrible idea it would be to hit this asshole, when Tobias leans over and whispers in his ear. Eamon leans down to listen, then turns to look at him with a sadistic smile.

The sudden intimacy between them in that moment is strange, and off-putting. The more I watch whatever's going on there, the less I like it.

"You're right, Tobias. Okay, Boston. Here's my proposal."

CHAPTER THIRTY-TWO

FORD

S ilas does a good job of pretending everything is normal all day, which I appreciate. But I'm not shocked when Cade *happens* to drop by to work on his bike. He's also acting like nothing's out of the ordinary, but I can tell he's got his eye on both me and Silas whenever he thinks we're not working.

It's fair. I don't know the details, but I've picked up enough bits and pieces to know that Silas has a pretty dark history with his own mental health. If that includes being a danger to himself, it stands to reason that Cade would be extra-protective of him to make sure he's not triggered by all my bullshit.

It's sweet, really. And I don't have the energy to be annoyed by all the babysitting. After yesterday, I probably gave up the right to be pissy about a little extra supervision for a while.

I'd kind of forgotten what it felt like to have people around who cared. It's not as bad as I thought.

So Silas does the majority of the work while I catch up on paperwork and anything else that isn't too hard on my arm. Cade plops himself next to his bike on the middle of the shop floor, immediately making a mess and filling the silence with an unnecessary running commentary about whatever the fuck pops into his head.

It's not the worst way to spend the day, I guess.

The peacefulness of it all lulls me into a calm state, and I'm able to think about some of the shit from yesterday, but with more of a protective cushion between myself and the emotion of it. As if the threat of another existential meltdown is there, but held at a distance by the noise and chatter that currently fills the shop floor.

I don't let myself think about Tommy. The knowledge that he's free, that there's nothing I can do about it, and I'll probably spend the rest of my life flinching at shadows because of it... That sucks. I don't see a way around it.

The stuff about Dad is what's confusing me, though. Yesterday I felt like the foundations of my life were being shaken out from under me, because this man that I always idolized for getting his life together for my sake continued to be a criminal until the day he died.

But is it still awful if the only reason he did it was to keep taking care of me?

The thought makes me cringe, too many conflicting emotions jostling for space inside my head.

"Ford, you okay, buddy?" Cade's voice carries across the room, although he's pretending to still be focused on the same oil change that he's been working on for at least two hours.

Without letting myself second-guess anything, I ask him the question that's been burning in me all day.

"What did you think of my dad? Did you think he was a good person?" I sign to him, because I've been spending too much time around Tristan and I've gotten out of the habit of reaching for my phone.

Cade squints and I can see him trying to follow. They've both been trying to learn some ASL, which is actually really fucking sweet, but Silas has definitely picked it up faster than Cade. He has the patience for it, maybe.

Silas understood me, so he helps Cade with the words he didn't get, and then they both look at me while Cade tries to formulate an answer.

"I loved Noah. I mean, he was crazy, but that's why we loved him. He always treated me well, and..." Cade trails off, and he looks at me for a second, like he's evaluating whether to say what's on his mind. "I mean, it was always obvious how much he loved you. How many people do you know have a dad who isn't a total deadbeat? Not a lot. Sure, he was nuts. But his whole fucking world revolved around you. I was always jealous, to be honest. Why do you think I hung out here so much?"

"Because he undercharged you," I sign, making Silas snort before he tells Cade what I said.

Cade smiles and shrugs. "Yeah, because he was a good guy. Why do you ask? What happened?"

I don't know whether it's worth telling them. Part of me wants to keep Dad's secrets, and the other part of me feels like I'm so full of them that they're poisoning me, and if I just vomit it all out, then I'll be free.

When I bring up both hands to rub my face, I feel my sleeve tug down to reveal my bandage. I snap my hands back down, but it's too late. Warmth floods my face all the way to the tips of my ears, and embarrassment feels like it has my chest in a vise, slowly squeezing.

I don't know what's worse, them seeing the bandage, even though I know that they know what happened, or them seeing me getting flustered about it.

It's all a humiliation sandwich.

Turning around so they can't see my burning face, I pull out my phone and focus on typing something out. It takes a minute, because once I give myself permission to spill, it all comes tumbling out. But just getting it down feels a little better, and by the time I turn around and hand them the phone, the two of them huddling together to read the message, I feel a little lighter.

I knew that Dad used to do some shady shit with a motorcycle club or something before I moved here, but I thought he quit all that

and went legit for me. I found out yesterday that he's actually been keeping this place afloat by doing some terrible criminal shit on the side, working for the same creeps that shot Tristan. I don't know what I'm supposed to do with that information.

They both read through it in silence. I hold the phone out with my right hand, keeping my injured arm cradled against my chest. As if I can make it not exist, if it's sufficiently out of sight.

Silas and Cade look at each other over the phone for a long beat, sharing an unspoken communication.

At last, Cade breaks the silence.

"Well, you came to the right place if you want to join the 'daddy issues' club, I guess."

"Cade," Silas chides. Without thinking, I reach out with the hand that's not holding the phone to smack him lightly on the shoulder with a scowl.

Cade ignores both of us, though. He's used to being scolded.

"Hold, please," he says, sticking one greasy finger in the air before turning and heading to the bathroom. When he returns, his hands are mostly clean. He grabs his ratty backpack from where he dumped it on the ground when he first got here, then pokes me until I'm sitting on a stool by the counter that runs along the edge of the shop floor and joins it to the office.

I grunt in protest, but he ignores me.

"Hush, your bandage needs to be changed. It's already dirty and there's strike-through. We can talk about our collective family trauma while I do it. Silas, baby, do you want to start? Your dad is a piece of shit, yet you inexplicably refuse to let me murder him for you."

Silas huffs, but Cade ignores him in favor of pulling out some gloves and bandaging material that he conveniently happened to have in his bag today.

I keep glaring at him, but he seems unperturbed. When he pulls out my arm and rests it on the counter, I flinch.

The urge to pull it out of his hand and storm out of the room is almost overwhelming. But I know, realistically, that it won't change anything. Instead, I refuse to look at it, letting my brain pretend this isn't happening and ignoring the raw, over-exposed feeling of my ribcage being raked over hot coals. Cade quietly works on pulling off the bandage that Tristan placed and then cleans the wound that I didn't want any other human being to ever see.

Meanwhile, Silas starts to talk, and I immediately feel like I've fallen into the middle of a well-worn argument between the two of them.

"My dad isn't a piece of shit. He did his best with what he had; he just wasn't equipped to do a good job of raising a child. I'm glad he's gone, because I think it was bad for both of us to be around each other, but it's not like he hated me. He never hit me." Silas looks at Cade pointedly, but Cade keeps ignoring him. "He was just shitty at being a dad."

I let that sink in. Maybe I was overreacting when it seemed like a betrayal that Dad hadn't cleaned up his act for me. He was still doing illegal shit, but at least he was doing it for me. He was trying to take care of me the best way he knew how.

Cade interrupts my train of thought.

"Yeah, but how did he make you feel? Your dad made you feel like shit every day of your life, even if it was only with his words and his neglect. My dad made me feel like shit by literally beating me up. I don't see a difference. Their methods were different, but the result was the same: neither of us felt loved, or whatever. But I do think you have to cut people slack for trying their best. So, I guess you have to ask yourself, Ford, how did Noah make you feel? Do you think he was trying to take care of you? Because that's what it always looked like to me, from the outside."

When I let myself risk looking back, he already has a fresh bandage covering up the gnarly wound. I quickly tug my sleeve back over it and reclaim my hand, reaching for my phone.

Yeah. That makes sense. I never doubted that he loved me. I mean, he learned fucking sign language for me. He was the only person who told me I didn't have to learn to talk again if I didn't want to. He was the only person who didn't act like I was some broken, fucked-up kid, even though I was.

I take a deep breath, because there's a pressure behind my eyes that's threatening to betray my normally placid expression. None of these deep, dark parts of me were ever supposed to be exposed to other people. Cade and Silas are both looking at me intently. There's a lot of compassion there, but I've also just revealed more about myself in the last twenty seconds than in the entire time I've known them.

It's like a piñata that's burst open. The urge to shove everything back inside is there, but it's useless. The container is destroyed and flapping in the wind, while the innards of my fucking life are spilled all over the floor for them to see.

My throat tightens. I'm on a knife-edge of panic, waiting for a breeze to push me one way or the other.

But I'm saved from having to pick my next words, because Tristan chooses that moment to walk through the door.

He looks criminally exhausted, but he still has that fucking glow around him that only insanely, impossibly good-looking people get. Like he's walking around with his own personal ring light on him at all times.

As soon as he sees me, he smiles, and I smile back despite myself. There's a flutter of warmth inside my chest, and it's the first non-stressful emotion I've experienced for hours.

I can see the moment he clocks the medical supplies, though, and his expression immediately shifts.

"What's wrong?" He moves quickly, long legs eating up the space between the doorway and where we're all sitting. "What happened?" Tristan grabs for my arm as he says it, but I wrap my good hand around his bicep and give it a reassuring squeeze.

Because I'm apparently saturated with embarrassment already, I don't think twice about the fact that Cade and Silas are watching as I lean in towards him, place my mouth right next to his ear and *shh* him as gently as I can.

Cade's watching us with barely suppressed glee, but he has the decency to help me change the subject.

"It's fine dude, the bandage needed to be changed. Everything looks good. Your patch job is holding up fine. And Silas hasn't let him lift anything, scout's honor."

Tristan huffs. "No way in hell you were a boy scout."

"Fine, then honor among thieves or something," Cade says, laughing. "I swear. Anyway, we were talking about shitty dads. You seem like someone who knows a thing or two about daddy issues." He doesn't hide the way he eyes me up and down as he says it, completely ignoring the exasperated expression I give him. "Tell us, Tristan, what kind of piece of shit was your dad?"

Tristan frowns too, like he's debating whether it's worth getting into it with Cade about being a little shit. But he seems to decide it's not, because all he says is, "None, actually. I don't have a dad. Never did."

Cade's eyebrows raise, but another look from me clams him up before he can ask a follow-up question.

Just because we're sharing our feelings doesn't mean it's open season on everyone's trauma.

Without realizing it, I've got my arm wrapped around Tristan's waist, my fingers teasing at the hem of his shirt, and he's leaning his weight into me just slightly. It's not very noticeable, but it's not secretive, either. We still haven't discussed what we're doing about all of this in public, so this feels like a big deal, but also like if I mention it, it'll pop the bubble and send one or both of us into an intimacy-panic tailspin.

"So, children. How was everyone's day?" Tristan asks.

I make an affirmative noise, then move my fingers to trace little lines over the warm skin I find just above his waistband, making him sink into me a bit more.

"It was fine. I got work done, Ford got work done, Cade pretended to work on his bike while asking everyone inappropriately personal questions," Silas deadpans.

"Hey, I didn't start that conversation!"

"And yet you made it so no one else wanted to continue." Silas is smiling though, the teasing obvious in his voice, and he leans in to kiss Cade with a little more tongue than I would necessarily like for how close we're all sitting right now.

I clear my throat, and their attention snaps back to me and Tristan.

"So..." Cade says when he stands up from the stool, looking at the two of us expectantly.

"So, what?" Tristan asks.

Silas elbows him very subtly, but it's not subtle when Cade flinches and scowls at his boyfriend.

"No! You said I couldn't say anything as long as they were pretending they weren't together. They're not pretending anymore." He flaps his hands at both of us, where we're leaning against the counter, shoulders pressed together but otherwise not touching. "This is bullshit. I've been patient. I need the tea!"

He's practically bouncing on the balls of his feet, his tongue pinched between his teeth and his eyes wide as he waits for our answer.

Tristan glowers at him, but he's clearly overused that, because it doesn't even make a dent in Cade's enthusiasm.

"Fine. We're together, or something."

"Yes! I knew it." Cade jumps at us both, wrapping his long arms around us in an awkward hug that I have to duck down for. It's weird, but he means well, so I can't get too annoyed. Tristan, however, looks like he's trying to burn a hole in the side of Cade's head with his glare.

"You should kiss," Cade says, undeterred, when he finally lets us go.

"This isn't a peep show, kid. Go make yourself useful and clean up the mess you just made," he says, pointing at Cade's bike and the pile of parts and equipment strewn around it. There's no room for argument in Tristan's voice, and Cade pouts a little but doesn't hesitate to do as he's told.

I turn to Tristan, lifting up my hands to sign, "You know this is my shop, right? You're not the boss in here."

He looks at me with a devilish gleam in his eye and signs back so Cade can't hear. "Yeah, but I'm the boss of him. It's a force of habit."

Before Cade starts cleaning, he leans into Silas and whispers, "What's a peep show?" and I swear Tristan almost breaks.

Silas just shakes his head like he's exhausted by all of us.

"You should be glad I talked him out of glitter bombing you. Wish introduced him to *Drag Race* a while ago, and it's gotten so very out of hand."

I don't know why, but of all the stupid shit that's happened in the last two minutes, or even in the last two weeks, that's the final straw that makes me laugh. I don't make a lot of noise when I laugh, but it's normally enough to draw people's attention, which is one of the reasons I broke the habit of doing it a long time ago.

I'm so far past caring right now, though.

Silas looks shocked for a second, but then slips into a smile, and Tristan is grinning at me wider than I've ever seen him grin before. When I catch my breath a little, he grabs me by the back of my head.

I think he's going to pull me into a kiss after all, but that's not what happens. He pulls us together and then gently *thunks* his forehead against mine, staring at me with laughter in his eyes the whole time.

It feels weirdly intimate. Like profound, unalienable proof that he's right here with me.

But before I can finish that though, someone walks in through the open roller door and clears their throat. I look up, expecting a familiar customer.

It's no one I recognize. She's youngish, maybe Tristan's age, and she looks way too put-together to be from anywhere around here. She looks like she's never even seen the inside of a Walmart and is distinctly out of place inside my shop.

She's staring straight at us with an unnecessary intensity. It only takes me a second to realize what's happening. None of the four of us were exactly making out, but we also weren't being cautious about our physical affection.

This is the kind of attitude I liked skirting past by keeping my business to myself, but if she has a problem with who I fuck, I have no problem telling her to shove her business up her ass.

We're all staring, I realize. I lean towards Silas and elbow him to say something and break this awkward silence, which snaps him back to attention.

"Can I help you, ma'am?" he says with his *aw shucks* country boy customer service voice he's gotten so good at.

"I've been looking for you everywhere, asshole."

It's not what I expected her to say, and it feels like my mind is playing catch up as I look around the room, trying to figure out which one of us she's talking to. When my eyes catch on Tristan, I realize. My heart drops, even though I'm not sure why.

He's paled a little, and exhaustion seems to have immediately taken him over. He shakes his head at her and clenches his jaw tightly before he speaks.

"You can't just show up like this, Kaitlyn. What the fuck?"

Tristan always sounds like he has a Boston accent to me. It's worse when he's drunk or angry. But this woman's presence in the room seems to have cranked up the dial to maximum already, and it's making me feel like I'm so far removed from him and this situation that he's more of a stranger than ever before.

"I can if you refuse to answer the phone. How was I supposed to know you weren't eaten by a wolf or something?"

She looks around, like the forest is about to spawn something threatening any minute.

Tristan sighs deeply before looking at me.

"Can you give me a minute? I need to deal with her. I'll be right back."

I think I nod. I might be too baffled to nod.

Tristan doesn't kiss me, but I'm still not sure who this random, attractive woman is to him. Or whether we're kissing in public. He does reach out to touch my waist in an instinctual, unintentional way before he turns to walk away.

When he gets to Kaitlyn, she doesn't get the same gentle treatment. She's half his size, but that doesn't stop him from taking her firmly by the arm and marching her out of the shop. Not hurting her, exactly, but more forceful than I was expecting.

She's completely unperturbed, huffing and rolling her eyes like he's the one being dramatic in this situation.

Once they're out of sight, it leaves me, Cade and Silas looking at each other with equally shell-shocked expressions.

"What the fuck?" Cade asks the room.

"Yeah. Do you know who that was?" Silas adds.

I shake my head.

Tristan is as much of a question mark as he always has been, apparently.

"She's mean. But kind of in a super hot way."

Silas gives Cade a baleful look as soon as the words fall out of his boyfriend's mouth, but Cade ignores him.

"What? I'm just saying what we're all thinking. Hot chicks from Boston don't exactly fall out of the sky around here. I don't know who she is, but I think you should go stake your claim, dude."

Now it's my turn to roll my eyes. I sign at them both slowly and clearly so they understand.

"This isn't high school."

"I agree with Ford. You have to trust someone if you want to be with them. She could be anyone. He could have a sister we've never heard about. She could be his evil twin. It's Tristan, who the fuck knows."

Silas stops talking and silence falls over the three of us. I tap my fingers against the counter, listening to the wooden echo and trying not to let my imagination get the best of me.

I may never have been in a real relationship, but Silas is right. I trust Tristan. I don't trust this woman not to be fucking with him, though. The temptation to go out there and see what's happening is overwhelming, although it's less about claiming him and more about making sure he's okay.

And maybe a teeny-tiny little bit about claiming him.

"Just so we're clear, I don't have an evil twin," Cade says to Silas, because he's incapable of being silent for more than twelve seconds.

Silas snorts. "Sky is your evil twin. You were just born thirteen years apart."

"Mmm, actually, that's probably true."

This is infuriating. I hate feeling useless. He would have asked me for help if he wanted it, though, right?

Tristan O'Brien, master of asking for help, being vulnerable, and relying on others.

I bite my tongue, though. I can be mature. I don't have to run off half-cocked.

At least, until I hear the yelling.

Chapter Thirty-Three

TRISTAN

"What are you doing here?" I hiss at my mother as I drag her outside. She's annoyingly unflappable and wears the same expression she would if I'd invited her to a picnic.

"I told you. You didn't answer your phone."

"I answered you a week ago and told you to fuck off," I interrupt, turning to face her as soon as we're a safe distance from the shop. I tower over her by practically a foot, but she was never intimidated by me before. I don't see why anything would change now.

In her mind, I'll always be her faithful hound. Something she owns, that's supposed to come to heel when called.

"Which is why I'm worried," she continues. "I would have understood if you went back to the Army. Not that I ever understood why you joined in the first place. But why would you choose to live in this godforsaken mosquito farm in the middle of nowhere instead of with your family?"

Something snaps inside me, like a firecracker thrown against the concrete.

"My family is dead!"

I didn't mean to lose my temper. I meant to have a quiet conversation that ended with her leaving before she could do anything to blow up my life here, but she's always been able to push my buttons in ways no one else can.

There's a flicker of genuine hurt on her face before her expression shutters again. I scrub my hand over my face and sigh, forcing the anger out of me as I exhale.

"Look, Ma, I'm sorry. I didn't mean that. I love you, which is why I came home and took care of you after Conor died. But you were doing great when I left and you look good now, so can I just get five fucking minutes to take care of myself? Even if it is in the middle of nowhere?"

I can see her shuffling through possible reactions, trying to decide which one is going to get her what she wants. Even though I'm not sure exactly what she wants anyway, apart from my obedience. Which is not happening.

Before she can ramp up into a full-on performance and start either yelling or crying, I try to change the subject.

"How did you even find me, anyway?"

She snorts. "I know where you live."

"Yeah, the town. But how did you know I was *here?* How long have you been stalking me?"

"Mothers don't stalk, Tristan. We observe. With love. Besides, I only got to town today. I followed you here from that bar. It was depressingly easy. You've lost your edge. You need to pay attention to your surroundings, sweetheart. Especially if you're going to hang out with the kind of people you seemed to be cutting deals with back there. What was that about? I thought you were too good for all that. Isn't that why you left me and Conor alone to run off and play *Captain America?*"

My temper flares again, and I grab her by both arms before I can stop myself. I'm careful enough not to hurt her, but I pull her in close so she can't escape my gaze when I talk.

"It's none of your business. My life is none of your business. Everything that's fucked up about my life is because of how you raised me. Everyone assumes the Army made me cold and violent and emotionally unavailable, but no. That was all you. You're the one who raised me to believe that love is for the weak, men exist to be manipulated, and life is one giant, endless con that we're all trying to survive. You're the one who taught me that I can only rely on myself, so here I am, relying on myself. And fuck you, it feels great. You don't get to escape the guilt of getting one son killed by suddenly growing a conscience and showing up to meddle in my life. You did your damage a long fucking time ago. You ruined your own childhood by getting knocked up, so I had to pay the price for it, right?"

I knew it was a low blow, but I said it anyway. And when the tears well in her eyes, I get the feeling they're genuine, because she tries to stop them.

Jerking out of my grasp, my mother shoves my chest as hard as she can, enough to make me rock back a step. She doesn't slap me, but I can see that she wants to.

Self-control. Good for her.

The escalation to a physical confrontation makes me slump in place, even though technically I'm the one that started it. This is a well-worn pattern with us, even if it's been a while.

If I engage, it'll only get worse, and she's the one who will push me even though she's the one most likely to get hurt. Instead, I stay still, my eyes downcast as she pushes me another couple of times, unleashing whatever vitriol she's been storing up for the past year.

"You little fucking brat! I'm not the one who ran away and abandoned my family. I could have left the two of you any time I wanted, but I didn't. I did my best. I was a kid, too, you know! And you left us to run around the world pretending to be a hero. When you know that you're just as scummy as the rest of us, you just put a uniform on over the top. And now you came out here so you can get worshipped by these fucking rednecks, instead of being responsible for anything, for once in your life. You're still a little kid! All you do is run away."

She's crying for real as she shout-sobs the last part, pushing me harder and harder to unleash the frustrations of letting her own family slip through her fingers.

My arms are crossed over my chest, and my face is pointed down. I can't look at her when she's like this. I don't even want to hear. I'm retreating into my mind, letting her wear herself out until we can get back to a rational conversation.

But I'm pulled out of my familiar withdrawal by the thunder of footsteps behind me.

Ford runs over from the garage, obviously drawn by all the yelling. His face is furious, and for a second I'm worried that this is just going to escalate everything, but when he reaches us he manages to do a complete 180 with his energy.

Stepping in between us like a brick wall, Ford holds his hands out to Kaitlyn but doesn't touch her. She steps back, looking up at him with a little intimidation showing.

She's not easy to intimidate. She's spent a lifetime working with big, scary criminals. But Ford is a sight to see, especially for the first time. Those feral eyes would give anyone pause.

Once the yelling and shoving has stopped, Ford huffs air like a bull, slowly turning his back on her to look at me. He reaches out and tips my face up to his, hovering in my space.

The world smells like him. It's a mixture of motor oil and that weird, aggressively lemony soap he uses, and it's already slowing down the way my heart was hammering in my chest.

He mouths *you okay?* to me, and I nod. Unconvincingly, probably, but still.

There's a pause, then Ford takes a big step back so he can keep both me and Kaitlyn in his eyeline. He gives me a once-over, then looks to her, where she's still sniffling and glaring in my direction.

"T, who the fuck is this woman?" he signs to me.

I'm opening my mouth to reply, but my mother cuts me off, signing and yelling at him at the same time.

"I'm his fucking mother. Who the fuck are you?"

Ford freezes, his eyes wide. He looks between us several times.

I get it. I was going to explain everything once I got rid of her, but she didn't exactly give me the chance, and I wanted to talk to him without an audience.

Letting out a big sigh, I hold out my hand to introduce them in probably the least pleasant conversation I've had since getting shot.

"Ford, this is Kaitlyn. Kaitlyn, Ford. Now, can we all please stop yelling?"

I think I sound tired. I feel tired.

"You call your mom 'Kaitlyn'?" he asks me.

I need a fucking drink. I wave my hand in her direction, pointing out the obvious.

"She was only fourteen when I was born. She liked to tell people I was her little brother, and the habit just stuck. It's not like she ever did much to act like a mom, anyway."

"You are such an ungrateful asshole," she snaps. She reaches out like she's going to smack me again, and I know it won't hurt. She's never actually beat me up. She just tends to lose control of her temper and take it out on whatever's closest. But Ford envelops her slim wrist in his massive paw and shakes his head with an expression that this isn't up for discussion.

"No," he signs, snapping his fingers at her. "No more hitting. From anyone."

He looks at me too, and a flicker of guilt skitters through me. She definitely brings out my worst possible decision-making, that's for sure.

Kaitlyn interrupts the thought by opening her trap again.

"Can you leave us alone? I'm trying to talk to my kid."

But Ford shakes his head. "T is my business. I'm not leaving you alone with him if you're going to behave like that. Plus, this is my shop. So you can say whatever you have to say, but if you touch him again, I'll escort your ass back to Boston myself. Understand?"

She huffs, clearly annoyed that it's two against one. I'm too busy staring at Ford like he's my own personal hero.

I've faced about a thousand people that are scarier than my 5'3", 120lb mother. And when we were dealing with the Banna, Ford was pretty much shaking in his boots while I was trying to deal with the situation.

Which was fine. I wanted to protect him. I always want to protect him, and I'm good at those situations in ways that most people aren't. He shouldn't have to deal with that shit.

But watching him stand up for me, instead of letting me listen to her screech and shove me for another twenty minutes until she eventually tires herself out, somehow makes me feel more safe and protected than if he'd pulled out an AK-47 and stormed the fucking beaches at Normandy in my name.

I don't know why. All I know is that it's making me want to curl up on his lap and never leave. I'm able to stand a little taller and breathe a little more clearly, just because he's standing there.

If this is what you get by not running away from relationships, I've really been fucking myself over all these years.

Ford looks at me with an expression that anyone else would think is blank, but I can see the warmth and affection there. He's letting me take the lead here, but he's got my back.

Without letting myself second-guess anything, I do what I wanted to do this whole time and slip my hand into his. His palm is warm and dry, and he squeezes my fingers as they lace between his.

"He's my partner. Or boyfriend. Whatever you want to call it. So he stays. Now, can we please talk like adults?"

My mother looks at our joined hands and then between the two of us, surprise obvious on her face. Although, if I had to guess, it's more that I'm in a real relationship than that it's with a man.

Still, there's a hint of childish fear, trying to take root inside me.

"I swear to god, Kaitlyn, if you say one fucking homophobic thing, I will remind you of every man you made me flirt with for the sake of one of your scams."

"You know I don't care about that," she snaps. Her expression is serious, evaluating me, but not angry anymore. "I'm just surprised."

The fear flickers out. I didn't need her approval. It's not like I have it for anything else. But it's one less fight to have, and that's a relief I appreciate right now. I let myself smile at Ford and get the smallest smile from him in return.

"So, is he a criminal, too? Or does he not know what you've been getting up to in shady bar rooms while he's at work?"

Well, that was a peaceful three and a half seconds.

My eyes close themselves, because I'm too tired to deal with this shit right now, but Kaitlyn hasn't exactly given me a choice. I feel Ford pull his hand away from mine, and then he's jostling me until I look at him while he signs.

"What is she talking about?"

He looks confused, not angry, but that won't last long.

"Fuck you," I spit at Kaitlyn, which doesn't seem to bother her at all. She's watching with intense interest as I face Ford again and answer him.

The temptation to lie is so strong. I can make something up. Or say that she's making it all up. She's not exactly coming across as someone super trustworthy right now.

But I feel like Ford and I just figured out what we are, and that it's worthwhile. I already felt guilty about going behind his back to talk to Eamon. It's been eating at me all day. I told myself it was for his own good, and I was doing it to protect him.

Lying to his face about it doesn't feel like something he would forgive me for, if he ever found out. And he'd be right.

"Please don't be mad." I feel small as I say it, chewing on my bottom lip. I'm not used to being in this position, because I don't normally allow myself the luxury of having things I care enough about to be scared to lose.

This is a new, unsteady feeling, and I don't like it.

Ford's eyes flick from side to side, like he's trying to synthesize a lot of information in his brain at once. His face settles into a neutral expression, and he looks at me and nods.

"Just tell me, and we can figure it out."

That eases the pressure a little.

I open my mouth and blurt out the truth as quickly and factually as possible. That I went to see Eamon behind his back and arranged to work for him to absolve Ford from any kind of fake debt that might have been assigned to him on his father's behalf. Then I hesitate, because I almost want to just keep the last part to myself, but I force the words out.

"And I told him to keep his end of the bargain he made with Noah. About Tommy."

Ford's face goes blank. Completely blank. It's scary, really. I can usually read him at least a little, even when other people can't. But right now, he might as well be made of stone.

With a stiff spine and without looking me in the eye, Ford turns away from me and Kaitlyn and walks back inside, not saying another word.

CHAPTER THIRTY-FOUR

FORD

I'm not sure where I'm going. I'm not sure how I feel, except that it's like the weirdest echo of all the things I was just wrestling with about Dad coming back to haunt me.

I think that when he died, I genuinely believed there would never be another person who cared about me enough to take care of me. I told myself I didn't need taking care of anymore. I liked being alone.

Which is why right now, my first thought is how much I love that Tristan put his dumb ass on the line to keep me safe. No matter how stupid it was or what the consequences could be.

I love Tristan.

From the moment we met, he's put an almost pathological amount of energy into trying to take care of me. Even if it's in the most unpredictable, chaotic and ill-advised ways possible, most of the time. And even if he's often caring for me by letting me take care of him and boss him around.

Ridiculous, unhinged man.

Who I love.

He finds me in the office. I think I walked past Cade and Silas in a daze, not answering them if they spoke to me. I'm not sure what he did with Kaitlyn, but hopefully he left her with the boys so she can be supervised and not fuck anything else up. In case she insists on lingering around here like a toxin.

That's a whole other situation to deal with. First, I watch Tristan approach me slowly, his hands outstretched, like you would walk towards a wounded animal.

His green eyes are wide, and I can see there's a shine to them even in the dim light of the office. His face is a little blotchy, and I feel like there have been too many emotional peaks and valleys for one day for him to deal with. Tristan normally sequesters himself from vulnerability. All this must be wearing on him.

It makes me want to throw this conversation out of the window and take him home instead, but I can't. I have to understand the implications of what he did.

When I turn to face him fully, he looks so distressed, my heart cracks open a little. Whatever sludge had been fermenting in there my whole life leaks out, and I let myself feel how much I love him, even while I also feel incredibly fucking angry.

Both things can be true. And probably will be again, because it's Tristan.

"Come here," I sign, keeping my expression gentle. He moves hesitantly, but when he gets close enough, I pull him close and wrap my arms around him. Immediately, he sinks into me like his bones have turned to mush. I feel him shake once, like he's swallowing the urge to sob, and he buries his face in my neck the way he loves to do.

We stand like that for a long time. I lean against the wall, taking his weight until I get tired. Then I slide down, taking him with me until we're both splayed on the floor. He's half across my lap, and it seems to break the spell of silence that had fallen over us.

He grabs my face with both hands, looking into my eyes with just as much intensity and desperation as before.

"I'm sorry I lied," he says, his voice raw. "I just couldn't walk around and not do anything. Knowing that those Banna assholes were going to keep dogging you about your dad, knowing that Tommy being out there was going to keep haunting you. I had to do something. I can handle it. I can deal with this shit. Let me handle it for you. Please," he begs.

I push his hair back where it's getting long enough to fall into his eyes. Words are escaping me right now, so I kiss him instead. In that kiss, I pour all the affection and reassurance that I can into him.

When we finally come up for air, we're both a little breathless. Tristan's cheeks are colored, and he's crawled even further into my lap. There are only a few inches between our faces and I don't want to pull away from him, so I squeeze my hands in between us to sign, small and silent.

"I know you want to protect me. But your actions have consequences, and if we're together, then they affect both of us. You have to understand that. What would I do if you went to jail? I don't need a protector, or my dad's car back, or Tommy dead, or anything else. I need you, dumbass. You're the thing that I can't live without."

Tristan looks at me intently, vulnerability shining in his eyes, and for a second, I think he's going to crumple.

When he kisses me again, it's fierce. It's all tongue and teeth, his hands grabbing at me everywhere he can, like he's trying to pull our bodies together until we occupy the same space in the universe.

"I'm sorry," he pants, and then kisses me again before breaking away. "I can't lose you either. I'll do anything to protect you. Please, just let me protect you. I love you so much, Cujo. All of you: scars, paranoia, talking or not talking, the whole package. I'll kill anyone to keep you safe."

My heart feels like he reached into my chest and squeezed it.

I kiss him, but this time I keep it gentle, and don't let him deepen it. When we break apart, I force the air through my throat and let the words come out in a hoarse, almost voiceless whisper.

"I love you, too. Stay with me."

Tristan thunks his forehead against mine like he did before, and I feel him nod more than see it. We're both taking up all of each other's space, like nothing exists beyond our reach.

"I'll fix it," he whispers. "We'll figure it out. Okay? Just let me keep you safe."

He kisses me again, but after a minute I pull back and sign.

"It goes both ways. I have to keep you safe as well."

Tristan looks uncomfortable for a second, but then nods.

"Deal."

Tristan and I spent about twenty minutes making out and basking in mutual affection, and then maybe another twenty minutes arguing about who was going to be in charge of pulling our asses out of the dumbass deals we'd both made with the Banna.

I can't completely blame Tristan for all this. I'm the one who went to Eamon first, begging him for information about my dad and putting myself in his pocket. Tristan just did what he always does and took it way, way further.

Involving murder.

I can't believe that Dad was going to pay to have Tommy killed. I mean, I can. The man killed Mama. Who wasn't Dad's wife or anything, but was still someone he cared about, once upon a time. And watching me slowly tear myself apart over the fear of his memory can't have been easy.

For someone who was trained to kill and spent a lifetime doing it, I can see the logic there. I can even see how Tristan could also have gotten on board, as twisted as it is.

I just can't let anyone go through with it.

I want to stop ruining my life over Tommy's memory. But I think that's only going to happen if I stop being afraid of him. All this time he's been in prison and unable to reach me hasn't stopped my brain from treating him as an ever-present threat. I don't see why him being dead would magically fix that, either. And letting myself or Tristan be responsible for his death would just be piling on an already-disastrous situation. My conscience is muddy enough as it is.

It took me a while to convince Tristan of this, but eventually, he got on board. Letting me go with him was a non-starter, though. After our arguing drew the boys' attention, we conceded that Cade would go with Tristan, because he grew up here and was the closest to *connected* out of the four of us, in Possum Hollow terms.

Which leaves me and Silas to sit here and lose our minds.

Oh, and babysit Kaitlyn. Who is possibly the most frustrating person I've ever met. She's like all of Tristan's impulsiveness and selfishness, without any of the redeeming qualities that normally soften those edges on him.

We've closed up shop for the day, and we're basically just waiting for them to come back. That hasn't stopped her from wandering around, touching anything she wants and ignoring me whenever I warn her not to. I don't trust her for a second, and the only reason I'm not kicking her out is because I'm convinced she'll be more destructive for Tristan if she's not being supervised.

"Are you always this childish?" I sign to her, after she plays with something I told her to put down for about the fifth time in the last hour.

"I'm bored."

Now that I know they're related, I can see the resemblance. It was less noticeable at first because of the size difference. She's petite, and very delicate, which is part of the reason I think she looks so much younger than she is. But they actually have similar features. The same features that look very feminine on her are what make Tristan fall on just the masculine side of pretty: full lips, high cheekbones, long eyelashes.

I bet they looked more similar when he was a kid. I can't imagine having a fourteen-year-old for a mom. I didn't exactly have a classic suburban childhood, but still. That's a lot.

In between the kissing and arguing, Tristan told me a little more about her. He said she's bipolar, but only got diagnosed as an adult. When he was a kid, especially when it was just the two of them and she was still a teenager, he thought she was just really fun. Between that and their crime-adjacent lifestyle, his tendency to be pathologically impulsive and also unfailingly independent starts to make sense.

These are all the things I let myself think about, so I'm not thinking about whether he's possibly getting murdered right now.

When that thought dies off, I snap to get Kaitlyn's attention. I'm sick of her taking up space here without telling us her real agenda. It's like having an exotic bird caged in the shop. You don't know whether it wants to be admired, to come over and bite you, or maybe just take a shit on the floor. Silas is watching the whole thing, apprehensive, like he doesn't quite know what to make of this woman.

That makes two of us.

"What do you want from Tristan? Why are you here?"

She throws herself onto a toolbox and slumps dramatically, like the question exhausts her.

"I told you. He hasn't been answering my calls. I was worried. I wanted to see him."

"If that were true, you wouldn't have started yelling and hitting him as soon as you showed up."

She glares at me for a moment before going back to picking at her manicure.

"It's not my fault he sets me off. If he hadn't been so rude, I wouldn't have yelled."

"There's no way you came all this way just to fight with him. Tell me, or I'll call the cops and tell them you broke in. Seriously, why the fuck are you here?"

Kaitlyn looks away from me, staring at the closed roller door, her jaw clenched.

"It doesn't matter. You've obviously decided that whatever I say is a lie, so why should I bother?"

Jesus. I did not wake up this morning prepared for emotional manipulation, but here we go. I sigh and try to force myself to let go of any lingering aggression I feel towards her.

"I'm sorry. I was pissed that you came here and immediately started pushing him around. But if you tell me the truth, I promise I'll believe you."

She looks at me for a while, and I can't read what she's thinking at all. When she finally speaks, I find myself wanting to believe her.

"I—I miss him. It's lonely without him or Conor. I want him to come home."

We hold each other's gaze for a while. I can feel the emotion behind the words sinking into me, even though she's trying to hide it. And it makes sense. She went from having two sons around to having none. That's a lot of silence for anyone to deal with.

I sigh and decide to extend an olive branch on Tristan's behalf. If he gets to arrange contract murder 'for my own good', the least I'm allowed is a little latitude when it comes to meddling with him and his mother.

"I don't think he wants to come back. But maybe you should stay and visit for a while. You can see what his life is like here. He's doing good for himself. Really."

She stares at me, her mouth hanging open a little in surprise, although I can see the mistrust in her green eyes. At that moment, she looks so much like Tristan, it's a little scary.

"But there will be absolutely no more fucking hitting, or yelling, or name-calling," I add. "This can be a fresh start for both of you. As adults."

She nods, silent for once in her life.

Thank fuck.

There's a little more awkward silence, but finally there's a sound as the side door clicks open and Tristan and Cade appear.

I run over, running my hands over him and checking for injuries. He laughs and kisses me, but lets me keep petting him, because at some point he turned into a bit of an attention whore for me.

"I'm fine, Cujo, I'm fine. More than I can say for smart mouth, here."

He points at Cade, who has the beginnings of a black eye. Silas already has his face in his hands, inspecting it, and Cade is wincing dramatically.

"What happened?" I ask, signing to Tristan and mouthing the words to Cade at the same time.

"He sassed Eamon when he shouldn't have and got a back-hand for his troubles. But it could have been worse. We're all intact."

I can already hear Silas and Cade arguing about whether he was an idiot, so I pull Tristan away from them and into the office. I also don't need Kaitlyn peering at us for this.

"Tell me everything," I sign as soon as we have a little privacy.

Tristan blows out a breath, but his face is pretty relaxed, all things considered.

"Well, the motherfucker lied to me, for one thing." Tristan looks at me, his brows knit together and his mouth set in a thin line. "I don't know how you're going to feel about this, but I think it's fair to say that however you feel is okay. It is what it is, and we'll just have to deal with it as best as we can."

I give him a quizzical look, because I don't follow, so he continues.

"Tommy's dead. He's been dead for a while. He died in a prison fight around the same time as your dad had that stroke. Victim Services probably sent you another notice, but it got lost in the shuffle of everything else. Eamon knew, but he took the opportunity to string me along and see how much he could squeeze out of me, the piece of shit."

My heart ka-thunks in my chest a few times, like sneakers in a tumble dryer.

He's dead?

I can't decide if I feel better, worse, or nothing at all.

"I triple-checked to make sure it's true. Which I should have done before, I'm sorry. I got too caught up. But yeah, he's gone. It's done, I guess." Tristan looks at me, his eyes searching for some sort of reaction.

"Okay."

It's the only thing I can think of to say.

"How do you feel?"

"I don't know. I'm okay. I don't know." The words aren't coming out in a way that makes sense, and my hands are shaking, so he takes them in both of his and holds them for a second.

"It's okay, Cujo. You're safe. We're all safe."

I nod, taking in a few deep breaths and letting myself settle into the familiar sights and sounds of the office until I feel less like I'm floating. The tang of motor oil in the air. Tristan's stupidly perfect smile in front of me. The crack in the laminate under my feet that I've stood on a million times before. I feel like this is going to take weeks to sink in completely, so for now I focus on the other issues that I can actually do something about.

"And everything else?"

Tristan grimaces.

"Yeah, he's not letting us off the hook. I didn't get the chance to tell you, but it wasn't a coincidence that Tobias and his friend broke into your shop. Eamon's been trying to get to you ever since Noah died. He's convinced that you belong with them, or something. Something about your birthright. I wasn't able to talk him into leaving us alone. It's like he's locked into you. But I did get him to promise to keep the shop safe and keep us safe from whatever weird war they've brought to town with them."

There's something he's not saying, and I raise my eyebrow at him when he doesn't say anything else.

Tristan winces again as he speaks, like he knows how much he's about to piss me off.

"I'm going to work for him. For a while. Nothing super dangerous, just medical care off the books when they need it." My chest feels tight with fear, and Tristan's words spill out as he rushes to reassure me. "Don't worry. I know how to handle guys like this. I can keep this all off the cops' radar and eventually we'll extricate ourselves from the situation. Besides, someone like Eamon can't have a long life expectancy. I get the feeling this is more personal on his part than the Banna as an organization giving a shit about us. We'll bide our time, I'll patch a few of them up, that's it. We'll get out. Nothing dangerous."

"Famous last words." Kaitlyn's voice interrupts us before I can tell Tristan exactly how much I hate this or propose going to the cops.

"Last time I checked, a closed door means 'fuck off'. Don't you have a flight to catch?" Tristan asks, not bothering to hide the vitriol in his voice.

Now it's my turn to wince.

"I may have invited your mother to stay for a little while."

Tristan looks at me with more shock and awe than I knew he had in him.

"What the fuck?"

Kaitlyn saunters over to us, trying to put her hand on my shoulder and looking only a little disgruntled when I shrug her off.

"Your boyfriend has manners, unlike some people. And thank fuck, too. Because it sounds like you need help." Kaitlyn pauses, and some of the artificial honey-ed tone slips from her voice. "I miss you, Tristan. Let me stay for a while. I'll help you negotiate whatever dumb-fuck situation you've gotten yourself into. You know, sweet-talking brain-dead criminals is my specialty. And maybe we can have a conversation that doesn't end in screaming before we both die of old age. I promise, that's all I want. Hand to God."

Tristan looks between me and her, exhausted.

"I don't want to play the dead mom card," I sign to him. "But seriously. You should at least try to have a relationship while you still can. If she's awful, I'll drag her out myself."

I direct the last sentence at her, but she pretends to ignore me.

She continues to pick at her nails and give off a regal air of superiority, despite the uninterested audience of only me and Tristan in the room. "Now, tell me about whatever you've fucked up here."

Tristan ends up shaking his head, ignoring her for a second while he pulls me into a hug. "I see. This is how it's going to be from now on? You make all my decisions?"

I push him back a little so I can pull my hands between us.

"Absolutely. You make terrible decisions that get you involved with criminals or shot. I'm in charge now, brat. You'll thank me when you don't die young."

Tristan smirks at me and shrugs.

"Fine." He turns towards his mother and begins to tell the whole story, starting with the day we met.

I watch as he talks. He's so animated right away, even though he insisted he didn't want to talk to her. And she matches his energy immediately. They shadow each other, both falling into jokes like this tale of us stumbling into organized crime and him getting shot in the process is one long calamity, and not a life-or-death disaster.

I'm not entirely sure what family I've ended up getting myself attached to. But I'm also not sure what kind of family I really came from, so fuck it. I'm sure Tristan will continue to find plenty of creative ways to bring trouble to my doorstep. I guess it just gives me more excuses to beat the brat out of him.

As often as he wants me to.

EPILOGUE

Two Weeks Later

FORD

"Please," Tristan begs, but I ignore him. He's been begging for hours. I'm not giving in now.

His body is covered in sweat, he's visibly shaking, and his cock is swollen and painful-looking, almost purple at the tip. I tied his hands loosely to the headboard with a ratchet strap I found lying around. He's stretched out across the mattress in a way that makes me want to pause and admire his beautiful body some more, but his panting breaths tell me it might be time to let him come.

Although I got Tristan to agree to his mother staying for a few weeks, I didn't like the idea of them being under the same roof without supervision. They're too volatile together, and there's still too much anger and resentment between them for that situation to not be a powder keg.

It only made sense for her to stay at Tristan's house while Tristan stays with me. I think it also makes him feel better to be able to keep an eye on me, in the wake of all the shit I'm still trying to process that went down with my dad and Tommy.

He doesn't live here. It's only temporary. It doesn't mean anything.

We have, however, discovered that sharing the same space all the time is really fucking distracting. Now that the barriers between us have fallen away, neither of us feels the need to hide how much we want the other. Which means whenever we're not working, we're pawing at each other relentlessly. It feels like making up for lost time.

My dick is practically chafed raw from overuse, but I don't care. I want to keep exploring Tristan inside and out until... Well, until forever. There's nothing that could make me want to stop.

Which is why I spent the first half of today making him come again and again until he was so exhausted he could barely stand. Then, when I got him excited for what he thought was one final round, I started edging him to the point of insanity.

Watching him unravel like this has been the highlight of my week.

Tristan lets out another long, high-pitched whine. Apparently, he's beyond words. His thighs are shiny with the precum he's been leaking for hours, and I make a mental note to make him rehydrate when we're done. In the meantime, I keep jerking him loosely. Just enough to keep him hard and desperate for release, but not enough to push him over the edge when he's already come so many times today.

His hips jerk and buck off the mattress, accompanied by an adorable squeaking sound. He's so oversensitive. Every time I touch him, it's like a firecracker going off.

"Cujo, I'm begging you. You can fuck me any way you want as long as you let me come in the next thirty seconds. Please."

I pause my work for a minute to lean over him and sign.

"Oh, I think we both know you'll always let me fuck you any way I want. And you're a big boy. You know how to tap out if you really want to. If not, be good and let me play with you however I want."

Tristan whines again, but otherwise stays quiet. He's so adorable when he's finally quiet. Flushed red from his face down to his chest, quivering and boneless, and all for me.

I take pity on him.

Leaning over his face, I put my mouth right up against his ear to whisper, "Good hole."

I take pleasure in the way he shivers. I still don't have any interest in talking like a 'normal' person, but sometimes when it's just Tristan and me, I feel like a few words can come out, and it's nice. Especially because I can see how much it means to him. Even though he's careful not to make a big deal about it.

When I move back down his body, I don't bother with the hand job. I swallow him immediately, engulfing him in the heat of my mouth and sucking him with purpose. I slip two fingers into his hole, working over his prostate as soon as I find it, and he's jerking so hard I have to use my free arm to hold him in place.

It takes a while for him to get there. He's writhing and moaning the whole time, and I'm drinking in every sound that fills the room.

I've worked him so hard that when he finally comes, there's hardly anything left inside him to fill my mouth. Just a small spurt of saltiness on my tongue, and then his violently tremoring body, let me know he's done.

I take my time licking his poor, swollen cock clean. He keeps jerking away from me because he's oversensitive as hell, but the mumbling noises he's making tell me he likes it. When I eventually finish and lie down next to him, releasing his wrists from the restraints, he immediately curls into my chest in a ball of shivering, overworked disaster-human.

"Well, that was one way to spend my day off," he says when he finds his voice again. "Although I may need another weekend to recover from this one. Or possible a spare emergency dick to swap out with this one. You were not fucking around."

I don't say anything. Nothing needs to be said. I smile to myself, and when Tristan raises his head to look at me, he's smiling, too.

"Do you want to take a shower and go to sleep?" I sign to him, because it's early, but he looks completely spent.

Tristan doesn't say anything, just makes a whiny noise and buries his face in my chest in a way that tells me he can't make up his mind. When he bites the tender skin near my armpit I wince. Sometimes I regret that I'm comfortable being naked in front of him now.

Not really, obviously. But he's so fucking bitey.

Tristan doesn't have to decide, though, because we're interrupted yet again by the sound of the door.

TRISTAN

It's not someone knocking at the door. It's someone letting themselves in. Into the locked house, and interrupting my post-multiple-orgasm buzz. Which could only mean one person.

"Tell me you did not give her a key," I say, raising my body enough to look at Ford.

Ford snorts. "No. But I get the feeling that was never going to stop her," he signs.

"Boys! Put your pants on. There's work to do." The sound of my mother's voice carries upstairs, officially dispelling the last of my afterglow.

I have just enough time to yank a blanket over us, because I know Kaitlyn well enough to know that she's not going to bother knocking. And I'm right. She lets herself into the bedroom, standing in the doorway expectantly like we've somehow inconvenienced her by not being downstairs to greet her in her unplanned drop-in.

I can practically feel Ford glowering at her from behind me.

"We need to talk about boundaries, Kaitlyn," I see him sign out of the corner of my eye.

"Please," she sighs. "Like I haven't seen worse."

Her eyes find the ratchet strap that Ford just discarded on the bedroom floor, the one that's still impregnated with my sweat and possibly cum. And of course, she picks it up, gives an evaluating little *hmm* noise and then says, "kinky."

Like any of this is an appropriate way to interact with your child.

"What do you want?" I snap, running out of patience.

Kaitlyn's demeanor shifts until she's all business.

"Eamon needs you. Right now, it's an emergency. Put on some pants, grab your biggest med kit and I'll drive you there."

Words cannot describe how much I hate that she's inserted herself into this situation. It's bad enough that I'm in the Banna's pocket, but my mother wiggling in there as well can only spell trouble. I can't decide if she's better off here, where I can at least monitor her criminal activity, or at home where she'll undoubtedly be doing the same thing, but I can go back to pretending I don't care about it.

"Fine. Wait for me downstairs. And put that down!"

When she doesn't move quickly enough, I throw a pillow at her, making her drop the ratchet strap and earning myself a glare. But it gets her to leave, at least.

Before I get out of bed, I turn to look at Ford. We've been trying to be optimistic about this situation. I still think it's going to be okay. I'll work off Eamon's imaginary debt, and he'll eventually get distracted by something else and I can extricate myself from the situation.

But I know it worries Ford a lot more than me.

"Are you going to be okay while I'm gone?" I ask.

Ford grimaces. "No. I'll be worried. But I'd probably be more worried if I went with you, and I'd be a distraction. Can you just text me every hour or two, so I know you're okay?"

I nod. "Of course."

There's a long pause, and I can tell he's turning over his various worries in his mind.

"Are you pissed that I asked Kaitlyn to stay? I can see now that she's a little more intense than I expected. I know you said she was involved with criminals, but I didn't expect her to get out there and deliberately stick herself in the middle of all this for no reason."

I shrug. He looks so concerned, I wish I could assuage it but it's difficult to explain.

"It's not your fault. I'm not pissed, and I do agree with you that I should try to make the best of our relationship while I can. She's just chaotic. It's how she is. She's going to do whatever she's going to do. Don't let yourself shoulder any of it or you'll be buried in her bullshit forever. I promise."

He nods solemnly, but I'm sure we'll circle back to this conversation a few more times. For someone who claims to hate talking, I've figured out pretty quickly that being extremely straightforward and just telling Ford how I feel about things is the easiest way to quiet his mind when he's twisted up about something.

"I'll go, I'll help them, and I'll be home before you know it. Kaitlyn can do whatever she wants. I'm only worried about us. Got it?"

He nods again, and I pull him into a tender kiss.

"It's just you and me, Cujo," I whisper to him when we pull apart. "We'll figure the rest of it out. I promise."

Up Next

<u>Running Feral, Possum Hollow Book 3</u>

Coming November 29th 2024

Tobias & Gunnar

Available for Pre-Order Now

<u>Possum Hollow Book 4</u>

Release 2025

The second half of Silas & Cade's love story

<u>Possum Hollow Book 4.5</u>

Release TBD

Rebecca & Wish Novella

Savage, Sins of the Banna Book 1

Available now as a serial on REAM along with other subscriber benefits and Possum Hollow bonus content.

Micah & Savage

Will be published on Amazon once complete in early 2025, turn the page to read the first chapter.

SINS OF THE BANNA

Book One: Savage

SAVAGE - SINS OF THE BANNA, BOOK ONE

When you think of the mafia, you probably think of glamor and violence. It's fast-talking New Yorkers wearing shiny suits and making deals over smoky backroom poker games. Or stony-faced Russians eliminating their competition with brutal efficiency. Pablo Escobar surrounded by tigers and cocaine.

They're all dropping the bodies of whoever gets in their way and looking fucking sexy while they do it.

It's what TV and books have been shoving down our throats for decades. I can walk into any Target right now and find books with some doll-faced heroine being swept off her feet by a gorgeous Armani-clad mafia prince with a BDSM habit and a secret heart of gold.

Well, I'm the mafia prince of Oklahoma.

If that's not life kicking me in the balls, I don't know what is.

There is no glamor in what I do. There are drug deals, and constant infighting, and an endless fucking stream of enemies that my father expects me to eliminate. Violence is messy. Dead bodies fucking stink. Hacking them up is the kind of workout that would make an Olympian pass out from exhaustion, and I'm really fucking sick of it.

I'm quitting. I know the tattoos that cover my neck and face are supposed to mean *blood in, blood out*; but for all the shitty things my father has done to me, I don't believe he'll kill me. Not if I do it right and go to him first. This job is eating me from the inside out, and if I keep going, I don't think there will be much left of me to keep doing his dirty work.

I'll kill anyone he wants. I'll pull any dirty job, anything he asks for. I'll fake my own fucking death. As long as he lets me go.

It's bad enough I'm already pulling a Tony Soprano and seeing a shrink in secret, because I need the meds to survive. If anyone found that out, I'd be a laughingstock. A vulnerable one. Let alone if they found out about any of my other embarrassing peccadillos.

Banna Lieutenants are supposed to be the cornerstones of our organization. We're a brotherhood. *Banna* means bond in Irish. It's supposed to be unbreakable. Except I don't think our ancestors accounted for many of us living past the age of twenty-one and having enough time for our demons to hook their claws into us.

"You alright, Savage?"

My second-in-command is staring at me, probably because we've been sitting outside the courthouse for a couple of minutes, and I have yet to make any attempt to step out of the car.

Even my name sounds stupid. All the lieutenants are given these code names when they're promoted. They're supposed to sound bad-ass I guess, but I think that on average, for professional criminals, we probably just take too much meth. It's a stupid name, and I'm stuck with it for life.

Not only because the Banna is my entire life, but because no one can pronounce my given name. Tadhg. Like 'tiger', without the -r. Not hard, but how many people in Oklahoma City do you think can wrap their heads around it?

My ignorant father was born here. I'm pretty sure we have as much Chickasaw blood in our family as Irish, but the man loves to play the part and he thinks using the old-country names makes us look more legit. It's the same reason his birth certificate reads 'Patrick', but he'll break a man's nose for saying anything other than Pádraig.

I think it's the fact that we murder anyone who gets in our way that keeps us in power. No one cares how *Irish* the Irish Mafia is but him, as long as we're still supplying the region with guns and drugs.

"I'm fine, Colm. Let's get this over with."

He nods gruffly, but he doesn't look convinced. His dark eyes are still on me, but I can't tell if it's concern or suspicion that he's trying to mask. With my brothers-in-arms, either is possible. His fingers tap out a rhythm on the back of the passenger seat, where he's twisted to look back at me. He has ink from his first knuckles up, just like me, except the letters across his fingers spell out "KNOW HOPE".

Mine say "SAVAGE", followed by the Banna snake. Because nothing's cooler than having your own fake name tattooed across your hands.

"Let's get this over with," I repeat, reaching for the car door.

Today is the one rare day I'm actually wearing a suit. It's fucking uncomfortable. Normally, I wear clothes with enough give that I can fight in them. I have no idea how all those mobsters in the sixties were out there kicking each other's asses while wearing loafers; I swear to God. But today I have a court appearance I wasn't able to wiggle out of.

The DA has pulled me in to testify against our biggest rival: the Aryan Brotherhood. I'm not going to say shit, of course. I know it and she knows it, but I think she's throwing me on the stand anyway in the hopes that I'll cave at the last minute and, *"Do the right thing, Mr. Moynihan."*

As if I'm physically capable. Father beat that ability out of me a long, long time ago.

I'll go up there, swear in, say I saw nothing, and then move on with my life. The DA can rest easy knowing that justice will be served regardless of the verdict. Our way may be messier, but it's much more to the point. The Aryan Brotherhood don't get away with anything when they're in my territory.

I step out of the car with a sigh, buttoning up my jacket as I move towards the entrance. It's a drab, gray building that looks like it's more suited to issuing parking citations than staunch justice. But what do I know?

As I walk—Colm hot on my heels—I rehearse what I'm going to say to Father tonight. How I'm going to plead with him for my freedom. I have to imply that it's a matter of life or death, which I'm beginning to feel like it is, without saying it outright. Letting him on to the truth of my mental state would be disastrous.

The man can scent weakness like a bloodhound, and he might be inclined to correct me. It's something he hasn't done since I grew taller than him and added about eighty more pounds of muscle to my frame, but the threat always exists. Lurking in the back of my mind and memories, even if it's not real.

I'll go up to him, stand strong, make my case for why I deserve to exit the organization with a little dignity, and then escape this fucking exhausting life for good.

Fuck knows what I'm going to do after that, but that's a problem for Future Savage.

I'm so in my head that I hear the commotion thirty seconds after everyone else does.

Normally, I'm trained to be on high alert at all times. It's been instilled in me since I was a little boy protecting my step-brother from Father's rages, long before my formal training began. For as long as I can remember, it was instinct. But protecting Micah was a worthy cause. Probably the only worthy cause I ever had.

Nowadays, all the misery that I've been drowning in has left me sluggish, and saving my own hide isn't enough motivation to switch that instinct back on. This thirty-second delay is a prime example of that. As soon as I clock it, I realize it's probably about to cost me my life. I've become slow and vulnerable, and the Aryan Brotherhood must have sensed it.

I reach for my Glock, but it's not there. The courthouse. I had to leave it in the car for the metal detectors.

Fuck.

Four men with their faces covered in cheap bandanas are charging up the steps. The courthouse security guards are moving at the speed that only fat courthouse rent-a-cops would. They look like they'd rather run for their lives than put themselves in between two groups of criminals about to battle it out on their doorstep.

The wall of sound hits me first. Then the acrid smell of blood and gunpowder fills my nose, and I find myself face down on the concrete without any awareness of how I got there. My shoulder throbs, and so does my stomach, so I must have been hit.

Each gasping breath of air I try to take is thick with dirt and dust. My lips graze the rough ground, and I wonder if the last sensation I'm going to experience in life is tasting the boot prints of everyone who's gone up and down these steps before me.

Fuck this. I wasn't even going to say anything. I was going to keep my mouth shut, and then get out. And now I'm surrounded by nothing but yelling and bright, gripping pain. I see Colm at an awkward angle, but it looks like unlike me, he was still carrying when they attacked. He's firing at someone now, so maybe there's a chance of us getting out of here alive. Or at least him.

I hope Colm doesn't die. I don't have any friends in this business, but if I did, he might be it.

In a flash of clarity, I wish it had been Father here to go down with me instead of anyone else. He's the one who deserves this kind of undignified end.

Well, I deserve it too. After everything he's made me do.

Right before the world goes black, I have one final thought. I hope at least I don't have to see him when we both make it to Hell.

About the Author

Erin Russell is a queer writer living in Los Angeles. They write hurt/comfort queer romance novels with the occasional horror story thrown in the mix. Connect with Erin on social media and check out the 68 Whiskey playlist on Spotify, using the QR code below.

I could not have finished this story without the help of my incredible betas: George, Ash, Stacey, Lauri, Chelsea, Michelle, Katie & Amy.

www.erinrussellauthor.com

www.ingramcontent.com/pod-product-compliance
Lightning Source LLC
Chambersburg PA
CBHW020934260626
47169CB00006B/1715